New York Times and *US...* **Dunlop** has written mor... including the acclaimed... Mills & Boon Desire. H... hit bestsellers lists. Ba... Romance Writers of An...

Teresa Southwick lives with her husband in Las Vegas, the city that reinvents itself every day. An avid fan of romance novels, she is delighted to be living out her dream of writing for Mills & Boon.

Brenda Harlen is a multi-award winning author for Mills & Boon True Love who has written over twenty-five books for the company.

First Published in Great Britain 2019
y Mills & Boon, an imprint of HarperCollins*Publishers*
1 London Bridge Street, London, SE1 9GF

HRISTMAS SECRETS © 2019 Harlequin Books S. A.

The Missing Heir © 2014 Barbara Dunlop
rick's Christmas Homecoming © 2012 Harlequin books S.A.
A Very Special Delivery © 2013 Brenda Harlene

thanks and acknowledgement to Teresa Southwick for her
n to the *Montana Mavericks: Back In the Saddle* continuity.

ISBN: 978-0-263-27999-3

1219

MIX
Paper from
responsible sources
FSC™ C007454

k is produced from independently certified FSC™
er to ensure responsible forest management.

nformation visit: www.harpercollins.co.uk/green

Printed and bound in Spain
by CPI, Barcelona

THE MISSING HEIR

BARBARA DUNLOP

For Mom

One

Cole Henderson propped himself against a workbench in Aviation 58's hangar at the Juneau, Alaska, airport and gazed at the front page of the Daily Bureau. He realized news of the Atlanta plane crash deaths should make him feel something. After all, Samuel Henderson had been his biological father. But he had no idea what he was supposed to feel.

A nearby door in the big building opened, letting in a swirl of frigid air and blowing snow. At ten o'clock in the morning, it was still dark outside this far north.

His business partner, Luca Dodd, strode in, crossing the concrete floor alongside the sixty-passenger Komodor airplane that was down for maintenance.

"You looking at it?" Luca asked.

"I'm looking at it," said Cole.

Luca tugged off his leather gloves and removed his wool hat. "What do you think?"

"I don't think anything." Cole folded the paper and tossed it on the bench behind him. "What's to think? The guy's dead."

A drill buzzed on the far side of the hangar, and the air compressor started up, clattering in the background as two maintenance engineers worked on the engine of the Komodor.

"He was your father," Luca pointed out.

"I never met him. And he never even knew I existed."

"Still…"

Cole shrugged. His mother Lauren's marriage to billionaire Samuel Henderson, whose family owned Atlanta-based Coast Eagle Airlines, had been short-lived and heartbreaking for her. She'd never hidden Cole's heritage from him, but she'd certainly warned him about the Henderson family.

"Eight dead," said Luca, spinning the paper so the headline was right side up.

"Sounds like it all went to hell in the final seconds." As a pilot, Cole empathized with in-air emergencies. He knew the pilots would have been fighting to safely land the airplane until the very end.

"Early speculation is a combination of icing and wind shear. That's freakishly rare for Atlanta."

"We all know how bad that can go."

"An Alaskan pilot might have helped," said Luca.

Cole didn't argue that point. Pilots in Alaska had more experience than most in icy conditions.

He glanced over his shoulder at the headline once again. On a human level, he felt enormous sympathy for those who'd lost their lives, and his heart went out to their friends and family who had to go on without them. But for him personally, Samuel Henderson was nothing but a stranger who'd devastated his mother's life thirty-two years ago.

By contrast, when his mother, Lauren, had passed away from cancer last year, Cole had mourned her deeply. He still missed her.

"They put up a picture of the baby on the website," said Luca.

The article had mentioned that Samuel and his beautiful young wife, Coco, had a nine-month-old son, who, luckily, hadn't accompanied them on the trip. But Samuel's aging mother and several company executives had been on board when the family jet had crashed into the Atlanta runway.

"Cute kid," Luca added.

Cole didn't answer. He hadn't seen the picture, and he had no plans to look at it. He wasn't about to engage in the Henderson tragedy on any level.

Luca leaned forward, putting his face closer to Cole's. "You do get it, right?"

"What's to get?" Cole took a sideways step and started walking toward a hallway that led to the airline's offices. November might be Aviation 58's quietest month, but there was still plenty of work to do.

Luca walked beside him. "The kid, Zachary, is the sole survivor of that entire family."

"I'm sure he'll be well cared for." For the first time, Cole felt an emotional reaction. He wasn't proud, but it was resentment.

Immediately after their secret marriage in Vegas, Samuel had succumbed to his parents' pressure to divorce Lauren. As a young woman, she'd walked away, newly pregnant. With only a few thousand dollars to her name, she'd boarded a plane for Alaska, terrified that the powerful family would find out about her baby and take him away from her.

Hidden in Alaska, she'd scraped and saved when Cole was young. Then he'd worked night and day to put himself through flight school and to build his own airline. Zachary, by contrast, would have an army of nannies and protectors to ensure he had everything a little boy could need—from chauffeurs to private schools and ski vacations in Switzerland.

"He's all alone in the world." Luca interrupted Cole's thoughts.

"Hardly," Cole scoffed.

"You're his only living relative."

"I'm not his relative."

"You're his half brother."

"That's just an accident of genetics." There was nothing at all tying Cole to Zachary. Their lives were worlds apart.

"He's only nine months old."

Cole kept on walking across the cavernous hangar.

"If the Hendersons are as bad as Lauren said they were..." Luca's voice trailed off again, leaving the bangs and shouts of the maintenance crew to fill in the silence.

Cole picked up his pace. "Those Hendersons are all dead."

"Except for you and Zachary."

"I'm not a Henderson."

"You looked at your driver's license lately?"

Cole tugged the heavy hallway door open. "You know what I mean."

"I know exactly what you mean. The jackals in Atlanta might very well be circling an innocent baby, but you'd rather walk away from all this."

"I don't *have* to walk away from this. I was never involved in it to begin with."

Cole's operations manager, Carol Runions, poked her head out of her office. "One seventy-two has gone mechanical."

Cole glanced at his watch. Flight 172, a ninety-passenger commuter jet, was due to take off for Seattle in twenty minutes. "Is maintenance on board?" he asked Carol.

"They're on their way out there now. You want me to prep Five Bravo Sierra?"

"What's the problem?" Luca asked her.

"Indicator light for cabin pressure."

"Probably a faulty switch," said Cole. "But let's warm up Five Bravo Sierra."

"You got it," said Carol, heading back into her office.

"If we take the Citation, we can be there in four hours," said Luca.

Cole stared at his partner in confusion. "There are ninety passengers on 172." The Citation seated nine.

"I meant you and me."

"Why would we go to Seattle?" And why did Luca think it would take them four hours to get there?

"Atlanta," said Luca.

Cole's jaw went lax.

"You gotta do it," said Luca.

No, he didn't. And Cole was done with talking about the Henderson family. Without answering, he turned to walk away, shaking his head as he went.

"You gotta do it," Luca called after him. "You know as well as I do, the jackals are already circling."

"Not my problem," Cole called back.

The Atlanta Hendersons had gotten along perfectly well without him up to now. He had no doubt their *i*'s were dotted and *t*'s crossed for every possible life or death contingency. They didn't need him, and he didn't want them.

Amber Welsley folded her hands on the top of the massive inlaid-maple table in the formal dining room of the Henderson family mansion. She was one of a dozen people riveted on Max Cutter at the table's head. Max's suit was well cut, his gray hair neatly trimmed and his weathered expression was completely inscrutable as he drew a stack of papers from his leather briefcase.

From the finely upholstered chair next to hers, Amber's friend Destiny Frost leaned in close. "Six lawyers in the same room. This is not going to end well."

"Seven lawyers," Amber whispered back.

Destiny's glance darted around. "Who'd I miss?"

"You. You're a lawyer."

"Yeah, but I'm the good guy."

Amber couldn't help flexing a tiny smile. She appreciated the small break in the tension.

Max was about to read Samuel Henderson's last will and testament. The others gathered in the room had an enormous amount at stake—about a billion dollars and control of Coast Eagle Airlines. But the only thing that mattered to Amber was Zachary. She hoped whatever arrangements Samuel and her stepsister, Coco, had made for the baby's guardianship would allow Amber to stay a part of his life.

Amber was ten years older than Coco, and the two had never been close. But Amber had been instrumental in her stepsister meeting Samuel at a Coast Eagle corporate function two years ago, and Coco's pregnancy had brought them closer together for a short time. Since then, Amber had felt a special kinship with Zachary.

Across the wide table from her, vice president of operations Roth Calvin shifted in his seat. Since the day the company's president, Dryden Dunsmore, had been killed in the plane crash, the three vice presidents had been running the show. Now Samuel's will would reveal who would get control of Coast Eagle.

Whoever it was would control Roth Calvin's future. Much further down the corporate ladder, as assistant director of finance, Amber didn't much care who took over the helm of the company. Her day-to-day job as an accountant wasn't about to change.

"My personal apologies for the delay in scheduling this reading," Max opened, his gaze going around the room. "But there were several complexities to this case due to the number of deaths involved."

Amber's throat thickened. She quickly swallowed to combat the sensation. Poor Coco had only been twenty-one.

"I'll start with Jackie Henderson's will," said Max. "I'll follow that with her son, Samuel's, which was written jointly with his wife, Coco. In addition, there is a small codicil, executed by Coco alone. I would caution you all to draw no conclusions until I've finished reading all three."

Max straightened the papers. "Aside from some small bequests to friends and long-time staff members, and a generous donation of ten million dollars to the Atlanta arts community, Jackie Henderson has left her estate to her son, Samuel, including her twenty-five percent ownership of Coast Eagle Airlines."

Nobody in the room reacted to Max's statements, and they gave only a cursory glance to the list of bequests handed around. That Samuel was Mrs. Henderson's heir was completely expected. And though Mrs. Henderson had been an exacting and irritable old woman, she had long been a patron of the arts.

"As to the last will and testament of Samuel Henderson…" said Max.

Everyone stilled in their seats.

Max looked down at a page in front of him. "Mr. Henderson has also left a list of small, specific bequests, and has made several charitable donations, also ten million dollars to the Atlanta arts community, along with an additional ten million dollar scholarship to the Georgia Pilots Association."

Max took a sip of water. "As to the bulk of Mr. Henderson's estate, I'll read directly from the document. 'My entire estate is left in trust, in equal shares, to my legitimate children. So long as my wife, Coco Henderson, remains guardian of my children, and until they reach the age of majority, business decisions pertaining to the children's interest in Coast Eagle Airlines will be made by Dryden Dunsmore.'"

There was a collective intake of breath in the room, followed by murmured sidebar conversations.

"Well, there's a complexity," Destiny whispered to Amber.

It was obvious Samuel had not contemplated Dryden Dunsmore dying along with him.

Max cleared his throat, and everyone fell silent.

"'Should my wife predecease me,'" he continued, "'guardianship of my minor children will go to Roth Calvin.'"

The room went completely silent, and a dozen gazes swung to Roth. He held his composure for a full ten seconds, but then an uncontrollable smile curved his thin lips, gratification glowing in the depths of his pale blue eyes.

A buzz of conversation came up in the room.

Roth turned to the lawyer on his right. His tone was low, but Amber heard every word. "With Dryden out of the picture, do I have control over the shares?"

The lawyer nodded.

Roth's smile grew wider and more calculating.

"The codicil," Max interrupted the various discussions.

People quieted down again, and Roth's expression settled into self-satisfaction.

"To give some context to this…" said Max. "And I do apologize for being so direct on such an emotional matter. Samuel Henderson was pronounced dead at the accident scene, while Coco Henderson was pronounced dead during the ambulance ride to the hospital."

Amber's stomach tightened. She'd been assured Coco had not regained consciousness after the crash, but she couldn't help but be reminded of the fear and horror her stepsister must have experienced in those final seconds while the plane attempted to land in the storm.

"As such, Samuel is deemed to have predeceased his wife." Max held a single sheet of paper. "Given that fact, Coco Henderson's codicil is legal and valid. It modifies the joint will in only one way." He read, "'I leave guardianship of my child or children to my stepsister, Amber Welsley.'"

Amber could feel shock permeate the room. Jaws literally dropped open and gazes swung to her. Roth's glare sent a wave of animosity that nearly pushed her backward.

Beneath the table, Destiny grasped her hand.

"What about business decisions?" Roth barked. "That woman is in no position to run the company. She's an assistant."

"Assistant *director,*" Destiny corrected.

Amber was in a management position, not a clerical one.

Roth sneered at them both. "Samuel clearly wanted someone qualified in charge of business decisions on behalf of his son."

"It's a valid question," said Max. "For the moment, Amber Welsley has guardianship over Zachary, including all rights and responsibilities to manage and safeguard his ownership position in Coast Eagle."

"But—" Roth began.

Max held up a hand to forestall him. "For any changes to that, you'll need a decision from a judge."

"You can bet we're going to a judge," spat Roth.

Amber whispered to Destiny, "What does this all mean?"

"It means we're going to court to duke it out with Roth. And it means he just became your mortal enemy. But right now, it also means you get Zachary."

Amber's chest swelled tight. Zachary would stay with her. For now, nothing else mattered.

Walking through the entrance of the Atlanta hotel ballroom, Cole gazed at the crowds of people attending the Georgia Pilots Association annual fund-raiser. Tonight was the formal recognition of the new Samuel Henderson Memorial Scholarship, so he knew the who's who of Coast Eagle Airlines would be in the room.

Luca was beside him, dressed in a formal suit. "You'll be glad you came."

"I'll mostly be glad if it shuts you up."

Cole had told himself a thousand times that the Hendersons of Atlanta were none of his business, and he still believed it. But Luca had kept after him for three long weeks. Finally, Cole had given in and checked out a picture of Zachary on a news site.

The baby was cuter than he'd expected, and his face had seemed strangely familiar. But Cole chalked it up to the power of suggestion. When you started looking for a family resemblance, everything took on new meaning. Sometimes gray eyes were simply gray eyes.

But once he'd scratched the surface, he'd ended up reading the rest of the article, learning there was a court challenge for guardianship. He didn't necessarily agree with Luca that everyone involved was a jackal out to get the kid's money. But he did find himself analyzing the players.

In the end, his curiosity won out, and he agreed to make the trip to Atlanta. He had no intention of marching up to the front door and introducing himself as a long-lost relative. He was staying under the radar, checking things out and returning to Alaska just as soon as he confirmed Zachary was safe.

"Right there," said Luca. "In the black dress, lace sleeves, brown hair, kind of swooped up. She's at the table below the podium. She's moving right now."

As Cole zeroed in on Amber Welsley, she turned, presenting him with a surprisingly pretty profile.

Her diamond jewelry flashed beneath the bright lights, accenting her feminine face. Her dress was classic, a scooped neckline, three-quarter-length lace sleeves that blended to a form-fitting bodice and a narrow skirt that emphasized her trim figure.

From this distance, she surprised him. She wasn't at all what he'd expected. She was younger, softer, insidiously captivating. While he stared at her, the wholly inappropriate thought that she was kissable welled up in his mind.

"You want to go over and say hi?" asked Luca.

The true answer was no. Cole wanted to get on an airplane and fly back to Alaska.

He might as well get this over with. Checking out Amber and all the other characters in this family drama was his purpose in being here. There wasn't any point waiting.

"Let's do it," he said.

"Roth Calvin's at the next table," said Luca as they walked. "He's facing us, talking to the guy with red hair, in the steel-gray jacket."

"I think you missed your calling as a spy."

Luca grinned. "I'm calling dibs on the one named Destiny."

"Who's Destiny?"

"She was in a couple of the photos with Amber Welsley. She's hot. And with a name like that, I'm definitely giving her a shot."

Cole shook his head. "She's all yours, buddy. I just want to make sure the kid's okay." Then any duty he might have as a blood relative would be done.

"By kid, you mean your baby brother?"

"Yeah, that's not a phrase we'll be using."

"Boggles the mind, doesn't it?"

"You're going to have to be boggled all by yourself. I won't be here long enough."

"You want a wingman for the intro?"

"Sure. But don't use the name Henderson."

"Undercover. I like it."

"I'll use Cole Parker. My middle name."

"Right behind you, Cole Parker."

The closer they drew to the Coast Eagle tables, the more beautiful Amber became. Her hair wasn't brown, but a rich chestnut with highlights that shimmered under the bright stage lights. It was half up, half down in a tousled bundle with wisps flowing over her temples and down her back. The scalloped neckline of her dress showed off an expanse of creamy skin, while the lace across her shoulders played peekaboo with his imagination.

Her eyes were deep blue, fringed with dark lashes. Her full lips were dark red, her cheeks enticingly flushed. He had a sudden vision of her clambering naked into his bed.

She turned as he approached, caught his stare and gave him an obviously practiced smile. He realized hundreds if not thousands of people must have introduced themselves and offered their condolences in the past weeks.

"Amber Welsley?" he asked her, offering his hand.

"I am."

"I'm Cole Parker from Aviation 58. My condolences on your loss."

"Thank you, Mr. Parker." She shook his hand.

The soft warmth of her palm seemed to whisper through his skin. He felt a ripple of awareness move up his arm and along the length of his body. Her expression flinched, and for a second he thought she'd felt it, too. But then her formal smile was back in place, and she was moving on.

Cole quickly spoke again to keep her attention. "This is my business partner, Luca Dodd."

"Please call me Luca."

"And I'm Cole," Cole put in, feeling like an idiot for not having said it right away.

"Aviation 58 was looking to contribute to the Samuel Henderson fund," said Luca.

Cole's stomach twisted, and he shot Luca a glare of annoyance.

Where had that come from? There was no way on earth Cole was contributing to something with Samuel's name on it.

"It's a very worthy cause," said Amber. But then she caught Cole's expression. "Is something wrong?"

"No," he quickly answered.

"You look upset."

"I'm fine."

She canted her head to one side, considering him. "You don't agree that the pilot scholarship is a worthy cause?"

"I believe what Luca meant is that we're thinking of setting something up in parallel. With Georgia Pilots, but not necessarily..." How exactly was he going to phrase this?

"Not necessarily in honor of Samuel Henderson?" Amber finished for him.

Cole didn't know how to respond to the direct challenge. He didn't want to lie, but he didn't want to insult her, either.

"You have a spare ten million hanging around to match Coast Eagle?" she asked.

"Ten million is a little out of our league," Cole admitted.

Her blue eyes narrowed ever so slightly. "Did you know Samuel?"

"I never met him."

The suspicious expression didn't detract at all from her beauty, and Cole experienced an urge to sweep back her hair and kiss the delicate curve of her neck.

"So you disliked him from afar?" she asked.

"I didn't…" This was getting worse by the second. Cole gave himself a mental shake. "I knew people who knew him."

"Amber?" prompted a man at her elbow.

Cole clenched his jaw at the interruption.

"Five minutes to introductions," said the man.

"Thanks, Julius." She glanced at Luca for a moment before settling her attention back on Cole. "It looks like I need to take my seat. It was a pleasure to meet you, Cole Parker."

"Are you always this polite?"

"Do you want me to be rude?"

Cole was the one who'd been rude. "This conversation didn't go the way I expected."

"Maybe you could try again some other time."

"What are you doing later?" He hadn't intended the question to sound intimate, but it did.

She didn't miss a beat. "I believe I'm eating crab cocktail and chicken Kiev, giving a short, heartfelt speech on behalf of the Henderson family, then relieving the nanny and going to sleep."

"Zachary?" Cole took advantage of the opening.

"He'll be having his bath about now. He likes splashing with the blue duck and chewing on the washcloth."

"Are you staying for the dance?"

"I doubt it."

"*Will* you stay for the dance?"

She hesitated. "You think you'll do better if we're dancing?"

"I'll try not to insult the evening's deceased honoree."

"You set a high bar."

"Underpromise and overdeliver."

The man named Julius returned, touching Amber's arm. "Amber?"

"Goodbye for now," she told Cole with a smile.

Though her expression was more polite than warm, he decided to take the words as encouraging.

"What the hell was *that?*" Luca muttered as she walked away.

"Contributing to his *scholarship?*" asked Cole. "Where did you expect me to go from there?"

"You choked."

"We are *not* contributing to his scholarship."

"You made that much clear."

They turned to wind their way between tables.

"She's not what I expected," said Cole as they returned to the back half of the big ballroom.

"She has two arms, two legs, speaks English. What did you expect?"

"I don't know." Cole struggled to organize his thoughts. "Snobbish, maybe, polished and conniving."

"She looked pretty polished to me."

"She's beautiful, but that's not the same thing."

"She's a knockout. Do you actually think she'll dance with you?"

"Why not?"

"Because you choked, and I'm sure she has other offers."

"I'm staying optimistic."

As the lights went dim and the applause came up, Cole made up his mind to approach her as soon as the dinner was over. This was by far his best chance to mingle with the Hendersons and Coast Eagle without revealing his identity, and he wanted to get it done and over with.

Two

Amber couldn't wait to get out of the ballroom. Her first choice on a Saturday night was to stay home with Zachary, tucked in her jammies with a cup of hot chocolate and an old movie. But she was the closest thing there was to a member of the Henderson family, and somebody had to graciously accept the pilots association's thanks.

Unlike her sister, Coco, Amber never attended highbrow events. Consequently, everything she wore tonight was new. Her feet were killing her in the ridiculous high heels. Her push-up bra was digging into her ribs, the lace scratching her skin. And the tight dress, chosen by Destiny, who insisted it was perfect, was restricting her movements so that she couldn't even cross her legs under the table.

The MC ended a string of thank-yous with a request for applause to compliment the catering staff. As the clapping died down, the music came up, signaling the start of the dance.

Amber breathed a sigh of relief. All that was left was to politely make her way toward the exit, find a cab and get home. She stood, tucking her tiny purse under her arm.

A fiftysomething woman she vaguely recognized grasped her hand to shake it. "Lovely speech, Ms. Welsley. Lovely speech."

"Thank you."

The woman's expression turned serious. "Even in such tragic circumstances, the Henderson family is having a positive impact on the community."

"Samuel was a very generous man," Amber responded by rote, though she had her own private thoughts on Samuel's character, most particularly his decision to marry her beautiful, impetuous, nineteen-year-old stepsister.

Amber had initially kept her distance from the couple, regretting many times the decision to bring Coco to the company party where the two had met. But then Coco had become pregnant, and Amber had been drawn back into the drama of Coco's life.

"Excuse me, Ms. Welsley," came a male voice.

The woman seemed reluctant to step back to give way.

"Good evening." Amber smiled at the new man, taking his offered hand, mentally calculating how long it would take her to run the gauntlet to the exit. It would be an hour or more at this pace. She truly didn't think she could stand that long in these shoes. For a nonsensical moment, she pictured herself toppling over onto the ballroom floor.

"I'm Kevin Mathews from Highbush Unlimited. I wonder if I might give you my card."

Amber kept her smile in place. "Certainly, Mr. Mathews."

He dug into his inside pocket for a business card. "We're a charitable organization, focused on environmental rehabilitation, primarily in the northwest. I know a lot about Mr. Henderson and Coast Eagle, and I can't help imagining that he would have been a supporter of the environmental rehabilitation."

Amber doubted that Samuel had given much thought to the environment, since he flew around in a private jet, air-conditioned the heck out of his mansion and owned several gas-guzzling luxury cars.

But she took the card the man offered. "I'd be happy to pass this along to Coast Eagle's Community Outreach Unit."

His expression faltered. "If you have some time now, I could outline for you our—"

"There you are," came a deeper male voice. "I believe it's time for our dance."

Cole Parker appeared by her side, his arm held out, a broad smile on his face.

Amber couldn't tell if he was rescuing her or about to pitch something himself. But she quickly estimated that the dance floor was more than halfway to the exit. That was progress. She returned his smile and took his arm.

"Please excuse me," she said to Kevin.

Kevin's expression faltered, but he had little choice but to let her go.

Cole guided her through the crowd, keeping their pace brisk enough to discourage the people who looked as though they might approach. It was hard on her feet, particularly her baby toes, but there was no option but to keep walking. Gradually, the crowd thinned near the dance floor.

"Am I out of the frying pan and into the fire?" she asked him.

"I'm not hitting you up for a donation, if that's what you mean."

"Good to hear." She wasn't sure what he wanted, but he was persistent enough that he had to be after something.

"I brought you a gift," he told her.

"Bribery? That's a bit blatant, don't you think?"

"I believe in getting straight to the point." He lifted his palm.

She glanced down, squinting. "You bought me a pair of... socks?"

"Dancing slippers. I got them from a vending machine in the lobby." He glanced down at her black-and-gold four-inch heels. "Unless I miss my guess, those are two-hour shoes."

She grimaced. "Is that what they call them?" It was an apt name.

She knew she should be suspicious of his motives, but she couldn't help but feel grateful.

"Over here." He pointed to a couple of empty chairs at the edge of the dance floor. "Have a seat."

She eased down, deciding to accept the gift and remove the torture chambers from her feet. How much could she possibly be indebted to him for a pair of vending-machine dancing slippers?

She unbuckled the straps and slipped her feet free.

"I went with medium." He handed her the black-satin, ballet-style slippers.

Slipping them onto her feet, she nearly groaned out loud. "They're so soft."

He bent to pick up her shiny heels, dangling them from his fingertips for a moment before setting them down. "These are ridiculous."

She rose with him. "This is an important event for Coast Eagle. And Destiny says they make my calves look longer."

"Your calves are already the perfect length." He set the shoes on the chair.

"You're not even looking at them."

"I can tell by your height." He offered his arm again. "Shall we?"

"I suppose it's the least I can do, since you saved my feet. But you have to make me a promise."

"Sure."

She took his arm. "After the dance, walk me to the exit." She glanced discreetly around. "For some reason, nobody's bothering me when I'm with you."

"Were they bothering you before?"

"All evening long." She'd never experienced anything like it. "Donations, jobs and pictures. Why on earth would anybody want their picture taken with me?"

"Because you're beautiful?" He drew her into his arms.

"Ha, ha." Coco had been beautiful. Amber was, well, sensible. She was very sensible.

Not that sensible was a bad thing. And she truly didn't mind her looks. Her eyes were a pleasant shade of blue. Her nose wasn't too big. Her hair was slightly curly and had its good days and bad days. Today it had been tamed by a team of professionals, so it looked pretty good. She had to say, though, she wasn't crazy about the sticky feeling from all the products they'd used at Chez Philippe.

"I wasn't joking," said Cole.

"We both know you've got a lot of ground to make up for from earlier," she said, settling into the rhythm of the music.

"True," he agreed.

"So anything you say or do is suspect."

"You're pretty tough to compliment, you know that?"

"There's no need. I'm over the fact that you didn't like Samuel."

He paused as if weighing his next words. "You're a very good dancer."

She couldn't tell if he was mocking her or not. She'd certainly never spent much time perfecting dance steps. Was he trying to kowtow, or was he simply making small talk? Or maybe he was just getting off the topic of Samuel.

"So are you," she answered neutrally. "I can't remember where you said you were from."

"Alaska. Are you changing the subject?"

"From me to you? Yes. You're about out of things to compliment. Unless you like my hair."

"I like your hair."

"Good. It cost a lot of money to get it this way. Now back to you."

"Aviation 58 is in Juneau. The state capital. It's on the panhandle."

"You're a pilot?"

"I am. I'm also one of the owners of the airline."

"I've never heard of it."

Coast Eagle flew to Seattle and California, but they didn't venture into the north. "We're regional."

She tipped her head back to look at him. "And what brought you to Atlanta, Cole Parker?"

He gave a small shrug. "It's December. Have you seen a weather report for Alaska?"

"Not recently. Maybe never."

"It's cold up there."

"So you're on vacation?"

"For a few days, yes."

For the first time, she allowed herself to take a good look at his face. She realized he was an astonishingly handsome man, deep gray eyes, a straight nose, square chin, all topped with thick, dark hair, cut short and neat. She couldn't detect aftershave or shampoo, but there was something fresh and clean about his scent.

He was probably six-two. His shoulders were square, body fit and trim. And his big, square hands seemed strong and capable where they held her. In a flash, she realized she was attracted to him.

"Amber?" His deep voice startled her. That sound was another thing she liked about him.

"Yes?"

"I asked if there was anything in particular we should see." Had he? How had she missed that?

She quickly corralled her thoughts. "The botanical gardens are beautiful. Or you can do outdoor ice-skating. My favorite is Atlantic Station. A little shopping, a little Christmas-light gazing, some hot chocolate." She couldn't help thinking about Zachary and the Christmas events he might enjoy as he got older.

She'd easily come to love seeing him every day. He was a bit fussy in the evenings, but the poor little guy had been through a lot. His mother and father were both gone, and he had no way of knowing why it was happening.

She was doing her best to substitute. And she'd wrapped her head around the possibility of raising a baby. Though she couldn't yet imagine her life with a child, a school-age child, then a teenager, then a young man. When she thought that far ahead, she feared she wasn't capable of pulling it off. But she knew she had to come through for him. She was all he had.

She felt a sudden urge to rush home and hold him in her arms, reassure him that she'd figure it out.

"Are we close to the exit?" she asked Cole, thinking she could slip out and get herself home.

"I'll dance you over there," said Cole. "Tired?"

"Partly. But this isn't exactly my thing."

"I thought the über-rich thrived on fresh crab, Belgian torte and champagne."

"I'm not über-rich." Though she could understand how he would make that mistake. Lately, everybody seemed to assume that guardianship of Zachary made her an instant billionaire. It was far more complicated than that.

"Right," he drawled.

She didn't want to have this debate. "Thank you for the dance, Cole."

His expression turned serious. "I did it again, didn't I? Stuffed my foot in my mouth?"

"Not at all. I am tired, and I really appreciate you escorting me across the ballroom. It was going to take hours at the rate I was going."

"I'll get you to the front doors," he offered.

"That's not necessary."

"It's my pleasure." His hand dropped to the small of her back. "I'll glower at anyone who tries to talk to us along the way."

She couldn't help but smile at that. And, to be truthful, it did seem like a prudent course of action. The lobby and foyer were full of people. Her name and face had been in the news for the past three weeks, so she was easily recognized.

"Then, thank you," she told him.

"Let's go."

He picked up the pace, drawing her across the mezzanine floor lobby and down two sets of elevators. People stared as they passed but didn't approach them. For a fleeting moment, she wondered if he'd consider a permanent gig as her escort. This was certainly more pleasant than her trek into the event.

"The doorman will get me a cab," she told Cole as they came to the glass front.

"No need. I have a car right here."

"Cole—"

"And a driver," he finished, moving through the front door. "I'm not plotting to get you alone. I'll get you home safe and sound, nothing else."

As she stepped onto the sidewalk, she felt its cold hardness through the dancing slippers, and her memory kicked in. "My shoes." She turned. "I left my shoes upstairs."

"I'll go back for them," he offered. "You don't need to walk all that way again."

"Taxi, sir?" the doorman inquired.

"I've got a car waiting," Cole answered, handing the man a tip. "A sedan for Aviation 58."

"I'll have it brought around," the doorman answered.

"I can't take your car," said Amber. How had this gotten so complicated?

"Where are you going?" asked Cole.

"Fifth Avenue and Eighty-Ninth."

"It'll only take ten minutes to get you there."

A black car pulled up in front of them and Cole opened the door.

Amber decided to go with the flow. The sooner she got going, the sooner she'd be home with Zachary. She climbed in, and Cole shut the door behind her.

But before they pulled away, he surprised her by hopping in the other side.

"I thought you were going back for my shoes."

"I'll do that after we get you home. Fifth Avenue and Eighty-Ninth," he said to the driver.

"That's ridiculous."

She couldn't understand why he'd make the round trip for nothing. Unless he was worried she'd commandeer his car for a joyride. Though she doubted the driver would let her do that.

As they pulled out of the turnaround and onto the street, she clicked through other possibilities. He'd been intensely persistent, awfully complimentary and easy to get along with, and he'd stuck to her like glue. What could he be after?

And then it came to her. The man owned an airline, a small regional West Coast airline that was likely looking to expand. She instantly realized the vacation story was a cover. Cole was here to do business.

She angled herself in the seat, facing him. "You're after our Pacific routes."

"Excuse me?"

"I figured it out. You're thinking Samuel's death makes Coast Eagle vulnerable. You're hoping we'll be looking to downsize, and you think you can get your hands on the Pacific routes to expand Aviation 58."

He stared at her for a long moment.

"You've been way too friendly," she elaborated. "You over-played your hand."

"Maybe I'm simply attracted to you."

She gazed down at the fancy dress. She did look better than

usual, but Cole was still out of her league. "There were far more beautiful women at the event tonight."

"I didn't see them." The sincerity in his expression was quite impressive.

"Nice try. It's the routes."

"You see that as the only possible explanation?"

"I do."

"Then, I admit it. It's the routes. Will you sell them to me?"

She leaned back in the seat. "I don't know why everybody thinks I have so much power. I'm the assistant director of finance. There's still a board of directors in place, and the vice presidents are in charge of operations until they name a new president."

"But as Zachary's guardian, you control board appointments."

"Theoretically."

If she kept custody of Zachary, that would be true. But before that could ever happen, she had a big fight with Roth on her hands.

"There's nothing theoretical about it," said Cole. "The board answers to the shareholders, and the president answers to the board, and everyone else answers to the president. You can do anything you want."

"But I won't. I have my own job at Coast Eagle, and I'm not about to muscle in on anyone else's."

"It's your responsibility." There was an unexpected hardness to Cole's tone. "It's your responsibility to Zachary to take control of the company."

She turned to look at him again. "It's my responsibility to Zachary to ensure the company is well run. That doesn't mean I make any particular decision."

His dark eyes were implacable. "Yes, it does."

"Well, Mr. Cole Parker, owner of Aviation 58 in Alaska, you are certainly entitled to your opinion. And I'm more than entitled to ignore it."

He opened his mouth but then obviously thought better of speaking.

The car came to a halt at the curb.

"The Newmont Building?" the driver asked. "Or are you in Sutten's Edge?"

"This is it," said Amber, feeling anxious to get away. "Joyce Roland is the director of planning," she said to Cole. "You can ask her about the Pacific routes, but she may not take your call."

The driver had come around and now swung open her door.

"Thank you for the ride. Good night, Cole."

A small smile played on his lips. "You're very polite."

"So I've been told."

"Good night, Amber. Thank you for the dance."

A sudden rush of warmth enveloped her, and she found her gaze dropping from his eyes to his lips. For a fleeting second, she imagined him kissing her good-night.

She shook away the wayward feeling and quickly exited the car. Zachary was upstairs waiting, and Roth was in the wings with a team of high-priced lawyers. Amber didn't have time for kisses or fantasies or anything else.

Cole advanced through the hotel lobby, heading for the escalators that would take him back to the ballroom.

It didn't take him long to spot Luca coming the other way, a pretty blond woman at his side.

"There you are," said Luca as they met. "I wondered what had happened to you."

"I left something in the ballroom," said Cole.

"This is Destiny Frost. Turns out, she's a friend of Amber Welsley." Luca's expression was inscrutable.

Cole played along, pretending Luca hadn't planned to meet Destiny. "Nice to meet you." He offered his hand.

She shook, and hers was slim and cool. "It's a pleasure."

"I offered Destiny a ride home," said Luca. "You coming with us?" His expression told Cole a third wheel would not be particularly welcome.

Cole tipped his chin toward the escalator. "I have to grab something upstairs. Can you swing back and get me later?"

Luca gave a satisfied smile. "Will do."

"Luca says you're from Alaska?" asked Destiny.

"We are," Cole replied.

"I've never been there."

"It's beautiful, magnificent."

"It must be cold."

Luca stepped in. "I've already offered to keep her warm."

Destiny smiled and shook her head. "He's shameless."

"But harmless," said Cole, intending to be reassuring, but also being honest. Luca was a perfect gentleman.

"I'll text you on the way back?" asked Luca.

"Sounds good." With a nod to both of them, Cole headed for the escalator.

He was going against the crowd, most people on their way out of the event. So he easily made it to the ballroom and headed for the chair where they'd parked Amber's shoes.

To his surprise, they were gone.

"Seriously?" he muttered out loud.

He glanced around at the departing crowd. At an event this highbrow, somebody was going to steal a pair of shoes?

Then he caught a glint of gold in one of the waiter's hands. He squinted. It was definitely Amber's shoes. The man was headed toward a side exit.

Cole made a beeline after him, feeling better about human nature. The waiter obviously thought they'd been abandoned and was taking them to the hotel's lost and found.

Cole wound his way through the tables and took the same exit, coming out into a long dim hallway. One direction obviously led to the kitchen, the other down a narrow flight of stairs. It seemed unlikely that the lost and found was in the kitchen, so he took the stairs.

At the bottom, he spotted the guy about thirty yards away. He called out, and the man turned.

"The shoes," called Cole.

Before he could say anything more, the man bolted, running a few steps before shoving open a side exit.

"Are you kidding me?" Cole shouted, breaking into a run.

He burst through the side door, finding himself in an alley.

He quickly scanned the area and spotted the guy at a run. He sprinted after the man. When he caught up, he grasped the guy's left arm and spun him around, bringing him to a sliding halt.

"What's going on?" Cole gasped. "You're stealing a pair of *shoes?*"

"They're my girlfriend's." The man was gasping for breath.

"They're *my* girlfriend's." As he spoke, Cole couldn't help but take note of the man's unshaven face, and the rather wild look in his eyes. "You're not a waiter."

The man reached in his pants pocket and pulled a knife, flicking open a six-inch blade and holding it menacingly out in front of him.

"They're *shoes*," said Cole, adrenaline rushing into his bloodstream. Admittedly, they were nice shoes. And given the Hendersons' wealth, they were likely ridiculously expensive. But what could they possibly bring this guy on the black market?

The man snarled. "Do yourself a favor and walk away."

No way was that happening. Cole was returning Amber's property to her. "Give me the shoes."

"You want to get *hurt?*"

Suddenly, a low growl sounded next to Cole. His skin prickled, and he glanced cautiously down. But the mangy dog was staring at the man with the knife. It didn't seem to be threatening Cole.

"He'll go for your throat," Cole lied.

The man glanced furtively at the dog.

The dog growled again.

"Drop the knife, or he'll attack."

The man hesitated, and the dog took a step forward. The knife clattered to the ground, along with the shoes, and the man took two rapid steps backward. Then he spun around and ran.

Cole took in the medium-size dog that was now wagging its tail, obviously feeling proud of himself.

"Good job," he told the mutt, patting its head, finding sticky, matted fur.

He looked closer and realized the animal was painfully thin.

It had a wiry, mottled coat, mostly tan, but black on the ears and muzzle. Its brown eyes looked world-weary and exhausted.

"You a stray?" Cole found himself asking.

He moved to pick up the shoes. When he straightened, the dog was watching him patiently.

"You probably want a reward for all that."

The dog blinked.

"I don't blame you." Cole blew out a breath. He supposed the least he could do was buy the animal a burger.

"Come on, then." He started down the alley toward the brightly lit street. The dog trotted at his heels.

At the front of the hotel, Cole reported the incident to one of the doormen, who sent someone to retrieve the knife. Cole learned that they'd had previous trouble with a thief impersonating a waiter at large events. If the knife had fingerprints on it, they might be able to catch the guy. It seemed likely he'd stolen more than just the shoes tonight.

Duty done, Cole and the dog then made their way down the street until they came to a fast-food restaurant.

Thinking it was a fifty-fifty shot the mutt would wait, Cole left it outside while he purchased two deluxe hamburgers. He was hungry after the fancy little portions at the pilots association event, and a burger didn't seem like the worst idea in the world.

When he returned to the street, the dog jumped to attention. It wolfed down the burger in two bites, so Cole gave it the second one, as well.

His phone chimed, and a text message told him Luca was sending back the empty car. Luca and Destiny were stopping for a nightcap.

Cole smiled at his friend's luck, tossed the wrappers in the trash and headed back toward the hotel. Predictably, the dog followed along. It was sure to be disappointed when a meal didn't appear at their next stop.

Cole took the animal back to the alley at the edge of the hotel property and pointed. "Go on, now," he told it.

It looked up at him uncomprehendingly.

"Go home," Cole commanded.

It didn't move.

He made his voice sterner. "Go on."

The dog ducked its head, eyes going sad.

Cole felt a shot to his chest.

He tried to steel himself against the guilt, but the effort didn't pay off. He crouched down in front of the dog, scratching its matted neck and meeting its eyes. "I don't know what you expect here."

It pushed forward, nuzzling its nose against Cole's thigh.

"Those are rented pants," said Cole.

It pushed farther forward.

"I live in Alaska."

Its tail began to wag.

"Crap."

"Mr. Parker?" The driver appeared in Cole's peripheral vision. "Are you ready to go, sir?"

Cole stood, drawing a deep sigh. "We're ready."

"We?"

"The dog's coming, too."

The driver glanced down at the scruffy animal. He hesitated, but then said, "Of course, sir."

"Do you have a blanket or something to protect the seat?"

"I'll get a newspaper from the doorman."

"That'll work," said Cole. He looked to the dog. "You want to go for a car ride?"

Its head lifted. Its brow went up. And its tail wagged harder.

"I'll take that as a yes." Cole knew he was making a stupid, emotional decision, one he'd likely regret very quickly. But he couldn't bring himself to leave the animal behind.

He closed his eyes for a long moment. All this for a pair of shoes.

Three

The next morning, Cole headed for the Hendersons' penthouse apartment to return Amber's shoes. He took the dog with him, thinking maybe he'd stop by the shelter on his way back and drop it off. He told himself they were in the business of finding stray animals good homes.

The dog looked much more appealing since Cole had given him a bath in the hotel's carwash bay. He smelled better, too, considerably better. And he'd probably put on five pounds between the room-service steak last night and the bacon and sausage breakfast.

The animal had been meticulously well behaved, and now stood quietly by Cole's side while Cole rang the bell.

A minute later, Amber answered the door. She was dressed in faded blue jeans, bare feet poking out at the bottom. A stained T-shirt stretched across her chest, and she had what looked like oatmeal smeared in her hair. Zachary was bawling in her arms.

"The doorman said it was a delivery," she told Cole over Zachary's cries.

Cole held up the shoes. "It is a delivery."

She focused on the shiny creations while struggling to hold the wiggling, howling Zachary. "Honestly, I'd hoped somebody might steal them."

"You have got to be kidding." Cole didn't know whether to laugh or cry.

"Only partially kidding," she admitted. "They cost a lot of money, but I don't ever want to have to wear them again." She glanced down. "You have a dog?"

"I have one now," he said.

"Okay." She seemed to digest that while Zachary continued to wriggle. It was clear she had her hands full. "Could you maybe just bring them in and toss them down?" She glanced around the foyer.

"Sure." Cole moved through the doorway, spying a closet door. He opened it and placed them inside.

The baby's cries faded to whimpers behind him.

He turned back. "I'll have you know I practically risked my life to rescue these."

Zachary suddenly stiffened. He twisted his head to stare at Cole in what looked like amazement.

"The party got that wild?" Amber asked.

Zachary's silver-gray eyes focused on Cole like lasers. He went silent and stared unblinking, seeming to drink in Cole's appearance.

Then, suddenly, he lunged for Cole.

"Hey." Amber grappled to keep hold of him.

Zachary's own arms were outstretched, reaching almost desperately for Cole. He started to howl again, hands clasping the air.

"This is weird," said Amber.

Cole didn't have a clue how to respond.

"Do you mind?" She moved closer, glancing meaningfully at the baby.

"I guess not." Who would say no?

Taking Zachary from her arms, he cautiously brought him into his chest. Zachary instantly wrapped his arms around Cole's neck, squeezing tight. He nuzzled his sticky, tear-damp face against Cole's skin. Then he sighed, and his entire body went limp against Cole's chest.

Through his shock and surprise, Cole's heart started to pound, bringing a strange tightness to his chest. For some bizarre reason, his baby brother trusted him. How was a guy supposed to react to that?

"You're magic," Amber whispered. "Whatever it is you're doing, just keep it up."

"I'm only standing here."

"He's been crying for over an hour. He gets like that sometimes."

"He probably exhausted himself before I got here."

"I think he misses his parents," Amber said softly, her expression compassionate as she gazed at Zachary. She reached out to stoke the baby's downy hair. "But he doesn't understand what he's feeling, and he certainly can't put it into words."

Then she gave Cole a sweet smile. "You should come inside for a minute."

The dog seemed to understand the invitation. It padded gamely into the living room.

Amber's cute, disheveled appearance, the mutt's claws clicking on the hardwood and the baby powder scent of Zachary's warm body curled in his arms brought a sense of unreality to Cole.

"Sure," he answered, and followed her through the archway.

It took only seconds for him to realize this was a perfect opportunity to learn more about her.

"It was either this or the mansion." She seemed to be apologizing for the opulent surroundings. "We thought it would be less disruptive if Zachary kept his nanny, Isabel. She occasionally sleeps over, so there was no way we'd all fit in my apartment. It's one bedroom with a tiny kitchen. This place belonged to Samuel."

The furnishings were obviously expensive, but they were strewn with baby blankets and rattles, the floor decorated with colorful plastic toys.

"Sorry about the mess," she said.

"You don't need to apologize."

"And me." She looked ruefully down at herself. "Well, this is me. This is what I normally look like. Last night was the anomaly."

"Seriously, Amber. You have nothing to apologize for. You look great."

She coughed out a laugh of disbelief.

"Okay, you look normal. How formal do you think we get in Alaska?"

She seemed to consider that. "Can I get you something?"

"I'm fine."

He didn't want to put her to any work. Then again, judging by Zachary's even breathing and relaxed body, his excuse for hanging around had just fallen asleep. Maybe refreshments weren't such a bad idea.

"Do you happen to have coffee?" he asked.

"Coming up. Take a seat anywhere." She gestured to the furniture as she exited through another archway that obviously led to the kitchen.

Cole took in the massive living room. In one corner, a plush sofa and a couple of leather armchairs bracketed a gas fireplace. Another furniture grouping was set up next to a bank of picture windows overlooking the city. The room was open to a formal dining room at one end and a hallway at the other that obviously led to the bedrooms.

He decided to follow Amber into the kitchen. No point in wasting valuable conversation time here by himself.

The kitchen was also huge, with high ceilings, a central island, generous granite counter spaces, stainless-steel appliances of every conceivable description and maple cabinets interspersed with big windows that faced the park. There was a breakfast nook at one end, stationed beside a balcony door, and an open door at the other, leading to a big pantry.

"This is very nice," said Cole.

"I'm still getting used to the size." She closed the lid and pressed a button on the coffeemaker. "It's weird moving into someone else's stuff—their furniture, their dishes, their towels. It's crazy, but I miss my pepper mill." She pointed to a corner of the counter. "You practically need a forklift to use that one."

Cole found himself smiling. "You should move your own stuff in."

For some reason, her expression faltered.

"I'm sorry," he quickly put in. "It's too soon?"

She paused, seeming to search for words. "It's too something. I won't pretend I was close to my stepsister, and I barely knew Samuel. Maybe it's the court case. Maybe I don't want to jinx anything. But I'm definitely keeping my own apartment intact until everything is completely finalized."

Cole perched on a stool in front of the island. Zachary was

quiet and comfortable in his arms and surprisingly easy to hold. "Tell me about the court case."

"You haven't read the tabloids?"

"Not much."

"I'm in a custody battle with Roth Calvin. He's a vice president at Coast Eagle and Samuel's stated choice for guardian."

"I'd heard that much."

"Coco named me as guardian, and I won on a technicality, but Roth's fighting it."

"Is Roth close to Zachary?"

Amber pulled two hunter-green stoneware mugs out of a side cupboard. "Roth's close to Coast Eagle. You were right last night in the car. The person who controls Zachary ultimately controls the company."

"So you *can* get me my Pacific routes." Now that Cole had thought it through, he realized the cover story was perfect. It gave him an excuse to ask all kinds of questions without anybody growing suspicious.

"I have no intention of micromanaging Coast Eagle."

"We had a fight last night, didn't we?" Cole had become so focused on the shoes, and then the dog, and then on Zachary, he'd forgotten she'd left the car mad at him.

"You call that a fight?"

"I believe I questioned your commitment to Zachary's inheritance."

"My commitment is to Zachary. I want the company to stay healthy for him, sure. But I can tell when I'm not the smartest person in the room. There are a lot of committed, hardworking managers and employees at Coast Eagle. They need to continue running the company."

"Don't sell yourself short."

"I'm an assistant director, Cole."

He liked it when she said his name. "You're responsible for the well-being of the company owner."

Her gaze rested on Zachary, and her tone went soft. "Poor thing."

"Poor little rich boy?" It came out more sarcastic than Cole had intended.

"I honestly wish he'd inherited a whole lot less. That way nobody would fight me for him."

"So you're afraid you might lose?"

Her expression faltered, and she focused on pouring the freshly brewed coffee. "I try not to think about it." She turned back with both cups in her hands. "I can't believe you got him to sleep."

"I'm just sitting here breathing. You wore him out."

"Maybe he likes the sound of your voice."

"Maybe," Cole agreed.

Cole didn't like to think Zachary's behavior had anything to do with the genetic connection. But Cole supposed it was possible he sounded like Samuel. Maybe Zachary was subconsciously picking it up.

"You can probably get away with putting him down in his bed," said Amber.

"He's fine here."

Oddly, Cole didn't want to put Zachary down, at least not right away. This vulnerable little baby was his brother. And for some reason, the kid had instantly trusted him. Cole was suddenly acutely aware that there were two of them in the world. He could not have imagined how that would make him feel.

Amber's boss, Herbert Nywall's, expression was stern as he rose from the table in her compact office on the seventh floor of the Coast Eagle building.

Max Cutter was the company's chief lawyer, so Herbert had had no choice but to acquiesce to his request to speak privately with Amber. But it was obvious Herbert was becoming frustrated with the increasing interruptions of Amber's day-to-day duties.

She didn't blame him.

"Can this wait, Max?" she asked, earning a look of shock from Herbert.

"I'm afraid not. Sorry, Herbert."

"Not at all," Herbert responded with false cheer. "She's all yours."

"We're pretty busy today," Amber told Max as Herbert closed the door behind him.

"You can't pretend this isn't happening." Max took the chair across from her at the two-person meeting table. It was wedged between her desk and a bookshelf in the windowless room.

"Believe me, I'm not pretending anything isn't happening." In the past three weeks, her life had been turned completely upside down.

Nothing was remotely normal, and now Cole Parker had appeared, somehow insinuating himself into the circumstances. She didn't quite know what to make of him. He was opportunistic, that was for sure. And he had definite designs on Coast Eagle.

But Zachary's reaction to him had been astonishing. And her own reaction was just as bizarre. Yesterday, she'd fought a ridiculous urge to throw herself into Cole's arms and trust him completely.

Max got straight to the point. "Roth's pressuring the board to appoint him president."

The news surprised Amber. It also worried her. "I thought they were going to wait to choose a president."

"That was the agreement. But he wants it bad, and half of the board members are convinced he'll win the custody battle. If he does, he'll be the guy deciding who stays on the board. They want to ingratiate themselves now while they have a chance."

Amber understood their dilemma. She even sympathized. If Roth obtained custody of Zachary, he'd be ruthless in his revenge on board members who'd stood against him.

"Plus," Max continued, "they see strength in him, decisiveness and intelligence. They think he'll make a good president."

"I don't like him," Amber blurted out. "And I don't think he'd make a good president."

Max sat back in his chair. "That was definitive." He seemed to be considering her words. "Is it because of the situation with Zachary? Because that would certainly be understandable."

"It's because he recklessly spends company money. He wants to refurbish or replace the entire fleet with no regard whatsoever for the debt load. He's a shopaholic on a massive scale."

Max quirked a smile. "Interestingly put, but not inaccurate from what I've seen."

"They can't make him president."

"The board's deadlocked. We need to appoint another board member to break the tie."

Amber shook her head. Max had broached the subject of board appointments with her two weeks ago.

"You know I don't want to do that."

"I know you don't."

"I don't want to run Coast Eagle." She knew she wasn't qualified to take the helm of the company.

"Well, you're the only one who doesn't."

Amber came to her feet, taking the three steps that brought her flush against the front of her desk. She turned back. This was a terrible office for pacing.

Max spoke again. "If you appoint the right person, a majority will agree on a different interim president and Roth will have to back down. If you don't appoint anyone, MacSweeny will flip. It's only a matter of time. And then Roth's in."

Amber spoke more to herself than to Max. "And the spending spree begins."

For some reason, her thoughts turned back to Cole Parker. In the car Saturday night, he'd said it was her responsibility to take control of the company for Zachary. She'd disagreed with him at the time, but the advice stuck with her.

She let the memory take shape, and his image came clear in her mind. The streetlights had played across his handsome face. He was sexy in a suit, sexier still in his blue jeans the next morning at the penthouse. And the memory of him holding Zachary? The tenderness had touched a chord deep down inside her. It shouldn't have turned her on, but it did. The truth was, everything about Cole turned her on.

All that probably meant she *shouldn't* take his advice.

She looked at Max, bringing herself back to the present. She had to agree that letting Roth plunge the airline into debt wasn't in Zachary's best interest. Any thinking person could see that. And what Max said was true. At the moment, she was the only person who could legally appoint a new board member.

If she didn't do it, no one could.

"Who?" she found herself venturing. "If I was to appoint someone, who would that be?"

It had to be someone they could trust. It also had to be someone who didn't have to fear Roth if he won the custody battle. It had to be someone who understood the airline, who brought true value to the board and who could be strong in the face of divided loyalties, uncertain times and extraordinarily high stakes.

She couldn't think of a single person who fit the bill.

"You," Max told her softly.

"No." She gripped the back of her chair and shook her head. "No." It was unthinkable. *"No."*

"You underestimate yourself, Amber."

"Coco chose me because she knew I would love Zachary. She had no idea it would put me in this position with the company."

"Coco had no idea about anything," said Max.

Amber didn't know how to respond to that. Her sister wasn't the most analytical person in the world. It was fair to say that Coco had operated on emotion rather than logic. It was also fair to say that Coco had never really grown up. She'd wanted what she'd wanted, and she'd usually wanted it right away. She'd never spent much time worrying about the impact on others.

"There's no one else," said Max, spreading his palms.

"There has to be."

"It's one vote. You take the appointment. You go to one meeting. You vote. You leave. And the new president takes over the reins." He glanced around her small office, all but wrinkling his nose. "You can come back here an hour later and take over your regular duties."

"There's nothing wrong with my job."

"Nobody's saying there is. Though not many new billionaires would keep working in this particular office."

"I'm not a new—"

"Amber, please. I can see that your instinct is to be humble. But you're Zachary's guardian. Anytime you want to exercise it, you have control of a billion-dollar company."

"Temporarily."

"Maybe. But maybe not."

She slid back into her chair, propping her elbows on the table. "It's not that simple."

"It's very simple."

She couldn't, wouldn't, didn't dare let her head run away with any aspect of the situation. There was too much at stake for her to let her guard down.

She tried to explain her feelings to Max. "I can't let myself think it's real until it's really real. You know?"

"Amber, this is no time to be superstitious."

"I can't jinx custody of Zachary. I can lose anything else, but not him."

"Coast Eagle needs you to step up."

Her stomach went hollow, and her pulse began to pound. It wasn't exactly what Cole had said, but it was close. Two apparently smart men were telling her the same thing.

"How long do I have to decide?"

"Twenty-four hours. After that, we may lose MacSweeny."

"Let me think about it."

Max gave a sharp nod. Then he rose. "I'll be back tomorrow."

"I'll be here."

"Max is a very intelligent lawyer," said Destiny over Zachary's cries.

They were in the penthouse kitchen, Amber jostling Zachary and Destiny doling out linguini and salad.

"You're a smart lawyer, too," said Amber.

"Sure, but I'm looking after your interests. Max is looking after the interests of Coast Eagle. From the perspective of what's in the best interests of the company, you should absolutely take the board appointment."

"And from the perspective of me?"

"You'll make a lifelong enemy out of Roth."

"I've done that simply by breathing."

Destiny grinned, while Zachary's cries increased.

Amber jiggled harder. She was growing exhausted. "I swear, if I had Cole Parker's phone number, I'd call him up and beg him to come over."

"He's the other Alaska guy?"

"Yes, the one who put Zachary to sleep Sunday morning without lifting a finger." Amber knew she should feel miffed by that, because it sure didn't seem fair.

Destiny picked up her phone. "I've got Luca's number."

"Yeah, right," Amber chuckled.

But Destiny raised her phone to her ear. "Luca? It's Destiny."

"Don't you dare," said Amber.

Destiny stopped talking and smiled. "Thanks."

Amber shook her head in warning.

"That's not why I'm calling," said Destiny. "No. It's really not. I'm looking for Cole."

Amber shook her head more frantically, moving closer.

"Not even close," said Destiny. "Tell him Amber needs him to put Zachary to sleep."

"She's joking," Amber called out, causing Zachary to cry louder. She turned away, walking toward the living room. "Shh, shh, shh," she whispered in his ear. "I'm sorry, baby. I didn't mean to scare you."

"Hi, Cole," said Destiny from behind her. "Yes, Amber needs the baby cavalry. Can you come?"

Amber couldn't believe this was happening. Cole was a stranger. You couldn't ask a stranger to drop everything, drive over and soothe your baby. The world didn't work like that. With any luck at all, he'd be bright enough to say no.

"They're on their way," called Destiny.

"You've lost your mind."

Destiny set down her phone and moved to the wine rack recessed in the kitchen wall. "How's Zachary been doing with the nanny?"

"Sometimes he's good with Isabel, sometimes not. Evening

is always the worst. We're been helping each other, but tonight's her night off."

Perusing the shelves, Destiny chose a bottle. "Do you think maybe we could give him a little of the merlot?"

"I wish. But definitely pour me a glass."

Destiny located the corkscrew, peeled the foil and opened the bottle. She moved two glasses to the center of the island and poured, placing them next to the two plates of linguini.

Then she slid onto a stool while Amber jiggled her way back to the island.

Amber knew there was no point in sitting down. Zachary had a built in altimeter. His preferred height was precisely five feet off the ground, not four feet, not four and a half. And his preferred swaying arc was approximately nine inches. Any deviation from the pattern brought an immediate vocal protest.

Luckily, Amber had become adept at simultaneously standing, swaying and eating. She lifted her fork and swirled a bite of the seafood linguini.

"Say I was to appoint myself to the board," she ventured.

"Say you were."

"Would it hurt my custody argument? I mean, would it look like I was the kind of person who used Zachary to gain power in Coast Eagle?"

Destiny thought for a moment. "Maybe. I mean, we'd spin it that you were willing to step up and look after Zachary's interests."

"Would a judge believe that?"

"Maybe. It's a fifty-fifty shot. Then again, a judge might just as easily take you *not* joining the board as a sign you weren't a suitable guardian."

"Problem is we can't separate the two." Amber set down her fork to free her hand for a drink of wine.

Zachary batted his arm out, nearly knocking the glass from her hand. She gave up on the drink.

"If you do it," said Destiny, "Roth will spin it that you're power hungry. If you don't, he'll spin it that you're incapable. But Coco wanted you, and that's important."

"But Samuel wanted Roth."

"He did," Destiny agreed.

"And in a character and intellect debate, Samuel is going to win out over Coco every time."

Destiny took a drink, and Amber couldn't help but feel envious. She settled for another bite of the linguini.

A knock sounded on the door.

"That was fast," said Amber, starting for the path through living room.

"They're staying at the East Park."

With a tired and tearful Zachary on her shoulder, Amber crossed to the entry hall. She checked the peephole and opened the door to Cole and Luca.

She couldn't help but smile at the sight of the dog at Cole's heels. He'd told her about the shoe altercation, and his decision to take the animal back to the hotel. She also knew he'd been planning to drop the scruffy dog at a shelter. He hadn't done it yet, and that was somehow endearing.

His expression was sympathetic as he gazed at the pathetically sobbing Zachary.

"I hear you've got trouble?" he said.

Zachary instantly perked up. He straightened in Amber's arms, turning to Cole and blinking his watery eyes. Then he lunged for him.

Cole reflexively reached out, stepping forward to catch the baby. "Hey there, partner."

"It's hard not to take this personally," said Amber, even though her arms and shoulders were all but singing in relief as the weight was removed.

For some reason, Luca was grinning ear to ear as he took in the sight of Cole and Zachary. "Nice to see you again, Amber."

"Hello, Luca. I'm really sorry that Destiny called you guys. It wasn't a fair thing to do."

"No problem at all," said Luca. "She in here?" He brushed past Amber.

The dog kept his position next to Cole.

"In the kitchen," Amber called to Luca's back.

Cole moved into the entry, and Amber shut the door behind him. Zachary heaved a shuddering sigh and laid his head on Cole's shoulder.

"Do babies always react to you like this?" she couldn't help asking.

"I don't know. I'm not usually around them. Mostly, they ignore me."

"Do you mind if I have something to eat while you hold him?"

"Not at all." Cole shrugged out of his jacket, draping it over the brass coat tree. "Do whatever you want. Have a bath. Take a nap."

"Tempting," Amber admitted. "But I've got a glass of merlot in there with my name on it."

Cole and the dog followed her into the kitchen, where Destiny had dished up some linguini for Luca.

"Peace and quiet," she noted, taking in Zachary's posture.

His little hand was stroking one side of Cole's neck, his face buried in the other.

"Hungry?" Amber asked Cole.

"You go ahead. But I'd pour myself a glass of wine." He took the remaining of the four stools, and the dog curled up at his feet.

Amber took a satisfying sip of wine and another bite of linguini. It was wonderful to have the use of both hands.

"What's his name?" Destiny nodded to the dog as she poured wine for the men.

"I don't know," said Cole, looking down. "We met in the alley after the dance, and I wasn't really planning to keep him."

"I think he's planning to keep you," said Amber.

"That's because I fed him a burger that first night."

"Cole's got plenty of room in Alaska," said Luca.

"You're taking him home with you?" asked Destiny.

Cole glanced down and seemed to contemplate. "I suppose I am. I'm not liking his chances stacked up against those adorable puppies at the shelter. I don't know who would choose him."

"He's not that homely." Amber sized up the square, tan muzzle, the floppy, uneven ears and wiry, mottled coat. "Okay, maybe Alaska's not such a bad idea."

"You're so diplomatic," Cole said with a smile.

"He'll need a name," said Amber.

"Rover?" Cole asked the dog.

It didn't react.

"Spot?"

Nothing.

Amber smiled as she ate and drank.

"Lucky? Butch? Otis?"

The dog glanced sharply up.

"Seriously?" asked Cole. "Otis?"

The dog came up on its haunches and lifted its chin.

"Otis wins," said Destiny.

"Otis it is," said Cole, reaching down to pat the dog's head.

It sniffed at Zachary's bare foot.

Zachary looked down with curiosity, and the two stared at each other for a long moment.

"Sizing up the competition?" said Destiny.

"Which one?" asked Amber.

Zachary looked suspicious of Otis, and Otis looked suspicious of Zachary. The adults all chuckled at the picture.

Amber quickly polished off her dinner, knowing it wasn't fair to take continued advantage of Cole.

She moved her plate to the sink. "I should give this little guy his bath."

"I'm guessing you mean Zachary and not Otis," said Luca.

"Definitely Zachary." She couldn't help but picture Coco's reaction to Otis in her expensive bathtub.

Cole shifted Zachary on his lap. "Otis had a bath in the hotel car wash the first night I found him."

"Did he mind?" asked Amber.

"Didn't seem to. He smelled pretty bad, so I bribed the valet."

She couldn't help admire his ingenuity.

"Smells a little like Showoff Gold now, but it's a big improvement."

Zachary reached for Otis, grabbing a handful of his ear.

"Careful there," said Cole, gently pulling Zachary back. But Otis just gazed at Zachary, not seeming the slightest bit concerned.

Much as Amber hated to disturb Zachary when he seemed so happy, it was getting late. She moved toward him.

"Time for a bath?" she asked, a lilt to her voice as she smiled brightly, trying to send him the message that something fun was about to happen.

She held out her arms. "Bath?"

Zachary shrank against Cole, his face scrunching up in discontent.

"I can come with you," Cole offered.

"That seems like a cop-out," said Amber. She was already feeling a bit inadequate as a guardian.

Cole rose. "It's a bath. No big deal. Sometimes it's good to just go with the flow."

She couldn't deny she was tempted. "Okay, maybe just this once. But I'm supposed to be convincing a judge that I'm the best guardian for Zachary. I'd hate to have to tell him it was you instead."

"Definitely just this once," Cole answered. "I can hardly give the kid a bath from Alaska."

"In that case, let's make my evening easier."

She led the way down the hall to the main bathroom.

It was easy to tell which of the rooms had been redecorated by Coco. The living room and kitchen were luxurious, with the finest appliances and handcrafted furnishings. But they were subdued and sophisticated, with the obvious touch of a professional decorator.

The master bedroom and the three bathrooms were in stark contrast. They were bright and flamboyant, every feature an extravagance of brilliance and color.

"I should probably prepare you for this," she told Cole.

He was behind her in the wide hallway, followed by Otis.

"I don't mind a mess," he answered.

Amber couldn't help but laugh. "I wish I was talking about a mess."

The bathrooms were very well cared for. Samuel had employed the same housekeeper at the penthouse for nearly a decade, and Amber had no intention of letting the efficient woman go. She paused with her door on the handle.

"What's wrong?" Cole asked.

"It's purple."

"Okay?"

"Very purple." She pushed the door wide and pressed the light switch, watching for his reaction.

The floor tiles were a deep, mottled violet. The wallpaper was mauve with violet pinstripes. Two ultramodern sinks were purple porcelain on clear glass.

The skylight glowed with perimeter lighting, while spotlights twinkled above the shower, sinks and tub. In addition to the complex purple tile work, the walls were decorated with pink-hued abstract paintings, while violet-scented candles and whimsical figurines were placed on glass tables.

"This is very purple," Cole agreed, moving inside as he gazed around in obvious amazement.

She followed. "The tub in here is a relatively manageable size."

She pushed up the sleeves of her sweater and twisted the taps on the oval tub. "The one in the master bedroom is nearly a pool."

Cole grinned. "I guess if you've got the money, you can do whatever turns your crank."

Straightening, Amber retrieved a couple of thick towels and a facecloth from a recessed cabinet, balancing them next to a pink porcelain cat. For all its size, the room was hopelessly impractical. There was only one small cabinet, and the counter space was minimal, most of it taken up with decorations.

"It was pretty interesting to see what Coco did when she was suddenly presented with money," said Amber.

"Did you offer your opinion?" Cole asked, shaking his head at the outlandish decor.

"I didn't see this room until after she died."

Cole perched himself on the edge of the tub and began to

pop the snaps on Zachary's one-piece suit. "But you don't think your stepsister handled money very well?"

"I think it overwhelmed her. She grew up in downtown Birmingham without a lot of advantages. She was nineteen when she met Samuel."

"He must have been fifty."

"At least."

There was an edge to Cole's voice. "Nice."

"She was pretty, stunningly beautiful, actually. She was outgoing and fun loving, and she seemed to idolize Samuel. I'm sure a psychologist would have a field day with the relationship."

"I'm sure," Cole agreed.

Amber knelt down and tested the water temperature with the inside of her wrist. She shut off the taps. Then she suction cupped Zachary's bath safety ring to the bottom of the tub and dropped a couple of brightly colored plastic fish into the water.

"Based on my single college psychology elective," said Amber as Cole lowered the naked Zachary into the ring, "I would say Samuel was everything Coco's father was not. Conversely, I suspect Samuel secretly feared he'd never have children and saw Coco as someone he could care for and protect."

"And sleep with," said Cole.

"He did marry her. I have to give him credit for that."

Zachary grabbed for the green fish, sending splashes of water over the edge of the tub, dampening Amber's sweater and jeans.

"To be fair," she continued, "from what I saw, he genuinely loved Zachary. I think he'd have had more children if Coco was willing."

Cole had gone silent, his attention fixed on the baby.

After a long moment, he spoke. "You liked Samuel?"

"Not really. I mean, I barely knew him, but it's hard to admire a fiftysomething man who marries a nineteen-year-old. Especially one who…" Amber tried to reframe her thought, but there was no way to put it that wasn't insulting to Coco.

She stretched to retrieve the facecloth, dampening it in the bathwater then squirting some rose-scented soap from a china dispenser.

"So how is it that you and Coco became stepsisters?" Cole asked.

Amber started to wash Zachary's back, relieved that he'd let her blow past the nonanswer. "My mother died when I was a baby. When I was seven, my father remarried. But shortly after, he was killed by a drunk driver, and then it was just Tara and me."

"I'm sorry to hear that."

"Thank you." At first, Amber had been inconsolable over the loss of her father, while Tara had seemed overwhelmed by the responsibility of Amber. So Amber had grown up fast, accepted the situation and learned to be strong.

She continued with the story. "Shortly after he died, Tara remarried and got pregnant with Coco."

"Did you and Tara have a good relationship?"

Zachary splashed happily, cooing in the tub while Amber washed him.

"We didn't fight or anything. She worked as a waitress. I was in after-school care. She made sure I was fed and had clothes. Meanwhile I was a pretty good kid, and stayed out of her way."

"That sounds lonely."

Amber shrugged. "It was okay. I didn't really know any different until Coco came along." She dampened Zachary's soft hair and rubbed in a dollop of baby shampoo.

"What happened?"

"I saw a different approach to parenting."

"Let me guess, Coco was the golden child."

"She was the princess of the family. She was their biological baby. While I was ten and didn't belong to either of them."

"I'm so sorry, Amber."

She gave herself a mental shake as she removed Zachary from the bath ring. "It was a very long time ago. I don't know why I'm even going into it."

"Because I asked."

Crouched over the tub, she leaned Zachary along her arm to rinse his hair. He squirmed but didn't cry.

"I never knew my father," Cole said from beside her.

"Divorce?" she asked.

"Yes. Before I was born."

"Did you have a relationship with him?"

"None."

"Why not?"

"My mother wanted nothing to do with him, and neither did I."

"Do you still feel the same way?"

"I do. But it wouldn't matter."

Amber guessed at what Cole meant. "He passed away?"

"He did."

She stood Zachary up, checking to make sure he was squeaky-clean. "Any regrets?

"Not a one. He never knew about me. My mom was absolutely fantastic. It was just the two of us, but she was hardworking, loving, supportive."

"That's nice to hear." Amber lifted Zachary from the tub, wrapping him in a fluffy mauve towel.

He cooed happily, but then spotted Cole. He wriggled in her lap, reaching out and whimpering.

"This is definitely insulting," she said.

"You're great with him."

"I'm not sure about that." She was honest. "But I'm what he's got, and I do love him."

Cole rose from the edge of the tub, reaching out to take Zachary in one arm and then helping her to her feet. It took him a minute to speak.

"Sometimes," he said softly, "families just happen."

His hand was warm and dry beneath hers, broad, strong and slightly callused. He didn't immediately let her go, and a strange feeling surged up her arm, pushing into her chest.

Time seemed to stop. She stood still and drank in his appearance. He was such a gorgeous, sexy man. His smoke-gray eyes were warm with emotion. She noticed once again that his shoulders were broad, arms strong, chest deep. He seemed to radiate a power that was more than just physical.

She fought another urge to throw herself into his arms.

"Amber," he breathed.

He lifted his hand to brush her damp hair from her cheek.

His touch was featherlight, but she felt herself sway toward him.

He leaned in, slowly, surely.

Then he touched his lips to hers.

He tasted like fine wine, his lips warm and firm. The scented steam rose between them while his fingers slipped back, delving into her hair.

The kiss deepened, and her desire skyrocketed.

"Gak," called Zachary, his hand smacking her ear.

She jerked back in shock.

"Gak," Zachary repeated, pressing his feet against her as if he needed space.

"All right, partner," said Cole. "You have my attention." But his gaze stayed fixed on Amber.

Embarrassment flooded her. "I don't know what happened there."

"I do," said Cole. He held her gaze for a long beat. "And I've never taken a single psychology course."

Then he backed away to the bathroom door, leaving her awash in arousal and confusion.

Four

Cole sat across from Luca at a small table in the festively decorated lobby lounge in the East Park Hotel. A blue-and-silver Christmas tree towered thirty feet above them. Lit reindeer bracketed the entrance. Strings of garland and clusters of icicles cascaded from the high ceilings, while the windows were frosted with scenes of ice and snow.

Carols played softly in the background as guests enjoyed the breakfast buffet.

"There's not a doubt in my mind that Amber is the right guardian for Zachary," said Cole.

He couldn't help but worry about Amber's description of her stepsister, and how Roth's legal team might use Coco's background and reputation. Amber was definitely going to have a fight on her hands in court.

"This is what I'm talking about," said Luca, seeming not to have heard Cole's comment as he swiveled his laptop around to face Cole. "That's Samuel at the age of thirty-three, a year older than you are now."

Cole focused on the picture of his biological father. The eyes were similar, but Samuel's hair was lighter, his chin narrower and his nose had a bit of an upturn.

"It's only there if you're looking for it," he said. "And nobody's looking for it."

"You've been outed by a nine-month-old baby."

"Yeah, well, I think we can count on him to keep quiet."

"He'll learn to talk someday."

"Not before I leave town."

"And listen to this." Luca turned the laptop and punched another key. "It's Samuel giving a speech twenty years ago."

"…once the plan is fully implemented, the new routes will take us to Britain, France and Germany…"

"Okay, that's a bit uncanny," Cole had to admit. He'd heard

his own voice recorded on numerous occasions, and Samuel's was very, very close.

"The kid knows you're family."

"At least that explains why he's latched on to me."

Luca took a sip of his coffee. "But you're still just going to walk away?"

"No."

Luca drew back in clear astonishment. "You're not?"

"First, I'm going to make sure Amber wins custody. Then I'm going to walk away. Involving myself in the Henderson family was never part of the plan."

Cole was heading back to his life in Alaska just as soon as things were under control here. Showing up in Atlanta was about him doing his duty. It wasn't some family reunion, and he wasn't about to upend his and Zachary's lives by acknowledging their biological connection.

Kissing Amber last night might have momentarily thrown him off track. He still couldn't believe he'd done it—in a purple bathroom of all places, with Zachary in his arms. How ridiculous was that?

His plan was to keep complications to a minimum. Not that a single kiss had added some huge complication. In fact, he'd already put it into perspective.

Sure, Amber was pretty. She was sweet and kind and compassionate. And she'd had a rough time of it growing up. Her stories had engaged his sympathies.

But lots of people had a less-than-stellar upbringing. She was fine now, and she loved Zachary. And Cole was right to leave the two of them to get on with it.

"You're sure that's what you want?" asked Luca.

"I'm positive it's what I want." Cole pulled his thoughts back to his earlier point. "Roth will try to prove that Coco was unfit to name either a guardian for Zachary or the person to control Coast Eagle."

"On the bright side," said Luca, "I don't think many wills are overturned because they're foolish."

"I hope not." Just then, Cole wished he knew more about the law.

"So what do you think of Destiny?" he asked Luca. "I mean, other than she's hot. Can you see past the fact that she's hot? Because you should declare a conflict of interest if you can't be objective." Cole wanted to be sure Amber was getting the best possible legal advice.

Luca was all but laughing as he cut into his waffle. "I don't need to declare a conflict of interest. I know she's smart."

"Are you sure? How do you know?"

"I asked her a few questions last night."

"And?"

"And she had a ton of technical information at her fingertips. But she wouldn't tell me anything about Amber specifically."

"You didn't make her suspicious, did you?"

"No. I pretended I was curious about what I'd read on social media. There's a lot out there on social media." Luca set down his cutlery and pressed a few more keys on the laptop. "For example, this, here. There are new rumors that Roth Calvin will be named interim president of Coast Eagle."

Cole reached out to turn the laptop to face him again. "I thought Amber was in charge?" Letting Roth step up as interim president couldn't be a good move for her.

"It's a board decision," said Luca.

"Which tells us Roth has the ear of the board." Cole didn't like the thought of that.

"It does seem like he's got the power at least temporarily."

Cole dropped his napkin onto the table and stood. "I need to get a handle on the guy."

"Where are you going?"

"Coast Eagle's corporate headquarters. I want to look Roth Calvin in the eyes."

"Right now? Without an appointment?"

"I'll talk my way in. I'm a fellow airline owner."

"You want some help?"

Cole considered the offer. But then he shook his head. "He's less likely to have his guard up if it's just one guy."

"Whatever you want."

Cole shrugged into his jacket. "See what else you can find out about the law."

"Can I talk to Destiny again?"

"As long as you're oblique."

Luca's eyes lit up. "Covert operations. Roger that. This is kind of fun."

Cole couldn't help but grin in return. "Seduce her if you have to."

"I'm all in for you, buddy."

Cole skirted the Christmas tree, made his way past the reindeer and exited to the sidewalk. It was easy to hail a cab, and it was a short ride to Coast Eagle.

He took a few fast steps across the lobby, purposefully blending in with a group of employees to pass unnoticed by the security counter. Then he entered the elevator, pretending he knew exactly what he was doing. Taking the chance that Roth's office would be on the top floor, he pressed the button.

The rest of the group exited on twelve. Cole continued up to a big, brightly lit reception area. It had gleaming hardwood floors, a bank of windows overlooking the city and a pair of immaculate saltwater fish tanks bracketing a long reception counter staffed by one woman.

"Good morning." She was immaculately dressed and thirty-something, and she smiled as she greeted him.

Cole strode forward and held out his hand. "Good morning. I'm Cole Parker, owner of Aviation 58. We're a midsize commercial airline out of Alaska. I was told Roth Calvin was the man to speak with at Coast Eagle."

"Do you have an appointment, sir?"

"I'm afraid I just got into town."

The woman's smile faded a little. "I'm sorry, but Mr. Calvin doesn't have any openings today."

Footfalls and male voices rose up behind them. The woman's surreptitious, worried glance to the group told Cole one of them was likely Roth Calvin.

He quickly turned, talking the man in the middle of the group to be the guy in charge. It had to be Roth.

Again, Cole strode forward, offering his hand. "Roth Calvin. I'm Cole Parker."

Roth's expression was guarded, and his critical glance flicked to the receptionist. Cole figured it was only a matter of moments before security arrived on the scene.

"I was speaking with Amber Welsley the other day. She suggested you were the person to discuss Coast Eagle's Pacific routes? I'm Cole Parker, Aviation 58 out of Alaska."

"Amber told you to see me?" Roth asked.

"She did," Cole lied. "She speaks very highly of you."

Roth's eyes narrowed, and Cole feared he might have gone too far. He was trying to arouse Roth's curiosity, and maybe put him off guard with the mention of Amber.

Roth looked at Cole. Then he looked to the receptionist. "Sandra, push the Millsberg meeting by fifteen minutes."

"Yes, sir," the receptionist answered.

"Right this way, Mr. Parker." Roth gestured to a doorway off the reception area.

"Please, call me Cole." Cole entered an airy meeting room that housed a round table for four with leather and chrome chairs, coffee service on a marble side counter and a sofa grouping near the picture windows.

Roth gestured to one of the chairs at the round table, then took the one opposite. "How can I help you, Cole?"

"I understand you're about to be named interim president," Cole opened.

A smug smile formed on Roth's face. "You've been listening to rumors."

"I find, more often than not, rumors tend to be based on some truth. I'll be honest, Roth, Aviation 58 is looking to expand along the West Coast. With the shakeup at Coast Eagle, I wondered if you might be interested in discussing some of your less-profitable routes in the West."

"All of our routes are profitable."

Cole had checked out Coast Eagle's public information on

the ride over, and now he made some assumptions and guesses. "Seattle to Vancouver is barely break-even. You've been losing market share in Portland. And your passenger load is low on anything northbound out of LA. Entering into a lease or code-share deal with Aviation 58 could boost your cash flow and profits considerably."

"You've done your homework, I see."

"I have," said Cole. "And it tells me Amber Welsley is a short-term play. You're the guy with the ear of the board."

Roth didn't answer, but he did nod.

"I haven't seen the actual will, of course. But I can guess where that's going. A trophy wife is all well and good, but nobody's under any illusions. Samuel would never have allowed a situation where Coco's decisions could run Coast Eagle into the ground."

Roth chuckled, and his expression relaxed. "You strike me as an intelligent man, Cole Parker."

"I'm also a patient man. I get that your attention has to be on the home front for a few months."

Roth gave a shrug. "These things can be expedited."

"That's good to hear."

"A word here, a conversation there. It's all about who you know, and who knows you."

"I understand," said Cole. "The sooner you get custody of the kid, the better." He paused. "I mean, the better for Coast Eagle, of course."

"Once the big question is settled, we will be looking for an early cash influx," said Roth, coming to his feet.

Cole rose with him. "That's good to hear, I'll—"

Suddenly, the meeting room door flung open, and Amber burst in. She glared at Cole, cheeks flushed, nostrils flared. "You went behind my back?"

"Amber." Roth's voice was stern and patronizing.

"You suggested I follow-up," Cole said to Amber, purposefully mischaracterizing their conversation.

"This is a private meeting, Amber." Roth's tone grated on Cole's nerves.

Amber ignored Roth and spoke to Cole. "I suggested you follow up with Joyce Roland."

"Amber," Roth all but shouted. "Can you please *excuse us?"*

Cole had to steel himself from demanding that Roth shut up.

The receptionist appeared in the doorway. "Mr. Calvin? They're waiting. The Millsberg meeting?"

Roth looked to Cole. "I do apologize."

"No problem. Thank you for seeing me. I'll be in touch."

Roth looked to Amber, obviously waiting for her to leave.

She folded her arms across her chest, standing her ground. Cole wanted to applaud.

Roth gave in and left the room, followed by the receptionist.

"How dare you," Amber whispered.

Cole wished he could tell her he was on her side. "It was an initial courtesy call. Nothing sinister. I told you up front that I was interested in the Pacific routes."

"And what were you doing last night? Pumping me for information? Are you actually using Zachary's trust to gain an inside advantage?"

"You called *me* last night," he reminded her.

"And you were only too happy to show up."

"To help with Zachary."

"That's how you played it, all right." There was something in her eyes, a veiled hurt that made him think of their kiss.

He took a step forward. "Amber, I'm sorry."

"For lying to me?"

"I didn't lie to you. Last night was all about Zachary." He paused. "I mean, it was *mostly* all about Zachary."

She gave her hair a little toss. "You don't need to explain."

But he did need to explain. He wanted to explain. "I like you, Amber."

"Well, I don't like you."

He moved closer anyway. "Yes, you do."

"Go away."

He shook his head. "I understand that it's complicated."

"It's not complicated."

"It's Zachary. It's business. It's you, and it's me." Even as he spoke the words, he asked himself what on earth he thought he was doing. He needed to leave this alone, not ramp it up.

"There is no you and me." But her expression instantly shifted, telling him otherwise. Her lips parted, her blue-eyed gaze going bedroom soft.

Cole glanced at the open door, debating pushing it closed and pulling her into his arms again. But that would be a stupid move. The receptionist, Sandra, would certainly report the closed door to Roth. It would complicate things even further for Amber.

But she was so enchanting, and his memory of kissing her was so incredibly strong, he couldn't stop himself. He reached past her and gave the door a shove. Her eyes went wide as it clicked shut.

Without giving her a chance to protest, Cole pulled her into his arms, bringing his thirsty lips down to hers and kissing her soundly. She gasped, but she didn't pull away. After a moment, her lips softened. She kissed him back, and her arms wound around his neck.

He pressed their bodies close together, feeling the sweet heat of her thighs and the softness of her breasts. He teased her lips with his tongue, and she responded, parrying with him, a small moan burbling in the back of her throat.

His hand went to her cheek, cradling the soft skin, holding her in place while he plundered her mouth. He forgot where they were, forgot everything except the sweet taste and scent of Amber. His other hand moved to her waist, sliding beneath her linen blazer, along her silk blouse, feeling the heat of her skin through the thin fabric.

Suddenly, she pushed back. "We can't."

Cole sucked in a breath. Of course they couldn't. What was he thinking? They were in her place of business.

"I'm sorry," he said.

But she shook her head. "My fault, too." Then she glanced at her watch. "I have to go. There's a board meeting." She stopped talking. Inhaled a deliberate breath and took a step back. "That was foolish. I don't know what got into me."

"Amber—"

"Goodbye, Cole." She moved for the door.

"Can I call you later?"

"No." She shook her head and pulled open the door.

From behind her desk, Sandra's sharp gaze went to Amber, then to Cole. He tried to look casual, innocent, as if nothing more than a brief conversation had taken place between them.

But it was hard to put his finger on the exact expression and posture that would convey those things. So he simply left the room, bid a brief goodbye to Sandra and took the elevator back to the lobby.

Smoothing back her hair and mentally pulling herself together, Amber reached for the door handle to Coast Eagle's main boardroom.

She couldn't believe she'd kissed Cole again. She couldn't believe she'd done it in the office. And she sure couldn't believe she'd enjoyed it.

She tugged open the door.

"There you are," said Max, rising from his seat at the head of the long boardroom table.

The other eight members of the board nodded politely, their gazes fixed on her. They were all men, fortysomething to sixtysomething, longtime members of the Atlanta business community and the aviation industry. She knew most of them by sight, but she'd shared little more than a passing greeting with any of them.

Max moved away from the head chair, gesturing for her to sit down in it. "Please, Ms. Welsley."

She hesitated over the bold gesture, but Max gave her an encouraging smile.

She told herself she could do this. For Zachary, she could do this. She lifted her chin, walked forward and took the power chair.

Max took the chair to her right.

She stared down the center of the table, fixing her vision on the photograph of a red-and-white biplane at the far end of the room. She had no idea what to say.

Luckily, Max opened for her. "Per article 17.9 of the Coast Eagle Articles of Incorporation," he said, "Ms. Welsley is exercising her right as majority shareholder—"

"She's not the majority shareholder," said Clint Mendes.

Max peered at Clint. "According to the State of Georgia, she represents the majority shareholder."

"But that's under appeal," said Clint.

"And until that appeal is settled, Ms. Welsley represents the interests of Zachary Henderson. Now, as I was saying—"

The boardroom door swung abruptly open, revealing Roth in the threshold, his eyes wide, face ruddy, and his jaw clenched tight.

"Mr. Calvin," said Max, a clear rebuke in his tone. "I'm afraid this is a private meeting."

"Is this *a coup?*" Roth demanded.

A hush came over the room as everyone waited to see what Amber would do.

She immediately realized she had to step up. She couldn't let Max defend her against Roth. She was going to be a board member, and she had to stand her ground.

If she lost the court case, Roth would have her fired within seconds. He would have done that anyway. She had nothing left to lose.

She came to her feet, turning and squaring her shoulders. "Please leave the meeting, Roth."

The silence boomed around her.

Roth's jaw worked, his face growing redder. "Are you out of your—"

"Please leave," she repeated. "This meeting is for board members only."

"You're not a board member," Roth all but shouted.

"I'm the majority shareholder, Roth. That's as much as you need to know. *Now leave.*"

Nelson MacSweeny coughed, but said nothing.

Roth glared at the man.

Then he fixed a biting, narrow-eyed stare on Amber.

But he seemed to understand that he'd lost the round. He stepped back, banging the door shut.

Knees shaky, Amber sat down. Everyone was still looking down the table at her. But something in their expressions had changed.

It might have been her imagination, but there seemed to be a level of respect in their eyes. She gazed levelly back. Her heart was pounding and her palms were sweating, but she wasn't about to let anyone know that Roth had rattled her.

"Ms. Welsley is exercising her right to appoint herself as a board member," said Max. "As current majority shareholder, she will sit as chair. As chair, she will break any tie over the appointment of an interim president."

"So not Roth," said Clint.

"Then who are we talking about?" Nelson asked.

"Are we taking nominations?"

"I've given it a lot of thought," said Amber. "I'd like to discuss Max Cutter as the interim president."

Max drew back in his seat. "I can't—"

"Turns out you can," said Amber. "I spoke to a lawyer this morning."

"You'll have to leave the room for the discussion," Nelson said to Max.

Max fixed his shrewd gaze on Amber. She didn't flinch. If she could sit as chair of the board, then he could sit as president. There was no one else she'd trust.

"Very well," said Max. He rose and gathered his briefcase.

As he passed, he paused behind her and leaned down. "I guess we'll go down together."

She turned her head to whisper. "Then I guess you'd better help me win."

"I was always going to help you win." He gave her a friendly pat on the shoulder as he walked away.

The door closed behind him and another board member spoke up. He was Milos Mandell, a former commercial pilot and internet entrepreneur.

"Can we speak freely?" asked Milos.

"I would think we'd better," said Amber.

"You seem like you understand what you just did."

She couldn't help flexing a small, resigned smile. "I believe I know what I just did."

"He's going to come after you," said Nelson, clearly referring to Roth.

"He's right to go after her," said Clint, glancing around at his fellow board members. "This *is* a coup."

Milos sat forward. "The coup would have been Roth taking over as president without the support of the major shareholder."

Clint stared hard at Amber. "You're jumping the gun, and it's going to cost you."

"While Roth will know you sided with him, so I guess you're safe." She let her words sink in for a moment.

Clint was smart enough to realize the opposite was also true. Amber now knew he was in opposition to her.

His jaw dropped a fraction of an inch. "I don't mean… That is, I'm not…"

"Any discussion on Max?" Amber asked the group.

She didn't have time to worry about Clint. She needed to get Max settled in as president, then she needed to focus on the court case, do justice to her day-to-day work and make sure Zachary stayed clean, fed and as happy as possible. The alliances, machinations and power plays at Coast Eagle were going to have to take a backseat.

On the staircase in front of Coast Eagle headquarters, Cole appeared and fell into step beside Amber. It was six o'clock. She was exhausted, and he was the last person she wanted to see.

Ironically, he was also the person she most wanted to see. The conflicting reactions were due to the kiss they'd shared in the meeting room.

"I read the press release," he opened, turning right along with her as she headed down the crowded sidewalk toward the transit station.

"I think that was a good move," he continued. "There's an

element of risk, but there's nothing about this situation that's not risky."

She stopped to turn on him, forcing the flow of people to part around them. The man had gone behind her back, kissed her senseless, and now he wanted to analyze her business decisions? "Is that really what you want to say to me?"

Her words seemed to catch him off guard and he hesitated. Horns honked and engines revved on the street as cars breezed past.

"Yes," he answered.

"Well." She coughed out a chopped laugh. "It's so *very* nice of you to approve of my decision."

"Are you still upset?"

"I'm also tired, and I'm busy, and I'm going to miss my train."

"Then you should get moving."

He was right. She turned abruptly to march toward the station.

He kept pace. "I have a hard time believing the Hendersons don't have cars and drivers."

"Are you going to pretend it didn't happen?"

"That you joined the board of directors?"

She rolled her eyes.

"That I kissed you?" he asked.

"That you betrayed me."

"I didn't betray you. I told you I was after the Pacific routes."

"Don't pretend you're stupid, Cole. And don't pretend I'm stupid, either."

"You're not stupid."

"I know."

"Except when it comes to transportation. Can I offer you a ride home?"

"You cannot."

"Why?"

Because he had her rattled. The memory of his kiss had taunted her all afternoon long, messing with her concentration. She wanted to know the kiss had rattled him, too.

"It'll get you home faster," Cole offered reasonably. "You'll be able to spend more time with Zachary."

"Go away." She fixed her sights on the train platform.

"Not what I was planning."

"What were you planning?" The question was automatic, and she instantly regretted asking it.

She didn't care about his plans. She wanted him out of her life. At least, a part of her wanted him out of her life. The other part wanted him to kiss her again. She nearly groaned in frustration.

"You're having a tough week," he said. "You need to have some fun."

She dodged her way around a group of pedestrians, then skirted a trash can and a stroller. "What? This doesn't look like fun?"

"Well, I'm having fun."

"What do you want, Cole?"

"To take you on a date."

His words shocked her to a halt.

He took her arm and drew her under a shop awning, next to a brick wall and out of the flow of pedestrians. "I can only guess at how hard you're working and how tired you must be. I want to help you take a break. Come out with me tonight. Let's walk through Atlantic Station, see the lights, drink hot chocolate. Or we can go skating. You said skating was your favorite."

"I don't like you, Cole."

"To be fair, you don't know me."

"I know enough."

"You only think you know enough." His gaze captured hers again, and the noise and commotion of the sidewalk seemed to fade.

"I'll sweeten the pot," he said. "We'll go to the penthouse. I'll work my magic and put Zachary to sleep. Can Isabel stay for the evening?"

"You're bribing me?"

"Absolutely."

"Why, Cole? The jig is up. I know you were using me to worm your way into Coast Eagle."

"Amber, I don't need you to worm my way into Coast Eagle. I walked through the front door and got a meeting with the soon-to-be president without an appointment."

"Roth's not going to be president."

"Good decision."

"You just switch your opinion on a dime, don't you?"

"I never thought he should be president."

She didn't know what to say to that. She didn't care what Cole thought. Still, for some reason she was glad to hear him agree with her.

"You need to get out for a while," Cole continued. "Take a break. Forget about everything."

She fought a smile at the absurdity. "What I want to forget is you."

His expression faltered, and she felt a stab of guilt.

"I'm sorry to hear that, Amber."

She was sorry she'd said it.

Wait, no, she wasn't. No good could come of her attraction to him. A date? The idea was absurd. He lived in Alaska, and her life was a mess.

The best they could hope for was a one-night stand. Which, when she thought about it…

Hoo, boy. She reached out to grip the brick wall.

"You okay?"

"I'm perfectly fine." She paused. "No, make that confused. Why do you want to go out with me? And why do you still want to help me with Zachary?"

It took him a moment to shrug. "Why not? I like you, Amber. I like Zachary."

"That's too simple an explanation." Amber raked her hand through her hair to tame it in the freshening wind.

"I'm not complicated."

"I am."

"It's ice-skating, Amber. What could be simpler than ice-skating?"

"You're trying to get your hands on our Pacific routes."

"Only if you want to sell them."

"I don't."

"Fair enough. Did you know you missed your train?"

It was pulling smoothly away on the tracks. He really was the most infuriatingly distracting man.

"My car is only a block away. What do you say?"

She wanted to say yes. She suddenly, desperately wanted to leave her troubles behind for a few hours and go ice-skating with Cole.

She gave in. "Okay."

He grinned, and she couldn't shake the feeling she'd been outmaneuvered.

Five

As they passed by the lit trees that lined the outdoor skating rink, Cole turned backward so that he was facing Amber. She wore a short white puffy jacket, blue jeans and bright yellow knit hat.

"Impressive," she told him with a smile.

He was grateful that she seemed relaxed. "Hockey."

Since it was barely below freezing, he'd gone with a windbreaker and a bare head. The fresh air felt good in his lungs.

"You're a hockey player?"

"Snow and ice sports are big in Alaska. I also snowboard and ski cross-country." He glanced over his shoulder to make sure the path was still clear as they rounded a corner.

"I swim," she said.

"Competitively?"

"At resorts, usually in the leisure pool, sometimes on the lazy river."

He brought up a mental image. "Impressive."

"Yeah, I float with the best of them."

"I was picturing you in a little yellow bikini. It was very impressive."

"That's just mean."

"Why?"

"Because I'll never live up to your imagination."

"Sure you will." His gaze took a reflexive tour of her trim figure. "Wait a minute. Do you intend to try?"

She laughed, and he loved the sound.

"Not this time of year," she singsonged.

"If I come back in June?"

"Maybe." She twirled neatly around. "You're pretty good yourself."

"Flatterer." But her smile was bright.

"You're beautiful, too."

"I'm not interested in a one-night stand."

The statement took him by surprise. "Excuse me?"

"Just so you know. I wouldn't want you to get to the end of the night and be disappointed."

"Is that what you think this is about?"

He didn't know whether to be insulted or just plain disappointed. He hadn't invited her out to get her into bed. But he didn't deny he'd give pretty much anything for an unbridled night of passion in her arms.

"You're not staying in Atlanta," she said.

"True," he agreed, even though he kind of now wished he was.

"And you're putting in an awful lot of effort flirting with me."

"Also true." But only because flirting with her was so much fun.

"So the options are limited."

"Maybe I'm trying to romance the Pacific routes out from under you."

"You know that will never work."

It was true. Cole couldn't imagine her falling for something so simplistic. Then again, he wasn't remotely interested in the Pacific routes.

He and Luca were following a carefully planned and meticulously orchestrated expansion scheme for Aviation 58. It was on track, and he had no intention of deviating from it for the next few years. He'd never make a knee-jerk decision based on random availability.

"You're great with Zachary, you know." Cole didn't want to talk business.

"*You're* great with Zachary. I'm mostly treading water." Then she frowned. "But if you're ever called to testify, the correct answer is that Amber is *fantastic* with Zachary."

"I've never seen such incredible natural mothering instincts," he said.

Her frown deepened. "I'm not his mother."

"I didn't mean that," Cole quickly corrected the innocent comment. "I only meant that it's obvious that you love him."

She skated in pensive silence for a moment, the lighthearted music and bright lights suddenly seeming out of place.

"I'm sorry," he offered, moving back to her side, reminding himself that she had grown up without the love of either of her natural parents.

"He's so young," she said softly. "He won't remember either of them."

Cole reached out and took her hand. "He'll remember you."

"It's not the same thing."

There was a deep sadness in her eyes, and it wasn't at all what he'd planned for her tonight.

"Hot chocolate?" he asked, nodding toward the strip of shops and cafés. "I'll spring for whipped cream and orange brandy."

Her expression relaxed again. "Sure."

They coasted to a stop, exchanged their skates for boots and made their way through the colored lights and happy crowds. It felt natural to take Amber's hand again as they strolled along the pedestrian street. He helped her pick out a stuffed dog and a soft rattle for Zachary. They waited while the clerk gift wrapped the toys, and Cole slung the package over his shoulder.

"That looks nice." He pointed across the street to a fenced restaurant patio with padded chairs and glowing propane heaters.

"Sold," said Amber.

They crossed through the crowds and were shown to a table near a festively lit garden.

He glanced at his watch. "I read there were fireworks at ten."

"Perfect timing." She glanced around. "I love it down here at Christmas."

"There's nothing like this in Juneau."

"Too cold?"

"During the holidays, yes. We do fireworks on the Fourth of July, but they lose something since it doesn't get completely dark at night."

"Not at all?"

"A sort of twilight look around 2:00 a.m. But you can golf at midnight on the solstice."

"I can't even picture it. Do you like living there?"

"I love living there. Juneau has a great sense of community."

"Tell me about your mother."

Cole brought up fond memories. "She was very pretty. She was kind and cheerful. She worked hard. Looking back, I realize just how hard she had to work when I was young."

"She never went after your father for support?"

"She didn't want him to know I existed."

The statement clearly piqued Amber's interest. "Why not?"

Cole immediately realized his mistake in letting Samuel get into the conversation. He purposely kept the rest of his answer casual. "She thought he'd be more trouble than he was worth."

Amber nodded her understanding. "I hear you."

How she said it made him wonder if she'd had bad experiences with men. He wanted to ask, but just then, the waitress arrived with magnificent mugs of hot chocolate, decorated with whipped cream and chocolate sprinkles.

"Dessert in a cup," said Amber with a happy smile.

Cole took the opportunity to shift the conversation away from his father. "Tell me about your dad."

She thought for a moment while she spooned a dollop of the whipped cream into her mouth. "He was tall. He had this booming, infectious laugh. I remember him flipping pancakes in the air, and how he used to trot around the yard, whinnying like a horse, with me on piggyback."

"Little girls like that?"

"I did."

"My mom baked bread on Friday nights," said Cole. "I'd hear her in the kitchen after I went to bed. She'd let it rise all night, then bake it in the morning. Best breakfast of the whole week."

"I'm trying to picture you young."

An image of Zachary came to his mind, and he hoped she wasn't trying to picture back that far. He'd hunted the internet for more photos of Samuel, found many and he realized there was a significant family resemblance. Then he'd had a friend back in Alaska send him some of his own baby pictures to compare to Zachary. They were all but identical.

Amber took another spoonful of the whipped cream. "I can't picture it. You must have always been old."

"Old? Thanks a lot."

"How old are you?"

"Thirty-two. You?" He already knew, but it seemed logical to ask.

"Thirty-one. So I guess you're not so old."

"Gee, thanks."

She grinned. "But I'm surprised you're not married, or at least in a relationship."

"There's no current or likely future Mrs.—" He caught himself. "Mrs. Parker. You?"

"Married?" she scoffed.

"I meant in a serious relationship?"

"Nope."

"What about in the past?"

"These questions are getting quite personal."

"They are, aren't they?" He didn't apologize or retract it.

She wrapped her hands around the mug. "Nobody of note." After a pause, she kept talking. "I left home right after high school, worked days, went to school at night to get my accounting designation. I might not be a vice president, but my job at Coast Eagle is significant."

He stirred the whipped cream into his hot chocolate. "I never doubted it was."

"I oversee six branch offices and several dozen staff members."

"Have I said something wrong?" He couldn't figure out what had made her defensive. He had nothing but admiration and respect for what she'd accomplished in her professional life.

She took a sip. "Not you. Roth, I guess. And some of the other executives. Sometimes I think they assume I'm just like Coco. They all knew her, while most of them had barely met me before the crash. They seem to have forgotten that I was at Coast Eagle before she met Samuel. I sometimes get the impression they think Coco got me the job."

He could imagine that would be frustrating.

"I decided the best defense was to ignore it," she continued. "And to do a good job, hard work and success would prevail and all that."

"Did it work?"

"Not really. And then the plane crashed. And now everyone thinks there's a ditz at the helm."

"They're wrong."

"They don't know that."

"Fair enough. But you know what I think?"

Her expression seemed to relax a little. "What do you think, Cole Parker?"

"I think they'd better learn. They'd better learn to respect your intelligence and your tenacity."

Anyone could see she was the perfect guardian for Zachary. The judge was going to see that, too. And soon she was going to be in charge of all of their lives.

"You're good for my ego, Cole."

"I'm trying."

"But, wow, did I ever get off topic." She took another sip. "That was a very roundabout way of explaining that I didn't have time for boyfriends. It's not that I never had offers."

"Of course you had offers." He couldn't figure out what made her so insecure. "You're amazing. And you're gorgeous. And I never meant for a second to hint that men didn't seek you out. I meant… Okay, I was fishing around for the competition."

She drew back. "Competition for *what?*"

"That didn't come out right. I'm attracted to you, Amber. I know I'm not staying in Atlanta. But I think of this as a date. And I guess it's a reflex for guys to wonder about who else might be out there in the wings."

"There are no wings. I mean, I have no wings. At least none with guys waiting in them." She closed her eyes and shook her head. "I'm making this worse and worse, aren't I?"

Cole struggled not to smile. "You're making it better and better."

"Tell me some more about you instead."

"Sure. What do you want to know?"

She settled back into the chair. "Women."

The first volley of fireworks burst in the night sky, and Amber laughed.

"Timing," she said.

"I *wish* my love life was that exciting."

"Give."

"Marcy Richards," he said.

"She is?"

His memory was warm. "My high school sweetheart. Tall, lanky, long red hair, a few freckles. She was captain of the girls' basketball team."

"What happened?"

"Tragic story, really. Senior year, she met a guy from Skagway. He was in town for a tournament. He kissed her. I punched him. She cried. But then four months later they both went off to U of Alaska. They're married now with two kids."

"Do you miss her?"

"Not really. She's my accountant, so I see her every week. She's great. And so, it turns out, is her husband, Mike."

"You're saying you're over the heartbreak?"

"I went off to flight school and had a series of short but satisfying relationships. Turns out, women can't resist a pilot."

"How short?"

"Hours, sometimes days."

"That's appalling."

"I was recovering from heartbreak. I was young and vulnerable."

"*Vulnerable* isn't the word I'd use."

He grinned. "You'd be right."

"And now?" she asked, brandishing her nearly empty mug.

"A few dates here and there, nothing that's ever turned into anything but a friendship. I'm pretty busy with Aviation 58, and Juneau's population is not that huge. A lot of the women my age have moved on."

"You ever think about moving on?" she asked.

He shook his head. "I love it there. And given how much Aviation 58 has grown, my roots are pretty deep."

"Maybe you can find a nice girl in Atlanta and take her home with you." There was a glow in her blue eyes that seemed to reach right down to his soul.

"Good idea. You doing anything for the next thirty or forty years?"

She set down the empty mug. "I know you're joking, but that's a pretty good line."

He wished he was certain it was a line. He pointed to her mug. "You want another?"

"I need to get home so Isabel can leave."

Six

As Isabel left the penthouse, Amber made her way down the hall to where Cole had gone in search of Otis. The dog had apparently plunked himself down in Zachary's open doorway and gone to sleep.

She found Otis there, with Cole inside the bedroom, tucking a blanket over the sleeping Zachary. Cole rubbed a gentle hand across Zachary's forehead before turning away from the crib. In the doorway, Amber stood to one side, her chest strangely warm.

"Sound asleep," Cole whispered as he stepped over Otis.

The dog opened one eye but didn't lift his head.

"Isabel said he slept right through," Amber whispered in return.

"Good for him." Cole stopped right in front of her.

He was close, too close, but she didn't want to move. Instead, she inhaled deeply, letting his fresh, masculine scent fill her lungs. It was a fight to keep from reaching out to touch him.

"Hi," he breathed.

She lifted her chin to gaze up at him, wishing he would kiss her, but knowing any more intimacy was a very bad idea. Her life was complicated, and he was leaving, and she needed to keep her focus on the court case. But the temptation to lean into his arms and forget everything for just a little while was almost overwhelming.

He brought his palm to her cheek, and the warmth of the contact seemed to flow through her entire body. Her breasts tingled and she parted her lips, subconsciously inching toward him.

His free arm slipped around her waist, and he slowly dipped his head to meet hers. "Is this just a kiss good-night?"

"I don't know." She grasped the sleeves of his shirt, anchoring herself.

"Fair enough." His soft lips captured hers.

His kiss was everything she remembered and more. It was

more than his lips, more than his tongue, more than his taste. Every pore on her body drank in his essence. Her heart rate increased. Her blood heated. She pressed herself against him, nipples beading against his hard chest, thighs molding to his, hands twining around his neck, into his hair then back again, tracing the planes and angles of his face.

She wanted to memorize his skin. She wanted to touch him everywhere, imprint every contour onto her brain.

Arousal swiftly pushed away reason.

Needing to get closer still, she worked her hands between them, struggling in the tight space to release the buttons on his shirt. In answer, his hands slid down her back, across her waist, cupping her rear, pulling her tight against his body, letting her know how strongly he desired her.

She stripped off her sweater. Her tank top followed. And she was before him in a white lacy bra.

He drew back and his pupils dilated, his breathing labored. He swore under his breath, then stripped off his shirt and backed her tight against the cool wall. He lifted her there, bringing her legs around his waist.

He flicked the catch on her bra, pulling it from between them, and they were skin to skin. She was in heaven.

His voice was a rumble against her mouth. "Amber?"

It was a struggle to speak. "Yes?"

"This is more than just a good-night kiss."

"Yes," she rasped. "Yes."

He worked his way down her neck, kissing the curve of her shoulder, then the swell of her breast. His lips fastened onto her nipple, and her body bucked, fingertips curling hard into his muscular shoulders. He switched sides, and her head tipped back, legs going tight around him.

"Which way?" he asked.

"Left," she rasped. "My left. End of the hall."

He scooped her into his arms and paced to the bedroom door, pushing it open and crossing to the big bed.

There he tossed back the covers and set her down. In a split second, he was with her, covering her body with his, kissing her deeply, his hands roaming her skin.

She went on an exploration of her own, following the hard definition of his shoulders and biceps, to his pecs and his washboard stomach. She unsnapped his jeans. He immediately did the same.

Then he pulled back to look into her eyes.

Without a word, he dragged down her zipper.

She followed suit, the backs of her knuckles grazing him as she went.

He sucked in a tight breath, eyes as dark as coal while they watched her.

She tugged down his jeans, and he kicked them off.

He pulled off her pants, palms skimming across her silk panties, back and forth, until she twitched in reaction. She moaned his name.

He kissed her breasts, and her arms stretched out, hands clenching into fists. And then her panties were gone. His boxers disappeared, and he had a condom. Thank goodness he had a condom.

He was on top of her, pressing into her, so slowly, so exquisitely. She arched against him, wrapping her arms and legs around him. She'd never felt anything that came close to Cole Parker.

He smelled of fresh air and wide-open spaces. He tasted like chocolate and brandy. His callused fingertips were rough and hot as he caressed every intimate spot on her skin. His body was shifting iron beneath her hands.

His weight felt good. His thrusts were focused, and her body reflexively adjusted its angle to accommodate him. He whispered her name. Then his arm braced the small of her back, pressing them tighter and tighter together.

Everything else was forgotten except the sensations cresting endlessly through her body as she climbed higher and higher. Colors glowed behind her eyes while white noise roared in her ears. Her world contracted to their joined bodies, tighter and tighter, until the dam exploded. The colors turned to fireworks, and sound boomed like a symphony as Cole called out her name.

Her pulse was in overdrive, and she was dragging in oxygen. Her limbs lost all feeling as she sank deeper and deeper into the soft mattress.

"You still with me?" Cole asked from what seemed like a distance.

"I think so. I'm not sure. Are we in Kansas?"

He chuckled. "I was *definitely* over the rainbow."

Reality floated its way back. "Oh, my."

"Don't second-guess," he warned.

"That was a lot more than just a kiss."

He brushed back her hair and looked into her eyes. "It felt kind of inevitable."

She knew what he meant. Every second they spent together seemed to draw them closer and closer.

"Maybe it was good to get it over with," she ventured.

"At least we're not wondering anymore."

"Were you?" she couldn't help asking. "Were you wondering?"

"Absolutely. From the first second I laid eyes on you. That's why I botched it so bad that night at the dance."

"It was a rocky start," she agreed. "But you rescued me. Then you rescued my shoes."

"You hate those shoes."

"True. But you do get points for trying."

He skimmed the backs of his fingers along her side. "Are those points redeemable?"

His touch was distracting, and his eyes were taking on that dark glow again.

"For valuable prizes," she told him.

He traced the curve of her hip. "What do I get?"

"What do you want?"

He seemed to hesitate for a moment. "To stay."

A shimmer of anticipation warmed her chest at the thought of sleeping in Cole's arms, waking up next to him, having breakfast together with Zachary.

"Are you serious?"

"Absolutely."

"Okay."

Cole awoke to the feel of Amber spooned in his arms and the realization that he had to tell her the truth. Up until last night, he'd been prepared to breeze into town, make sure Zachary was settled and breeze back out again. But things had changed. She had changed them.

She rolled onto her back, blinking her eyes in the dim light from the window.

"Morning," he said softly.

A pretty smile grew on her face. "Morning."

Otis whimpered at the door.

Then Zachary let out a cry down the hall.

"Is Isabel in yet?" Cole asked.

Amber craned her neck to look at the bedside clock. "Not for an hour."

Otis whined more insistently and Zachary's cries grew steady.

Cole grimaced. "I'll walk the dog if you feed the baby."

"Sorry," said Amber.

"Not your fault at all." He sat up, shaking off sleep. "We jumped from a one-night stand to an old married couple in the blink of an eye."

"Not the morning you had in mind," she asked from behind him.

He turned, already smiling. "Oddly, it feels like the perfect morning. Shall I pick up some bagels while I'm out?"

She rose from the other side of the bed, gloriously naked and indescribably beautiful. "Make mine blueberry."

"You got it." He forced himself to look away and pulled on his jeans.

Otis's leash was at the front door, along with Cole's jacket. They took the elevator, and once they were on the sidewalk, they headed to the park.

Cole let the fresh air clear his brain. While they walked, he formulated and discarded several versions of a speech to Amber. Should he plunge in with the fact that he was Samuel's long-lost son? Or should he go about it chronologically, outline his motivation and rationale before hitting her with his real identity?

He didn't want to upset her. He didn't want to worry her. And he certainly didn't want to make her distrust or dislike him any more than he already had. But last night had been too amazing for anything less than complete honesty.

He and Otis ended up on the opposite side of the park. They made their way down the block to a bakery Cole had found a couple of days ago. He left Otis outside and chose a variety of bagels, then they started back to the penthouse.

He found himself wondering what Zachary ate. Would he like to try a bit of bagel? Or did he stick to pureed foods?

Cole knew absolutely nothing about babies or toddlers. All he knew was that Zachary was adorable, and that he was curious about the stages of development to come. He hoped once he told Amber the truth, she'd be willing to send him pictures and videos. Maybe he could even come back occasionally and check up on Zachary.

The more he thought about it, the more he realized acknowledging their blood relationship was the right thing to do. He wasn't sure why he waited so long.

Nearly an hour had gone by before he returned to the penthouse. Amber had given him her spare key, so he let himself in, wondering if Zachary would have finished his bottle and might be having a morning bath. He hoped he wasn't being fussy for Amber.

When Cole opened the door, he did hear Zachary's cries. But they were interspersed with adult voices. At first he assumed Isabel had arrived. But it was a man speaking, then another answering.

Cole and Otis rounded the corner to the living room to see Roth Calvin and four other men standing with Amber in the middle of the room. Two of the men were on cell phones, while Amber was holding a crying Zachary. Cole reflexively moved forward to take the baby.

"What's going on?" he asked, worried that something had gone wrong in the court battle.

"Thank you," whispered Amber as Zachary's cries quieted. "Isabel's running late, and we've got a problem."

Cole glanced at the other four men. "What's wrong?"

"A Coast Eagle flight is in trouble," said one of them.

Cole went instantly on alert. "What kind of trouble?"

"Hydraulic failure," said the shortest of the three. "The landing gear won't come down."

"What's he doing here?" Roth demanded, ending his call, seeming to have just recognized Cole.

"I brought bagels," said Cole.

"Zachary likes him," said Amber.

"What kind of plane?" Cole asked.

"We've got work to do here," said a large, rotund, fiftysomething man with gray hair and a bulbous nose.

"Cole," said Amber. "This is Max Cutter. He's our interim president. This is Sidney Raines and Julius Fonteno, both vice presidents. You know Roth."

"What kind of plane?" Cole repeated. The size of the plane dictated the scale of the problem.

Julius, the large man, frowned. "Shouldn't you go change a diaper or something?"

Cole braced his feet apart. "It'll be faster if you just answer the question."

"Boonsome 300 over LAX," said Sidney, the shorter, younger man, glancing up from the screen of his phone. "They're reporting twenty minutes of fuel left."

Cole's stomach sank. A Boonsome 300 was a passenger jet. There were up to two hundred souls on board.

Max Cutter ended his own call. "The pilot's leaving the holding pattern and bringing her in."

Cole looked to Amber. She was still and pale.

"Are you a pilot?" he asked Sidney.

"Yes."

"They've checked the pump circuit breakers?" Cole knew

the answer would be yes. But he couldn't help going through the diagnostics in his mind.

Sidney gave a nod.

"Any visible leaks?"

"None," said Sidney. "Foam's down on the runway."

"They'll cycle the gear again?"

"They will."

Cole stepped closer to Amber, wishing he could reach out and take her hand. A belly landing in a plane that size was incredibly risky.

"Gear's down," said Sidney, grasping the back of the sofa even as he uttered the words. "They cycled the gear one last time. They've got hydraulic pressure back."

Relief rushed through Cole.

Amber dropped into an armchair, a slight tremor in her hands. "Thank goodness."

"They're on short final," said Sidney, putting his phone to his ear. "Tower's patched me in."

They all waited, watching Sidney closely until he gave the thumbs-up. "Wheels down. It's all good."

"Yes," hissed Max.

"Relief valve, do you think?" Cole posed the question to Sidney.

"They'll have to go through the whole system."

Roth spoke up. "Amber, get the communications director on the phone."

Cole bristled at Roth's abrupt tone, but Amber moved to the landline.

Roth continued talking. "We'll call it a minor delay in the deployment of the landing gear. All safety procedures were followed, and it was an isolated incident."

Amber stopped, looking back over her shoulder. "An isolated incident?"

"Yes."

"We know this how?"

"Because we've been flying the Boonsomes for nearly ten years, and it's never happened before."

"I don't like the word *isolated*," said Amber.

Roth's eyes narrowed.

"I'd suggest replacing that clause with everyone on board is safe, and there were no injuries. Once we've confirmed that's the case."

Roth squared his shoulders. "The whole point of a press release is to reassure the public—"

"I agree with Amber," said Max.

"Of *course* you agree with Amber," said Roth. "You're her appointee."

"I agree with Amber, too," said Sidney.

Roth set his jaw.

"I have to side with Roth on this," said Julius. "The more reassurance we can give our passengers, the better."

"It's early days," said Cole. "Better to mitigate your words until the investigation is complete."

"Who let this guy in here?" asked Julius.

"I'm an airline pilot," said Cole. He might not be a Coast Airlines employee, but he knew the industry.

"Bully for you," said Julius.

"It might be better if you excused us," Roth said to Cole.

Cole looked to Amber. He could go or he could stay, but he was taking his cue from her, not from Roth.

"What about the other Boonsome 300s in service?" asked Max. He was scrolling through the screen on his phone. "Here. Midpoint Airlines just grounded theirs."

"That was fast," said Sidney.

"Kneejerk," said Julius. "It's not like there's a pattern."

"They've got a total of three Boonsomes," said Roth. "It's an easy decision for them to make."

"It puts pressure on us," said Sidney.

"We're not caving to pressure," said Roth. "We've got twenty-four Boonsomes. It's a quarter of our fleet."

Amber's hand was resting on the telephone. "We could have lost two hundred passengers."

"We didn't," said Julius.

"We're *not* considering this," said Roth with finality. "Unless the federal regulator orders us, we are *not* grounding twenty-four airplanes."

"It's a publicity grab from Midpoint," said Julius.

Cole couldn't help jumping in. "Depending on the problem."

"We'll find the problem," said Roth. "And we'll fix it. Nobody's suggesting we send that particular plane up again without a thorough overhaul."

"And if something happens with another Boonsome?" asked Sidney.

"Nothing's going to happen," said Roth.

"You're playing the odds," said Amber.

"I play the odds every time I get out of bed," said Roth. "You want one hundred percent certainty? We lose a million dollars a day with those planes on the ground. *That's* a certainty. It'll take two weeks minimum to get any answers on an investigation. Anybody want to do the math?"

Max looked to Amber. "What are your thoughts?"

"That's a lot of money," she said. "But it's a lot of lives to risk, too." Her gaze moved to Cole.

Julius gestured to Amber, disdain in his tone. "*This* is our leader?"

"She's looking for input," said Max. "I'm looking for input, too."

Roth's face twisted into a sneer. "My input is don't bankrupt the company while you're temporarily in charge."

Cole clamped his jaw to stop himself from speaking.

"The plane is at the gate," said Sidney. "And the terminal is full of reporters."

"We have to put out a statement," said Roth.

"We have to make a decision," Amber told him.

"We don't have a choice," said Julius. "Nobody's giving up a million dollars a day."

"Say that again after we lose a plane full of passengers," said Sidney.

"Do you want my opinion?" Cole asked Amber.

"Yes."

Roth let out an inarticulate exclamation.

Cole ignored him. "Ask yourself this. Before the inspectors identify the problem, would you risk putting Zachary on a Boonsome 300?"

Amber shook her head.

"We ground the planes," said Max.

"Have you *lost your minds?*" asked Julius.

Amber squared her shoulders and gave Max a sharp nod of agreement.

Pride swelled up inside Cole's chest.

"This is amateur hour," Roth spat. "Believe me, you haven't heard the last of it."

"We'll request an expedited investigation," said Max. "But for now the decision is final."

Amber focused in on Cole, moving closer to speak in an undertone. "I have to go to the office."

"I know." He realized their conversation about Samuel would have to wait.

"Can you stay with Zachary until Isabel gets here? She thought maybe noon."

"Don't worry, I'll stay."

Relief flooded her eyes. "Thank you."

"No problem. Talk to you later?"

"I'll call you."

"Good luck."

"Everyone's safe. That's a whole lot of luck already."

The group moved toward the door, Amber grabbing her purse and throwing a coat over her slacks and sweater. When the last of them left and the door latched shut, Cole turned his attention to Zachary.

The baby was sucking on the sleeve of his stretchy one-piece suit.

"You like bagels?" Cole asked.

"Gak baw," said Zachary, grabbing at Cole's nose.

Amber's day went from frightening to stressful to downright infuriating. At six o'clock, Destiny was sitting across from her at her compact office meeting table.

"*That's* how Roth spent his day?" she asked Destiny.

Destiny pushed a sheaf of papers across the table. "I don't know how they did it, but they got an emergency court date. The custody hearing starts at nine tomorrow morning."

"I thought we'd have weeks to get ready." Amber gave the paperwork a passing glance, but she trusted Destiny's assessment.

"We have hours to get ready."

"Can we do it?"

"Not as well as I'd like. But we can work hard tonight. And Roth's side is under the same deadline."

Amber's cell phone rang.

"Remember," said Destiny, "the fundamentals remain the same. Coco's codicil is legal and valid. They have to prove you're not a fit guardian."

Amber didn't recognize the calling number. "Hello?"

"Amber, it's Cole."

She glanced to Destiny, feeling a small spike of guilt about last night. "Hi, Cole."

Destiny's interest obviously perked up.

"I need to talk to you about something."

"Is it Zachary?"

"No, no. He's fine. At least, he was fine when I left him with Isabel this afternoon. Can you meet me for dinner?"

She wished she could. "I'm afraid not. Destiny and I are going to be busy."

There was silence on his end. "It's kind of important."

"I'm sorry."

"Maybe later?"

"Tonight's not going to be good. We'll be working really late."

"Is everything okay?"

"Yes." She hesitated. "No." She knew she shouldn't share, since she barely knew him. But she felt like she owed him an explanation. "It's actually not okay. Roth's convinced the judge to hold an emergency hearing tomorrow morning. He's going after custody."

"Tomorrow morning?"

"He's going to use my decision on the Boonsome 300s as proof I'm unfit to control Coast Eagle."

"He'll lose, Amber."

"I hope so." Her stomach was already beginning to cramp up.

"Is there anything I can do?"

"Ask me out again in a few days?"

Destiny's brows went up.

"Happy to," he answered. Then his tone changed. "I really wish I could see you now. Even for a short time."

"That would be nice. But we're pretty much pulling an all-nighter here. I'm about to call Isabel and arrange for her to stay over."

"I could stay at your place, wait for you there."

"Not necessary." She wasn't going to let herself presume any more on Cole's good graces. He didn't come to Atlanta to be a babysitter.

He was quiet again. Then he blew out a breath. "Okay. A couple of days, then."

"Thanks."

"Nothing to thank me for. Good luck."

"Thanks for that." She'd take every scrap of luck she could get. "Bye, Cole."

"Bye."

She pressed the end button and set down the phone.

Destiny spoke. "We're going to take thirty seconds of our valuable time here, and you're going to tell me what's going on with Cole. Then I'm putting it completely out of my mind until after the hearing." She glanced at her watch. "Go."

"I like him. He likes me. We went skating last night, then we drank killer hot chocolate. We went back to my place, slept together, which was pretty killer, too. Then he stayed over, went out for bagels and then all hell broke loose. He wanted to see me again tonight, but…" She spread her arms.

"Holy cow," said Destiny in obvious awe. "We are definitely going to talk more about this. But right now we've got a whole lot of work to do."

Seven

Cole and Luca slipped into the back of the courtroom. Word had obviously gotten out about the hearing, because the room was packed with reporters and onlookers. He couldn't help but feel bad for Amber. It was stressful enough to have Zachary's custody on the line without an audience of one hundred.

Predictably, Roth's side attacked Coco. They started by disparaging her motivations in marrying an older, wealthy man, then they called witness after witness, painting an unflattering picture of her intellect. Cole knew from conversations with Amber that Coco was emotional and sometimes erratic, but the witnesses made her sound unstable, unprincipled, even dishonest.

Luca tipped his head closer to Cole. "How much do you think is true?"

"She did marry a billionaire nearly three times her age. And I don't think she was a rocket scientist."

Cole imagined a lot of what was being said about Coco's temper and her behavior at parties was accurate. Then again, if she'd been at a frat party like most nineteen-year-olds, instead of at a posh charity function or the opening of an art museum, nobody would have raised an eyebrow.

"Doesn't mean she wasn't a good mother," said Luca.

"And it doesn't mean her wishes shouldn't be respected." Nothing Cole had heard so far would indicate mental incompetence on the part of Coco.

Roth took the stand, and the gallery's attention seemed to heighten. Cole guessed most people here knew the pivotal players in the drama.

Roth's own lawyer questioned him first.

"Did you and Samuel Henderson ever discuss his future plans for Coast Eagle Airlines?" the lawyer asked.

"Extensively and on many occasions," Roth answered.

"Did he ask your advice?"

"Yes, he did."

"To your knowledge, did he ever ask his wife, Coco Henderson's, advice on Coast Eagle Airlines?"

Roth smirked. "Never."

"You're certain?"

"Positive."

"Objection," said Destiny.

"Sustained," said the judge.

"I'll rephrase," said the lawyer. "Did Samuel ever say anything directly to you regarding his opinion of his wife's advice on Coast Eagle?"

"He told me she knew nothing about business. He said he never discussed it with her."

The lawyer gave a satisfied nod. "Did Samuel Henderson indicate to you that he wanted his son to one day take over the business?"

"Yes. Samuel loved his son deeply. I've never seen him so happy as when Zachary was born. He talked about keeping the airline in the family for another generation. It was his fondest wish that Coast Eagle be protected and preserved for his son."

Destiny rose again. "Objection. The witness is not in a position to know Samuel Henderson's fondest wish."

"That's what he said to me," said Roth.

"Overruled," said the judge.

"Did Samuel ever speak to you about his wife having any kind of a hand in running Coast Eagle Airlines in the event of his death?"

"He did," said Roth, and an odd expression flicked in his eyes.

Cole found himself doubting Roth's honesty on the question.

Roth answered, "He said the only people he trusted with Coast Eagle and with his son were Dryden Dunsmore and me. He said someone needed to control Coco because she had the decision-making ability of a twelve-year-old."

"He said that directly to you? Those were his words?"

"Yes. And they're supported by his will, which included

both Dryden and I in guardianship or controlling positions in Coast Eagle."

"A little too convenient," Cole whispered to Luca.

"I can't tell if the judge is buying it or not."

Destiny cross-examined but wasn't able to poke holes in Roth's story. Cole and Luca slipped out at the lunch break, picking a restaurant several blocks away to avoid being seen by Amber or Destiny. By late afternoon, Amber was the only witness left.

Roth's lawyer started with Amber's competence at Coast Eagle. It went as expected. There was no getting around her lack of experience, but Cole thought she held her own, particularly on yesterday's decision to ground the Boonsome jets. Yes, it was a financial loss, but risking passenger lives was too dangerous.

Unfortunately, it then came to light that their closest competitor had not grounded their Boonsomes, and Amber's decision had, at least in the short term, put Coast Eagle at a competitive disadvantage. The lawyers successfully framed her decision as emotional and even brought Cole into the equation, accusing Amber of taking advice from a competitor on a confidential corporate matter.

It wasn't going well for Amber's side.

"You were ten years older than your stepsister?" the lawyer then asked her.

The question obviously surprised Amber, and it seemed to take her a moment to regroup. "Yes."

"And you left home when she was eight years old?"

"I did."

"How often did you see her after that?"

"Not often."

"Once a week, once a month, once a year?"

"Maybe once a year," Amber admitted, causing a small flurry of whispers in the courtroom.

"Until you introduced her to Samuel Henderson."

"Yes," said Amber.

"And why did you introduce them to each other?"

"Coco was in town. When I mentioned the corporate Christmas party at Coast Eagle, she asked to go with me."

"She asked to go with you?"

"Coco enjoyed parties."

"Yes, I think we've established that already."

"Objection," said Destiny.

"I withdraw the comment," said the lawyer. "After she began dating Samuel Henderson, would you say you and your stepsister grew closer?"

"We did."

"And you saw each other how often then?"

"A couple of times a month. She was busy. And she was newly married. And she had a lot of obligations."

Cole wanted to tell Amber to stop talking. She was sounding defensive, as if she was embarrassed that they weren't closer.

"Tell me, Ms. Welsley, how did Coco feel about her baby?"

"She loved Zachary very much."

"As mothers do."

Amber didn't answer.

Cole applauded that decision.

"What about before he was born?"

She went still, and her face paled a shade. "I don't understand."

"I don't like this," Cole muttered beneath his breath. Something was clearly wrong.

"Before Zachary was born. How did Coco feel about being pregnant?"

"She was healthy. There were no particular problems, morning sickness or anything."

"I'm not talking about her physical health, Ms. Welsley. I'm talking about her emotional health."

Again, Amber stayed silent.

"Was your stepsister happy to be pregnant with Zachary?"

Cole got a cold feeling in the pit of his stomach.

"She was surprised," said Amber. "She hadn't planned on it happening so soon."

"Surprised or upset?"

Amber paused. "She was upset at first."

"Upset enough to get an abortion?"

Amber's hesitation said it all.

"Damn it," Cole ground out.

"She didn't get an abortion," said Amber.

"Did she want an abortion?"

"Objection," said Destiny.

"I'll rephrase," said the lawyer. "Did she ever tell you she wanted an abortion?"

The silence was unfortunately long.

"Once," Amber admitted.

"Did you talk her out of getting an abortion?"

"I gave her my opinion."

"Which was?"

"That babies were always good news. And that she was going to be a wonderful mother."

"Is it fair to say you changed her mind?"

Amber didn't answer.

"Ms. Welsley? Is it fair to say you changed your stepsister's mind, talked her out of getting the abortion she desired?"

"She wasn't serious," said Amber. "She was upset. She was newly married, and being pregnant came as a shock to her."

"Did she make an appointment at an abortion clinic?"

"No."

The lawyer waited.

"She didn't."

"Perhaps not to the best of your knowledge. But I can tell you she *did* make an appointment at an abortion clinic."

A collective gasp went up in the gallery, followed by whispered comments.

The judge pounded his gavel, and the room returned to quiet.

The lawyer returned to his table, lifting a piece of paper with a flourish. "I have here a copy of an appointment card for Coco Henderson for the Women's Central Health Clinic."

"Where did you get that?"

"From the Women's Central Health Clinic."

"Coco obviously did not have an abortion."

"Because you talked her out of it. Like so many of your step-sister's childish, ill-informed impulses, had you not been there to persuade her otherwise, the consequences would have been catastrophic. She would have had an abortion, and Zachary would never have been born."

The sick feeling of defeat was written across Amber's face. Cole fought an urge to go to her. He wanted to pull her into his arms and tell her everything was going to be okay. But he couldn't. And it wasn't.

"That was a body blow," said Luca.

There was nothing Destiny could do to counter the revelations. Both lawyers walked through closing arguments, but there wasn't a single person in the room who trusted Coco's judgment, nor was there anyone who truly believed she had her son's best interests at heart.

Samuel had been shown to be a loving father, thrilled from minute one that they were expecting a baby. Coco looked selfish and petulant, her intelligence and judgment suspect.

Destiny sat down and put an arm around Amber's shoulders.

"You have to do it," Luca whispered.

"Do what?"

"Tell them who you are."

Cole shot Luca a look of astonishment. *"What?"*

"Now. Right now. Put in a bid for custody. You're a blood relative."

"Custody?" Had Luca lost his mind?

"At the very least, it'll throw a wrench in it, slow things down. If you don't, if the judge rules on this—and it looks like he's about to rule—then it's done."

Adrenaline shot into Cole's system, and his stomach clenched. How could he do it? How could he not?

"Ms. Welsley," said the judge, "I have no doubt as to the love you feel for Zachary. However—"

"Do it!" Luca hissed.

Cole shot to his feet. "Your Honor."

The judge drew back in obvious shock. "You're out of order, sir."

"Go, go, go," said Luca.

Cole moved into the aisle and walked forward.

Amber and Destiny both turned to stare. But he didn't dare look at them.

"Bailiff," called the judge.

Cole knew he had only seconds. "My name is Cole Parker Henderson. I'm Samuel Henderson's son."

Amber felt her world dissolve beneath her.

Cole continued walking to the front of the courtroom. He continued talking. He didn't even bother to look her way.

"I want to petition the court for custody of my half brother," his voice boomed.

"He's a competitor," Roth cried out, coming to his feet.

"Order," called the judge, bringing down his gavel.

The bailiff seemed uncertain of what to do.

Destiny whispered in an undertone, "What the—?"

"I'm *such* an idiot," said Amber.

"Can it possibly be true?"

Cole came to a stop at the little gateway.

Amber took in Cole's expression. "That's no bluff."

He was firm and resolute. She realized he had to have planned this all along. And she'd let him in. She'd trusted him. She'd armed him with all kinds of information. She'd left him alone in the penthouse, alone with Zachary.

"This is preposterous," said Roth. "It's a stalling tactic."

Cole glared at him. "It's easy enough to prove. DNA, for example."

"That'll take time. And we're losing money by the hour. Your Honor, this can't possibly be legal."

Roth's lawyer stood. "Your Honor, you were about to rule."

A voice came from the back of the room. "We have a DNA test."

Cole spun.

Luca came to his feet. "Your Honor, I have the results of a DNA test by Central Laboratories, proving Samuel's paternity."

"What do we do?" asked Amber, panic beginning to build deep in her stomach.

"Wait," said Destiny, watching the judge closely.

The judge finally spoke. "I'm not persuaded that a genetic relationship alone alters the merits of this case. Samuel Henderson could have any number of illegitimate children—"

"They were married," Cole's deep voice intoned.

Silence followed the pronouncement.

"My mother and Samuel Henderson were married." He shot a sharp look to Roth. "Again, very easy to prove."

Luca spoke. "I have a copy of the marriage certificate and the divorce decree."

Cole turned to stare at Luca for a long moment.

Destiny leaned close to Amber. "*This* is a whole new ballgame. Hang tough."

Destiny came sharply to her feet. "Your Honor, we ask for a recess."

Roth's lawyer jumped in. "*We* ask for a ruling."

But Destiny wasn't finished. "Under the terms of the will, as a legitimate child of Samuel Henderson, Cole Henderson is entitled to half of Samuel's estate."

The courtroom erupted.

"Order, order," the judge called over the din. "Court is in recess until such time as Samuel Henderson's will can be reviewed." He looked to Cole. "Mr. Henderson, if you do not already have a lawyer, I suggest you get one."

Everybody left their seats, and the courtroom turned into a mob scene. Cole stood still, the crowd jostling around him. He was nearly chest to chest with the bailiff guarding the low gate.

"Get me out of here," Amber said to Destiny. "I can't see him. I can't talk to him."

"We can take the side door." Destiny grabbed her briefcase.

All Amber wanted to do was get back to Zachary. For a horrible moment there, she'd known she was about to lose him. Zachary had almost been ripped from her care and given over to Roth. She was still shaking with reaction.

"Amber," called Cole.

She refused to look at him. "Go away."

"I wanted to tell you. I tried to tell you."

She let out a short, high-pitched laugh. "When? *When?* It's not like you lacked opportunity."

"We need to talk."

"We've talked enough. I've told you enough." She turned away.

"Amber," Cole tried again.

Luca's voice interrupted. "Destiny, we need a copy of the will."

"Not *now*," said Cole.

Destiny's tone was sharp. "As if you haven't already read it."

"We haven't," said Luca.

"Why the theatrics?"

"You were about to lose," said Luca.

"Amber?" Cole tried again.

Destiny appealed to Cole. "This is not a good time."

"I don't particularly care. You can't ignore this."

Amber glared at him. She wanted to yell at him. He'd deceived her. He'd slept with her. He'd let her think he cared about Zachary.

But before she could do anything stupid, she forced herself to turn and walk away.

She left the courtroom and all but ran down the hallway to the foyer. It was full of reporters, but she ignored their questions. She ignored everything, striding blindly for the exit.

Destiny caught up. "You're doing great. Just keep walking. My car's to the left, one block up."

"I remember. I need to see Zachary."

"We'll go there first."

"Ms. Welsley, did you have any idea Samuel had another son?"

"Did your sister know Samuel had another wife?"

"Did Coco have any other abortions?"

Destiny hit the unlock button and pulled open the passenger door for Amber. Amber climbed inside and slammed the door, not particularly caring if she smashed someone's camera.

And then Destiny was inside, too. She started the car, and the reporters finally backed off.

"You okay?" she asked, reaching out to touch Amber's shoulder.

"I'm terrible," Amber answered.

She felt trapped, desperate. For a wild moment, she thought about sneaking Zachary out of the country, hiding out on a beach somewhere where nobody could find them.

"What happens now?" she asked, her voice shaking.

"First, we comb through the will."

"Does Cole really get half?"

"Unless there's something I'm remembering wrong, yes, he does."

Amber's voice broke over the next question. "Will he get Zachary?"

"I don't know, honey. I honestly don't know."

Amber's mind scrambled, zipping from Zachary to Coast Eagle, to the Boonsome 300, and then to Cole.

"I have to talk to Max," she told Destiny. "I have to get back to the office."

"Do you want to go home first?"

Amber shook her head. "I'll call Isabel. Roth will go straight to Coast Eagle, and who knows what move he'll try to make next." She realized in a rush that despite everything, she feared Roth more than she feared Cole.

Back at the office, Roth had fought with Max. Julius had argued with Sidney. Each of the board members had called to express their concern. Though, thankfully, all had agreed that Max should stay in place for now as interim president.

Destiny had reviewed Samuel's will and was now on her way to the penthouse to meet Amber. It was nearly ten by the time Amber finally made it through the door, exhausted and starving.

She kicked off her shoes, shrugged out of her steel-gray blazer and dumped her purse on a table in the living room. Destiny had promised to bring a large pepperoni and mushroom, while Amber was in charge of margaritas.

She called out to Isabel, then, without stopping, she went directly to the kitchen and dumped a tray of ice cubes, lime juice, tequila and orange liqueur into the blender and set it on high.

The doorbell rang, and she padded through the living room to greet Destiny.

"Extra cheese?" she asked hopefully as she eyed the large cardboard carton.

"You bet."

"Come on in."

While Destiny settled the pizza on the kitchen island and retrieved the plates, Amber poured the margaritas into two large glasses.

"I've been seriously thinking about strapping Zachary into his car seat and heading for the border," said Amber.

"Which border?"

"Does it matter? I can't help but think we'd be better off if nobody could find us."

"You might be better off, but I'd have a legal nightmare to unravel."

"I suppose."

The fight suddenly went out of Amber, and exhaustion set in. She climbed onto one of the stools and helped herself to a slice of the gooey pizza.

"You could try to make a deal with Cole," Destiny suggested. She started with a sip of the slushy drink. "It's pretty clear he's after Coast Eagle."

"Do you think Samuel knew about him?" In her few spare moments this evening, Amber couldn't help but wonder if Samuel had shunned Cole and kept him a secret or had been oblivious to his existence.

"Interesting wording in the will," said Destiny. "Either Samuel knew, or at least suspected he had a child with his first wife, or he was planning more children with Coco."

"He definitely wanted more children," said Amber.

There was more silence.

"An abortion?" asked Destiny.

"I almost couldn't talk her out of it."

"For future reference, that's the kind of thing you want to share with your lawyer."

"I had no idea it would ever come out."

"Everything always comes out eventually."

"I didn't know she'd made an appointment. She didn't tell me that. It was one night—one long, horrible night where we argued. And then she changed her mind. I don't remember any of the staff being around. I thought nobody knew but me."

"She might have told Samuel."

Amber gave her head a decisive shake. "She knew how much he wanted children. If she'd had an abortion, it would have been in secret. She'd never have admitted to him she'd had doubts."

They both fell silent, chewing their way through the pizza slices.

"We were about to lose, weren't we?" Amber asked.

"We were about to lose big-time. Roth knows how to run Coast Eagle, and Samuel was way out front in the character debate."

"Just because Coco was self-centered doesn't mean she was wrong to choose me."

"I agree," said Destiny, helping herself to another slice. "We need to figure out Cole's plan. I can guess at Roth's next move. Between Samuel and his mother, the Hendersons controlled sixty-five percent of Coast Eagle. The other shareholders are minor, mostly companies, none with more than seven percent. But Roth still has a play. If he gets custody, therefore half of the Henderson family shares, and if he can bring the other shareholders on side, he'll control the board and get himself appointed as president."

"He doesn't care anything about Zachary."

"True, but all but impossible to prove," said Destiny. "Samuel named him guardian for some reason."

"If Cole gets custody, he controls all sixty-five percent. He's invincible." Amber paused. "But why the ruse?"

"He was obviously looking for information, solidifying his position. That has to be why Luca was cozying up to me."

"Did you tell Luca anything?"

"Nothing that wasn't already public. Cole obviously saw you as his primary rival rather than Ross. I'm guessing he was either going to co-opt you or take you out."

"He must have been shocked when it went in Roth's favor."

"And had to suddenly change the game plan. I don't think they planned it like that."

"They did have DNA and a marriage certificate at the ready."

"True," said Destiny.

Amber took a drink, appreciating the hit of alcohol warming her system. "What do we do now?"

"We need more information on Cole."

"Maybe I could seduce it out of him. No, wait. I already tried that."

Destiny gazed at her for a moment, the tone of her voice going softer. "How was it?"

"Seriously?"

Destiny gave a helpless shrug. "What can it hurt to tell me now?"

Amber set down her half-eaten slice of pizza, regret enveloping her. "It was great. He was funny, romantic, totally into me." She swiped back her hair. "At least he seemed totally into me. Too bad he was faking the whole thing." Every time she thought about their night together, the humiliation returned. "I'm not sure I can face him again."

"I could talk to Luca instead. He might give me something we can use."

"Did you sleep with Luca?"

"Almost. He tried pretty hard."

Amber held up her glass in a toast. "You're a stronger woman than me. And you've still got that as leverage."

"I'd have said yes eventually."

"But you won't anymore, right?"

"I won't anymore," said Destiny. "Well, unless I think it'll make him talk. Then, well, okay, I'd be willing to take one for the team."

Eight

"I know she's here," Cole said to Luca as he pulled open the steel door of the Coast Eagle hangar. "And she'll have to be polite."

He knew Amber wouldn't dare step out of line at the Coast Eagle children's Christmas party. She'd have to listen to him.

He walked inside.

Carols chimed from unseen speakers, while soap bubbles drifted around them like snow. White lights and colored balls domed over the ceiling, swooping down in swirls and shapes to meet the concrete floor, which was covered in artificial snow.

There was a giant Christmas tree in the center of the hangar and a forest full of lighted trees and friendly elves. A cookie-decorating station took up one big corner of the room. Another group of elves painted Christmas shapes on the children's faces. And, of course, Santa was in his castle, posing for pictures and handing out presents.

The festive scene jarred with the frustration swirling inside Cole's head. In the three days since the hearing, a group of lawyers had poured over Samuel's will. This morning, they'd all agreed that Cole was a beneficiary, entitled to half of Samuel's estate.

Cole didn't want an inheritance. When he'd come forward and announced himself, he hadn't the slightest inkling he'd be included in the will. He wasn't here to take anything away from Zachary. Still, he'd use the position if it gave them leverage.

"There she is," said Luca. "Beside the Christmas-tree forest."

Cole spotted her. As always, he was immediately struck by her beauty. She wore a bright red dress with white piping. It clung to her slender curves.

He was here to talk. But talking was far down on his wish list. For starters, he wanted to haul her off somewhere and kiss her senseless.

"Mr. Henderson," Sidney Raines greeted him cheerfully, shaking his hand. "I heard the estate was settled this morning in your favor."

"Call me Cole. It's nice to see you again, Sidney."

Of all the vice presidents, Sidney was easily the more savvy and most reasonable. Cole also liked Max. He was less impressed with Julius, and he was prepared to fight long and hard against Roth.

"It's probably early on to broach the subject," said Sidney, glancing around the huge building, "and I realize this isn't the time or the place, but have you given any thought to what role you'll take on in the company?"

"It isn't the time or the place," said Cole. "But you're right to ask the question. Would you be able to meet over the weekend?"

"Absolutely. You just name the time and place."

Cole took out his cell phone. "If you give me your cell number, I'll call you later on."

Sidney dictated his phone number, then bowed out.

"It's a good question," said Luca.

"I know," said Cole as the two men started toward the brightly lit forest.

"Do you have any idea what you are going to do?"

Cole's thinking hadn't made it past the first couple of moves. "I'm going to find a permanent president."

He worked fourteen-hour days taking care of Aviation 58. He had to get back there as soon as possible. But he'd accepted that he now had a role in protecting Zachary's inheritance.

The closer they got to Amber, the more beautiful she became. No surprise to Cole.

Zachary was in her arms, also dressed in red and white, a goofy little hat on his head. Cole couldn't help but smile at how Zachary reached for the twinkling lights of the closest tree. He'd really missed the little guy.

But then Amber saw him.

Her smile instantly disappeared, and her blue eyes went cold. She took a step, and it was obvious she was going to flee.

Cole quickly crossed the space between them, wrapping a hand around her arm and keeping her close.

Luca wisely hung back.

"Everybody's watching," he cautioned her in a low tone. "Smile. Pretend it's all good between us."

"Go away."

"Not a chance. Smile."

Zachary zeroed in on Cole.

"Gak baw," he called, lurching toward Cole.

Cole reflexively reached for him. His arm brushed her breast, and the contact sent a surge of energy through his body.

He ordered himself to calm the heck down. "You heard the decision on the will?"

Amber put a brittle smile in place, but her tone was flat. "Congratulations."

"We have to talk."

"I don't have time. I promised Zachary we'd decorate some gingerbread." She reached for the baby, but he turned his head, clinging tighter to Cole.

"It'll be easier if I come with you," said Cole.

"No, it won't."

"I'm on your side."

She scoffed out a laugh. "Is that a joke?" Then she held out her arms to Zachary. "Come on, pumpkin."

The baby stayed firmly latched to Cole.

Cole couldn't help feeling sympathetic. "As much as I hate to think about it, I must look like Samuel. Or maybe I sound like him, or smell like him."

"Zachary loves me, too, you know."

"Of course he does."

"He's known me since birth."

"It's a case of mistaken identity," said Cole. "Somewhere in his subconscious, he sees me as family."

"You are family."

Cole was growing more and more conscious of the interest in their conversation. Nobody had dared come within hearing distance, but there was a lot of pointing and whispering going on amongst the staff.

"Let's go decorate some gingerbread."

"Why can't you just leave?"

"If I give him back, he's going to make a scene."

"Was that your plan? I mean today's plan—use Zachary against me?"

"There was no plan."

"Do I strike you as stupid?"

"Amber, please. Gingerbread. Let's just do the gingerbread."

There must have been a note of desperation in his tone that got her attention because she glanced around, seeming to become aware of the onlookers.

"Right," she agreed. "Let's go."

They moved casually to the rear corner of the hangar. People eyed them speculatively as they did so, but held back. Luca disappeared, obviously understanding that Cole needed to speak with Amber alone.

"Mr. Henderson, Ms. Welsley, Merry Christmas!" called a middle-aged woman as they passed.

"Merry Christmas," Cole automatically returned.

"Notice you got top billing," Amber muttered.

"I'm carrying the little rich kid."

"You are the little rich kid."

The greeting seemed to break the ice, and they were bombarded with well-wishers all along their route.

Amber was right. While the employees were completely polite and respectful to her, Cole was getting the lion's share of the attention.

Finally, they came to the cookie-decorating station. The attendants quickly cleared a stand-up table for them, spreading out a new paper cover and bringing an assortment of gingerbread, sugar-cookie shapes, icing and colorful candies.

"Go for it," said Cole. "Pretend you're completely absorbed in the cookies, and maybe people will stay away."

She stared at the tabletop without moving.

"The tree," Cole prompted. "Decorate the tree with the green icing."

Amber picked up a plastic knife.

He focused on keeping his expression agreeable as he spoke. "I'm going to need your support."

She gave another strained smile as she iced the sugar cookie tree. "Like that's going to happen."

"I didn't know about the will."

"Yes, you did."

"How would I know? Tell me how I would know."

"There were ten people in the first reading. Obviously someone leaked the details to you."

"None of them knew I existed."

"So you say."

His voice rose. "I don't just say. It's true."

"The red candies?" she asked him sweetly. "Or the blue and white?"

He took a calming breath. "The red."

"I like the blue and white."

"Seriously? You want to argue about candies?"

"I don't want to argue about anything. I want you to go away. Preferably far away. I hear Alaska's nice this time of year."

Cole shifted Zachary in his arms. Happily, the baby was fascinated by the lights, the sounds and the people moving around.

"If you'll listen to what I have to say, you'll understand why you need to help me."

"No, Cole. If I believed what you had to say, I might be inclined to help you. But that's never going to happen. I'm never going to trust you again."

"I want what's best for Zachary."

"You want what's best for Cole. And congratulations, you're halfway there."

Cole regrouped. "Roth can still take control of the company."

She dropped a handful of blue and white candies on the freshly iced tree and pressed them firmly down with her palm.

For a moment, he thought she'd crush the cookie.

"I can see you've done the math on the share ownership," she said.

"Do you have any influence with the minor shareholders?"

She flashed another phony smile. "None whatsoever. I'm the lowly assistant director of finance and the stepsister of a flaky trophy wife. Why would anyone listen to me?"

"We can still help each other."

"Have a cookie, Cole. It's all you're ever going to get from me."

She suddenly scooped Zachary out of his arms.

It took the baby a second to realize what had happened. Then he immediately opened his mouth and let out a cry.

If not for the staff members surrounding them, Cole would have gone after her. Instead, he watched her march away and disappear into the crowd.

Zachary's cries were soon swallowed by the cheery carols and happy shouts of the other children.

Luca appeared beside him. "Didn't look like that went too well."

"She has *got* to be the most stubborn woman on the planet." Cole's gaze fell to the slightly mangled cookie. He picked it up and took a bite.

"Fighting with Amber makes you hungry?"

"It makes me something, that's for sure."

He crunched down on the sweetness. Fighting made him want to grab her and squeeze her tight, kiss her hard and press their bodies together. It didn't matter what insanity swirled around them, he couldn't forget the night they'd made love, and he couldn't quell the overriding urge to do it all over again.

Amber wasn't going to crack.

It was nearly ten o'clock at night. Zachary had barely napped during the afternoon. He'd fussed through dinner and pouted through his bath. She'd even given him an extra bottle, going through their entire bedtime routine a second time in the hope he'd catch on.

Now he was in his crib, kicking his feet and sobbing. His

covers were on the floor. His head was sweaty, and his hands were wrapped tightly around the painted bars.

Her phone rang over the noise, and for a crazy second she hoped it was Cole. If he called her and asked to come over, it wasn't the same as giving in, was it?

Unfortunately, the number was Destiny's.

She moved into the hallway, and Zachary's cries increased behind her.

"Hi," she said into the phone.

"How're you doing?"

"Not great."

"Is that Zachary?"

Amber leaned against the wall of the hallway, sliding down to sit on the plush carpet. "He doesn't want to settle."

"I'm sorry."

"Not your fault. Not even his fault. Honestly, I feel like sobbing right along with him."

"Luca said you saw Cole today?"

Amber knew she should remember his annoying behavior, her anger and his new set of lies. But instead she remembered his touch, his voice and those now-familiar gray eyes.

"At the kids' party," she answered Destiny. "Wait, when did you see Luca?"

"Earlier tonight."

"Why?" What was going on?

"Nothing's going on. I like Luca, Amber. I'm not giving him any information. He's not even trying to ask. We both know we have to be circumspect."

Amber clunked her head back against the cool wall. "I'm sorry. You're entitled to a personal life."

"He did say something, though."

"What's that?"

"He said that by not helping Cole, you're de facto helping Roth."

Amber gave a slightly hysterical laugh. "I thought you were going to say something much more personal. Like you had beautiful eyes or he wanted to see you naked."

"Oh, he definitely wants to see me naked."

Amber firmly pushed her own problems away. "You should let him."

"Excuse me?"

"You want to. I can hear it in your voice."

"There's nothing in my voice that says—"

"Go for it. Your celibacy won't help me. In fact, it'll probably distract you from helping me."

"You want me to have a one-night stand?"

"I had one." The memories rose one by one in Amber's mind. Into the silence, Destiny's tone turned reflective. "You think you're the better for it?"

"Not at all. But I'm stuck in the middle of a preposterous circumstance. You'll be fine."

"You want some company? Need some reinforcements?"

"You don't need to come all the way over here."

Not that Amber wouldn't welcome the support. Maybe Destiny could take a turn holding Zachary. He was still crying, and it was all but impossible to steel herself against his sadness.

"I'm five minutes away," said Destiny.

"You are?"

"Just left a meeting at Bacharat's. You know, that private lawyers' club? You're on my route home."

"Then, yes, sure. Stop by."

"Sounds good. It might take me a few minutes to park."

"See you then." Amber disconnected the call.

Feeling a bit lighter, she headed back into Zachary's bedroom. He had pulled up on his feet and was gripping the top of the crib rail. His cheeks were flushed red and damp with tears.

"Oh, sweetheart," she said out loud, lifting him into her arms. "How can I help?"

He cried harder.

She racked her brain. "What about some music? Want to watch videos?"

Zachary seemed to have a fondness for country and western, especially the drawling male singers.

With no better ideas, she carried him to the living room and tuned in the country station. It didn't fix the problem, but at least it gave something to blend with his cries.

Then the knock came on her door.

"I know you're too young to understand," she said to Zachary as they crossed the living room, "but my arms are about to get a rest, and that's a very good thing."

She swung open the door.

Cole stood in front of her, Otis at his heels.

She was stunned. "You're supposed to be Destiny."

"I saw her in the lobby."

At the sound of Cole's voice, Zachary swung around.

"She said she'd give me ten minutes," said Cole.

"Destiny sent you up?" Amber didn't want to believe it.

Zachary reached for Cole.

"You want me to take him?"

Amber caved. "She'll be up in ten minutes?"

Cole cracked a smile. "I bet he's asleep by then. He looks exhausted."

Amber was weak. In fact, she was defeated. "He's the one and only reason I'll let you in."

"I'll take it." Cole gathered Zachary against his shoulder and moved into the foyer.

"What's goin' on here, partner?" Cole rumbled.

Zachary laid his head onto Cole's shoulder and his cries turned to shuddering breaths.

She couldn't resist. She smoothed the sweat from Zachary's forehead, brushing her fingers across his downy, fine hair. "Poor little guy."

"You're very patient," said Cole.

"Not always."

There were times when she couldn't help feeling frustrated and resentful. She was doing everything she could for Zachary, but it wasn't enough. Sometimes she thought he was being miserable just to make her jump through hoops. But in her saner moments, she knew he was far too young to be manipulative.

"You need to do anything?" he asked her as they walked to the living room. "Hungry, thirsty?"

"Don't be nice."

A smirk appeared on his face. "Okay."

"You know what I mean. Don't try to ingratiate yourself by helping me with Zachary. It won't work."

Otis picked a spot beside an armchair and flopped down.

"Then do you think you could whip something up for me?" asked Cole. "Maybe a dry martini and a few hors d'oeuvres?"

"Shut up and mind the baby."

Cole grinned. "He's doing fine."

"I hate that you can do that, you know." It wasn't fair at all.

"Accident of genetics." Cole lowered himself into an armchair.

It was yet another thing that ticked her off. When she was soothing Zachary, she couldn't sit down. She had to stand and sway or he'd cry his head off.

"This whole thing is an accident of genetics," Cole repeated.

"You want some hot cocoa?" she asked. She couldn't help remembering the last time they'd shared that particular beverage, but she needed something soothing right now.

"I was just messing with you. Don't go to any trouble."

But it wasn't any trouble. "It'll only take a minute, and I'm having some."

He hesitated. "In that case, sure."

She left for the kitchen.

"You need any help?" he called behind her.

"You're already helping."

"Points for that?" he asked.

The question stopped her cold. She couldn't help remembering the last time they'd joked about points. He'd asked to spend the night, then they'd slept curled together in her bed. If only they could go back to that moment, even just for a little while. Because what she really needed right now was a broad shoulder to lean on. Unfortunately, leaning on Cole's shoulder was out of the question.

She heated up the cocoa and returned to the living room.

"Sorry," he told her.

"For what?" She set a steaming cup down on the small table beside him and took the end of the sofa opposite to where he sat.

"For making that points crack."

He obviously remembered the last time.

The sweetened air seemed to still around them. Her mouth went dry, and her heartbeat thudded thickly in her chest. She braved a look at his face, and their gazes held. The ticking of the clock seemed to grow louder.

Cole broke the silence. "The reason I'm here..."

She was half afraid, half excited about what he might say. She distracted herself with a sip.

"The reason I'm here," he began again, "is because we can't let Roth win, and that means I need your help."

She didn't want Roth to win. But she didn't want Cole to win, either. Her throat closed up, and her chest pierced with pain.

She had a desperate urge to rip Zachary from his arms. She didn't care if he cried. She didn't care if she never slept again. She wanted to hold him every second of every day from now until someone forced her to stop.

"I..." she tried. "How can..." To her mortification, a tear slipped out.

She rose from her chair, surreptitiously swiping the tear away. "He's asleep. We can put him in his crib now."

"Sure," Cole agreed easily, rising with Zachary in his arms, watching her closely.

She walked down the hall to the nursery. There, she straightened the rumpled sheets and folded a fresh blanket onto the mattress.

A yellow nightlight glowed in the corner, highlighting the cartoon giraffes, elephants and lions on the wall. Soft stuffed animals decorated every surface.

Cole moved beside her and eased Zachary down onto the white flannel sheet. He pulled his arm from beneath Zachary and stepped back. The baby didn't stir. Amber covered Zachary with a knit blanket and a patchwork quilt. Then she stroked her palm over his warm forehead.

"Good night, sweetheart," she whispered.

She straightened, her heart aching all over again. She gripped the top of the crib rail, struggling to draw a breath.

Cole's strong hand came down on her shoulder. "Are you okay?" he asked softly.

She swallowed. Her voice came out on a pained whisper. "I'm so frightened."

"I know."

She shook her head. "No, you don't. You can't possibly understand."

She was going to lose Zachary, and there wasn't a thing she could do about it.

He gently turned her. She didn't stop him as he drew her into his arms. It didn't seem to matter that he was one of the enemies; she accepted the strength he offered.

His voice was deep and steady. "I know you can't let yourself believe anything I say. But I want what's best for Zachary. I promise I'll do what's best for Zachary."

She tipped her chin to gaze up at him. She wanted so badly to believe it was true. She needed some hope to hang on to.

Minutes ticked slowly past.

He reached up to brush her chin, his voice low and sexy. "You are amazing."

She knew she had to pull away. She had to shut this down before it went any further. His eyes were smoldering, his desire completely obvious. His hand crept into her hair. His gaze zeroed in on her lips, and he bent his head.

He was going to kiss her.

She wasn't going to stop him.

His lips touched hers, warm, soft and gentle.

She stretched up, leaned in, let her arms twine around his neck as he took the kiss deeper. She'd missed him. She couldn't believe how much she'd missed him.

Her world was dissolving around her, and he felt like the only anchor point. His hand splayed her back, pressing her close. A moan rose up from her chest, and she met his tongue. Flicking flames of desire rose up inside her, heating her body, sensitizing every nerve ending. She needed to get closer, to feel his skin.

But suddenly, he drew back. "We can't do this."

She was mortified. What was she thinking? What was she doing, throwing herself into his arms?

He braced his hands around her upper arms, putting a few inches between them. "We need to talk."

"Talk," Amber managed to agree.

He put a hand lightly on the small of her back, guiding her from the nursery, down the hall, back to the living room.

She went straight to the far corner of the sofa, struggling to pull her dignity around her.

She could feel Cole's gaze on her from where he sat in the armchair. But she couldn't bring herself to look at him. She couldn't imagine what he thought of her. He'd deceived her, used her to gain information about Coast Eagle, Samuel and Zachary. And yet she'd been willing to leap into bed with him a second time.

There was something terribly wrong with her.

"What will Roth do?" Cole asked into the silence. "If he wins custody, what will he do?"

Amber struggled to move past emotion to logic. "I expect he will hire a nanny. I hope he keeps Isabel, but I don't know that he will." She had to stop for a breath. "Then he'll use the power of his guardianship to get appointed president of Coast Eagle."

"He won't want to be chairman of the board?"

"He wants to be hands-on. He wants to run the company day-to-day. His first plan is to update or replace the entire fleet. He thinks he'll be able to increase our market share enough to cover the debt."

"You doubt that?" asked Cole.

"His projections are dangerously optimistic."

Cole gave a contemplative nod.

Amber forced herself to ask the burning question. "What will you do?"

His gaze was level and honest. "I don't know."

"How can I trust you?"

"You can't. You shouldn't."

She scoffed out a laugh at that.

He took a sip of his now-cool cocoa. "All you can do right now is go on what's certain. Roth's got the advantage over me, and he cares about Roth, first, last and always."

"You're saying you're the lesser of two evils."

"I know you can't bring yourself to trust me yet. But you know for certain you can't trust Roth."

"That's not at all comforting."

"I know. But it's all you've got."

Amber knew he was right. She hated it. But it was true.

Nine

As a significant shareholder in Coast Eagle, no matter how things turned out in the long term, Cole knew he needed to understand the company. He and Luca had both been in daily contact with Aviation 58 since arriving in Atlanta, but Luca now offered to take over as much as possible on the Alaska operation.

Luckily, even leading into the busy holiday travel season, things seemed well under control at Aviation 58. There were no unexpected maintenance issues, passenger load was as predicted and the Alaskan weather was cooperating surprisingly well.

Cole entered the Coast Eagle building and was immediately recognized. Security greeted him and called up to the executive floor to announce his arrival.

As he exited the elevator, he was greeted by the receptionist, Sandra, who was exceedingly welcoming and polite this time. She introduced him to Samuel's personal assistant, a fiftyish man named Bartholomew Green. Bartholomew had a British accent and was dressed in a dark formal suit, a matching vest, crisp white shirt and a gold tie.

Samuel's office was also ostentatious, with a huge, ornately carved cherrywood desk, and a massive credenza with cut-glass decanters. A sofa and two armchairs had diamond tufted, dark leather upholstery, while expensive oil paintings hung on the walls. Cole couldn't help wonder how his down-to-earth mother had fallen in love with the man he was learning about.

"Will you be moving into the office today, sir?" asked Bartholomew.

"I will," said Cole.

The last thing in the world he wanted to do was step into his father's shoes. But he needed to make a statement. Roth, the judge and everybody else had to see he was taking the reins—even if it was only temporary.

He took in Bartholomew's attire once more. He supposed

he'd have to update his own wardrobe, and he was going to make the same recommendation to Amber. She was next on his list of things to deal with at Coast Eagle.

"Can you set up a meeting with Max and the vice presidents for this afternoon?" Cole asked Bartholomew.

"Do you have a preferred time, sir?"

"Two o'clock." Cole couldn't have cared less about the time, but he needed to be the guy making the decisions.

"The east boardroom?"

"Sounds fine. Can you direct me to Amber Welsley's office?"

"She's in accounting. That's on the seventh floor. Shall I show you the way?"

"Is it overly complicated?"

Bartholomew seemed to allow himself a small smile. "Left when you get off the elevator, first hallway on your right."

"I think I can manage. No need for a tour guide."

"Very good, sir."

"Anything else I should know?" Cole asked, curious to know where Bartholomew's loyalties would lie.

"What would you like to know?"

Cole paused to gauge the man's expression. "What do you think is important?"

An intelligent light came into Bartholomew's eyes. "Mr. Henderson had a lot of faith in Sidney. I believe that was appropriate. He also had a lot of faith in Roth. I believe that faith may have been misplaced. He also understood the need to deploy Julius in certain situations."

"Such as?"

"Would you like me to be blunt?"

"Always."

"Julius is a pit bull. But he's Coast Eagle's pit bull."

"What about Max Cutter?"

"Max Cutter will be completely up front and honest with you. If I had to guess, I'd say he can't wait to get out of the president's role and back to the legal department."

Cole agreed with that assessment. Max had said as much himself.

"And Amber Welsley?" Cole asked.

"I knew Mrs. Henderson a lot better than I knew Ms. Welsley."

"Impressions?"

"She has always struck me as hardworking but below the radar. I'm not certain she thought very highly of Mr. Samuel Henderson."

"He married her baby sister."

"Indeed. Though I'm not certain she was a fan of Mrs. Henderson, either."

"May I rely on your discretion, Bartholomew?"

"You may."

"Good to know." Cole was impressed with the man so far.

"If I may, sir?"

"Yes?"

"You haven't asked about Samuel Henderson."

"That's because I don't want to know."

Bartholomew was silent for a moment. "Very good."

"Is that a problem for you?"

"Not at all."

Cole looked through the doorway to the outer office and Bartholomew's desk. "Give me the lay of the land here."

Bartholomew moved to stand beside him. "You've seen reception, and my desk is right there. The office to your right is the president's. Max isn't using it, because he already has an office on this floor. Around the corner to your left is Roth, next to him is Julius, and Sidney is around the corner from the president's office. The east boardroom is next to Sidney, and the west meeting room is next to Julius. After that, you're through reception to the director's offices and the executive lunch room."

"Is everyone in today?"

"As I understand it, yes."

"Thank you, Bartholomew." Cole exited the office and made his way to the elevator in the reception area.

Under Sandra's veiled curiosity, he pressed the button for seven. He could well imagine the conversations and speculation would start the second the door closed behind him. That was good. He wanted people to wonder.

On the seventh floor, he took a left then a right, quickly finding Amber's office.

Her door was open, and he was taken aback by the small size. She sat at her desk, head down, writing on a financial sheet.

"There's an adding error on report sixteen," she said without looking up, obviously hearing him arrive. "I know we have to pull the soft commitments in manually, but we need to make sure the formulas are—"

She spotted Cole in the doorway. "Sorry." His presence seemed to fluster her. "I assumed you were my assistant."

"Nope." He walked in.

She sat up straight and set down her pen. "You're here."

"I'm here." He glanced around. "More to the point, you're *here*."

"I'm usually here."

"This is your office?"

"It is."

"So the office of the assistant director of finance?"

"That would be me."

He braced himself on the desk across from her. "Not anymore."

She drew back. "Have I been fired?"

"Promoted. Or haven't you been paying attention?"

"Being temporarily nominated as guardian is not a promotion."

"You're chair of the board."

"For the next five minutes."

"If you want people to take you seriously, you need to look the part."

"Pretending I'm the real chair of the board would be embarrassing for everyone involved."

He straightened. "I don't get you."

"I'm not that complicated."

"Yes, you are. But that's not my point. We need to use every weapon at our disposal. One of the strongest, if not *the* strongest we have is the fact that, for now, we *are* in charge. Get up."

Her brows shot up. "Excuse me?"

"There's an empty office on the top floor—you're moving in. Right now."

"You can't order me to—"

"Amber."

She set her jaw.

He ignored the expression. "Your biggest weakness is that nobody can picture you at the helm."

"That's because I'm not capable of taking the helm."

"Who says?"

"Reason and good judgment?"

"They're wrong. And you're wrong." His tone hardened. This was too important to mess up. "And if you don't march yourself up to that corner office right now and start giving orders, then you haven't done your best by Zachary."

"I have done everything—"

"No, Amber. You haven't. Right now, between the two of us, we control sixty-five percent of Coast Eagle. Let's start acting like it. Let's let the world see us at the helm. That way, they'll know we can do it."

She glanced around her office, the three computer screens, the stacks of reports. "But—"

"First stop, your boss's office to give him permission to replace you."

"Give away my job?" The prospect clearly distressed her.

"Temporarily. Trust me, Amber. And if you can't trust me, trust Destiny. Phone her now. I know she'll agree."

Amber's lips compressed as she obviously thought through the situation.

"Being seen in charge is our best weapon," he reiterated. "Don't throw it away."

"Okay." She came to her feet, expression determined. "I'm willing to try anything."

Cole felt a surge of relief. He'd known she was stubborn. But he'd also known she was smart. Luckily, smart had won out.

* * *

"I've never even set foot in this store," Amber whispered to Destiny.

The next step in Cole's stated strategy was to deck both of them out in what he called a power wardrobe. From what Amber could see, that meant spending a whole lot of money.

"I've never shopped here, either," Destiny answered. "But I know some of the senior partners do. I've heard them mention the name."

"I don't dare look at the price tags," said Amber, glancing around at the gleaming floors, marble pillars and leather furniture groupings with complimentary designer water and champagne.

"What price tags?" asked Destiny. "If you have to ask, you can't afford it."

"I think I might break out in hives."

Cole and Luca entered the store behind them.

"This ought to do it," said Luca with obvious satisfaction.

Cole took in the high, brightly lit ceilings. "It's nothing like the Fashion Farm back home."

"Are you two going upstairs?" Destiny nodded to the sign for menswear.

"And miss the fun?" asked Luca.

"Let's get Amber decked out first," said Cole. "I want to make sure she doesn't hold back."

"You doubt my powers of persuasion?" asked Destiny.

"You'll make me self-conscious," Amber told Cole.

"What better means to cure you? If you can get comfortable in front of me, the rest of the executives will be easy." He pointed to a headless mannequin in a blazer and skirt combination. "What about that?"

The skirt was short and black, scattered with tiny white flecks. The blouse was white with a braided scooped neck. And the blazer was solid black, fitted, with the sleeves pushed up the forearms.

"I like the necklace, too," said Cole. "And the belt. Why not try on the whole thing?"

"You don't think the skirt's a little short?" Amber asked. Though she would admit, the outfit looked fun.

"Shows you have confidence," said Cole.

"I don't have confidence."

Cole turned to Destiny. "You see what I'm dealing with?"

"It would work with black stockings," said Destiny.

Cole opened his mouth, but Luca elbowed him in the ribs.

A sales clerk arrived. "Do you need any help?" she asked with a broad smile.

Amber couldn't help wondering what Cole had been about to say on the topic of black stockings. She also couldn't seem to stop a shimmer of sexual awareness.

"She needs a whole new wardrobe," said Cole, gesturing to Amber.

Amber shifted under everyone's scrutiny. "Oh, I wouldn't say I need an entire—"

"Shut up," Destiny interrupted. She gestured back to Cole. "He's buying, and we need her to look like a million bucks. Literally."

"Daywear, evening, office?" the clerk asked.

"Yes," said Cole.

"This is getting out of hand," said Amber.

She understood the principle behind his strategy. And now that she'd had a few hours to think about it, she agreed with it. But still, it wasn't necessary to go overboard.

"She's been appointed to chair the board of a billion-dollar company," said Cole.

Amber opened her mouth to disagree, but his look stopped her. Fine. Okay. She was going to stop telling people she was a fraud. She was still a fraud, but she could fake it for Zachary's sake.

"Bring it on," she said to the clerk. "I need to look good in the office. I have several evening meetings scheduled, and given the season, there are a few formal events, as well."

"She'll need shoes and purses," said Destiny.

"Don't forget jewelry," said Luca.

"Do we want to do something with her hair?" asked Cole.

Amber glared at him. "Careful. You're next."

"I'm perfectly willing to get a haircut."

"He's the…" Amber paused. "What is your title? You're going to need a title. I'm thinking a big, brass plate on the office door, Mr. Henderson."

"The Big Cheese?" joked Luca.

Destiny gave him a thumbs-down.

The clerk smirked as she began looking through the well-spaced racks.

"Grand Pooh-Bah," said Cole.

"I'm not joking," said Amber. "This is your plan. You need to buy all the way in."

"We've got a president. We've got a chair. Executive board member?"

"You can be the chair," said Amber. "I'll be an executive board member."

"Cochair," said Luca. He pointed to Amber. "Cochair of the board." Then he pointed to Cole. "Cochair of the board."

Amber and Cole looked at each other.

"Okay by me," she said. It would be better than doing it alone.

Cole shrugged. "I'll order the brass nameplates."

"What do you think of these?" asked the clerk, holding a gold dress and a black blazer in one hand, and a navy-and-white outfit with a nautical flair in the other.

"The stuff on the mannequin, too," said Cole.

Amber gave in. "Sure. Bring me whatever you think will work. I'm new at this."

The clerk showed her to an airy changing room with a settee and a triple mirror.

"Come out and show us," Cole called.

"I'm going in to help," said Destiny, slipping past the velvet curtain.

The professional outfits were easy to find. But once they switched to dresses, things bogged down. There were simply too many choices, and all of them were gorgeous. Once she made it past her cost worries, Amber actually began to enjoy herself.

After an hour, Cole headed to menswear. Once he was gone,

Destiny dived into the fun, trying on a few of the dresses herself. The women were close enough in size that they could swap back and forth. Destiny was a little bigger in the bust while Amber had the longer legs. Some of the swaps were quite comical.

Amber had accepted a glass of champagne, and now wandered over to where it sat on a glass table. She was trying on a flirty, strapless cocktail dress that was unlike anything she'd ever worn before.

The bodice was snug, wrapping her in silver beading and sequins. It had a high waist of deep jewel blue with a chiffon skirt that flowed to midthigh. Her back was mostly bare, crisscrossed in shiny, beaded straps, ending in a drop V waist. She'd also found a pair of high-heeled silver shoes that were surprisingly comfortable and seemed to go with a lot of outfits.

"*This* is a keeper," said Destiny from behind her.

Amber turned to see Destiny do a runway turn in a glimmering, full-length gold sheath with a slit up the leg.

Luca's voice drawled from the armchair where he'd stayed back to watch. "Have you got a month's pay to blow?"

"I was going to let Cole buy it," Destiny answered with an impish grin. "The man just inherited half a billion dollars. He's not going to notice one little dress."

"Sure," came Cole's unexpected voice. "Dresses are on me."

Amber turned to find him looking her up and down. "Buy that one."

She felt suddenly self-conscious, particularly knowing he'd had a good view of the back.

"I'm just messing around," she told him. "I've already picked out more than enough."

"Buy it," he repeated. "It looks good on you."

"I don't have anywhere to wear it."

"You will."

"I don't think you have a good feel for my social life."

"The Coast Eagle Christmas party is on Friday. It's formal." She glanced down at herself. "You call this formal?"

"What do you call it?"

"Nightclubbing."

"Nobody's going to complain." He moved in a bit closer, his voice going low as Destiny and Cole engaged in their own conversation. "I'm sure not going to complain."

The familiar shiver of arousal teased her limbs. "Stop."

"You done?" he asked.

She nodded.

"Got shoes, purses, jewelry? Whatever else Destiny says you need?"

"I wouldn't trust Destiny if I was you."

"She's right. I did just inherit a ridiculous amount of money. And this is important." There was something in his tone, some combination of reluctance and tenacity.

"Are you okay?" she asked.

"I'm fine."

"Are you still wrapping your head around it?"

It took him a moment to speak. "I don't think I've started wrapping my head around it. I'm going one step at a time. You hungry?"

The question took her by surprise. "Hungry?"

"For tonight, I think that's the next step."

"I could go for a pizza," she admitted. It would feel nice to climb back into her jeans and be normal.

A grin spread across his face. "I like you, Amber. All this, and now you want to go out for pizza."

"Double cheese if you don't mind. And maybe a beer?"

Cole tipped his head to the sales clerk. "We'll take everything she liked, including the dress she's wearing." Then he nodded to Destiny. "Her, too. She's got an important court case coming up, and she needs to look good."

The clerk's eyes went round.

"Cole," Amber protested, horrified to think that the woman might take him seriously and ring up everything.

He ignored her protest, instead speaking to Luca and Destiny. "We're going for pizza and a strategy session. Now that we look the part, we have to act the part. Amber and I need to make a decision. Something important, positive and significant, and we have to be able to implement it fast."

"You mean change company policy?" asked Amber.

"Absolutely," said Cole. "You two get changed, I'll pay the bill."

Amber renewed her protest. "Cole, you can't buy everything."

He slipped an arm around her shoulder. "I know this is hard for you. But we're doing it. And honestly, I'm through having this argument with you."

A spurt of anger jumped to life inside her. She opened her mouth to retort, but something in his eyes stopped her cold.

Fine. He wanted to blow his money? That was up to him. She was through trying to save him from himself.

In her new clothes, and at the head of the boardroom table, Amber looked fantastic. Cole had to struggle to keep from chuckling at how the vice presidents kept shooting surreptitious looks her way. She was wearing a steel-gray blazer and skirt set, with a white blouse underneath. Lace along the scooped neckline kept the outfit from being too severe.

She'd changed her hairstyle, too. Strands were braided at her temples and partially pulled back to a knot at the nap of her neck. She looked sophisticated and professional. She also looked sexy, and it made him want to kiss her.

Then again, pretty much everything made him want to kiss her these days. Last night, watching her bite into a slice of double-cheese pizza had turned him on.

He dragged his gaze away from her, focusing on business. He and Amber both looked the part now, and they were going to act it, too, starting with some small but definitive strategic directions for the company.

"Thank you all for joining us," Cole opened politely, although everyone in the room was fully aware their attendance at the senior management meeting had not been optional.

"Ms. Welsley and I realize this is a temporary situation," he continued. "However, our expectation is that the status quo will continue into the future."

"Excuse me?" Roth piped up.

Cole sent him a glare and kept speaking. "My interest in Coast Eagle is not in dispute, and I'll be relying on Ms. Welsley for continuity."

Roth opened his mouth, but Cole spoke right over him. "For the moment, Ms. Welsley has made a few decisions about passenger compensation."

"Thank you, Cole," said Amber, her tone crisp, her posture straight. "As most of you know, new guidelines on passenger compensation were developed by the U.S. Consumer Association in October of this year."

"Voluntary guidelines," said Roth.

"Roth," said Cole. "If you could please hold your comments."

Roth's eyes blazed at the rebuke while Max obviously fought a smirk. Sidney also looked like he was enjoying himself.

"Accounting has done a comparison between overbooked flights, passenger compensation and lost passenger revenue due to last minute cancellations. Bartholomew, can you put up the slides?"

Bartholomew, who also looked a bit smug, brought up the graphic slides on the side screen.

"As you can see," said Amber, "with a change in our policy on flight overbooking, actual monetary loss will be manageable, while the marketing and social media attention, not to mention the customer confidence and goodwill could be significant. Therefore, we'll immediately adopt the new guidelines on passenger compensation and suspend the policy that allows overbooking. That way, our customers can be completely confident in their travel plans."

She stopped speaking and looked levelly down the table.

Cole felt an immediate surge of pride. She was damn good at this.

"May we speak now?" asked Roth, sarcasm dripping from his tone.

"Yes," Amber answered, even though the question was directed at Cole.

Cole's pride in her increased.

"The monetary losses will be significant," said Roth.

"Loses will be compensated for in the long run," said Amber.

"Maybe in a best-case scenario. But passengers don't want certainty. They want low prices. If you drive our prices up by even ten dollars a ticket, they leave for the competition in droves."

"I'm not suggesting we change our prices," said Amber.

"You're living in fantasyland," Roth all but shouted. "Do you have any idea what kind of a mess you'll leave for me to clean up?"

Though he was trying to let Amber take the lead, Cole couldn't help himself. "You?"

Roth seemed to catch himself. "Us."

"Well, *us*," said Cole, "is Ms. Welsley and me. And I agree with her assessment."

"I agree with it, too," said Max. He looked to Sidney. "Can you work up a marketing plan? We'll need to hit the ground running as soon as the announcement is made."

"I want to announce right away," said Amber with both clarity and confidence. "I want passengers to know their remaining holiday travel plans will not be disrupted by overbooking."

"The Friends and Family campaign is nearly finished," said Sidney. "We can easily incorporate this as a marquee element."

"Done," said Max.

"Hold on," said Roth. "We haven't heard from Julius."

Julius's chin came up. He looked a bit like a deer in the headlights. It was clear he didn't know where to jump.

"Julius reports to Max," said Cole. "Max has made his decision."

"That's not how it works," Roth shouted.

"That's how it works now," said Cole. "This meeting is adjourned." He turned his attention to the president, clearly dismissing everyone else. "Max, do you have a second?"

"I do," said Max.

Fury in his eyes, Roth rocked back from the table and stomped from the room.

With an admirably contained smirk, Bartholomew closed the door behind them all, leaving Cole, Amber and Max alone.

"At the risk of speaking out of turn," said Max, "that was fun."

Amber blew out a breath and slouched down in her chair. "That's not the word I would use."

Cole gave in to the urge to place a hand on her shoulder. "You did great."

"He is out for blood."

"He was always out for blood," said Max.

"You don't think he'd ever take it out on Zachary, do you?"

The slight tremor in her voice told Cole just how brilliantly she'd been acting while the vice presidents were in the room.

"He won't have the chance. Because we're going to win." Cole refused to contemplate anything else.

He turned his attention to Max. "They're resuming the custody hearing on the twenty-eighth."

"Next week?"

Cole nodded.

"Who's representing you?"

"Since Amber is supporting my petition for custody, Destiny has agreed to represent me. She knows the background and circumstances better than anyone else I could hire."

Max's brow furrowed. "She's not the most experienced choice."

"Her firm has assigned a senior partner for support. And they've earmarked their top research team. I'm guessing they want my future business."

"Then that's the best of both worlds," said Max, his expression relaxing.

"That's what we thought." Cole covered Amber's hand with his.

Hers was cold.

Max spoke up. "You know Roth's out there soliciting the support of the minor shareholders."

"He's got the advantage in that," said Amber, sliding her hand from beneath Cole's.

"He does," Max agreed. "They all know him. And Samuel's vote of confidence goes a long way. And, I'm sorry to be so blunt, Amber, but they all knew Coco. That doesn't work in our favor."

"We've got genetics on our side," said Cole.

Cole felt no admiration whatsoever for his father. But he'd quickly come to care about his half brother. And he cared more about Amber than he could have imagined. She was desperately trying to do the right thing, and the jackals were circling her now.

"Can you see any problem with the policy change?" he asked Max.

"None," said Max.

"Any questions?" asked Cole.

"Not yet." Max paused. "Anything else you need right now?"

Cole looked to Amber, and she shook her head.

"We're good," said Cole.

Max rose to leave, closing the door behind him and leaving them alone.

"You did it," said Cole.

"I sure hope it works."

"It will. And so will the others. This one was a good idea, a solid business decision. As the first airline to adopt the guidelines, you're going to get some really positive buzz. The policy change will garner loyalty—maybe not all of your passengers, but enough. And those passengers will be the frequent fliers. That's huge. It was a smart move you made."

"We made."

"It was a smart move, Amber. Don't sell yourself short. They know who's in charge now, and it'll spread around the building like wildfire."

"You think?" She seemed to ponder. "Sidney might tell someone. But Roth will never admit it. And Bartholomew doesn't strike me as a gossip."

"I'm willing to bet Bartholomew knows exactly when and how much to gossip."

"Phase three underway?" she asked.

"Phase three well underway." He jokingly held out his hand. She accepted it and shook.

The contact made him instantly recall what it was like to hold her close. He wished he could pull her in for a hug. He longed to kiss her. He longed to stroke her hair and feel the length of her body pressed up against his.

"Destiny will be here in an hour," she said, retrieving her hand once again.

Cole accepted her withdrawal, shaking off his wayward feelings. "Destiny's been looking up precedents for blood relatives being given preference in custody cases. Do you know if Roth spent any amount of time with Zachary?"

"Not that I heard about, but Coco didn't tell me everything."

"I've been trying to predict his thinking," said Cole. "With you, his best ammunition was that you were too inexperienced to run Coast Eagle. With me, he'll go after my capability as Zachary's guardian. I'm vulnerable there."

"Not if they ask Zachary."

Cole chuckled at that. "It is too bad that Zachary can't talk."

"It's too bad Zachary's not a puppy."

"Excuse me?"

"With a puppy, you put him down between the two people and both call him. Whoever the dog runs to wins."

Cole grinned. "I do like my chances with that."

"Sometimes the simplest solutions work best."

"Can we suggest it to the judge?"

"Only if you want him to order a psychological evaluation."

Ten

Christmas Eve, Amber and Destiny had settled down in a corner of the penthouse living room in front of the twinkling tree and the gas fireplace, cups of eggnog in their hands. Zachary was bathed and wearing red-and-white snowflake pajamas. They'd already snapped a few pictures of him looking so adorable, and now he was busy pulling himself up on pieces of furniture, trying to toddle from one handhold to the next, falling down on his diapered bottom with each attempt.

"At least he's tenacious," said Destiny.

"Stubborn," said Amber. "And not always in a good way."

But she had to admire him in this. He picked himself up again, gripped the coffee table, made it to standing, then set his sights on the ottoman.

"Is it just me," asked Amber, "or does he seem extraordinarily intelligent?"

"He seems extraordinarily intelligent."

"I thought so. I only had to tell him once to leave the tree alone."

"And here I thought the pine needles prickled his hands."

"Maybe," Amber allowed. "Do you mind very much that we're staying in tonight?"

Over the past few years, she and Destiny had always travelled somewhere fun for Christmas. Last December they'd gone snowboarding at a great resort in Switzerland. This year, travelling would have been a lot more complicated with Zachary along. Amber knew it would be better relaxing at home. She also wanted to keep him in his routine, since tomorrow would be such an exciting day.

She knew he had no concept of Santa and wouldn't even realize the presents had appeared overnight. Still, she found herself looking forward to the morning. She was certain he'd take to unwrapping just fine. And she hoped he'd like playing with the toys she'd picked out.

"Not at all. This is fun, too," said Destiny. "The eggnog's fantastic. And the view from here is great."

"What about Luca?" Amber asked. She'd been curious about their budding relationship for days now. But whenever she and Destiny were together, the court case had taken all of their attention.

"He's still in town," said Destiny.

"I *know* he's still in town. I see Cole every day at the office. What I'm asking is if anything has happened between you two?"

"Define *happened*."

"Have you kissed him?"

"A few times." Destiny covered a smile with a sip of eggnog.

"And?"

"And what?"

"And anything more than kissing?"

"Not yet."

"But soon?"

"I don't know. Something's holding me back. I guess I'm not the flinging kind. Who knew?"

"Turned out I was," said Amber. "Who knew?"

Destiny's attention perked up. "Again?"

"No, not *again*. The once. I haven't slept with him since I found out the truth."

"But you want to."

"Who wouldn't? But he deceived me, and he's trying to take Zachary away."

"He's trying to keep Zachary away from Roth. That's not quite the same thing."

"It's not," Amber agreed. "I suppose I should be grateful."

"Are you grateful?"

"He's a fascinating guy, Dest. He's incredibly strategic, and unbelievably bold. In less than a week, he's got the entire company in awe of him."

"Controlling the company will do that to people."

"Yeah, but it's more than just that. He's got a certain presence. You should have seen him shut Roth down." Amber remembered the expression on Roth's face. "If Roth ever gets a chance, he's going to annihilate Cole."

"I don't think he'll get the chance," said Destiny.

Amber looked closely at her expression. "Are you really that optimistic? Or are you trying to make me feel good on Christmas Eve."

"Both. But I am optimistic. There are a lot of precedents out there for blood relatives winning custody."

Amber's gaze caught on Zachary. "Look!"

Zachary took a step, then another and another. He sort of toppled into the ottoman, but stayed upright. Then he turned to Amber with a massive, self-satisfied grin on his face.

"Good boy," said Amber, beaming with pride.

"There'll be no stopping him now," said Destiny.

A knock sounded on the door.

Destiny rose. "I'll get it. You keep watch in case he does something else amazing."

Zachary slapped his hands against the leather ottoman. Amber guessed he was gearing up for the next excursion.

Then, suddenly, his face broke into another grin. "Gak baw!" He let go of the ottoman and toddled forward.

"Hey there, partner."

Amber twisted to see Cole entering the room, a couple of brightly wrapped packages tucked under his arm.

Zachary made it three steps, then four, then his pace sped up. A split second later, things got entirely out of control.

Cole shot forward to grab him before he could go head over heels. Otis stayed a safe pace behind.

"Nice job," Cole praised Zachary.

"He just started doing that," said Amber. She found herself ridiculously happy to have Cole share the moment.

"Merry Christmas," came Luca's cheerful voice.

He and Destiny emerged from the foyer, Luca's arm firmly planted around her waist, a sappy grin on his face. Her cheeks were slightly flushed, and her lips were slightly swollen. No

need to guess who'd come up with the idea of dropping by tonight.

"I brought you a present," Cole said to Amber.

Her glance went to the packages, instantly guilty because she
hadn't bought anything for him. "Oh, Cole, you shouldn't have."

"Oh. Uh...no." He looked contrite. "These are for Zachary."

In his arms, Zachary was already plucking at the ribbons.

"I'm your present."

"Excuse me?" She couldn't believe she'd heard him right, or
that he'd made such an outrageous statement in front of Destiny and Luca.

"I'm here to make sure Zachary gets to sleep tonight."

She felt relieved. Or maybe it was disappointed. Sure, it
would be mortifying to have Cole show up and announce he
wanted to sleep with her. Then again, it would be awfully exciting to have Cole show up and announce he wanted to sleep
with her.

She realized everyone was staring at her.

She quickly reined in her wayward thoughts. "You didn't
have to do that."

"No trouble. Can I put these under the tree?"

"Sure. Of course. But I can't guarantee Zachary will stay
away from them."

Cole looked at the clock. It was coming up on eight.

"He can sit with me for a while," he said. "That should keep
him out of trouble."

Otis selected a spot near the tree in front of an armchair and
curled up to watch.

"Mind if I steal Destiny?" Luca asked. "We've got a car and
a driver, and I want to take in the lights."

"Ask Destiny," said Amber.

"Do you mind?" Destiny asked her.

"Go, go. Have fun. I've got the baby whisperer here to make
my life easy."

Luca tugged Destiny against his side. "Your chariot awaits."

Cole set the gifts under the tree while Destiny and Luca all
but scampered out the front door.

"Did he drag you here?" asked Amber.

Cole rose, Zachary happily bopping him on the top of the head. "What? Who?"

"Luca. He was pretty single-minded about getting Destiny out the door. I'm assuming you're the sacrificial lamb."

Cole smiled as he lowered himself into an armchair. "I volunteered for the gig."

"You're a good friend."

"I am," he agreed. "Got any more eggnog?"

"I do."

"I can get it myself."

She scooped up Destiny's empty cup. "Oh, no, you don't. You're on baby duty. Just sit tight."

He lifted Zachary into a standing position on his lap. "Oh, I like this," he said to the baby. "You and I hang out here. Your auntie does all the work."

She poured a fresh glass of eggnog and added some spiced rum, stirring the concoction together.

When she returned to the living room, Zachary was sitting facing Cole, playing with the buttons on his denim shirt.

She handed Cole the glass. "Don't let him taste it."

Cole's eyes squinted down. "I wouldn't do that. I won't give him anything without asking you."

"There's rum in it. That's all I meant." She hadn't meant to sound picky and possessive.

Cole took a drink. "Good." Then he set the glass out of reach of Zachary.

The awkward moment passed.

"Nice pajamas this guy's got going on," Cole said easily.

"I couldn't resist them. They were so cute."

"Did you take some pictures?"

"I did."

"Will you take one of the two of us?"

The request surprised her, but she quickly recovered. "Sure." Her phone was on a side table, and she reached to retrieve it.

"How about in front of the tree?" Cole asked Zachary, sitting down on the floor. "Any chance you'll hold still and pose for the camera?"

"Gak baw."

"As always, I'm going to take that as a yes."

Amber lined up the camera, taking various poses from various angles. While she snapped the pictures, the family resemblance between the two became startlingly evident. She was half amazed, half afraid.

It was obvious they belonged together. It was just as obvious that she'd have little say in the matter. And a win for Cole still left her up in the air. Or maybe it was out in the cold.

"Did you get any good shots?" asked Cole, setting Zachary down on his feet.

Zachary clung to his fingers, teetering on his feet before letting go and taking a single step away.

Amber scooted toward Cole, settling beside him, scrolling her way through the pictures.

"Those are pretty good," said Cole.

"I can see now why he thinks you're familiar," she admitted. "It's absolutely there."

He turned to look at her. "You think?"

"I do."

Something clunked loudly on the floor, and they both looked up.

Zachary was clinging to the coffee table, slapping his palms against a puddle of eggnog while the glass rolled away.

"Oh, no," Amber groaned, quickly rising to her feet.

Otis immediately seized on the opportunity, jumping up to lap at the spilled eggnog.

"Otis, no," Cole commanded, following Amber. "This walking thing is going to take some getting used to."

The dog looked disappointed, but obediently went back to lie down.

Zachary stuffed his fingers into his mouth, breaking into a grin at the taste.

Amber reached for him, pulling the fingers free. "No rum for you, young man."

Cole gazed around. "You want me to take care of the baby or the mess?"

She felt a surge of gratitude for his offer. "Do you think you could give him a quick bath?"

"I'm on it." He took Zachary carefully into his arms, facing the messy parts away from his shirt and pants as he carried him down the hall. Otis followed along behind.

Sighing in resignation, Amber went to the kitchen storage room for paper towels and the mini steam cleaner.

Twenty minutes later, Cole's shirt was soaked through. But Zachary was clean and happy, tossing little plastic ducks around the tub. The kid had an arm, so some of the ducks flew across the purple bathroom. Cole wasn't about to leave Zachary's side, so they were running out of ducks.

"About done there, partner?" Cole asked, reaching forward to lift him.

Zachary grinned and kicked happily, sending a few final splashes toward Cole, one of them hitting him in the face and dampening his hair. Cole quickly wrapped Zachary's wiggly, wet body in a mauve towel, rubbing him dry before settling him on one hip. Then he leaned down to unplug the tub and used his free hand to gather up the errant ducks.

They made their way into the living room to find Amber on her hands and knees. The rumble and hiss of a steam-cleaning machine obscured the Christmas music. Her brow was sweaty, and her blouse was mussed as she pushed the appliance back and forth on the carpet.

She glanced up to see them. Then she rocked back, hitting the machine's off switch and swiping a hand across her forehead.

"I think I got it clean," she said.

Cole peeled his wet shirt away from his rib cage. "I'm not sure we've quite got the hang of this billionaire lifestyle."

She grinned. "He looks happy."

"He's happy. I'm soaking wet."

She came to her feet, dusting off her knees. "When it comes to babies, trust me, bathwater is the least of your problems."

"I'll keep that in mind."

"You want to take on diaper and pajama duty? Or do you want to put away the steamer?"

"Your choice. But after that, I want champagne and maybe some Belgium chocolate truffles sprinkled with gold flakes."

She shook her head in obvious confusion.

"Something billionaires would eat."

She moved to the wall to unplug the steamer. "That's a thing? Gold flakes on chocolate?"

"Real gold, apparently."

"And you eat it?"

"Well, I've never tried myself. But I hear tell it's expensive."

She coiled the cord. "Alright, Midas. You take diaper duty. I'll check the wine rack and pantry for things that are expensive."

"We can send out," he offered.

He didn't want her to go to any work. That was his whole point. Christmas Eve wasn't the time for cooking and cleaning.

"You're going to send out for gold chocolates?"

"For whatever you want."

"Let me see what we have first. And you might want to get the kid into a diaper before too long."

Cole glanced down at Zachary. "Right. Good advice."

Realizing the risk, he wasted no time in getting to the nursery. His diapering job was awkward but adequate, and he easily found a new pair of soft, stretchy pajamas.

Soon, they were back in the living room, then into the kitchen in search of Amber.

She turned from the counter, obviously hearing them arrive. "This brand comes in a wooden box and a gold bottle." She opened the lid of the champagne case to demonstrate. "It should be expensive enough to meet your standards."

"I was only joking."

She gave a shrug. "There's nobody around to drink it but us. And I don't think champagne keeps indefinitely."

The microwave oven beeped three times.

Amber pointed to the sound. "Zachary's Chateau Moo 2014 is in the microwave."

"Got it," said Cole, crossing the kitchen.

"We have fresh strawberries. And I found a few bars of dark chocolate. The label's in French, so I'm guessing they're imported. And this…"

Cole approached with the formula bottle in his hand.

"Gold-colored sugar sprinkles. Yellow, actually."

"You take me way too literally." But he couldn't help but be impressed by her ingenuity.

He perched himself on a stool, used his best guess on how to position Zachary and offered him the bottle.

Fortunately Zachary knew the drill. He snagged the bottle with both hands and relaxed into Cole's lap.

"I'm going to melt the chocolate, dip the strawberries and sprinkled them with gold."

"You clearly did not understand my point."

She blinked at him with a wide-eyed, ingenuous expression. "I thought you wanted gold-covered chocolate."

"Sure you did. I wanted luxury to come to us with no effort. That's how billionaires live."

She separated the halves of a double boiler, filling the bottom with water at the sink. "So far, for me anyway, the billionaire lifestyle is pretty much like any regular lifestyle. Except that it's a ridiculously long walk from the kitchen to the master bedroom. My tea is cold by the time I get there."

"You take tea to bed?"

"I sip jasmine while I read. It's very relaxing."

"I sip single malt while I watch the sports news. Very relaxing."

She lit a gas burner under the double boiler.

"You are actually making chocolate strawberries."

"It is Christmas Eve." Then a look of concern crossed her face. "Have you had dinner?"

"We grabbed a burger on the way over. You?"

"Late lunch."

"I really can order something in. You want a steak or some pasta? Or you seem to have a thing for pizza."

She pouted. "Okay, now you're making me hungry."

"Pizza it is." He paused, gazing down at Zachary. "I think this guy's out for the count."

Her expression softened, and she moved toward them. "I can take him if you'll watch the chocolate."

Cole extracted the bottle from Zachary's pursed mouth. He sucked a couple more times before sighing in his sleep.

"I've got him," he told her quietly. "I mean, if you're okay with me putting him to bed."

"Of course I'm okay with that." She brushed a hand across Zachary's forehead, then she followed it with a tender kiss.

Emotion tightened in Cole's chest. For the first time in his life, he actually got it. He'd seen men with their families, watched them care for their children. But he'd never had an inkling of the strength of those instincts, the flat-out intensity of the desire to protect.

"You sure?" he found himself asking.

He was little more than a stranger to Amber, and it suddenly seemed unfair to ask her to trust him with Zachary.

She smiled. "Go for it. Then order that pizza. We're going to need something that goes with five-hundred-dollar champagne."

"Is that seriously the price?" It struck Cole as ridiculous.

"That's what it says."

"How can any taste be worth twenty dollars a swallow?"

"You tell me. You're the billionaire."

Cole rose. "I guess we're about to find out."

He gently parked Zachary over his shoulder. Zachary's little body was warm and soft, molded trustingly in his arms.

Minutes later, he finished tucking Zachary into his crib, leaving Otis posted across the open doorway, and returned to the kitchen to find Amber with a dozen chocolate-dipped strawberries lined up on waxed paper. She was sprinkling "gold" on the sticky chocolate.

"I'm impressed," he told her, coming up behind her.

"They turned out pretty good." She sounded happy, and that made him smile.

The scent of chocolate and strawberries floated around them. Her hair brushed his arm. He knew he was standing too close, but he hadn't the slightest desire to move.

He wanted to touch her, to wrap his arms around her, kiss the back of her neck, then turn her around and kiss her mouth. Forget the strawberries, he wanted to strip her naked and make love to her all night long.

"I was thinking a pesto pizza," she said. "Maybe with mushrooms and dried tomatoes, nothing too overpowering."

"Whatever you want," said Cole, realizing he meant it in every sense of the word.

"And feta cheese?"

He could see the corner of her widening grin. "Why is that funny?"

"Makes it more expensive."

"Now you're catching on. We'll definitely get some feta."

It was time to step back. It was time for him to step back from Amber and call a pizza place. He drew a deep breath to brace himself, telling his feet to get a move on. But he inhaled her scent above the strawberries.

And then she turned. She turned, and she was right there, in front of him, her lips only inches away.

"Do you want to change out of your wet clothes?" she asked. "There might be something around here of Samuel's that—"

"No." The question was like a bucket of cold water. "I'm not wearing Samuel's clothes."

Amber looked slightly hurt. "Okay."

"I'm sorry. He wasn't good to my mother, but it's a long story." Cole extracted his phone. "I'll order the pizza."

"You don't want to talk about it."

He didn't. Then again, it wasn't some big, painful secret that he couldn't discuss.

Samuel was a jerk who never deserved Lauren's love. But Cole wasn't going to waste any emotional energy hating the man, either. He didn't care. And he hadn't cared for a very long time. There was no reason not to tell Amber the story.

"I'm fine to talk about it. But let's pour the champagne first."

Eleven

They were on their second glass of champagne, munching their way through the pizza before Amber asked him again.

"You don't mind telling me about Samuel?"

She was at one end of the sofa, Cole at the other. She'd turned sideways to face him, crossing her legs beneath her. His body was canted sideways, one leg up on the leather cushion.

"There's nothing much to tell. You know I never met him. All I know is what my mother told me."

"Did she hate him?" From what little Cole had said, Amber guessed his mother, Lauren, had gotten a very raw deal.

"She hated his weakness, that he caved to his family." Cole stretched an arm along the back of the sofa. "They fell quickly and deeply in love. But she didn't come from the right family, hadn't been to the right schools, didn't have the refined tastes and manners he knew his parents would look for in a daughter-in-law. So he married her without telling them, thinking once it was a done deal, his parents would be forced to accept her."

"They didn't," Amber guessed.

"They went ballistic. They ordered him to divorce her right away, and to never admit to anyone that she'd existed. If he didn't, they said they'd disinherit him. No surprise that he loved the family money more than he loved my mother."

"He didn't deserve her," Amber said softly.

"I must have said that to her ten thousand times."

Cole fell silent, looking sad, and Amber found her heart going out to him. "You don't have to talk about it."

"He was nothing to me. I mean, nothing. I was angry off and on, especially as a teenager. But then I realized he didn't even deserve my anger. As far as I was concerned, he might as well have not existed. When he died…"

Cole lifted the crystal flute and took a drink of his champagne. "This sounds terrible, but when he died, I didn't care. I knew I should. But I didn't. I wasn't sad. I wasn't glad. I didn't expect his death or anything about the Henderson family to be even a blip on my life. Things were going to carry on as normal."

"It didn't occur to you there might be an inheritance?"

"Not even for a second."

She set down her half-eaten slice of pizza, exchanging it for the glass of champagne. "So why did you come to Atlanta?"

"Luca kept after me. Then one day, I gave in. I looked at a picture of Zachary. I don't know. There was something about him, something in his eyes. I knew I had to at least make sure he was safe and secure."

Amber's chest tingled and went tight. "You came here to take care of your brother."

"And then I met you." The look in his eyes was tender. "And I knew Zachary was safe. It was just a matter of getting through the hearing without anyone figuring out who I was."

"But then I lost."

He nodded. "I didn't know what to do. I'd learned enough about Roth by then that I couldn't let him win."

"Thank you."

"There's no need to thank me. And I haven't defeated him yet."

"But you're trying. You really don't want Coast Eagle, do you?"

"I want what's best for Zachary. It's ironic, really. When I first heard about him, I resented him. All I could think was that he was going to have the easy life while Mom and I had struggled so hard to get by."

Amber set down her glass, impulsively shifting closer. "But now you care."

He gazed into her eyes. "It's pretty easy to care."

She reached for his hands and squeezed. "It's pretty easy to care about you, too, Cole."

She'd meant to be reassuring, friendly and comforting. But her tone had become breathy, and the atmosphere thickened between them.

Cole stroked his thumbs across the backs of her hands. Then he stroked the inside of her wrists, watching as he moved his way up her bare arm.

Arousal became a deep, base pulse in the center of her body.

He raised his head, and there was a tremor in his tone. "I know I have no right to ask."

She wanted him to ask. She desperately wanted him to ask.

"Just for tonight," he said. "Just for a little while."

She nodded.

"Can we stop fighting it?"

She nodded harder.

"Oh, Amber." He leaned forward, placing his lips against hers, tenderly at first, but then with unmistakable purpose. She came up on her knees, wrapped her arms around his neck, pulling forward to kiss him more deeply.

He turned her into his lap, his hand splaying across her stomach as his tongue teased hers.

Instinct took over, and her body arched reflexively toward him while their kiss continued.

"You are so beautiful," he breathed.

"You are so wet." She drew back to stare at his shirtfront. "You're still soaking wet."

He gave a soft chuckle. "I could take it off."

"Yes." She nodded, pretending it was merely a practical suggestion. "You should take it off."

He flipped the buttons open, making his way down the pale gray shirt. She glimpsed his chest, then his abs. Then he peeled the shirt away, revealing his muscular shoulders and arms. He was an incredibly magnificent man.

"You're the one who's beautiful," she told him.

She gifted a lingering kiss on his smooth chest, flicking out her tongue to leave a wetter spot on his skin.

"Do that again." His voice was tight.

She kissed him again, tasting the salt of his skin, feeling his heat through the tenderness of her lips.

"I got your shirt wet," he rasped.

"That's too bad." She kissed a slow path across his chest.

One of his hands bracketed her hip; the other undid the buttons on her shirt.

"Are you fixing it?" she asked, lips brushing his skin as she spoke.

"I'm fixing it."

"That's good." She shrugged out of the shirt, revealing her white lace bra.

"All good." He released the catch on her bra, peeling it off. "All very, very good."

She knew she should be self-conscious, even embarrassed by her nakedness in the well-lit living room.

"If Destiny and Luca come back, we're…" She moved up to kiss his neck, bracing her hands on his shoulders, absorbing the feel of their taut texture.

"Oh, darling," he drawled. "They're not coming back."

"They're not?" Not that she was truly worried. She wasn't about to stop undressing Cole.

"Did you see their expressions?" There was a chuckle in his voice. "They're not coming back."

She unsnapped the top of his fly. "Just as well."

His warm hand closed over her breast. "I like the way you're thinking."

She bit back a moan. "What am I thinking?"

"That you want me." He narrowed his attention to her nipple.

A zing of sensation flashed to the apex of her thighs, and this time she did moan. "I do want you."

"I want you, too, very, very badly."

She wrapped her arms around his neck, bringing her mouth to his. "Oh, Cole."

"Amber." He tunneled his spread fingers into her hair, kissing her deeper and deeper.

She fumbled with her pants, while he got rid of his.

Then she was lying back on the sofa, pulling him to her, impatient and anxious to become one. But he made her wait, feathering his fingertips along her thighs, circling and teasing as he went.

"Now," she begged.

"Yeah?" he asked, his voice husky, breathing deep.

"Right now." The anticipation was too much.

"In a hurry?"

She knew how to stop this game. She raked her fingertips down his stomach, going lower until she grasped him, wrapping her hand smoothly around his length.

His body convulsed. "Okay."

"In a hurry?" she managed.

"Yes." He disentangled her hand, drawing her arms up above her head. "I'm definitely in a hurry."

Moments later, he was inside her, swift and sure, and she gasped at the strength of the sensations. His movements were steady and deep. Her reaction more and more intense.

He kissed her mouth, his hand going to her breast. She was bombarded with pleasure over every inch of her body. Time seemed to stop while she drank in his taste, scent and touch. She never wanted it to end.

"You're amazing." His lips brushed hers as he spoke. "I've never...ever...ever..."

"Cole," she gasped. "Don't stop. Please don't stop."

"I'm never stopping. Not...ever."

But she could feel it. She could feel her climax shimmering. Her body climbed higher and higher, her nerves extending, muscles tightening, until it all crashed into an apex of pleasure.

She cried out.

He groaned her name.

And their bodies peaked as one.

She was weightless at first, then exhausted, her limbs too heavy to move.

"That was your fault," he muttered in her ear.

It took her a moment to muster up the energy to speak. "What was my fault?"

"You ended it."

"I did. You're just too good."

"Oh, darling. That was exactly what I wanted to hear."

She cautiously blinked her eyes open, the twinkling Christmas tree coming into focus, then the fireplace and the champagne bottle.

Cole's weight pressed her into the sofa. For the first time in what seemed like forever, she felt safe, content and at home.

Cole eased himself into the giant tub in the master bathroom, settling at the end opposite to Amber. He'd lit candles all around and set the champagne glasses and the rest of the bottle on the wide tiled edge. The water was steaming in billows toward the box window that overlooked the city, mingling with the scent of citrus that filled the air.

"This *is* practically a pool," he couldn't help but note, stretching his arms to each side, his legs brushing lightly against Amber's beneath the water.

Amber lifted her champagne flute. "Are we behaving like billionaires now?"

Her hair was swept up in a messy knot. Her cheeks were flushed, her lips dark red and her lashes thick against the crystal blue of her eyes. Her breasts bobbed ever so slightly beneath the surface of the water. She had the most beautiful breasts he'd ever seen.

"Close enough," he answered. "I've got everything in the world I want right here."

She smiled. "Plus gold chocolates in the kitchen."

"I forgot about those."

She gave a mock frown.

"I mean," he said, attempting to properly appreciate her efforts, "I can't wait to try one."

She raised her glass in a mock toast. "Now you're catching on."

He drank with her. "So tell me what you have planned for tomorrow."

She looked puzzled. "Tomorrow?"

"Christmas Day."

Her expression said that she'd completely forgotten the date. He was going to take that as a positive sign.

"Presents for Zachary," she said. "And Destiny's coming

over. Luca, too, maybe? And…" This time a flash of worry creased her face.

"What?" he asked.

She shook her head.

"Something upset you. What was it?"

"Uh, you guys didn't…"

He wasn't following, and he gave his head a little shake.

She gestured to her naked body. "Please tell me you two didn't plan…this."

The question shocked him so much, it took several seconds to form an answer. "No."

Admittedly, it wasn't the most comprehensive answer in the world. He tried again. "We didn't plan a thing. Okay, yes, I know that Luca likes Destiny. And I guess he knows I like you. But we never talked about sex, and we sure as hell didn't plan out some Christmas Eve seduction scenario." Frankly, he was a little insulted by her suggestion.

"You don't talk to Luca about sex?"

Her question was so genuine that Cole's annoyance disappeared. "I don't talk to him about sex with you."

"Oh." She shifted under the water, looking decidedly guilty.

Wait a minute. "You talked about *me* with Destiny."

Amber blushed. "She asked me."

"And you told her?" He pretended to be affronted, but it was a struggle not to laugh.

"Sorry," she offered faintly.

He polished off his glass of champagne. "I'm the one who's sorry. I'm just messing with you. Tell anybody you want."

"I only told Destiny."

He gave a shrug as he reached for the champagne bottle. "I honestly don't care. But I won't tell Luca anything that makes you uncomfortable."

He gestured with the bottle.

She held out her glass. "I know it seems like the double standard."

"It *is* a double standard. But me and the rest of the male population have come to terms with it."

"Now I feel guilty."

"Don't. Believe me when I tell you, guilt is the last thing I'm going for here."

She seemed to relax and leaned back against the edge of the tub. "What exactly are you going for?"

"I have to say, I enjoyed the part where you said I was too good at sex." He paused. "And I liked the expression on your face when you said it. And I liked that I was holding you in my arms at the time. And that you were naked."

Arousal reawakened as he spoke.

He couldn't seem to get enough of looking at her, talking to her, touching her. But it was close to midnight, and he knew this interlude had to end—likely very soon.

"Come here," he told her softly.

Her blue eyes went wide in obvious surprise.

He set his glass aside. "Come sit with me."

It took her a minute to react. But then she braced herself on the edge of the tub and slipped across, candles flickering in the mist as she settled between his legs. The glass of champagne was still in her hand.

He wrapped his arms around her stomach, holding her naked softness to his body and kissed the crook of her neck. Her supple warmth, smooth skin and the subtle scent of her shampoo brought back memories of their lovemaking. He wanted her all over again.

"Tell me about Alaska," she said, relaxing against him.

"It's cold."

"How incredibly informative."

"Lots of snow, mountains, wildlife. The people are amazing. There's no road access to Juneau, so there's a very close-knit sense of community."

"You have no roads?"

"We have roads in the city, of course. But the only way to get there from the mainland is by ferry, boat or airplane. Good for business at Aviation 58."

"Is there much there? Can you shop?"

"We have stores, groceries, clothes, hardware, even car dealerships, certainly everything you need for day-to-day life. There are over thirty thousand people living in Juneau."

"That's less than a football game."

"That's why we have such a great sense of community."

"What do you do up there?"

"Mostly, I run a business and fly airplanes."

"And for fun?"

"Ski, snowmobile, mountain climb, swim, soccer. There's plenty of outdoor recreation, but we also have plays, music, restaurants, movie theatres, even fashion shows."

"Just like a regular city."

"Exactly like a regular city. But with more snow and more bears."

"I'd be terrified of bears."

"They're not exactly walking down the main drag in Juneau." He paused. "Well, not often."

"Are you serious? Or are you messing with me again?"

"It's rare. But it can happen. You should come and check it out."

As soon as the words were out, he felt the shift in atmosphere. He could have kicked himself. He and Amber were, right this moment, a tiny oasis in the midst of their bizarre situation.

"I'm sorry," he offered.

"It's okay."

"No, it's not. I didn't mean to hint we were going somewhere as a couple. That's just insincere and misleading, even manipulative."

Her tone went cool. "Don't worry, Cole. I won't be dropping in on you in Alaska."

"That's not what I meant, either. I'd love to have you come to Alaska."

Her body was growing stiffer by the second. "Isn't this where we came into this conversation?"

"I'm so sorry."

He smoothed back her hair. He couldn't help himself, he kissed her dewy neck. When she didn't rebuff him, he kissed her jawline. Then he tipped back her head and kissed her mouth.

The second he tasted her, arousal hijacked his senses. He kissed her deeply, turning her in his arms until she was facing him, straddling his lap, her wet breasts sliding along his chest. He sat up straight. He cupped her bottom, pulling her tight to the V of his legs.

He was right where he wanted to be. But the water was cooling off, and they were going to have to leave soon.

"I don't want to hurt you," he whispered.

"You're not."

"I want the world to go away. I want to stay right here and forget everything else. I don't want to let you go."

She nodded.

"Amber. You're incredible." He cradled her face, kissing her all over again.

Then he drew back, and they gazed at each other for a long, long time.

"Can I stay tonight?" he dared ask.

"I want you to stay."

His heart swelled with satisfaction, and he folded her into his arms.

Christmas morning, it wasn't clear to Amber which delighted Zachary more, ripping into presents or walking across the room on his own. He had no interest at all in any of the toys, but wandered from chair to table to ottoman with ribbons and bows in hands.

Otis stayed off to one side, looking stoic and long-suffering when Zachary grabbed at his fur or ears or tried to decorate him.

A few hours ago, Cole had had the presence of mind to put his clothes through the laundry. So while he was dressed the same as last night, the clothes, at least, were fresh.

Amber had given her hair a blow dry this morning, put on a little more makeup than usual and dressed in a pair of skinny black slacks and a shimmering red blouse. She'd chosen a funky pair of Christmas-ball earrings and felt überfestive. She had to admit, it was nice to have Cole around to entertain Zachary while she had spent the extra time getting ready.

Destiny arrived with Luca midmorning, and neither seemed surprised to find Cole on the floor with Zachary.

A couple of wrapped gifts in his hands, Luca headed for the tree. Destiny grasped Amber's arm to hold her back.

"Tell me what happened," she whispered in Amber's ear.

Amber pretended she didn't understand the question. "When?"

Destiny rolled her eyes. "Last night."

"What happened with you last night? I thought you'd come back."

"We had a great time, that's what happened with me."

"Great?" Amber asked. "Or *great?*"

Cole offered Luca a cup of coffee, and the two, along with Zachary and Otis, headed for the kitchen.

"Both," Destiny answered as the men disappeared. "We toured the lights, had a few drinks and went back to his hotel."

Amber filled in the blank. "And that's all she wrote?"

"I'm hoping we'll write some more."

Amber grinned and gave Destiny a one-armed hug as they moved into the living room.

"And you?" Destiny asked, brows going up as they each took a seat.

"Cole stayed the night."

"So it's better? You've made up?"

"*Made up* is not the right phrase. We didn't, don't have a relationship."

"What is it you have?"

Amber thought back to Cole's words last night in the tub. "I don't know. A mutual problem?"

"That doesn't sound very romantic."

Maybe not, but Amber was determined to see it for what it was and enjoy it for what it was. Last night with Cole had been amazing, and this morning had been fun. There was no point in speculating beyond that.

"You want coffee?" she asked Destiny.

"Please."

As Amber rose, she heard a phone ring from inside the

kitchen and recognized it as Cole's. Destiny followed behind her into the kitchen and took a seat at the island counter, where Zachary was in his high chair playing with a little pile of breakfast cereal rounds.

"When?" Cole asked into the phone. His tone was serious, and he gave a sideways glance to Amber.

She instantly knew something was wrong.

She glanced reflexively at Zachary, grateful he was right here beside her where she could see he was fine.

"How many?" Cole asked.

Amber found herself moving toward him.

He reached out and put a hand on her shoulder.

"Are you sure?" He paused. "Hundred percent?" He breathed a sigh. "Yeah. I will. You've got it. Call me if you hear anything else."

"What is it?" Amber asked, holding her breath.

"There was another hydraulic problem with a Boonsome 300."

Her tone went hushed. "The same thing?"

Cole nodded. "Astra Airlines. The flight was coming into O'Hare."

"Has it landed?" She swallowed. She couldn't bring herself to use the word *crashed*.

"Belly landing onto foam. Everyone got out, but there was a fire. The plane's destroyed. The federal government has grounded the Boonsomes, and they need complete access to the Coast Eagle plane at LAX."

"Absolutely," said Amber. "Whatever they need."

She stopped speaking and sucked in gulps of air, her mind galloping to what-if scenarios. What if she hadn't grounded the Coast Eagle fleet? Her decision had been based on her gut feeling, not on any technical expertise. She was an accountant, not an aviation specialist. What if she'd made the wrong choice, and a Coast Eagle flight had crashed and killed the passengers?

She felt the room spin around her, and a wave of nausea cramped her stomach.

Cole's hand tightened on her shoulder. "Amber?"

She pushed him off and bolted for the living room.

She made it as far as the hallway, and gripped the corner of the wall to steady herself.

Cole was instantly behind her, his hands on her shoulders.

"They're all okay." His tone was soothing. "Bumps and bruises, maybe a couple of cracked ribs. The captain did a spectacular job on the landing."

She swallowed the lump in her throat. "What if I hadn't?" she managed.

"Hadn't what?" He came around to look at her.

"What if I hadn't grounded the Coast Eagle fleet?"

"But you did. You made exactly the right decision."

"Because I listened to you."

"You listened to everyone in the room, and then you made the call."

"I'm scared, Cole," she admitted, starting to shake. "I'm not qualified to do this. I shouldn't be cochair of Coast Eagle. Nobody should be listening to me."

He drew her into his arms and smoothed a hand over her hair. "If they'd listened to Roth, a Coast Eagle plane might very well have crashed."

Amber digested that thought. She knew there had to be a counterargument to it, but she couldn't come up with it right now.

"They'll find the problem," said Cole, the certainty in his deep voice making her feel unaccountably better. "They'll fix it, and nobody else is going to get hurt."

"I want to go back to my regular job."

He looked down at her and gave her a smile. "You'd abandon me?"

"You made the right decision, right off, because of your knowledge and experience."

"Amber, the single most important attribute of being a good decision maker is listening—listening to the right people and weighing all the evidence. Nobody is an expert in everything. That's Roth's downfall. He won't listen to anyone but himself."

She had to concede that was true.

"It's Christmas," said Cole, rubbing her upper arms. "Everyone is safe, and the right people are out there doing their jobs. Let's take one more day to forget about the chaos all around us. Can we have one more day for us?"

She forced herself to break away from him. He was right. This was Zachary's first Christmas, and there was nothing that needed her immediate attention.

"Yes," she told him.

"Good. We should get outside for a while. Do you think Zachary would like a walk in the park?"

Amber knew Zachary would love a walk in the park. And so would she. Cole's instincts seemed bang on when it came to the two of them.

Twelve

By the time the judge called a recess, Cole could feel his blood pressure pounding inside his ears. Over Destiny's continued objections, Roth's lawyer had painted Cole as a conniving, opportunistic fortune hunter who had deliberately kept himself hidden from the Henderson family until there was some profit for him. The man had scoffed at the idea that Cole hadn't known about the will. And he'd railed about the unfairness of placing Zachary in the care of a man that neither of his parents had ever met.

It had taken all of Cole's self-control to stay quiet and seated. Now he shot up from his seat and rushed from the courtroom, keeping his gaze straight ahead as he passed through the gallery. He needed to bring his anger under control before he spoke with anyone.

He took long strides through the foyer, out onto the sidewalk, turning down the block where he could disappear into the crowd. He drew long breaths of the crisp air, trying desperately to clear his rioting emotions.

"Mr. Henderson?" a voice called from behind.

Cole didn't turn. The last thing in the world he needed right now was another nosey reporter. He wove through the busy sidewalks, lengthening his stride to put some distance between them.

"Mr. Henderson?" the voice repeated.

Cole took two more paces then decided to put an end to the intrusion. He pivoted, spread his feet and clenched his fists by his sides. "Do you mind—"

"Sorry to bother you. I'm Kevin Kent, president of Cambridge Airlines." The fiftysomething man huffed as he caught up.

The introduction surprised Cole.

"We're based out of London, England," said the man, holding out a business card.

Cole didn't take it. He didn't want to talk to anyone, not a reporter, not an airline executive, not Destiny, not anyone.

"Is there something I can do for you?" he snarled.

The traffic rolled past them, echoing against the pavement, while groups of pedestrians parted to go around.

"I've been watching the proceedings in the courtroom."

Cole didn't respond to the statement. The courtroom had been packed for a day and half, with a lineup outside. It seemed most of the city was watching the proceedings.

"I know you're taking a beating, but my money's on you."

If Kevin Kent wanted a thank-you for the vote of confidence, he was going to be disappointed.

"I've spent some time looking into your Alaska holdings," he continued. "Do you have a second to talk?"

"Here? Now? You want to talk about *Alaska?*" Who cared about Alaska? Zachary's future was on the line.

The man glanced at the multistory buildings around them. "There's a coffee shop on the corner."

"I'm not on a coffee break."

"Right. Okay. I'll get to it. I know you have a thriving airline in Alaska. That you built it from the ground up, and you have a partner and friend in that business with you."

Cole was getting impatient. So Kevin Kent could do an internet search. Big deal.

"When this court case ends, if you win, you're going to have a big decision to make."

Cole crossed his arms over his chest. No kidding. What else had the man deduced?

"I'm banking on you winning," said Kevin. "And I'm banking on your loyalty to Aviation 58."

"Are you working up to a point, Mr. Kent?"

"Call me Kevin. Yes. My point is you may be in the market to sell."

Cole drew back. "Sell Aviation 58?" There wasn't a chance in hell he'd sell his airline.

"No," said Kevin. "Coast Eagle Airlines."

Cole felt the ground shift beneath him; he dropped his arms to steady himself. The bustle of the downtown street went momentarily still and silent. "Sell Coast Eagle?"

"To Cambridge Airlines."

Cole wasn't sure he'd heard right. He was trying to save Coast Eagle for Zachary's future.

"I'm not in the market to sell," he assured Kevin. "I won't *be* in the market to sell."

"Perhaps not." Kevin seemed to be watching Cole closely. "Though I'm not sure you've had an opportunity to think through the complexities of running two separate airlines."

"I'm not going to—" Cole caught himself.

He hadn't thought of it in those terms. But if he won the custody battle, who *would* run Coast Eagle? He wasn't staying in Atlanta. He'd never planned to stay in Atlanta.

Max had made it clear he was temporary as president, and he wasn't the right fit anyway. Roth was absolutely not going to be in charge. Sidney was smart, but new to the VP post. Cole's take was that he needed several years of mentoring before taking on more responsibility.

"We have the corporate depth," said Kevin. "And we have the expertise. You'd have the choice to remain as a minor shareholder, of course. I won't lie to you, I think that would be a good investment. But we'd prefer to buy you out. Have you looked into Coast Eagle's net worth?"

Cole had not. Things had been moving ahead so quickly that he hadn't focused any attention at all on what happened after the court case. And at the moment, he was a lot more worried about the possibility of losing than of winning.

"You need to think about it," Kevin told him softly. "I'm not being opportunistic, and I'd fully expect due diligence on your side. But my take is that you need to win this. And my take is that you're going to fight with everything you've got. And when you win, I want to talk. Because I think you're going to have to make a choice—Coast Eagle or Aviation 58."

He offered his card again. "Call me anytime."

This time, Cole took the card. Kevin Kent gave him a nod and walked away.

Afterward, Cole stood still for a full five minutes.

How could he possibly sell Coast Eagle? Then again, how on earth was he going to run it?

"Mr. Henderson?"

Cole gave himself a mental shake.

This time the man who approached him was a reporter. "Frank Hast, Atlanta Weekly. How do you respond to the accusation that you're using your half brother as a pawn to get your hands on the Henderson fortune?"

Cole stared at the man, wondering what would happen if he simply slammed him into a wall.

"I don't," he said instead and began walking away.

The reporter paced alongside. "Then what do you say to reports that you're using a relationship with Amber Welsley to undermine Roth Calvin?"

The word *relationship* stopped Cole in his tracks. He almost rose to the bait, but he checked himself just in time. "Roth Calvin needs to worry about the facts, not about anything I have to say."

"What *is* your relationship with Amber Welsley?"

"Ms. Welsley is the guardian of my half brother."

"For the moment."

Cole began walking again.

"One more question, Mr. Henderson."

"I have to get back to court."

"But—"

Cole lengthened his stride.

The man hustled to catch up. "Do you agree that Roth Calvin was wrong to put profit before passengers' lives?"

Cole was tempted to answer that one, but he held his tongue and kept going. He was saving his arguments for the judge. The reporter finally gave up.

Luca was on the steps of the courthouse as Cole approached. He quickly spotted Cole and came forward to meet him.

"You okay?" he asked, glancing around as if gauging their distance from possible eavesdroppers.

"Not really."

Luca nodded his understanding. "Destiny was looking for you."

"I needed some air."

"Yeah."

Their conversation ended, but Cole's mind was clicking its way through information and options.

"Have you given any thought to what happens after?" he asked Luca.

"If you lose?"

"If I win."

Luca cocked his head. "No. And honestly, I don't think that's what you need to worry about right now."

"Maybe not," Cole allowed. They were a very long way from winning. But Kevin Kent had gotten him thinking.

"You're the underdog," said Luca.

Cole blew out a breath, telling himself to focus. "What did Destiny want?"

"To talk strategy."

"Are we changing it?" Cole didn't think that was a bad idea. They had hoped Cole's blood connection to Zachary would be their trump card, since the courts overwhelmingly sided with family. But Roth's attack on Cole's motivations and character had clearly turned the tide against them.

"She wants to demonstrate that Roth's sole interest in Zachary is his stake in Coast Eagle."

"So far, he's the one doing that to me."

"He's never spent any time with Zachary."

"Neither had I until last week." Cole knew he was sounding pessimistic. But he was feeling pessimistic.

Luca glanced at his watch. "She thinks it's the best bet."

Cole didn't think it was a huge strength. But they were running out of time and out of options. "I wish I had something better."

"So do I," said Luca. "We have to go back."

"And after?" asked Cole.

"Don't think about it."

"I have to think about it."

"Let's get through today. Whatever happens, we'll face it tomorrow."

Cole gave a reluctant nod. The best thing he could do for Zachary was to remain focused for the rest of the afternoon. If they got a decision today, whichever way it went, they'd start working through their next options in the morning.

Though the courtroom was packed, it was surprisingly quiet. From the third row, Amber focused on Cole's posture. His shoulders were tense, his body completely still as Roth's lawyer gave his summation.

"Samuel Henderson made his final wishes clear," the man's voice boomed with authority. "He named Roth Calvin as his son and heir's legal guardian. Samuel Henderson has known Roth Calvin for over a decade. He has put his trust in Roth Calvin." He made a half turn and pointed to Cole. "Nobody, not this man or anybody else, has the right to undermine Samuel Henderson's wishes on such an important, intimate and fundamental decision of who would raise his son in the event of his death. There is no ambiguity here, Your Honor."

As his voice thundered on, Amber's heart thudded harder. Sweat broke out on her palms. This was hopeless.

They were going to lose.

She was absolutely positive they were going to lose.

The room seemed suddenly hot, and her stomach churned with nausea. She rose from her seat. She could feel Luca watching her as she rushed to the back of the gallery, bursting through the double doors and heading for the ladies' room.

The length of the lobby felt endless, but finally she made it into the cool quiet of the restroom. She gripped the counter, staring at her reflection in the mirror, tears stinging her eyes as she willed her stomach to calm down. She didn't have time to fall apart.

"Think," she ordered herself. *"Think!"*

The marble counter was cold and hard, and her hands started to ache from the pressure of her grip. She ran through every wild and crazy solution, including grabbing Zachary and making a run for it.

Then, in a rush, it came to her fully formed. It was crazy. And it was a gamble, a huge gamble that might very well backfire on her. But at least it was something.

She let go of the counter and retrieved her cell phone from her purse. Then she pressed the speed-dial button for the penthouse.

It was silent, then it clicked, then silence again.

"Come on, come on, come on."

Roth's lawyer was probably finishing up, and there was only so much Destiny had to say.

Finally, the call rang through.

"Welsley-Henderson residence."

"Isabel?"

"Amber? Did they—"

"No. Not yet. But I need you to do something for me. And I need you to do it right now. It's important, and you have to hurry."

"Certainly, ma'am."

"Bring Zachary to the courthouse."

"He's asleep."

"I don't care. Wake him up. Don't stop to change him or to feed him. Tell the driver to go as fast as humanly possible. I'll meet you out front."

"But—"

"Just do it. There's not a second to waste."

"Okay," said Isabel. "Yes. I will."

Amber shut off her phone and tucked it away. She took a final, bracing breath, staring back at her reflection. This might be the stupidest move she'd ever pulled. But she didn't see any other possible hope. If she didn't do something, they'd lose.

She settled her purse strap on her shoulder. Then she left the restroom and made her way back across the big foyer. Her footfalls echoed against the high ceiling and the marble pillars. Sunlight streamed through a wall of glass above the main doors.

It was far too early to go outside to meet Isabel, but she was too jumpy to sit back down in the gallery. She stopped outside the courtroom. She cautiously cracked the door open and saw Destiny come to her feet. All she could hope was that Destiny had a lot to rebut.

She let the door swing shut again and began pacing in the opposite direction. She took a curved staircase to the second floor, walked the perimeter, then took the staircase back down again. She wandered through a side hallway and found an ancillary exit. She took it and walked the three blocks around the complex to the front courthouse stairs.

There she stood, telling herself it was still too early to expect Isabel and Zachary, but scrutinizing every dark sedan that came into view from the south.

She checked her watch. Fifteen minutes had passed.

"Come on, Isabel."

Another five minutes, maybe three minutes, and she'd let herself call Isabel's cell.

And then she spotted the dark blue sedan with Harrison at the wheel. She rushed to the curb, meeting it as it came to a stop, grabbing the back passenger-side handle.

It was locked. Her hand snapped away, and she had to steady herself.

"Ms. Welsley?" Harrison called, rising to look at her over the top of the car.

"Unlock," she called. "I have to hurry."

"Of course, ma'am."

The lock clicked, and Amber pulled open the door. She went to work on the car seat harness, tugging it free, releasing Zachary's arms and legs.

He blinked up at her, sleepy, puzzled.

"Is something wrong?" asked Isabel.

"I'm in a rush," Amber answered, pulling Zachary against her shoulder and stepping back. "They're almost finished."

She turned.

"The diaper bag," Isabel called after her.

"No time," Amber tossed over her shoulder, running up the stairs.

Zachary whimpered in her ear.

She didn't blame him. Poor little thing, dragged unceremoniously out of his bed, probably tired and hungry, likely with a very wet diaper.

"I'm sorry, sweetheart," she whispered in his ear. "But I have to try. I *have* to try."

She pulled open the door, still at a jog as she crossed the far-too-large foyer.

Zachary's whimpers become more insistent as she swung open the courtroom door.

Destiny was on her feet, back to the gallery, talking to the judge. "The precedent Chamber versus Hathaway clearly applies and clearly demonstrates…"

Amber's footsteps slowed as she experienced a rush of unadulterated fear. Was this stupid? Was she making a mistake? But then she focused on the back of Cole's head and forced herself to move forward.

Zachary started to squirm in her arms. His whimpers were turning into whines.

Luca stared at her as she passed the third row. But she ignored him. She ignored the stares of the spectators, and even the curious brow raise from the judge. She moved rudely in front of three people in the front row.

"Cole," she hissed. "Cole?"

He turned, and his expression faltered. "What's wrong?"

At the sound of Cole's voice, Zachary instantly swung around. He howled and lunged for him. As Cole had done a dozen times, he neatly reached out and caught Zachary in his arms.

Destiny turned, and then everything focused on the commotion.

"Order," called the judge, banging his gavel.

Zachary's arms wrapped tight around Cole's neck, and he buried his sobbing face against the crook of Cole's neck.

Destiny moved toward the pair. "Your Honor, this is Zachary Henderson."

The judge peered over the top of his glasses. "I will not allow this hearing to turn into a circus."

But Zachary's sobs were already subsiding, his little body relaxing against Cole's chest.

Roth's lawyer came to his feet. "Objection, Your Honor."

The judge swung his attention to the defendant's table. "What grounds are you going to choose?"

"The plaintiff is not permitted to use props."

"Props?" asked Destiny, with exactly the right note of surprise and censure in her tone.

"Props," the man repeated. "The plaintiff clearly believes that holding Zachary Henderson will make him look to the court like the more capable guardian."

"Mr. Henderson is the more capable guardian." Destiny nudged Cole. "However, if Mr. Calvin would rather hold the prop himself, we have no objection." She looked hard at Cole.

Cole was quick to pick up on the message, walking straight over to Roth to offer Zachary.

Roth jumped to his feet.

"Here you go," said Cole, holding the soggy Zachary out toward him.

As Roth recoiled, Zachary shrieked in obvious terror, reaching desperately for Cole.

"No?" Cole said to Roth.

He pulled poor Zachary back against his chest.

Zachary clung there, breaths shuddering in and out while murmurs came up all across the courtroom.

Destiny jumped back in. "In the interest of peace and order, I'd suggest we let Mr. Henderson hold his brother."

The other lawyer glared at her.

The judge banged his gavel.

Destiny turned to Amber. "Give me your phone. Quick."

Amber scrambled for her phone, handing it over to Destiny.

Cole sat down, and Zachary went mercifully quiet.

"Excuse me, miss?" A woman whispered behind Amber.

Amber turned to find the woman had scooted down to make room on the bench. She patted the spot.

Amber smiled her thanks and sat down.

Nobody seemed certain of what to do next, but Destiny spoke right up, talking while she glanced up and down from the tiny screen on Amber's phone. "Since arriving in Atlanta," she spoke loud and clearly to the judge, "Mr. Henderson has forged a special and intimate bond with his brother."

"Objection," said the other lawyer. "Their purported relationship is no more than hearsay. And it's his half brother."

Destiny glanced meaningfully down at Zachary cuddled up to Cole, obviously letting everyone make up their own mind about the relationship between the two.

"I'll rephrase," she said. "Since arriving in Atlanta, Mr. Henderson has spent a great deal of time with his baby *half* brother. This includes babysitting, feeding, bathing, diapering, playing with him and many hours of cuddling Zachary. In fact, Mr. Henderson spent Christmas Eve and Christmas Day with his half brother."

She took three paces to a small computer table. "I'd like to introduce into evidence some photographs." She swiftly plugged a cord into Amber's phone.

Amber couldn't help but smile.

Immediately, the picture of Cole and Zachary under the Christmas tree came up. Zachary looked adoringly up at Cole as he grasped Cole's nose, grinning. The expression on Cole's face was tender and loving.

"Objection," said Roth's lawyer.

As Destiny turned to acknowledge the lawyer's request, she obviously pressed a button on the phone. A candid shot came up, Zachary and Cole romping with Otis. It was even better than the first.

"On what grounds?" asked the judge.

"The plaintiff is clearly using these photos as a tool of manipulation. They're staged."

"They're family Christmas photos," said the judge. "Since

Christmas Day took place last week, I have no reason to doubt the voracity of the photographs."

Destiny immediately brought up the next photo. It was Cole holding Zachary wrapped in a fluffy towel. The baby was clearly fresh from the bath, and gazed happily into Cole's eyes.

Amber's heart warmed at the memory.

"As these pictures will attest—and we can certainly add witness testimony as well—with the exception of providing advice to Coast Eagle airlines in order to save passenger lives, Mr. Henderson has spent virtually every day with his half brother since arriving in Atlanta."

"Objection," Roth's lawyer repeated. "This isn't a contest to see who can rack up more baby hours."

Destiny countered, "This hearing is to establish who is the most appropriate guardian for Zachary. Time spent with the baby is absolutely relevant to that question."

"Ms. Welsley has obviously inappropriately used her temporary guardianship over Zachary to undermine my client's—"

"Ms. Welsley's conduct is not at issue."

Cole came to his feet. "May I speak, Your Honor?"

The gallery's attention swung to Cole, and both lawyers turned, as well.

The judge considered the question for a long moment.

"Yes," he said. "I think it would be valuable to hear from Mr. Henderson."

Destiny withdrew toward the plaintiff's table, clearly yielding the floor to Cole.

Zachary was quiet on Cole's shoulder, gently fingering his gray-and-red tie.

Cole took a deep breath before beginning. "To be perfectly candid, I have to say that when I read Samuel Henderson had died, I wasn't sorry. I didn't feel much of anything. All I knew about the man was that he'd broken my mother's heart. At that point, I wanted nothing to do with any of the Hendersons."

Cole shifted a couple of steps sideways to come out from behind the table. "As I've already stated, I didn't know about the will. And even if I had, I wouldn't have cared about it. I have a growing, thriving business of my own."

He absently rubbed Zachary's back. "When I finally did come to Atlanta, it was incognito and with the sole purpose of ensuring Zachary would be properly cared for. But from the first moment I met him, my brother insisted I pay attention to him."

Cole smiled fondly down at Zachary. "I don't know whether it was the sound of my voice, the smell of my skin or that I looked something like our father. But from that point on, this little guy has done everything in his power to tell me that he needs me, that it's my responsibility to take care of him, to protect him and to love him. He may not be able to talk, but he's made his desire clear."

Amber's chest went tight, and her throat closed over.

There was a catch in Cole's voice. "And he is right. He's so very right. No matter what you decide here today, Your Honor, Zachary is my brother. He will always be my brother. He will always need me, and I will always be responsible for his welfare. Not because I have to be, or should be, but because I love him, and I will fight with every breath in my body to keep him safe."

Cole went silent. If a pin had dropped in the courtroom, it would have echoed.

He stood a moment longer, then he sat down and placed a kiss on the top of Zachary's head.

Zachary tipped his chin and grinned up at him, gently patting the side of Cole's cheek. "Gak baw. Gak. Gak."

Amber nearly burst into tears.

"I agree, partner," Cole whispered softly. "I agree."

Everybody looked to the judge.

Even Roth's lawyer seemed dazed.

Destiny put her hand on Cole's shoulder.

The judge cleared his throat. "I find…" He paused, adjusting his collar, then rearranging a few sheets of paper in front of him.

He glanced to the bath picture that was still up on the screen. "This is a very unique situation. And I recognize that there is a lot of money at stake. I understand that Coast Eagle Airlines needs to be run effectively. And I understand that guardianship of Zachary Henderson is pivotal to the operation of the company and therefore to the safety and livelihood of thousands of employees and passengers."

Destiny's hand tightened on Cole's shoulder.

He turned to glance at Amber, and the worried expression on his face made her stomach sink. She blinked against tears all over again.

"However," said the judge, "the purpose of this hearing is to determine the best guardian for Zachary Henderson. I cannot let any of the complicating factors impact his well-being and his future." He lifted the gavel. "Therefore, I find in favor of the plaintiff. I grant full and permanent guardianship of Zachary Henderson to Cole Henderson." The gavel came down.

Amber didn't hear a thing as she burst from her seat at the same time Cole turned to face her.

She rushed through the little gate and flung her arms around both of them, her heart overflowing with gratitude.

Cole chuckled as he held her tight. "I can't believe you did it."

"Did what?"

"Turned Zachary into a puppy."

She pulled back and grinned. "I was so scared. But he went straight to you."

"You're a genius."

"It was a big risk."

"It worked."

"Well done, you two," Destiny chimed in, clapping one hand on each of them.

"Well done, you," said Amber in return. "You were brilliant."

"That was a great idea."

"So was using the pictures on my phone."

Roth marched past them, stone-faced, staring straight ahead.

Cole watched his back for a few seconds. "It's going to be an interesting day at the office tomorrow."

"I'm going to worry about *that* tomorrow," said Amber.

Cole gave her a nod. "Agreed. Tonight, we celebrate." A trace of concern seemed to flit through his eyes. "Tomorrow, we figure out the rest."

Thirteen

Cole set the champagne bottle on the fireplace hearth, handing one flute of champagne to Amber and taking the other for himself. "It's very convenient to have a well-stocked wine cellar."

"It is. And I finally managed to figure out the code," said Amber.

She was sitting beside him on the thick carpet, leaning back against the sofa. Zachary was fast asleep in bed, Otis on guard in the hallway outside his door, and the lights were dimmed throughout the penthouse. The flickering gas fire blended with the tiny white lights of the Christmas tree.

"Some of the wine is locked up?" Cole asked.

"I mean the color code to the price and vintage."

"Yeah?"

She raised her glass. "Oh, yes. We are enjoying a very fine vintage."

He didn't have the heart to tell her that champagne all tasted the same to him. "We have a lot to celebrate."

"You were brilliant."

"No, you were brilliant. I just picked up the ball."

"And carried it across the goal line."

"You threw the hail Mary pass."

She grinned. "I did, didn't I? To us, then, and our mutual brilliance."

"Don't forget about Zachary." If they'd scripted the event, the kid couldn't have pulled it off any better.

"He was perfect." She took a sip. "Oh, this is a good one."

Cole followed suit. It tasted like sweet, bubbly wine to him. "It is."

"I guess you're the chair of the board now," she said, stretching her arms out as she leaned back.

Cole felt an uncomfortable pull in his gut. "We should talk about something else."

"Did you see the look on Roth's face? He is both furious and terrified."

"I don't see him at Coast Eagle for the long term."

"Are you going to fire him right away?"

Cole took a swig of the champagne, wishing it was something stronger and less sweet. "That's a complicated decision."

And it wasn't a decision he was in a position to make. He'd have to be willing to stay at Coast Eagle for weeks, maybe months before he could figure out the quagmire of the company's inner workings. Not that he held out hope for Roth, but a knee-jerk reaction wasn't in the best interest of the company.

"You'll have to hire a president. Max is anxious to get back to the legal department."

Cole finished the glass and set it aside, fighting an urge to grab Zachary and drag Amber with them to the Alaskan border. Nobody else mattered.

"Can we talk shop tomorrow instead?" he asked, easing over beside her. "You look beautiful in the firelight."

Her blue eyes softened. "You think?"

"I know." He touched his finger to the bottom of her chin, lifting it ever so slightly to give her a kiss.

The champagne tasted a lot better on her than it had in the glass.

"Thank you, Cole," she whispered against his lips.

He scooted closer still and framed her face with his hands. "I'd do anything for you."

Her smile was beautiful. She was beautiful. She was smart and strong and capable. And she was the sexiest woman he'd ever laid eyes on.

He kissed her.

Then he kissed her deeper, longing radiating through him, pushing everything out of his mind, everything but Amber and how much he needed her.

When he came up for air, he reached for her glass, setting

it aside. Then he lay back, easing her on top of him, loving the press of her soft body against his. He ran his hands along her back, down to her thighs, remembering the exquisiteness of her form.

He slipped his hand beneath her shirt, touching the hot, supple skin of her back, stroking his palms upward.

"You're distracting me," she told him.

"That's the idea."

"We have to talk."

"I know."

"There are a thousand decisions to make."

"Not tonight."

"But—"

"Shh. Give me tonight." He could hear a note of desperation in his own voice. "The world will come apart soon enough."

"It won't be that bad."

But Cole knew it would. It was going to get very, very bad. He was Aviation 58, and she was Coast Eagle. And now he had Zachary.

When his office door burst open, Cole looked sharply up from his desk. He wasn't a stickler for protocol, but the action seemed rudely abrupt.

Then he saw that it was Roth.

He set down his pen and sat back in his chair.

Roth advanced into the room. "I *want* an explanation."

"Of what?"

The only unexpected thing Cole had done so far was to *not* fire Roth. And that was only because he wanted to leave that option for whoever became the next president. And he doubted Roth would demand an explanation for keeping his job.

"You were talking to Kevin Kent," Roth announced.

Cole was forced to hide his shock. Only Luca and Bartholomew had known about this morning's call. He couldn't imagine either of them telling Roth.

He bought himself some time while he mentally calculated both the damage and his next move. "And?"

Roth braced his hands on Cole's desk, leaning forward. "And we both know what that means."

"Do we?" Cole asked. His tone was mild, but his brain was still scrambling.

"It means you're looking to sell. Are you going to liquidate your interest, Mr. Loving Half Brother? Do you care so little about the Coast Eagle legacy that you'd sell it off, maybe break it up, whatever it takes to free up the cash that kid got you?"

"Leave my office," said Cole.

"If you're holding a fire sale, the senior management team deserves an explanation."

Cole felt his blood pressure creep up. "The senior management team will deal with whatever the *owner* decides."

"So you're selling out and pocketing the windfall," Roth spat.

"Leave," Cole ordered.

"No regard for *anyone* or anything else?"

Cole heard a gasp.

He glanced past Roth to see Amber in the doorway. Her eyes were wide and her face was pale as she clung to the doorjamb.

He swore under his breath, even as he vaulted from his chair. She was quick to turn away, dashing down the hall toward the elevator.

He followed at a run. When he caught her, she was frantically stabbing the down button.

"Calm down," he told her in an undertone.

She didn't look at him. "Is it true?"

"I'm not having this conversation in the foyer."

In his peripheral vision, he caught the interested look of Sandra, the executive receptionist. He remembered how friendly she'd been with Roth the first day he'd visited. And it occurred to him that she had a phone number readout on her switchboard.

Amber turned, jaw clenched. "Just tell me if it's true."

"Come back to my office."

"Tell me the truth. Are you going to sell Coast Eagle?"

He scrambled for a way out of the conversation. "It's complicated. We need to talk. And we can't do it here."

She pressed her lips together, staring at him with disdain.

"Come back to my office, where it's private. You can hate me just as easily there."

She didn't answer.

"Amber," he prompted.

"Fine."

He turned and gestured for her to go first.

He let the distance grow between them. Then he stopped at Sandra's desk. He pinned the woman with a furious glare. "If you *ever* research my phone calls again and report them to *anyone,* I'll fire you on the spot."

The color drained from her face.

Leaving, he followed Amber into his office.

She was standing at the window, back to him, staring into the sunny Atlanta afternoon.

He closed the door, composing and discarding opening lines. "I was going to talk to you tonight."

She turned. "I can't believe I fell for it—hook, line and sinker."

He automatically moved toward her. "You didn't fall for anything. I've barely decided. I only decided this morning that selling is the best thing for everyone."

"You mean the best thing for you."

"No, not for me." He amended that statement. "Yes, okay, for me. But only because I could never do it. It's not humanly possible to run two airlines. I wanted to do it. I thought about doing it. Believe me, I came at doing just that from every angle I could."

"Over an entire two days?" she taunted.

"And before."

"Before? You'd planned to sell out *before* we even went to court?"

"I didn't *plan* to sell out. I considered the possibility that I might *have* to sell out."

"You don't *have* to do anything, Cole."

He hated the coldness in her eyes. "I have a plan."

"Clearly, you've had a plan all along. Do you have a conscience? Do you have a soul?"

"A plan for us," he explained. "I want you to come to Alaska as often as you can."

She reached out to grip the window ledge. Her voice was a rasp. "Alaska?"

"To see Zachary. And me, of course." He hoped she'd want to see him. She had to want to see him. He'd come to need her in his life.

She scoffed. "Last time you invited me to Alaska, you admitted you were being insincere and misleading, even manipulative."

It took him a second to remember his words. But he did, and he regretted them deeply. "That was a long time ago."

"The truth is the truth, Cole. Like I said back then, you don't need to worry. I won't be dropping by Alaska to bother you."

"Will you hear me out?"

"I don't think so."

"For Zachary's sake, will you *please* hear me out?"

"Are you taking him away from me?"

"I'm taking him to Alaska, yes. But—"

"Then there's nothing more to say, is there?"

There was plenty more to say. But he could see that this was pointless. Maybe they could talk in a few days. Or maybe he should be patient and let things settle.

Zachary had to be his priority just then. And the Cambridge deal needed his immediate attention. He also needed to get back to Aviation 58. He couldn't stay away any longer.

He didn't want to wait to square this with Amber, but maybe it was for the best. She wasn't going to listen to him right now.

"I'm trying hard not to hurt you," he told her.

She moved for the door, her voice stone flat. "So nice that you at least tried."

* * *

Amber was never going to forgive Cole Henderson, and she'd probably never forgive herself. He and Zachary had been gone for nearly a week, and she'd rehashed every minute of the past month inside her head trying to figure out where she went wrong, and how she could have so thoroughly misjudged him.

"I should have realized," she told Destiny.

"Realized what?" Destiny was across the table from her at Bacharat's. It was Friday night, and the last thing Amber wanted to do was go back to the empty penthouse.

"I should have realized that with this much money at stake, all men would be ruthless."

Destiny toyed with her martini for a moment. She started to speak then stopped herself.

"What?" Amber asked.

"Don't shoot the messenger."

"Are you actually going to defend him?"

"No. But do you think maybe you should have heard him out?"

"Absolutely not." Of that, Amber was certain.

"Why?"

"Because he'd only make up more lies. You can't trust a liar."

"To be fair, you don't *know* he was lying."

Amber's voice rose. "I thought you said you weren't going to defend him."

"I'm not defending him."

"The man had a billion-dollar deal lined up less than forty-eight hours after he won the court case. You don't think that required a little preplanning?"

Destiny didn't seem to have an answer for that.

"I hate to say this," Amber continued, and she really did, "but Roth's right when he says it all looks suspicious."

Destiny paused a beat before responding. "Does it bother you that you're siding with Roth?"

It did bother Amber. But, bottom line, Cole had breezed into town for three short weeks, romanced her, then left with her nephew and a billion dollars.

"I made a huge mistake," she said, swallowing. "What if I never see Zachary again?"

"That's simply not going to happen," said Destiny.

"He's in *Alaska*."

"You can go to Alaska."

Amber shook her head. "No. No, I can't."

Destiny stared hard. "You can. You *will*. Not tomorrow and not next week, but you *will* go see Zachary."

"I'm mortified that I fell for Cole's act."

"I've known you for five years. You are not going to let your embarrassment get in the way of doing the right thing for your nephew."

"You sound like you have faith in me." Amber wasn't sure she deserved anybody's faith.

"I have nothing *but* faith in you."

"Thanks." Amber polished off her martini, trying to feel some faith in herself. "I think I need another."

"I'm with you." Destiny signaled for another round. "Luca has been texting all day."

"I'm sorry it went bad with Luca."

"It didn't go bad with Luca." Destiny's tone was a little sharp.

"I didn't mean—"

"It was too *short* with Luca." Destiny's tone mellowed. "But it was all good. I really do miss him."

"I don't miss Cole."

"That's a big fat lie. You might be ticked off at him, but you have to miss him."

"I'm—"

Destiny spoke overtop her. "This sharing-our-feelings thing isn't going to work if you're just going to lie to me."

Amber tried to wrap her head around the jumble of her feelings for Cole. "I can't miss a man who didn't exist."

"Tell me something," said Destiny, propping her elbow on the tabletop and her chin on her hand. "If Cole was real, if the guy you met was authentic, would you be in love with him right now?"

"That's a pointless question."

"I saw you at the courthouse," said Destiny. "How you looked at him. How he looked at you. In that moment, you were a goner."

Amber remembered. And she experienced the feelings all over again—the intense rush of pride and respect for his strength and honesty, the knowledge that Roth had been vanquished and Zachary was safe, the certainty that she didn't have to worry anymore, that somebody else would help shoulder the burden, and the way he'd immediately turned toward her, the emotion in his eyes, her absolute certainty that nobody else in his world mattered, just her and Zachary.

"Amber?" Destiny prompted.

"Yes," Amber admitted. There really was no reason to lie to Destiny. "If that guy, the guy from the courtroom… If that guy truly existed, I'd be a goner."

Destiny's phone chimed. She looked at the number display and then put the phone to her ear. "Destiny Frost."

She listened for a moment, and her eyes narrowed.

Amber selfishly hoped that whatever it was wouldn't drag Destiny away tonight.

"What kind of paperwork?" asked Destiny. She sent a puzzled glance Amber's way.

Amber frowned.

"Is there a rush?" asked Destiny. "I've had a couple of martinis."

Amber couldn't help feeling disappointed. She didn't want Destiny to leave.

"We're at Bacharat's."

We? Amber glanced around the room, looking to see if she recognized anyone else from Destiny's firm. She didn't.

"Sure," said Destiny. "We'll be here."

As Destiny ended the call, Amber gathered her purse.

"What are you doing?" asked Destiny.

"Getting out of your way." Amber started to rise.

"Well, don't. That was about you."

Amber sat back down. "What about me? Am I being fired already?"

"No. Good grief, where did that come from?"

"Roth's still a VP."

"And Cole still owns the company."

"Only until the deal is finalized."

"Don't be paranoid. You're good at your job, and the new guys are going to see that. And this has nothing to do with your job." Destiny grinned.

"So who was that?" asked Amber.

"Fredrick Galloway of Galloway, Turner and Hopple."

"That means nothing to me."

"He's Cole's new Atlanta lawyer."

A wave of apprehension washed over Amber. "What does he want?"

"He was pretty cagey. Galloway's the top attorney at the top firm in the city."

"I'm sure Cole can afford the best." Though she didn't need it, Amber took another sip of her martini.

"He's got some kind of paperwork for you."

"I don't know what more I can give him. I've already given him—" Amber suddenly teared up. "Oh, damn."

Destiny reached for her hand. "It's going to be fine."

Amber looked into her friend's eyes. "Why did I go and fall in love with him?"

"I wish I could—"

"Ms. Frost?"

Amber looked up to see a sixtyish, fit, well-groomed man standing next to their table.

Destiny came to her feet, purely professional and polite. "Mr. Galloway. It's a pleasure to meet you."

Amber managed a smile.

"I'm sorry to interrupt your evening," said Mr. Galloway. "And, please, call me Fredrick."

"This is my client, Amber Welsley."

"Ms. Welsley." He gave her a nod.

"Amber," she automatically corrected.

Fredrick looked around. "Reception was able to provide us with a private meeting room on the fourth floor. Would you mind joining me there?"

"We'd be happy to," Destiny answered.

Amber took her purse and her coat, doing a double check behind her to make sure she hadn't left anything on the table.

They made their way to the reception elevator, going up one floor to the club's meeting rooms. Fredrick led them down a quiet hallway to a large boardroom. The lights had been turned on and coffee set out on a side table.

Destiny poured herself a cup, but Amber decided to let her stomach rest for a bit.

Fredrick took a seat near the end of a long table. Destiny and Amber sat across from him.

"As I said on the phone," he opened, "you're welcome to take the package with you to read over the weekend. I'd appreciate it if we could talk again Monday morning."

"We can make that happen," said Destiny.

Amber slid a sideways glance at Destiny, gauging her reaction. She seemed impressed by the man, and not overly concerned about the paperwork.

"In a nutshell," Fredrick continued, "Cole Henderson is setting up a trust fund for Zachary."

Amber couldn't hold her tongue. "How incredibly magnanimous of him."

Fredrick gave her a surprised look.

Destiny grabbed her knee under the table.

"What?" Amber looked at them both. "He steals a billion dollars from Zachary, and now he wants to set up a trust fund? What is it, for college or something?"

She wasn't clear on what it had to do with her. Maybe Cole wanted her to believe he was taking care of Zachary so she wouldn't go gunning for him.

Wasn't that a rule of a good con? Make sure the mark's not too angry with you when you leave? She was sure she'd seen that in a movie somewhere.

Fredrick cleared his throat. "My client has requested that Ms. Welsley, Amber, be named trustee with full power to make all decisions regarding the trust fund until Zachary Henderson reaches the age of eighteen."

"Sure," said Amber with a careless shrug. "I'll make sure he gets to college."

This time, Fredrick seemed to be fighting a smile. He slid a sheaf of papers across the table to Destiny. "The trust fund will also provide a salary for Amber."

"I'm not taking any of the money for myself," Amber scoffed. "Just because certain other people believe it is perfectly acceptable to—"

"Amber," Destiny interrupted.

"—use a defenseless baby as a means to—"

"Amber!"

Amber snapped her mouth shut. "What?"

"It says all proceeds from the sale of Coast Eagle Airlines." The words didn't mean anything to Amber.

Destiny spoke slowly, articulating each word. *"All* the proceeds from the sale of Coast Eagle go into the trust for Zachary."

Amber cocked her head sideways, struggling to make sense of Destiny's words. "I'm not following."

"Cole is putting the whole billion into a trust fund for Zachary."

"Dollars?" Amber asked in a dry whisper.

"To be managed by you, as accountant, and he's suggested me as legal counsel, but you have discretion over that." Destiny sent a glance to Fredrick.

Fredrick nodded his confirmation.

Destiny continued, "Until Zachary is eighteen, at which time an orderly and gradual dispersal will begin to move control to Zachary."

Amber swiped her hair back from her forehead. "I know I'm

a little tired. But I thought you just said Cole put me in charge of *all* of the money."

"He did," said Destiny, a grin nearly splitting her face.

"And unlimited trips to Alaska," said Fredrick. He leaned forward and pointed to a spot on the page. "You get an annual salary, benefits and he was *very* specific about the unlimited trips to Alaska."

Amber instantly woke up. Her mind flashed back to the fight they'd had in Cole's office. *I have a plan,* he'd said. *A plan for us. I want you to come to Alaska as often as possible.*

Her hand flew to her mouth. "Oh, no."

"This is good," said Destiny. "This is amazing. I'm…" She looked helplessly to Fredrick.

"Mr. Henderson's instructions are clear and specific," said Fredrick. "And Galloway, Turner and Hopple is pleased to be working with you. This file will have my personal attention."

"He wasn't a fraud," said Amber, as much to herself as to Destiny.

Cole wasn't a fraud, and that meant Amber was in love with him. And she'd made a horrible mistake.

Cole now knew where he'd gone wrong. He never should have left Amber in Atlanta. And he should have brought her in on the decisions around Zachary from the very beginning. He knew she'd seen the trust fund documents; Fredrick confirmed he'd delivered them Friday night.

Cole had expected to hear from her. He'd expected her to understand his logic and like his solution. But it was Monday morning and there hadn't been a single word. Luca had called Destiny, but even she didn't respond.

It was late last night when he'd had the epiphany. Amber didn't want to be brought in at the end of the discussion. She wanted, needed and deserved to be a part of any decision involving Zachary. She also needed to be part of any decision involving Cole.

He knew he was in love with her, completely and forever.

That meant they'd be partners, completely and forever. So long as he could convince her to forgive him.

He wheeled his SUV into the terminal parking lot at the Juneau airport and turned to Zachary strapped into the car seat behind him.

"Got another trip in you?" he asked.

"Gak," said Zachary.

Cole grinned. "I'm going to take that as a yes."

He extracted Zachary, opened the hatchback to retrieve the small duffel bag he'd thrown together this morning. They were catching a scheduled flight, a big, fast jetliner that would get them to Seattle and then Atlanta as quickly as possible.

He balanced Zachary on one hip and lifted the duffel bag with his other hand, elbowing the hatchback closed. "Let's go get her, buddy."

It was a short walk to the main terminal entrance.

Cole would normally just hop in the back of the plane, not particularly caring about amenities. But with Zachary in tow, he'd gone with a first-class ticket. He'd been up most of the night figuring out his problems, and he hoped both of them could sleep for a few hours on the way.

He crossed the lobby toward the check-in lineups.

"Cole?" came a soft, familiar voice.

He stopped dead, not believing it could be true.

But when he turned, there she was, less than five feet away. She was smiling and her blue eyes shone. His heart lurched in his chest.

"Amber." He was in front of her in two strides, dropping the duffel bag to the floor.

"I was coming to see you," she told him.

Zachary immediately lunged for her. She caught him and pulled him to her chest.

"I was coming to you," said Cole. "I was so wrong. I'm so sorry."

Zachary patted her cheek, and she laughed.

"I'm the one who is sorry." She sobered as she told Cole, "I never should have doubted you."

"You had plenty of reasons to doubt me. I hoped you'd understand when you got the trust fund."

"I did understand. That's why I'm here." She gave a little laugh. "Well, that, and it was included in my salary package."

"I was wrong," Cole repeated.

Her expression faltered.

"About selling Coast Eagle," he quickly clarified. "That's not my decision to make alone."

She looked confused. "But you said you couldn't run them both."

"I know. And I can't. But I didn't explore all the options. I have now. And we have another option. But I'm not making this decision without you." He took a breath, steadying himself, realizing he was trying to tell her too much and all at once.

He stopped talking and drew her into his arms, her and Zachary, holding them both close.

"I love you," he whispered in her ear. "I love you so much. And I need you. And Zachary needs you. And you have to marry me. And you have to be his mother, because that's the only way this works. It's the only way he gets what he deserves out of life." He was talking too much again, but he couldn't stop himself. "You and I both had to compromise, but Zachary doesn't. He can have it all, Amber. But only if you'll marry me. I'm sorry. That was too much to throw at you. But once I started talking—"

"Yes," she said, drawing back. "Yes, I love you. And yes, I'll marry you. And of course, *yes,* I'll be Zachary's mother."

He kissed her deeply, until Zachary squirmed between them. "Gak!"

Cole chuckled, and Amber laughed as he drew back to give Zachary some space.

"Can you handle another thing?" he asked her.

"Things like you love me and want to marry me? Those kinds of things? Bring them on."

"We can merge the airlines."

She looked confused.

"But only if you want to do it. This is a decision we're making together. We can still do the trust fund instead. But Luca and I sat up all night last night. He's on board. We merge the airlines and run them together."

"Coast Eagle expands to Alaska?" she asked.

"No." Cole shook his head. "Aviation 58 expands to Atlanta. The head office stays here, but we live in both places."

"Yes," she said again. "Oh, yes."

"Can you handle one more?" Cole asked, feeling as if he was on a roll.

"*There* you are!" Destiny appeared out of the throng. "Hey, Cole. How did you know we were coming in on this flight?"

"I didn't," said Cole. "I was heading for Atlanta."

Destiny grinned at that. She turned to Amber. "I told you so. Did I not tell you so?"

"You did," Amber agreed with a smile.

"Hey, Zachary," Destiny greeted him.

"Does Luca know you're here?" asked Cole.

"I just called him."

Cole glanced at his watch. "Then, I expect he'll be here in about two minutes."

The Aviation 58 offices were on the far side of the airport grounds, but Cole knew Luca wouldn't waste any time getting to Destiny.

"So how're you two doing?" asked Destiny, jiggling Zachary's little hand.

"He's not selling Coast Eagle," said Amber.

Destiny froze, looking worriedly at Amber. "So you're out of a job?"

"She just agreed to marry me," said Cole.

"I was gone maybe five minutes," said Destiny.

"I work fast," said Cole. "We're going to run it together, as a family."

Luca appeared at a run, laughing as he scooped Destiny into

the air, kissing her hard and twirling her around. "I hope you don't plan to leave anytime soon."

Cole drew Amber close again. "You're not leaving, *ever*."

Fine by her. "I'm staying right here."

"I love you *so* much."

Zachary reached for Cole, and he lifted him from Amber's arms, settling him once more on his hip. Then he looped his arm around Amber's shoulder, realizing in a rush of happiness that he had a family. He had a perfect little family of his very own.

"That last thing?" he whispered into her ear.

"Yes?"

"Brothers and sisters for Zachary?"

"Just as soon as you're ready."

Cole was ready now.

* * * * *

THE MAVERICK'S
CHRISTMAS
HOMECOMING

TERESA SOUTHWICK

To my brothers—Jim, Mike, Dan and Chris Boyle.
I love you guys. Merry Christmas!

Chapter One

When he'd come to Thunder Canyon five months ago looking for his biological parents, Shane Roarke never expected
to find out that his father was in jail for stealing from the
town. So far his mother's identity was still a mystery, but
maybe that was for the best. Did he really want to meet the
woman who'd shown the bad judgment to hook up with a
criminal? And what did that say about his own DNA?

He'd arrived a city-slicker chef with a list of questions
about who he was. Now he had half the answers and a lot
to lose if anyone else found out. The information and what
to do about it weighed heavy on his mind.

In June he'd taken the executive chef position at The
Gallatin Room, the fine-dining restaurant at Thunder Canyon Resort. With successful restaurants in L.A., New York
and Seattle it had been a career step-down, but necessary
for personal reasons. Now he was the definition of a man

in conflict—part of him wished he'd never come, while the other part really liked this town.

"Oh, you're still here—"

Shane looked up from the glass of wine in front of him to the redhead who'd just walked into his kitchen. Gianna Garrison was a waitress and part-time bartender on his staff. In the big cities where he'd worked his name had been linked to models, actresses and celebrities, but he'd never seen a more beautiful woman than the one in front of him now, looking like a deer caught in headlights.

"I'm still here," he agreed.

"Like the captain of a ship."

"The last to leave." He smiled.

Gianna was wearing the black slacks and long-sleeved white shirt all the waitresses wore but it looked better on her. The tucked-in blouse accentuated breasts, not too big or too small, which only left just right. Her waist was trim, her legs slim and that curly, shoulder-length red hair always got his attention even from across a crowded room. Close-up was even better.

"Sorry to bother you." She started to back out of the room. "I'll just be going."

She wasn't bothering him. In fact she'd done him a favor. Shane realized the last thing he wanted was to be alone with his dark thoughts.

"Wait. We were a waitress short tonight." Pretty lame stating the obvious, but he'd just switched mental gears and it was the best he could come up with to stop her from leaving.

"Yeah, Bonnie has a bad cold. Coughing, sneezing and breathing germs on that party of ski executives from Switzerland seemed counterproductive to the goal."

Shane nodded. "Convincing them that Thunder Canyon

has the snow, slopes and service to make it a winter vacation destination for Europeans."

"Right. And have you seen any of those movies on the flu pandemic and how disease spreads? We wouldn't want Thunder Canyon identified as ground zero by the Centers for Disease Control. The Swiss would probably hear about it."

"That wouldn't be good. Bonnie was wise to call herself off."

The humor sparkling in her eyes made them almost turquoise. He hadn't noticed that before, which wasn't surprising. Between work, looking for his birth parents and feeling guilty about it on account of his real parents who loved him unconditionally, he'd been a little preoccupied. Now she was only a couple of feet away and he noticed that her eyes were wide and beautiful, like the Caribbean Ocean. If he wasn't careful, he could drown in them.

"So one waitress less means you worked twice as hard," he said.

She lifted one shoulder in a no-big-deal gesture. "I just moved faster, smiled more and dazzled them with the Garrison wit, hoping they had no idea it was taking just a little longer to get their orders delivered. The complimentary bottle of wine you sent over to the table didn't hurt, either. By the way, they raved about the food and seemed surprised. You'd think the invention of Swiss cheese entitled them to culinary domination of the universe."

"I'm guessing you didn't say that to them."

"No." She grinned.

"The head of the delegation complimented me on the food and service before they left. He promised me maximum stars, diamonds, happy faces, thumbs-up, however they designate their rating. Without you I couldn't have pulled that off, Gianna."

Her wit wasn't the only thing about her that dazzled. When she smiled, her face lit up like the town square decorated for Christmas. "I'm flattered you noticed."

"I make it my business to notice. It crossed my mind to come out to help serve, but I couldn't get away."

"Cooking is what you do. Delivering what you cook is my job."

"There's more to it than that. Even when the food is good it's not always easy to keep the customer happy. But you make it look easy. Tonight you did a fantastic job."

"I just handled it," she said modestly.

"You always do. You're one of my best waitresses. Thanks for all your hard work. I appreciate it very much."

"No problem. It's what you pay me for but it's nice to hear you say it." Gianna backed up a little more. "I'll just be going now."

No, he thought. Her dazzle kept the dark away and he wasn't ready for it to come back yet. He wanted her to stay. Saying that straight out might make her nervous, think he was hitting on her. That wasn't his intention. The pleasure of her company was his only goal; the question was how to achieve it.

All Shane could come up with was a delaying tactic. "Did you want something?"

"Why do you ask?"

"You came in the kitchen."

"Oh, that. It's just, you know—" Her shrug did interesting things to her breasts. "Tonight's special looked and smelled amazing so…"

"You're hungry." Of course. What other reason would she have for coming here when her shift was over. After a mental forehead slap, he said, "Doing the work of two people didn't leave time for a dinner break."

"It's my own fault. I missed the staff meal before service started. I'll just grab something on the way home."

"No." He stood and walked over to her. "The least I can do is feed you. And there will be a glass of wine involved."

"Don't make a mess on my account. The dishwasher and prep crew already cleaned up."

"But I'm the boss. I have a nice Pino Grigio already uncorked and it pairs well with the spinach and crab ravioli." He led her to the stool he'd just vacated then pressed gently on her shoulders, urging her to sit. The slight touch ignited a need in his belly and the instinct to pull her against him was unexpectedly powerful.

It was his business to notice workflow in the restaurant and he had. Just because it wasn't his job to be attracted to someone working the flow didn't make the attraction any less real. But he still wasn't hitting on her. This was just a gesture. A happy staff didn't quit and contented workers kept things running smoothly. Training a new waitress was time consuming and costly.

"I was going to have something myself. Please join me."

"Okay, then. Thanks." She rested her heel on the metal rung of the stool and crossed one leg over the other.

The movement was graceful, sexy, and it was an effort to pull his gaze away. On his first day at The Gallatin Room, Gianna Garrison had caught his eye, but for professional and personal reasons he'd resisted the impulse to act on the temptation. Until tonight.

Just before Thanksgiving he'd received conclusive proof that Arthur Swinton, the most hated man in Thunder Canyon, was his biological father. The information had weighed on him over the last couple of days and he was low on willpower. That was the best explanation he could come up with for this lapse in professional judgment. It was time to do his chef thing and take his mind off other things.

While he worked assembling plates, warming food, pouring wine, Gianna chattered away. He let her, liking the sound of her voice, the warm honey with just a hint of gravel. Then something she said tapped into his dark mood again.

"The Thanksgiving dinner you prepared last week for military families was amazing. Everyone in town is talking about it. Angie Anderson and Forrest Traub told me how thrilled the families were, how special and appreciated they felt for their loved ones' sacrifices."

He'd been more preoccupied than usual since that night. People had looked at him like he walked on water and he felt like a fraud. How could he be a walk on water type when Arthur Swinton was his biological father? The man had been convicted and sent to jail for embezzling public funds. Not only that, he'd perpetrated a conspiracy to ruin the Traubs, one of the most prominent families in town. If there was someone who didn't hate Swinton, Shane hadn't met them yet.

Gianna smiled at him. "They said it really helped because of missing their loved ones overseas so much, especially around the holidays."

"I know something about missing family," Shane whispered.

"What's that?" she asked.

He slid hot food onto two plates, then looked over his shoulder. "You're missing something if you don't eat this while it's hot."

"It looks wonderful and smells even better."

He put the two steaming plates on the stainless-steel countertop, then pulled up another stool and sat at a right angle to her. "Dig in."

"Okay." After she did, her gaze met his. "This is sinfully good. I don't even want to think about the calories."

"It's a little-known fact that when you do the work of two people calories don't count."

"Thank goodness. Because this tastes even better than it smells and it smells very fattening." She licked a drop of white wine sauce from her lower lip.

For a second, Shane thought he was going to choke on his own food. The look on her face was the most unconsciously erotic thing he'd ever seen.

A sip of wine kick-started his brain again and he managed to say, "I'm glad you like it."

The words almost made him wince. He had a reputation for being charming but tonight he wouldn't win any awards for witty repartee. It was a miracle that she didn't make an excuse and run for the hills.

"How do you like Thunder Canyon?" She took another bite and chewed.

"Actually, I love it."

"Seriously?" She stared at him as if he had two heads.

"Cross my heart. If it's not at the top of my list, it's very close."

"But you've been all over the world, no?"

"Yes."

"Where did you go to culinary school?"

"CIA."

"Does that mean you could tell me but you'd have to kill me?" The corners of her full mouth turned up.

"The Culinary Institute of America. Hyde Park, New York. About two hours from Manhattan."

"Convenient."

He nodded. "I got a degree in Culinary Arts management because I always wanted to open my own restaurant. But I went to Paris to learn baking and pastry arts. I've traveled to Italy and Greece to experience various cooking techniques like liquid nitrogen chilling, and experience different cuisines. CIA also has a campus in Napa where they specialize in a different area of food preparation and wine pairing."

"So you've got a well-rounded culinary education."

"Yes. My parents are well-to-do. I didn't have to worry about student loans and could indulge every aspect of my curiosity about business trends and cutting-edge themes in the food-service industry."

Her eyes filled with a little wonder and a lot of envy. "That sounds so exciting. How can the town square in Thunder Canyon, Montana, compare to the Eiffel Tower? The Louvre? The—everything—of France?"

"Paris is something to see. No question. But it's not fair to compare places in the world. The favorites just speak to your heart."

"And Thunder Canyon speaks to yours?"

"Yes." It was true, but she probably thought he was a poetic idiot.

He didn't understand his instant connection to this small town in Montana so far off the beaten path. It crossed his mind that the answer could be in his DNA, but that didn't make sense. Not really. Arthur Swinton was a greedy opportunist who only cared about himself and that had nothing to do with the place that filled up his son's soul.

"I'd like to hear about you," he said. "Are you from here?"

"Born and raised. My mother, father, sister and her family are still here." She put the fork down on her empty plate. "After getting a business degree, I went to New York."

"And?" He poured a little more wine in her glass. "What did you do there?"

"I opened a travel agency."

"So, you took a bite out of the Big Apple." Brave girl. He was impressed. His first business venture had been close to home in L.A. She jumped right into the big time. "Apparently I'm not the only one who's been all over the world."

She lifted her shoulder, a noncommittal gesture. "I was pretty busy getting the company off the ground."

"It's a lot of work, but incredibly exciting turning a dream into reality."

"Speaking of reality," she said, clearly intending to change the subject. "You certainly turned your appearance on that reality cooking show—*If You Can't Stand the Heat*—into culinary success."

"I was lucky."

"Oh, please. If you call talent, charm, good looks and a clever way with a wooden spoon luck, then I'm the Duchess of Cambridge."

He laughed. "So you think I'm not hard on the eyes?"

"Are you kidding? You're gorgeous." She looked a little surprised that the words had come out of her mouth. "But, for the record, really? That was your takeaway from what I just said?"

It was better than wondering where his looks had come from. "Beauty is as beauty does."

"What does that even mean?"

"You got me. Do you have someone running the travel agency?" Which begged another question. "Why are you here in Thunder Canyon?"

"Personal reasons." The sparkle disappeared from her eyes and she frowned before quickly adding, "I'm only here for a little while. Not much longer."

Shane understood personal reasons and the reluctance to talk about them so he didn't ask further. "Are you anxious to get back?"

"Who wouldn't be?" She took the stem of her wineglass and turned it. "There's a rumor that your contract here at The Gallatin Room is only six months."

"Yeah." He'd thought that would give him enough time to find out what he wanted to know, but he'd only found out half of it. Now the question was whether or not to keep going and what to do with the information he already had. "So it seems both of us have a time limit here in town."

It was weird, probably part of the pathetic, poetic streak kicking in tonight, but talking to her had made him realize that since coming here he'd been a loner. And suddenly he was lonely. But the last thing he needed in his life was a long-term romantic complication. She was beautiful, funny and smart. He wanted to see her again and she wasn't staying in town. That made her the perfect woman.

"I guess you could say I have a time limit here," she agreed.

"Then we shouldn't waste any time. Have dinner with me."

She looked at his empty plate. "Didn't we just do that?"

"Sassy." He grinned and added that to her list of attributes. "I meant something away from work. Monday is the only day the restaurant is closed and every place within a twenty-mile radius is, too. How about I cook for you at my condo? It's not far, here on the resort grounds."

"I know. But—"

"It's just a home-cooked meal. How does six-thirty sound?"

"I don't know—" Her expression said she was struggling with an answer.

That's when he gave her the grin that reality show enthusiasts had called his secret ingredient. "Doing double-duty tonight deserves a double thank-you."

"When you put it that way… How can I say no?"

"Good. I look forward to it."

Gianna had been looking forward to this evening since Shane Roarke had invited her to dinner. She took the elevator to the third floor of the building on Thunder Canyon

Resort grounds where his condo was located. After five months of nursing a crush on him she could hardly believe he'd finally asked her out. Or in. It felt surreal, with a dash of guilt for good measure.

What she'd told him about herself in New York was a little sketchy. She hadn't so much taken a bite out of the Big Apple as been chewed up and spit out by it. Apartments were small and expensive. The travel agency didn't survive, a casualty of the internet, with more people looking online, eliminating the middle man. And the recession. And she'd seen no point in sharing with Shane that she kept falling into the trap of choosing men who had no intention of committing.

She hadn't lied about personal reasons bringing her back to Thunder Canyon. It was the elaborating part she'd left out. Being unemployed and penniless *were* personal and her primary motivation in coming home. A job at The Gallatin Room was getting her back on her feet. She had a small apartment above the new store Real Vintage Cowboy and the only car she could afford was a fifteen-year-old clunker that she hoped would hold together because she couldn't afford a new one. Sharing all of that with a sexy, sophisticated, successful man like Shane Roarke wasn't high on her list of things to do.

After stepping out of the elevator she walked down the thick, soft carpeted hall to the corner apartment, the one with the best views.

"Here goes nothing," she whispered, knocking on the door. Moments later Shane was there. "Hi."

"You're very punctual." He stepped back and pulled the door wider. "Come in. Let me take your things."

She slipped out of her long, black quilted coat and handed it to him along with her purse, then followed as he walked into the living room. It was stunning. The wood entryway opened to a plush beige carpet, white overstuffed sofa, glass tables and twelve-foot windows on two sides. High ceilings held recessed lighting and the expanse of warm, wheat-colored walls were covered with artwork that looked like it cost more than she made in a year.

"Wow." Gianna had been nervous before but now her nerves got a shot of adrenaline. "This is beautiful."

"I think so, too." Shane's gaze was firmly locked on her face.

Her heart stuttered and skidded. His eyes weren't the color of sapphires or tanzanite, more like blue diamonds, an unusual shade for a stone that could cut glass. Or turn icy. Right this second his gaze was all heat and intensity.

"I've never seen you in a dress before. Green is your color," he said. "It looks beautiful with your hair."

Outside snow blanketed the ground; it was December in Montana, after all. But this moment had been worth the cold blast of air up her skirt during the walk from her clunker of a car. She'd given tonight's outfit a lot of thought and de-cided he saw her in black pants most of the time. Tonight she wanted him to see her in something different, see her in a different way. The approval on his face as he glanced at her legs told her it was mission accomplished.

"'Tis the season for green."

She'd never seen him out of work clothes, either. The blue shirt with long sleeves rolled up suited his dark hair and brought out his eyes, she thought. Designer jeans fit his long legs and spectacular butt as if made especially for him. For all she knew they might have been.

"Would you like some chardonnay?"

"Only if it pairs well with what you're cooking," she answered.

"It does."

She followed him to the right and into the kitchen with

state-of-the-art, stainless-steel refrigerator, dishwasher and cooktop. It was most likely top-of-the-line, not that she was an expert or anything. Ambience she knew something about and his table was set for two with matching silverware, china and crystal. Flowers and candles, too. The ambience had date written all over it.

"Good to know. Because I'm sure the food police would have something to say about nonpaired wine."

"I kind of am the food police."

"That makes one of us." She took the glass of wine and sipped. Not too sweet, not too dry. It was delicious. The man knew his wine and from what she'd been able to dig up on him, he knew his women, too. She was really out of her depth. "And it's kind of a relief that you know your stuff. Because you know that thing about actors wanting to direct? I don't think it works the same in food service. Waitresses don't want to be chefs. At least I don't. Boiling water I can do. Ham sandwich, I'm your girl. Anything fancy? Call someone else. Call you. You're famous in food circles for—"

He stopped the babbling with a finger on her lips. "Call me for what now?"

"You tell me." She took a bigger sip of wine and nearly drained the glass.

"You're nervous." He was a master of understatement.

"I didn't think it showed."

"You'd be wrong." He smiled then pulled chicken, vegetables and other ingredients from the refrigerator—all obviously prepared in advance—and stuff from a cupboard beside the stove, probably seasoning or spices. Or both. He took out a well-used frying pan and placed it on the stove. "But I'm pretty sure I understand."

"What?"

"Your nerves. Thanks to reality TV, exposure about everything from bachelors to swamp people, we chefs have earned something of a reputation."

"What kind of reputation would that be?" She finished her wine, then set the glass on the granite countertop.

"Bad boy." The devil was in the blue-eyed glance he tossed over his shoulder. "And I'm no exception."

"Oh?"

"Think about it. What I do involves sharp knives and fire. Very primitive." As he lit the burner on the stove, the fire popped as the gas ignited.

"I see what you mean." And how.

"On top of that I invited you to my place for dinner. But let me assure you that I have no intention of making you the dessert course."

"That never crossed my mind." But why not? she wanted to ask. It hadn't been on her mind until just now. Well, maybe a little bit when she saw him in that shirt and those jeans because that kicked up a curiosity about what he'd look like *without* them.

He glanced over his shoulder again while tossing in the air over the hot flame everything he'd put in that frying pan. "In spite of what you may have heard, I'm not that type. I like to get to know a woman."

If he really got to know her, chances were pretty good that he'd lose interest. And speaking of types, she probably wasn't his. She wasn't a businesswoman now, more the still-trying-to-find-herself variety.

"So, what are you doing for Christmas?" Changing the subject had seemed like a great idea until those words came out of her mouth. Would he think she was hinting for an invitation? The filter between her brain and mouth was either pickled or fried. Or both.

"My holiday plans are actually still up in the air," he said. There was an edge to his voice that demanded another subject change so she did. "What are you making for dinner tonight?"

"It's something I'm experimenting with."

"So I'm the guinea pig?"

"Think of yourself as quality control." He grabbed the two plates off the table, then slid half the contents of the frying pan onto each one and set them on a part of the cooktop that looked like a warming area. Then he put liquids into the sauté pan and stirred, fully concentrating on the job. After spooning what looked to her like rice from a sauce pan, he said, "Dinner is served." He glanced at her. "More wine?"

"Please."

After filling her glass and setting plates on the table, he held the chair for her to sit down. If a guy had ever done that before, she couldn't remember. Then he sat across from her. The star lilies and baby's breath with candles in crystal holders on either side gave it all a romantic feel.

Suddenly her appetite disappeared, but she was here to eat and figured she'd better do that. She took a bite of the chicken and the flavors exploded on her tongue. "Oh, my. That is so good. It's like a party in my mouth and I thought only chocolate could do that."

"I'm glad you like it."

"What's in here?" She chewed and swallowed. "Can you tell me or would you have to kill me?" At his wicked look she shrugged. "Bad-boy rep, remember? CIA. Fire. Sharp stuff."

"I'll make an exception for you." He picked through the food on his plate. "Chicken. Asparagus. Mushrooms."

"This looks like rice, but the consistency is wrong."

"It's risotto."

"Ah." The gleam in his eyes started pressure in the vicinity of her chest and she hoped it was nothing more than pre-indigestion.

They ate in silence for several moments before he said, "So how was growing up in Thunder Canyon?"

"It was great, but keep in mind that I didn't know anything else." She put down her fork and wiped her mouth on the cloth napkin. "The pace is slower here and kids don't need to grow up so fast."

"It's slower for grown-ups, too."

Gianna nodded. "Not everyone is happy about that. Maintaining the balance between status quo and development has been and probably still is a source of conflict here in town."

That started a discussion about everything from population growth to weather to large holiday groups scheduled at The Gallatin Room the following week. It was interesting to hear about restaurant management, all that went into a successful business besides just preparing food. Time seemed to both fly and stand still.

Finally Shane looked at her. "Would you like more?"

"No, thanks." Her plate was empty and she was so full. "I guess guinea *pig* was the correct term."

"I don't think so. Clearly you enjoyed the food. In some cultures burping is high praise and a compliment to the chef."

"And in some parts of the country it's a competitive sport."

He laughed, then stood and picked up his plate. She followed his lead and carried hers into the kitchen, where he took it from her and set them in the sink.

"What can I do to help?" she asked.

"Nothing. You're a guest and I have a housekeeper. Why don't we sit in the living room?"

"Okay." But when they walked in, the tall windows were filled with the sight of lights winking in the valley below and she walked over. "That is a pretty amazing view."

"I think so. Would you like to see it from the balcony?"

"Oh, yes." She might never have another chance.

Shane opened the French door, then let her precede him outside. The cold air hit her immediately, but when they moved to the railing and he stood beside her, his nearness and the warmth from his body took the edge off.

"Oh, Shane, this is so stunning. Is it always like this?"

"Well, the mountains are permanent and don't change."

"Duh."

He grinned down at her, then pointed. "See the spotlights over there? That's the slopes and they're always illuminated for night skiing. But in the last few days since Thanksgiving, people are putting up Christmas decorations so everything is even more beautiful."

She glanced at him. "There's something in your voice, an awe, a respect, as if you're whispering in church."

"It kind of feels that way," he admitted. "There's a sense of being in the presence of God. The natural beauty here…"

"Speaks to your heart?"

"Yeah. I do love it. Especially on a night like this."

She looked up at the moon and stars. "I don't know what's more beautiful, the sky above or valley below."

"Maybe it isn't either one."

There was a raspy quality in his voice that made her look at him. Their gazes locked and his sparked with heat and intensity. His shoulders were wide, his arms strong. Suddenly she was filled with an ache to feel them around her. She *wanted* to be dessert.

As if Shane could read her thoughts, his mouth inched toward hers and again time stood still.

Until it didn't.

One second passed with him just standing there, then two before he backed away even though the expression in his eyes hadn't changed. "It's getting late. I should probably see you to your car."

Gianna blinked up at him wondering what just happened. She wasn't so out of practice that she didn't know when a man was going to kiss her, and Shane had been about to do that. Something had changed his mind, but darned if she knew what it was. But clearly she'd been dismissed for unknown reasons.

"It is getting late. I'll just get my coat."

Shane got her things, and if the atmosphere at the restaurant was as awkward as the walk down to where she'd parked her wreck of a car, work was going to be even less fun than being one waitress short while feeding the Swiss delegation.

Chapter Two

Three days later Gianna was stewing in The Gallatin Room kitchen, which was ironically appropriate. It had been three nights since Shane had made dinner for her at his place. Three nights of seeing him at the restaurant where they both worked and he hadn't said a word to her—not about work, not even about things other than work. Even a hello, how are you, wasn't in his repertoire. In fact he was going out of his way to ignore her and she didn't understand why.

She also didn't have time to think about it. Waitresses were hurrying in and out of the kitchen with orders and busboys handled trays of dirty dishes, utensils and glassware. It was busy and noisy and she was putting together a basket of bread for the order she'd just taken. Shane stood by the stove concentrating on sautéing seafood over a hot flame. She stared at his back and felt like a lovelorn idiot, but she couldn't help it. When he was in a room her gaze automatically searched him out.

He, on the other hand, didn't even look at her when he wasn't cooking. Disappointment trickled through her and she felt incredibly stupid. Maybe she'd been hoping the third time was the charm—or third day post dinner he would finally break his silence.

No such luck.

Bonnie Reid pushed through the swinging doors separating the kitchen areas from the dining room. Her friend did break the silence.

"Wow, it's busy in there tonight, G."

"Tell me about it."

Gianna rested her hip against the stainless-steel worktable. She'd become good friends with the other waitress, a petite brunette with a pixie haircut and big brown eyes. They'd both been hired at about the same time and bonded over the good, the bad and the awe of their celebrity boss. The other night she'd thought he actually was awesome, but now? Not so much.

"I'm very glad you're over your cold and back to work." Gianna dragged her gaze away from Shane and looked at her friend.

There was sympathy in those brown eyes. "If I hadn't been too sick to crawl out of bed, I'd have been here. It must have been awful by yourself, serving that big party of Swiss businessmen."

"I managed." And now she heard Shane's voice in her head, telling her she always did. The words still made her glow, but she was doing her best to get over it.

"I hated leaving you shorthanded. You must have run your legs off."

Gianna looked down. "Nope. Still there. Cellulite, the extra two and a half pounds on each thigh and all."

"Yeah. Right." Bonnie grinned. "You're fit and fine, my friend."

"Not that anyone would notice." She glanced at Shane who still had his back to her.

"Did something happen while I was out sick?" Bonnie's tone was sharp with curiosity, but fortunately their boss was too far away to hear in the noisy kitchen. "What did I miss?"

"Nothing." That was the very sad truth, Gianna thought.

"I'm getting a vibe, G." Her friend glanced at Shane, then back. "Did Roarke the magnificent do something? Say something?"

"Said something, did absolutely nothing." Darn him. Gianna picked up the silver basket in which she'd artfully arranged a variety of herb-covered rolls and cheese cracker bread, then started to walk back to the dining room.

"Uh-uh. Not so fast." Bonnie shook her head. "You can't drop a cryptic comment like that and not elaborate. It violates every rule of friendship and is just wrong on so many levels."

"Really, nothing happened. I guess I just got the signals wrong. Wouldn't be the first time."

"You're trying to deflect me. Even if this is about all the time you wasted on too many men who have an allergy to commitment, it's not going to work. Did Roarke make a move on you?" Bonnie's eyes filled with indignant anger and she looked a little dangerous.

"Nothing like that." Gianna pulled her farther around the corner to make sure they couldn't be overheard even with the sizzle of cooking and banging of utensils. "We had a moment."

"What kind of moment?"

"When you called in sick I missed the staff dinner then did double duty and was starved at the end of my shift. I thought everyone had left and came in here to grab something to eat. Shane wasn't gone."

"You were alone with him? Did he try something?"

If only… "No. He made me food and gave me wine."

"To lower your resistance? I'll take him apart—"

"Stand down." Gianna couldn't help smiling at the thought of her tiny friend taking on tall, muscular, masculine Shane Roarke. "He asked me to dinner on Monday, at his place."

"How was it? His place, I mean. I've got more questions, but first things first."

"All I can say is rich people really are different."

"That good, huh?"

"The artwork. Furniture. Spacious floor plan and high ceilings. The lighting." She sighed at the memory. "And don't even get me started on the view."

"So he caught you in his web, or lair, or whatever, then pounced?" The fierce look was back.

"That's just it. He took me out on the balcony to show me the view of the mountains, the valley getting ready for Christmas. There was a moon and stars and lights stretching across said valley."

"Romantic with a capital *R*."

"Romantic with every letter capitalized and the whole word italicized." She sighed. "I was sure he was leaning in for a kiss and then—"

"What?"

"Nothing. He all but told me to go home, except he did it in his Roarke-like way. 'I'll see you to your car,'" she quoted.

"Bastard." Bonnie shook her head. "Gentleman bastard."

"I know." Gianna peeked at him again, busily sautéing something. "That was Monday night and he hasn't acknowledged me here at work since. I'm not sure which is worse. The let's-just-be-friends speech I'm used to or this cold shoulder."

Bonnie's frown went from fierce to puzzled. "I prefer the speech. At least you know where you stand."

Maybe that was her chronic problem, Gianna thought. If the relationship status wasn't spelled out, she went straight to hope. That meant she'd made no progress in breaking her bad habit of being a hopelessly romantic fool who wasted time on the wrong men.

"Anyway, that's the scoop." She angled her head toward the swinging doors. "I have to get back to work."

"Me, too." Bonnie gave her a sympathetic look. "I've got your back."

"Thanks."

Gianna put her shoulder to one of the kitchen's swinging doors, then opened it and walked into the quiet and elegant world where special service was the key to success. A beautiful setting during any season, The Gallatin Room was even more so, decorated for Christmas. A ten-foot tree with white lights, red, green and gold ornaments and shiny garland stood in the corner. All the tables had red poinsettias in the center on white linen tablecloths.

Now that Gianna had seen the view from Roarke's penthouse apartment, she knew this restaurant wasn't the most romantic place in Thunder Canyon, but she'd put it very high on the list. This was a weeknight but the place was nearly full, and that happened when you served the best food in town. That's what the two women at her table were after. Gianna had chatted them up while delivering menus and found out they were having a girls' long ski weekend.

She put the breadbasket on the table, then looked at the beautiful blonde and equally pretty brunette, both in their late twenties. "Have you decided or do you need another few minutes to look over the menu?"

"Too many tempting choices," the blonde said. "Do you know what you're having, Miranda?"

"I should go with salmon." She frowned, but her face didn't move. "But Shane's filet with that yummy sauce is to die for."

Gianna didn't recognize either woman and she had a good memory for faces. "So you've been here before?"

"Not here." Miranda shook her head. "But I've been to Roarke's in New York. Daisy and I do a winter ski trip every year and have been talking about trying the slopes in Thunder Canyon for a while. But we always decided on somewhere easier to get to that had restaurants with a reputation. Then we heard Shane Roarke was the chef here."

"He definitely is."

"Miranda says this menu is different from the one in New York," Daisy said.

"He's tailored his signature recipes specifically for The Gallatin Room. I can tell you that every one is fantastic."

"What's your favorite?" Daisy asked.

The chicken he'd made for her at his place. But that wasn't for public consumption yet. She smiled at the two women and hoped it was friendly because that's not the way she felt.

"It would be easier to tell you what's not my favorite. If you're in the mood for beef, the filet is excellent, practically melts in your mouth. And the sauce only enhances the flavor. I'm not a fan of lamb, but people who are rave about it here. The stuffed, grilled salmon is wonderful. And a little lighter, which would leave room for dessert."

"Tell me the chocolate, sky-high cake I had in New York is a choice."

"I don't know if it's the same, but there is one that will tempt you to lick crumbs off the plate."

"That does it." Miranda smiled in rapture. "Shane's desserts are the best. I'll have the salmon. Tell me about The Gallatin salad."

"It's greens with avocado, tomato and goat cheese in a very delicate dressing. So delicious you won't believe it's good for you."

"You talked me into it."

"Make it two," Daisy said. "And a bottle of the Napa Valley Chardonnay."

"Excellent choice." Gianna smiled at the two women. "On behalf of Thunder Canyon Resort and The Gallatin Room, I'll do everything possible to give you a perfect dining experience. If there's anything you'd like, just let me know. It's our goal to make this your ski vacation destination every year."

"Shane being the chef here made the difference in our choice this time," Miranda said.

"He's really something." Just what, Gianna wasn't sure.

"Is he by any chance here now?" Miranda asked.

"Every night."

"I'd love to say hello again." She looked at her friend. "And Daisy has never met him."

"I've certainly heard a lot about him," the blonde said. "Do you think he would come by the table?"

"I can ask." And that would give her an excuse to talk to him. "Although he's pretty busy."

"I understand. I'm not sure he'll remember me, but my name is Miranda Baldwin."

Gianna walked back to the kitchen and her heart was pounding at the thought of talking to Shane. Maybe it would break the ice. Give him a chance to say he'd just been too busy, up to his eyeballs in alligators what with Christmas parties and planning menu changes to shake things up with new dishes in January. It was a slim hope, but hope was something and a hard habit for her to break.

She went through the swinging doors into the kitchen and

saw Shane directing the sous-chef. He shifted to the cutting board on the stainless-steel table across from the stove.

"Can I talk to you?" she asked, moving beside him.

"What is it?" There was no anger or irritation in his tone. In fact there was no emotion at all, which was worse.

If only the world would open now and swallow her whole. Gianna felt her hope balloon deflate. His non-reaction made it unlikely that he would mention their dinner or anything about spending time with her. It was like nothing had ever happened. Situational amnesia. If he wasn't going to bring up the subject, neither would she.

"There's a Miranda Baldwin in the dining room who says she knows you from New York and wondered if she could say hello. I told her you might be too busy—"

"I can do that." He started toward the door and said over his shoulder, "Thanks."

"For nothing," she whispered under her breath.

In every serious relationship she'd had, the guy had strung her along and when it was time to fish or cut bait, she got cut. But Shane couldn't get away from her fast enough, which was a first. Apparently bad dating karma had followed her from New York and mutated.

Clearly he wasn't into her. Since she wasn't into wasting any more time, that should make her happy. Somehow it didn't.

Shane pushed through the double doors into the dining room and left Gianna behind in the kitchen with the hurt he'd caused evident in her eyes. She probably thought he was crazy and who could blame her? Certainly not him. He'd invited her to dinner, then stood with her looking at the night sky and wanting to kiss her more than he wanted his next breath. Every day since then he'd fought the urge to tug her into a secluded corner and see if her lips tasted as good as he imagined. There were times he wished he was as good with words as he was with food and this was one of those times.

He liked her, really liked her. The attraction was stronger than he'd felt in a very long time, maybe ever. He was still coming to terms with the truth about his father's identity so, for Gianna's sake, he wouldn't start something that he could really mess up. Cooling things was for the best and judging by the look on her face when he'd left the kitchen so abruptly, he'd done an exceptional job of it. The depth of emotion he'd seen proved that even though it would be temporary, she could get hurt and he wouldn't do that to her.

Looking over the bustling dining room a sense of satisfaction came over him. Revenue was up from this time a year ago and if that was because of him, he was glad. If the information about who his father was got out, that could keep him from drawing a local crowd, so he planned to enjoy this while it lasted.

Shane knew which tables Gianna had tonight and headed in that direction, then recognized Miranda. She was a beautiful brunette and asking her out had crossed his mind while he'd been in New York. Now she seemed ordinary compared to a certain redhead he wished he'd met while they'd both been there.

He stopped at the table. "Miranda, it's good to see you again."

"Shane." She smiled. "You remember me."

He didn't feel especially charming, but it was said that trait was what had won the reality cooking show and launched his career. He dug deep for it now.

"Of course I remember." He bent and kissed her cheek. "A woman like you is unforgettable."

"Then maybe it was my phone number you forgot. You never called me." Her eyes both teased and chastised.

"Believe me when I say that you're better off." It was easy to look sincere when telling the truth. "And there was no one else."

"Contrary to what the tabloids said."

"Because, of course, we all know that every word the rag sheets print is the honest truth." He grinned to take any sting out of that statement. "Truly, I had no personal life. It was all about opening Roarke's and keeping it open. I was practically working around the clock."

The blonde at the table cleared her throat, demanding her share of attention. "Hello, Mr. Roarke. I'm Daisy Tucker."

"It's a pleasure to meet you, Miss Tucker."

"Daisy. And the pleasure is all mine."

He didn't miss the flirty expression, the seductive tone, and there was a time when he'd have flirted back. Partly to fuel his reputation and get his name in the paper. Although he'd just mocked the tabloids, any marketing expert would tell you that even bad publicity is good, anything that gets your name out there. He was no expert, but knew the information that his biological father was a criminal would take bad publicity to a different, not good level.

"Shane," Miranda said, "after opening restaurants in so many big cities here in the States, I expected you to conquer London, Paris and Rome. It was really a surprise to find you were the executive chef here in off-the-beaten-path Montana."

"I had my reasons."

"But Thunder Canyon? What's the appeal?"

He spotted Gianna's bright hair across the room, just as she was coming out of the kitchen and a knot of need tightened in his belly. She wasn't the reason he'd taken the job but just being able to watch her was definitely appealing. The not-touching mandate was his cross to bear.

"That's difficult to put into words." He looked from one

beautiful face to the other. "I simply fell in love with Thunder Canyon."

"In that case," Miranda said, "maybe you could suggest some places to visit while we're here."

It was a hint for him to show them around and not a very subtle one. Even if he had the time, he wasn't interested. "It was actually love at first sight with Thunder Canyon. I haven't been here that long and haven't had time to explore much."

"Then maybe old friends from out of town is a good excuse to see the local highlights."

"As tempting as that would be, my schedule is really tight. I've got parties every weekend and several during the week until Christmas." It wouldn't be politically correct to tell her he wasn't interested. "You're better off checking with the concierge at your hotel."

"I'm very disappointed," she said.

"Me, too. You know what they say. This is the most wonderful time of the year."

"Ho, ho, ho." Miranda pretended to pout.

"It was wonderful to see you. Happy holidays." He kissed each woman on the cheek. "Duty calls."

He turned away and scanned the room, something he did frequently. It was a chance to make sure service was impeccable, that people were relaxed and happy. How he'd love to get a helping of happy for himself. Speaking of relaxed... He spotted a romantic booth for two and recognized the romantic couple occupying it.

Angie Anderson and Forrest Traub radiated love like a convection oven. That spontaneous thought begged the question: Where in the world had this recent poetic streak come from and when would he shake it?

He headed in their direction and when the two of them stopped gazing into each other's eyes for a moment, they spotted him. After weaving his way through the tables, he slid into the booth against the wall on the seat across from them. The other side had plenty of room for several more members of a platoon since Angie sat so close to Forrest, there was no space between them.

"Hi," he said to them.

"Merry Christmas." Angie was a college student and a volunteer at the town's teen hangout called ROOTS. In her early twenties, her shiny brown hair and dark eyes made her look like a teenager herself. "How are you, Shane?"

"Okay. What's up with you guys?"

"I'm counting the days until classes are over and it's vacation."

"Even with studying for finals she finds time to help the kids out with the holiday letters for soldiers." Forrest put his hand on hers, resting on his forearm. His hair was still military short and he had the muscular fitness and bearing of a soldier, even with the limp from a wound he'd sustained while deployed overseas.

"It makes me feel good to volunteer. What goes around comes around and I want this Christmas to be perfect for everyone," she said. "It's our first together."

"It's already perfect for me. Santa came early this year. I've already got everything I want." The depth of his feelings for this woman was right there in Forrest's eyes.

"Me, too." Angie leaned her head against his shoulder for a moment.

Shane felt like an intruder at the same time he envied them. *People Magazine*'s most eligible bachelor chef had never felt quite so alone before and he was sure that information would surprise the inquiring minds that wanted to know. It wasn't so much about this young couple as it was wanting to touch Gianna and not being able to. Denying himself the pleasure of kissing her under the stars seemed more than stupid when he looked at these two.

"Actually, Shane, I'm really glad they let you out of the kitchen tonight."

"It happens every once in a while." He grinned at them.

"We were hoping to see you," she said.

"Planning to hit me up to cater your wedding reception?" he teased.

"Maybe." Forrest laughed. "Seriously, we wanted to thank you again for all your hard work cooking such a fantastic Thanksgiving dinner for military families. Every single person said the only thing better would have been to have their son or daughter, father or mother home."

"He's right, Shane." Angie glanced at the man she loved, then back. "We can't thank you enough for what you did. You're the best."

"Not really."

He knew it was meant as a compliment but he wondered whether or not they'd feel the same if the truth came out that he was the son of Thunder Canyon's very own crook. He'd hurt Gianna tonight by brushing her off. If she knew the truth about him, she'd probably feel as if she'd dodged a bullet. Except for a strategically placed *R*, crook and cook were the same.

The burden of his father's identity still weighed heavily on him. For now it was his secret and keeping it to himself was the only way to control the flow of information. That meant not getting close to anyone.

Or kissing anyone. Immediately he thought of Gianna. Even her name sounded beautiful and exotic. The fire in her hair and freckles on her nose were a contradiction that tempted him every time he saw her.

And he saw her almost every day.

Chapter Three

At work on Friday Gianna was crabby and it was all Shane Roarke's fault. She'd seen him the previous night smiling his charming smile at the brunette and blonde, chatting them up as if they were the only two women in the world. That wouldn't bother her so much if he hadn't given her wine and food in this very kitchen and smiled his charming smile at *her*. Then he invited her to his place for a test run of a new recipe where he charmed her some more.

She loved being charmed but wished he'd kept it to himself because all of that attention had fed into her crush, the one now starved into submission because without fuel there was nowhere to go. She was doing her best to not think about him but that resolve was challenged earlier tonight when she'd seen him brooding. It was the same expression she'd noticed the night of her double duty, although what the handsome, successful, famous Shane Roarke had to brood about was beyond her.

She pushed through the double doors and he looked up from whatever he was sautéing. And that was the thing. He never looked up when he was cooking. The building could be on fire and he'd still focus on the food. A girl noticed stuff like that when she had a crush on a guy. For the last three days he'd ignored her unless special requests from a customer made a conversation necessary to get the order just right. Tonight Shane had looked at her every time she was around, no matter what he was doing.

Gianna ignored him as she put in the order for two salads with romaine lettuce and the most delicious croutons on the planet. The prep cook would toss it with Shane's special dressing, then add freshly grated Parmesan cheese. She picked up the wide, shallow bowls and set them on a tray. As she went to the double doors to go check on her tables a feeling prickled between her shoulder blades. Glancing over her shoulder she saw a hot and hungry expression in Shane's gaze. There was something up with him and she was involved.

As soon as she came back for the salads, she'd find out what was going on with him. After leaving the kitchen she walked through the maze of tables and stopped.

She knew these two, had seen them in here individually. Both were somewhere in their mid-fifties, and widowed. She saw they still had salad on the plates in front of them on the white, cloth-covered table. "Still working on those salads, Mrs. Bausch, Mr. Walters."

He was a big bear of a man with the calloused hands and leathery skin of someone who worked outdoors. "When are you going to call me Ben, little lady?"

"As soon as you stop calling me little lady. My name is Gianna."

"You got it, Gianna." There was a twinkle in his blue eyes.

"I haven't seen you two in here together before." She was curious.

"This is a blind date." Kay Bausch was characteristically direct. "Austin Anderson set us up. You probably know he's an engineer at Traub Oil Montana where I'm the secretary to the company president."

"Ethan?"

"Points to you, Gianna. That's the right Traub. And there are so many of them that sometimes it's hard to keep the names straight." She looked across the table at her blind date. "Ben has known him since he was a teenager. Austin, not Ethan."

"He's a good kid," Ben answered, his mouth curving upward to form a smile in his rugged face. "He was kind of lost after his mom died in a car accident when he was only a teenager. Turned out he just needed a steady hand."

"That's nice at any age." Kay's voice was a little wistful. "And now he's got his wife, Rose, Ethan's sister. They'll have their first anniversary on Christmas."

Gianna felt a twist in her chest that signaled a severe case of envy. She'd seen the couple in here for dinner and the glow of their love still radiated. It's what she had once hoped to find and now had all but given up on. Still, feeling sorry for herself was something she tried to do on her own time.

"Apparently Austin is quite the romantic."

"How do you mean?" Ben asked her, but the expression on his face said he knew where she was going with this.

"He fixed you two up. How's that working for you?" She looked at Kay, then Ben.

His grin was full of the devil. "So far I'm not sorry I put on this coat and tie."

"You look very handsome. And uncomfortable," Kay added. "The effort has not gone unnoticed or unappreciated."

"Good to know. Because it has to be said that there's no way to beat a comfortable pair of jeans."

"I couldn't agree more," his date said.

"Something in common already." Gianna nodded approvingly. "Can I get you anything else right now?"

"Nope. Got everything so far." Ben was looking at his companion, who smiled like a young girl.

"Okay, then. *Bon appétit.* You two enjoy."

Again weaving through the dining-room tables filled with people, she made her way back to the kitchen. Shane looked up as he was arranging shrimp in wine sauce over rice on two plates. Bonnie grabbed them, threw a nod of support, then left with the plates on a tray. She was alone with the chef and it was a sign, Gianna thought.

She marched over to where he stood in front of the stove and not all the heat she felt was from the cooking. "What's going on?"

"Excuse me?"

"Are you going to have me fired?" She folded her arms over her chest as she met his gaze. She didn't know where the question came from but her luck had been so bad it was best to get the worst case scenario out of the way first.

The surprise in his eyes was genuine. "What?"

"You keep staring at me and it's not a happy look. You're going to tell the manager to fire me, aren't you?"

"No."

She waited for an explanation, but it didn't come. "Then it's my imagination that you keep watching me?"

"No."

Again nothing further. He was the most frustrating, exasperating man she'd ever met and she had a talent for meeting exasperating men who frustrated her. "Then I don't get it. I don't understand what you want from me."

A muscle jerked in his jaw and his mouth pulled tight. He

was fighting some internal battle and it was anyone's guess which way things would go. Finally he all but growled, "Then I'll show you what I want."

He took her hand and tugged her down the short hallway and into the large, walk-in pantry where nonperishable, industrial-size supplies were kept. Canned goods, jars of olive oil, flour, sugar and spices were all stored in here on floor-to-ceiling metal shelves. Shane shut the door, closing them in.

"You know," Gianna said, her tone a little breathless, "you didn't need to bring me in here to yell at me. Public chastisement is okay. I can take it. Just tell me what—"

The words were cut off when he pulled her into his arms. "This is what I want to tell you."

And then he kissed her. His lips were soft, gentle, but there was nothing gentle about the effect on her senses. It felt as if a wave of emotions crashed over her and she was floating because her legs went weak. The scent of his spicy cologne mixed with the pleasant smell of oil, spices and fire. Blood pounded in her ears and the feel of her breasts crushed against his hard chest was simply scrumptious.

He cupped the back of her head in his palm to make the meeting of their mouths more firm, and the harsh sounds of his breathing combined with hers and filled the storeroom. She would have been happy to stay like that forever, but Shane pulled away. It could have been an hour or a nanosecond because time in this alternate sensuous universe was hard to quantify.

She blinked up at him and said, "Does that mean I'm not in trouble?"

"That's what it means." He leaned his forehead against hers. "I've been wanting to do that all week."

"Really?" Since her thoughts were smoking hot along with the rest of her, Gianna had trouble pulling herself together to call him on the fact that he'd ignored her most of the week. Somehow she managed. "You have a very odd way of showing it."

"You're right." He blew out a long breath and backed up a step, as if he needed distance to think clearly, too. "My behavior is inexcusable. Mixed signals."

"You think?"

"I don't think. It's a fact I've been running hot and cold."

"I noticed." After that kiss she definitely preferred hot, but given his recent mercurial moods it was best not to have expectations.

"Personal stuff in the workplace is a rocky road to go down. It's tricky to navigate. I was trying to take the high road, do the right thing. I'd never want to make you uncomfortable."

"You could have used your words," she pointed out, "said something. I know a thing or two about being conflicted regarding…personal stuff."

"Oh?"

"Yes." She lifted her chin a little self-consciously. In for a penny, in for a pound. Might as well use her words. Never let it be said she was a do-as-I-say-not-as-I-do person. "I understand how sometimes it's easy starting down a path, but the right time to turn off it can be tricky."

"Very Zen of you."

"Okay. Here's an example. I dated a divorce attorney for over two years before we had 'the talk' where I found out he never planned to commit. Should have turned off that path a lot sooner."

"I see."

"Then there was the accountant who saw too many joint checking accounts split, not necessarily down the middle, by messy breakups. There's a year and a half I'll never get back."

"Okay."

"The college professor who said up front that he was a loner. That one is my own fault."

"You've definitely had a conflict or two."

"Yes, I have. As with my job, I can handle it. You don't need to protect me. I'm a big girl."

"I noticed." His eyes were like twin blue flames with the heat turned up high.

"Don't hold back on my account."

"It won't happen again," he agreed.

"That was a very nice kiss."

One of his dark eyebrows lifted. "Nice?"

"Location, location, location." She looked around the storeroom and wrinkled her nose. "For the record? The balcony of your apartment has much better mojo."

"Everyone's a critic." He grinned. "Let me make it up to you."

"How?" She should be ashamed at being so easy, but darned if she could manage that.

"Meet me here after work and I'll show you."

"Okay." Way too easy. The end of her shift wouldn't come fast enough.

All it took was Shane's kiss to make her crabby mood disappear. Probably not smart, but definitely the truth.

After making sure everything in the kitchen was shut down and squared away to his satisfaction, Shane turned off the lights. Only the security ones were left on, making the interior dim. The frenzied chaos so much a part of the food-service business he loved was over for the night and eerie quiet took its place.

He waited for Gianna to get her coat and purse then meet him here. Keyed up from work, he paced while he waited. Part of him hoped she wouldn't show because he didn't need more complications in his life. Mostly he couldn't wait to see her. Fighting the temptation to kiss her had given him a lot of time to imagine what it would be like, but the actual touching of lips had been everything he'd expected and more.

What he hadn't expected was her straightforward sass and steadfast spunk. The way she'd challenged him about how peculiarly he'd been acting had surprised and charmed him in equal parts. He hadn't been surprised in a good way since the first time he'd seen Thunder Canyon.

With his parents' blessing, he'd hired a private investigator to find his biological parents and the guy had narrowed the search to this small town in nowhere, Montana. His restless need to connect the dots about himself had been stronger than his aversion to packing himself off to that small town. The surprise was his instant connection to the rugged beauty of the mountains and trees, being drawn in by the friendliness of the people.

He'd grown up in Los Angeles, for God's sake, where freeways, traffic and smog ruled. He wasn't a mountains-and-trees kind of guy. At least he'd never thought so. But the connection he'd felt had only gotten stronger in the five months he'd been here. That was already a lot to lose, and now there was Gianna.

That saying—the apple doesn't fall far from the tree—was a saying for a reason. And the sins of the father... The rest of the words eluded him but when sins were involved it couldn't be good. Something deep inside Shane rebelled at the thought of Gianna knowing who his father was.

The kitchen door opened and there she was, wearing a navy blue knit hat pulled over her red hair with curls peeking out by her collar. She had a matching scarf tied loosely around her neck and the ends dangled down the front of her coat. When she smiled, the beauty and warmth melted the place inside him that had started to freeze over.

"So," she said, "just how are you going to make it up to me?"

He wasn't quite sure, but when the moment was right, he'd know. "You'll just have to wait and see. Let's go."

"Okay."

There was a rear restaurant exit and she followed him past the pantry where he'd kissed her earlier and the big industrial-size refrigerator and freezer. He opened the outside door and let her precede him, then closed and locked it after them. The area was illuminated by floodlights at the corners of the building.

"That air feels so good," she said, drawing in a deep breath. "So clean and clear and cold."

"How do you feel about a midnight walk in the moonlight?"

Her blue eyes sparkled with merriment. "I feel like that's a promising start to making things up to me."

The restaurant employees parked here in the back and since they were the last two to leave, Shane figured the only car in the lot, an older model compact, belonged to Gianna.

He looked down at her. "You don't come out here alone after your shift, do you?"

"No. It usually works out that several of us leave together."

"Good." But tonight he would make sure she was safe. "Are you okay with leaving your car here?"

"Because someone might break in? I should be so lucky it would get stolen." She laughed and the cheerful sound magnified in the still night.

"Is it giving you trouble?"

"Trouble is too nice a word for what it gives me. Every

day I cross my fingers and say a little prayer that it will start and get me to work."

"If it ever doesn't, let me know. I can't afford to lose my best waitress."

"You might regret that offer," she warned.

They walked across the lot to the sidewalk that bordered an open grassy area. At least there used to be grass. He'd seen the green before winter rolled in and dumped a couple feet of snow. During the day the temperature was warm enough that the existing snow melted a little, wetting the walkway. The sun had gone down hours ago and it was freezing, making the sidewalk slippery. On top of that, a light snow had started to fall.

"So much for walking in the moonlight," she teased.

"I'm trying to feel bad about that. But for a boy from Southern California, the excitement of snow still hasn't worn off."

"All that sunshine and good weather must really get old."

"It's a dirty job, but someone has to live there."

She laughed. "Still, there's something to be said for Montana."

"Preaching to the choir, Gianna," he said. "And it's not just the landscape or weather. The people in this town are good, friendly, salt-of-the-earth types."

"I know what you mean." Her tone was serious and sincere. "I met people in New York. Still have a good friend there who used to be my roommate. But the city is so big and impersonal. There's an intimacy here that's unique."

"Everyone has made me feel really welcome, embraced me as one of them."

"Thunder Canyon spirit," she agreed. "But they can turn on you in a heartbeat if you let them down."

That's what worried him. But it probably wouldn't happen tonight. He made a deliberate decision to change the subject. "So, we had a pretty good crowd in the restaurant."

"We did." She glanced up at him. "Were you mad enough to spit when that man sent his steak back twice because it wasn't mooing on the plate?"

He shrugged. "People pay a lot of money for service and food. It's my job to make sure they're satisfied."

"For every persnickety person, there's a Ben Walters and Kay Bausch."

"I don't think I know them." When she slipped a little on the sidewalk, he took her hand and slid it through the bend of his elbow. It wasn't an excuse to stay connected. Not really. He was responsible for keeping her safe.

"Ben is in his mid-fifties, a rancher born and raised here. He's a widower. Kay is a transplant from Midland, Texas. She works for Ethan Traub and came with him when he opened Traub Oil Montana. She's a widow." She sighed. "I was their waitress tonight."

"Nice people?"

"Very. And the best part is they were on a blind date. Austin Anderson fixed them up."

"Angie's brother?"

"Yeah. It's really sweet. And I can't help wondering if the two of them were meant to meet and find a second chance at happiness. Romantic drivel, I know."

"Not here. To me it sounds like just another day in Thunder Canyon."

"On the surface that's sort of a cynical remark," she observed. "But digging deeper, I can see the compliment buried in the words."

They were walking by one of the resort's Christmas displays with lighted reindeer and Santa Claus in his sleigh. Animal heads moved back and forth and Rudolph's nose was bright red. The big guy with the white beard moved his hand in a wave. Old-fashioned, ornate streetlamps lined the walkways and the buildings were outlined with white lights.

"This is really a magical place, especially this time of year," he said.

"I know." There was a wistful tone to her voice as she stared at the decorations. "What is Santa bringing you this year? A Rolls Royce? 3-D TV with state-of-the-art sound system? Really expensive toys?"

Material things he had. And more money than he knew what to do with had paid for a private investigator to dig up information. But it was what money couldn't buy that made him feel so empty.

"I actually haven't written my letter to Santa yet."

"I see." She stared at the jolly fat man turning his head and waving. "Have you been naughty? Or nice?"

"Good question."

The mischief in her eyes turned his thoughts to other things and he looked at her mouth. The memory of those full lips so soft and giving convinced him that this was the right moment to make it up to her for not taking advantage of the romantic mojo on his balcony.

Shane lowered his head for a kiss, just the barest touch. He tasted strawberry lip gloss and snowflakes, the sexiest combination he could imagine. And he could imagine quite a bit. His heart rate kicked up and his breathing went right along with it. Gianna's did, too, judging by the white clouds billowing between them.

No part of their bodies were touching and she must have found that as dissatisfying as he did. She lifted her arms and put them around his neck, but when she moved, her foot slid on the sidewalk and she started to fall.

Shane shifted to catch her but couldn't get traction on the icy surface and knew both of them were going down. He managed to shift his body and take the brunt of the fall on his back in the snow while Gianna landed on top of him with a startled squeal. Then she started laughing.

He looked into her face so close to his and said, "That couldn't have gone better if I'd planned it." If he had, he'd have planned to be somewhere warm and for her not to have so many clothes on.

"So, you think it will be that easy to have your way with me?"

"A guy can hope."

Apparently the innocent expression he put on his face wasn't convincing because she chose that moment to rub a handful of snow over his cheeks.

He sucked in a breath. "God, that's cold."

"I'm so sorry." Clearly it was a lie because she did it again.

"Payback isn't pretty." He reached out to grab some snow, then lifted the collar of her coat to shove it down her back.

She shrieked again, then gave him a look. "You're so going down for that."

"I'm already down."

"Then we need to take this battle to a new level." She jumped up and staggered back a few feet, then bent down. When she straightened, she hurled a snowball with each hand, but missed him.

Shane rolled to the side and grabbed her legs, tackling her. "I learned to do that when I played football."

He looked down at her laughing face and thoughts of war and retaliation retreated. She was so beautiful he couldn't stop himself from touching his mouth to hers. Definitely going on Santa's naughty list this year.

He deepened the kiss and caught her moan of pleasure in his mouth as she slid her arms around his neck. They were already down so he didn't have to worry about losing his balance this time. That was fortunate because she felt so good in his arms, he had his doubts about maintaining emotional equilibrium.

He cupped her cold cheek in his palm and traced the outline of her lips with his tongue. She opened her mouth, inviting him inside, and he instantly complied. The touch sent liquid heat rolling through him and he groaned with the need to feel her bare skin next to his. The sensual haze lasted just until he felt her shiver.

He lifted his head and saw her shaking. "You're freezing."

"N-not yet. But c-close."

Shane levered himself up and to his feet, then reached a hand down to help her stand. In the streetlamp he could see that her coat and pants were wet. "You're soaked."

Her teeth were chattering, but she managed to say, "Th-thanks for the news flash."

"You need to get into something dry."

"I need to go h-home."

"My place is closer." The next words just popped out, but as soon as they did he knew how much he wanted it. "You could stay tonight."

"Oh, Shane—"

"Just a thought. No harm, no foul."

"I'd really like to." There was need in her eyes, but it was quickly followed by doubt. "But…"

There always was, he thought.

"I have an early day tomorrow," she said. "It's probably best if I go home. Rain check?"

"You got it." He'd never meant a promise more. "Now let's get you back to your car."

He hurried her to the parking lot and took her keys when her hand was shaking too badly to fit it in the lock. When she was in the driver's seat, she managed to get the key in the ignition and turn it. There was a clicking noise but the engine didn't turn over.

Shane met her gaze. "Did you forget to say your prayer this morning?"

"That's not the problem. This clunker is officially beyond the power of prayer. It's dead."

Chapter Four

Trouble wasn't a four-letter word but it should be when talking about her car, Gianna thought. On top of that, she was freezing. Rolling around in the snow with Shane had seemed like a good idea at the time, but not so much now.

He leaned into the open door and met her gaze. "I think the battery's dead."

"Of course it is because that's just how I roll—or in this case, don't roll. And dead is good."

"How do you figure?"

"It won't feel a thing when I beat it with a baseball bat."

"That won't help the situation."

"Says who? Hitting something would make me feel a lot better." She got out of the car, shivering when the cold air wrapped around her, then dug in her purse for her cell. "It's late. There's no way I can deal with this now. No garage will be open, so I'll call a cab to take me home."

He put a hand on her arm. "Not while I'm around."

"I don't want to inconvenience you."

If she'd taken him up on the offer to spend the night it would be very convenient, but she was pretty sure sleeping wasn't on his mind when he'd offered. It's not that she wasn't interested in sex, but this was too soon.

"I'm happy to help you out, Gianna. And I won't take no for an answer." He plucked his cell phone from the case on his belt, pushed some buttons and hit Send. A moment later he said, "Rob? Shane Roarke. Can you do me a favor? Bring my car down to the restaurant, the parking lot out back." Rob said something that made Shane grin. "Yes, a very nice Christmas bonus. Happy holidays." He put the phone back in the case. "The car will be here in a few minutes."

Gianna stared at him. "It must be amazing to be you."

"And who am I?" The words were meant to be glib and lighthearted but a slight tension in his voice made him sound a little lost.

Shane Roarke, celebrity chef and wealthy eligible bachelor? Lost? That was just nuts. She must have hit her head when they were wrestling in the snow. Or her brain was frozen. He was rich, famous, handsome. Women threw themselves at him. If this was a dream, she didn't want to wake up. And he was driving her home.

To her minuscule apartment above Real Vintage Cowboy. Yikes.

After seeing his place she was a little embarrassed to bring him inside hers. But that was just silly. After he pulled into the parking lot behind the store she'd just hop out and say thanks. There was no reason for him to know that her apartment was so small she could stand in the living room with a feather duster, turn once in a circle, and the place would be clean.

Headlights rounded the corner of the building then slowly

moved closer to them, finally stopping. A young man got out of the BMW SUV. "Here you go, Mr. Roarke."

"Thanks, Rob. Can I give you a lift back to the lobby?"

"No, thanks. The fresh air feels good, clears my head. That will help me stay awake and it's a long night ahead."

"Okay. Thanks again."

"Have a nice evening." He lifted his hand in a wave, then headed back the way he'd come.

"And just what is Rob's job title?"

"Concierge." He walked her to the passenger side of the car and opened the door. "One advantage of condo living is around-the-clock service."

"Does Rob's skill set lean toward replacing a dead car battery?" she wondered out loud.

"If you were one of my neighbors it would be his job to figure out how to do that."

"Rich people really are different."

He closed her door, walked around the front of the car and passed through the headlights, then slid in on the driver's side. "Where to?"

"Real Vintage Cowboy. It's on Main Street near the Wander-On Inn and Second Chances Thrift Store."

"I've been there. Isn't it closed this time of night?" He glanced over at her, questions and something else swirling in his eyes before he put the car in gear and drove out of the parking lot.

"My apartment is above the store. So you've been there?"

"Yes." Again his voice was tense. "I actually went shopping there. And for the record, rich people aren't different. I put my pants on one leg at a time."

"Okay. If you want to split hairs, I'll play," she said. "Have you ever been in the grocery store?"

"Here in Thunder Canyon, or ever?"

"Let's get wild. Here in town."

"No. I leave a list for the housekeeper."

"Of course you do." While he drove, she settled into the soft leather of the heated seat. Because Rob was Rob, he'd turned on the heater and the interior was warm in addition to feeling like a spaceship with all the dials and doohickeys on the dashboard. "I want a housekeeper and a Rob," she said wistfully.

"With great privilege comes great responsibility."

"Confucius says…" She glanced over at him, the rugged profile, the strong jaw and stubborn chin. There was something so appealing in his smile, a quality that tugged at her, made her want to touch him. "Would you translate that for me?"

"It means that money is a reward for hard work. A benefit of having it is being able to hire help so that when you're not working, complete relaxation is possible."

"So, getting into the milieu of my car, your batteries are recharged and you can go to work with renewed energy and make gobs more money."

There was irony in the glance he slid to her. "Something like that."

From where she was sitting, the rich were different, no matter what he said. That didn't mean their houses wouldn't burn in a wind-driven brush fire or their cars didn't break down. But when bad stuff happened there were no worries about the cost of fixing it. And you could hire someone to change a battery or flat without batting an eye.

Gianna would bet everything she had that the actresses, models and famous-for-being-famous women he dated wouldn't be fretting about how they were getting to work in order to earn the money to buy a car battery for a clunker. It was too depressing so she decided to change the subject.

"So, when you went to Real Vintage Cowboy, what were you shopping for?"

"I'm building a house."

That wasn't really an answer. "I heard a rumor to that effect. People talk about you."

"Because I'm different?"

"No. Because you're a celebrity." When the car stopped at a stoplight under a streetlamp, she saw the muscle in his jaw tighten. "So, because of the house-building rumor, I was a little surprised when you said you might not be renewing your contract at The Gallatin Room."

"All I did was confirm that it's only six months."

"Again you're splitting hairs." Now that she thought about it, he was pretty stingy with personal information. "If you're not staying, why build a house?"

"I found a great piece of land that was begging to be developed."

So, of course, he bought it and did just that, even though his time in Thunder Canyon might be limited. So much for his assertion that the rich weren't different. She thought about using what he'd just told her as evidence to support her statement, but decided against it. He would never understand.

The windshield wipers rhythmically brushed snow away as the car glided smoothly along nearly deserted Main Street. When they drove past The Hitching Post, Gianna tensed. The new and improved bar and restaurant had been thoroughly overhauled by new owner, Jason Traub. He'd managed to respect its Montana history and maintain the Western style while using reclaimed lumber and stones.

The upstairs, which used to be rooms for rent, had been converted into an intimate salon with overstuffed leather chairs, hand-carved rockers and antlers that hung on the wall. A large stone fireplace and cozy floor rugs made it a welcoming place for a quiet drink and conversation. None of that is what made her nervous.

A minute or two after going by, Shane turned the car into the lot behind Real Vintage Cowboy and pulled into a parking space closest to the building.

"Thanks a lot, Shane. I don't want to keep you." She started to open the passenger door.

"Let me turn the car off."

"Don't bother. You don't have to see me to my door. I'll just run upstairs. You've done enough already."

Her effort to make a smooth exit was wasted and she knew it when the car's dashboard lights revealed his amusement.

"If I didn't know better, I'd think you were nervous about something."

Not something, everything, she thought. "Not at all. I just don't want to take advantage of your kindness."

"Oh, please." He turned off the engine. "I'm not in the habit of barely slowing down to let a lady out of my car. Just so we're clear, I'm walking you to your door. No argument."

He'd left her no graceful way out of this and did it in such a gentlemanly way. Could be because he didn't know her very well and was on his best behavior. Could be an act meant to disarm her. If so, it was working. She was almost completely disarmed.

"Okay," she said. "But you should know. My apartment is on the third floor."

"Real men don't flinch at a second set of stairs."

"Don't say I didn't warn you."

Shane came around and opened her door, then walked beside her to the wooden stairs on the outside of the building. When they got to the landing, Gianna had her keys out. "Thanks, Shane. I had a great time tonight."

"Me, too." His gaze searched hers. "Did I redeem myself for first-kiss faux pas?"

She laughed. "Yeah."

"Good. Here's another better first."

He lowered his mouth to hers. It was soft and warm where their lips met, but the breeze swirled snow around them and made her shiver.

Instantly he pulled back. "I'm an idiot. Your clothes are still wet, aren't they?"

"Y-yes."

"You need to get inside. Good night, Gianna."

She nodded, but as he started to back away it hit her that she really didn't want him to go. A third kiss didn't mean she'd known him any longer, just convinced her that she wanted to spend more time with him. It wasn't smart, but the words came out of her mouth, anyway.

"You're cold, too. How about a cup of tea?"

"I wouldn't mind." He stared down at her, questions in his eyes. "But only if you're sure it's not too late. You've got stuff to do tomorrow."

His hand was on her arm; his gaze held hers. She was definitely sure. "It's not too late." Or maybe it was. "Just don't expect much. My apartment is nothing like your place."

Gianna unlocked the door and he followed her inside. She tried to tell herself that the actresses, models and TV personalities he dated probably had places this small but it didn't work.

The apartment was long, narrow and divided into two spaces—living room and kitchen, bedroom and bath. There was a window looking out on Main Street and the other faced the parking lot with rugged, majestic mountains in the distance. When you thought about it, she and Shane sort of shared a scenic view, but his was way better.

She'd separated her cooking and eating area with a hunter-green love seat. Braided rugs in green, coral and yellow were scattered over the wooden floor. The walls were painted a pale gold and had white baseboards and crown molding. Scattered pictures hung in groupings, a lot of them framed in cherrywood ovals. To shake things up, she'd put a two-foot section of a scaled-down ladder over the outside door and a hanging fixture over the stove held several copper pots and an orange colander. It was bright and cheerful, in her opinion.

She watched Shane, trying to gauge his reaction. "Be it ever so humble…"

"Have you ever heard the expression, 'it's not the square footage, but what you do with it'?"

She tapped her lip. "Is that like 'size doesn't matter'?"

"In a way." His grin was wicked and exciting. "You've created a space that's homey, comfortable and charming. A reflection of its occupant."

"So, let me see if I understand what you're saying. I'm homey and comfortable?"

"Don't forget charming," he said, looking around again, then coming back to meet her gaze. "Among other very attractive attributes. My place doesn't have this warmth…" He stopped. "And speaking of that, I'm an idiot. Get out of those damp clothes into something warm."

Your arms would be warm.

Gianna hoped she hadn't said that out loud and when his expression didn't change, she breathed a sigh of relief. "Okay. Let me get tea first—"

"I'll do it."

"But…"

"Do you have tea bags?" he asked.

"In the appropriately marked canister by the stove. It won't take a minute—"

"You don't trust me?" He shook his head. "I'm CIA. My culinary genius is the stuff of legend."

"Humble, too," she muttered.

"I think I can handle putting a couple of mugs with water in the microwave."

"Okay, then. Knock yourself out."

She walked through the doorway that separated the living room from her bedroom and bath. After closing the door, she stripped off her coat followed by the rest of her wet clothes. Still chilled to the bone, fashion and seduction were not her priority now. She pulled a pair of fleecy Santa Claus pants from her dresser and a green thermal shirt and put them on, then slipped into her oversize dark blue terrycloth robe, thick socks and fuzzy slippers.

In the adjoining bathroom she turned on the light and recoiled from her reflection in the mirror. "Oh, dear God."

Mascara from the lower lashes gave her "raccoon" eyes and her hair looked like she'd combed it with a tree branch. After washing her face to remove the makeup and free her freckles, she applied cream and ran a brush through her red hair. The cut that had layers falling past her shoulders was good, the color—not so much.

She was finally warm thanks to Shane getting her home as fast as possible. Inviting him in was equal parts boldness and stupidity. Conventional-dating protocol dictated three dates before sleeping with someone. Between dinner at his place and tonight's walk in the snow, they were barely at one.

She had no illusions about a future with Shane Roarke because he'd been honest about his uncertain plans. Still, she wanted him. That was the downside of giving him a first kiss do-over. The touch of his lips, the feel of his hard body pressed against hers had just made her want him even more.

And that was the stupid part of giving in to her boldness. Her heart was telling her to slow down; her head was saying take me now.

There was very little danger of him doing that, she

thought, looking at her reflection. The old robe and Christmas pants would prove to the seduction police that she hadn't dressed to lure him to her bed.

"You're comfortable and homey, the complete opposite of a temptress," she said to herself. "Charming is debatable."

With a sigh she opened the door and joined him in the kitchen. "I see you found everything."

"Yes." He'd removed his coat and settled it on the standing rack by the front door. Now he was leaning against the counter with two steaming mugs beside him. His jeans were fashionably worn and fit his lean legs perfectly. The white cotton shirt fit his upper body in the most masculine way. But what hiked up her pulse was the amusement in his eyes as his gaze scanned her from head to toe. "Love the outfit."

Looking down she said, "I'll start a new fashion trend. Montana practical."

"I think you look pretty cute." He traced a finger across her cheek. "Love the freckles."

"Yeah." She wrinkled her nose distastefully. "Me, too."

"What's wrong with them?"

"When I was in grade school, the boys wanted to play connect the dots on my face. That got really old. The curse of a redhead."

"Your hair is beautiful and unique."

"I always wanted to be a blonde or brunette."

"Boring."

The simple, straightforward word warmed her the way fleece, thermal and terrycloth never could. "Still, there's something to be said for blending in. Being different made me a target of teasing."

"It's a well-known fact that boys are stupid."

"You'll get no argument from me." She raised her gaze to find him watching her and a sizzle of awareness sprinted down her spine. When he moved closer, her heart started to pound.

"But we get smarter." He cupped her face in his hands and slid his lips over her cheek, soft nibbling kisses that made drawing air into her lungs a challenge. "How's that for connecting the dots?"

"Great technique." Her voice was a breathless whisper and she felt his lips curve into a smile. The only thing that would make this better was his mouth on hers. "Definitely smarter."

"But wait. There's more," he said a little hoarsely.

Gianna pressed her palm to his chest and felt the heavy beat of his heart then shivered at the heat in his gaze. "More sounds good to me."

Strangely enough she didn't agonize over the right or wrong of this. It just was. She wanted him, wanted to give herself to him. No questions; no regrets.

She felt his hand loosen the belt of her robe and slide inside, cup her hip. The good thing about oversize clothing was how easily you could slip it off.

When their gazes locked, she saw invitation in the smoldering depths darkening his blue eyes. "Do you want to see the bedroom?"

"Only if you want to show it to me."

Her answer was to take his hand and lead him through the doorway. The light beside the bed was on, illuminating her simple, white chenille spread. Throw pillows in light pink and rose gave it color, but she threw them onto the floor. Shane was the only man she'd ever brought in here and he seemed to fill the room, complete it somehow.

Gianna folded down the bedspread and blanket, revealing her serviceable flannel sheets. "Not sexy, just practical for a Montana winter. Otherwise I scream like a woman when I go to bed."

One of his dark eyebrows rose as his mouth curved into a wicked grin. "There's nothing wrong with screaming like a woman."

"I agree—when it's not from cold sheets."

"I promise you won't be cold." He traced his index finger along her collarbone and proved the truth of those words.

Shards of heat burned through her, warming her everywhere. Her toes curled and she stepped out of her slippers. But she hadn't let him be the first man in this room just to be a passive participant. She tugged his shirt from the waistband of his jeans and started undoing its buttons. Then she pressed her palms to his bare chest, letting the dusting of hair scrape across her hands, the nerve endings in her fingers.

The moan that built inside her refused to stay contained and Shane took it from there. He shrugged out of his shirt, then took the hem of hers and lifted it over her head.

He cupped her bare breasts and brushed his thumbs over the soft skin. "Beautiful."

She put her hands over his knuckles and gently pressed, showing him without words how perfect it felt. His breathing increased and the harsh sound of it mingled with hers. The scent of him, the heat of his skin, the feel of his hands all capsized her senses and drowned her in need. She backed toward the mattress and tugged him with her. Then she pushed off her fleece Santa pants and toed off her socks. His eyes darkened with approval and the heat of desire.

Gianna sat on the bed and even though the flannel sheets were cold on her bare skin, there was no screaming. Just acute anticipation. She watched Shane unbuckle his belt and step out of his jeans, then pull a condom from his wallet and set it on the nightstand. She wasn't sure he could see it in her eyes, but she most definitely approved. His shoulders were wide, his belly flat, his legs muscular. He was fit and fine and—for tonight—hers.

She held out her arms and he came into them, pressing her back on the mattress. He kissed her deeply and she opened, letting him stroke the inside of her mouth. While he ravaged her there, he slid a hand down her waist and belly, then her inner thigh. The touch tapped into a mother lode of desire and she could hardly breathe.

"Oh, Shane, I want—"

"I know."

He reached for the condom and covered himself, then rolled over her, between her legs, taking most of his weight on his forearms. Slowly he entered, filling her fully, sweetly. Her hips arched upward, showing him, urging him.

She could hardly draw enough air into her lungs as he stroked in and out with exquisite care. Then he reached between their bodies and brushed his thumb over the bundle of nerve endings at the juncture of her thighs.

The touch pushed her over the edge where she shattered into a thousand pieces. Shane held her and crooned words that her pleasure-saturated mind couldn't comprehend but knew were just right.

As if he knew the perfect moment, he started to move again. His breathing grew more ragged until there was one final thrust and he went still, groaning out his own release. Like he'd done for her, she wrapped her arms around him and just held on.

"Gianna—" Her name was a caress riding on a satisfied sigh.

"For the record—" She kissed his chin and the sexy scruff scraped her passion swollen lips in the nicest possible way.

"Yes," he urged.

"Boys really do get smarter."

She felt the laugh vibrate through his chest where their bare skin touched. Ordinarily that would have made her smile, but she couldn't quite manage. Boys might be smarter, but girls were notorious for making stupid choices. She had the emotional scars to prove she'd made the same ones multiple times.

She just hoped this wasn't a different kind of mistake, the kind that would make her sorry in the morning.

Chapter Five

Shane woke when Gianna mumbled in her sleep and moved restlessly against him. They were spooning, a term he used in cooking but liked a whole lot better in this context. If finding out his biological father was a criminal in jail was the worst thing since coming to Thunder Canyon, this was the best. He nuzzled her silky red hair and grinned.

Light was just beginning to creep into the room around the edges of the white blinds over the window and the number on the clock by the bed made him groan. Because his business was primarily done in the evening, he always slept in. His day usually started much later than this, but he had to admit it had never started better.

Gianna stretched sleepily then went still after her legs brushed against his. Without looking over her shoulder she asked, "Shane?"

"You were expecting someone else?"

"No." She cuddled into him. "I was sure I'd dreamed last night."

"A nightmare?"

"Oh, please. It was wonderful and you're very aware of that. I refuse to feed your ego."

"Then how about feeding me some breakfast?"

"I'll try. After I throw on some clothes. Meet you in the kitchen. Five minutes. I get the bathroom first."

Before he could ask a question or form any sort of protest, she'd thrown back the covers and raced from the bed. While waiting his turn, Shane thought about the situation. Sex was a very efficient recipe for stress relief and his body was really relaxed for the first time in longer than he could remember. That's not to say he hadn't been with women, but the vibe was different with Gianna.

Maybe it was more intense because their time together would be short. She wasn't staying and if information came out about who he really was, he wouldn't have to make a choice about his contract since it wouldn't be renewed. All he knew for sure was that as long as the two of them were in town, he wanted to see her.

Within the designated time frame, he joined her in the kitchen. She was wearing the same fleece pants, thermal top and robe from last night, which was both good and bad. She looked every bit as cute and he wanted to take the clothes off her again.

"Coffee?" She stood in front of the machine on the counter and glanced over her shoulder. When she met his gaze, a lovely blush stole over her cheeks as if she knew what he'd been thinking.

"I'd love it," he said.

"Coming right up." She added water, then put a filter and grounds in the appropriate place before pushing the start button.

"What did you mean about trying to feed me breakfast?"

"I'm not sure what I've got to cook," she explained.

"Let me have a look."

"Be my guest." She laughed. "Oh. Wait. You are my guest. And I'm the worst hostess on the planet if I let you do the cooking. There just may not be much in the refrigerator."

He slid her a wry look. "I won a reality cooking show by whipping up a gourmet meal with jelly beans, popcorn, granola, shrimp and instant mashed potatoes."

"Let me just say—eww." She folded her arms over her chest. "But far be it from me to stand in your way. Go to it, chef boy."

He lifted one eyebrow. "You do remember I'm the boss?"

"Not right now, you're not," she shot back. "At this moment you're my—guy in the kitchen."

"Good to know. Let's see what guy-in-the-kitchen has to work with."

The contents of her pantry and refrigerator were limited. It was the female equivalent of a bachelor's. Half a bottle of white wine. He grabbed the open milk container and took a sniff that told him it was still good. Individually wrapped slices of cheese. A couple of limp celery stalks and a few green onions. There was a loaf of bread touting fiber, low calories and weight control. Thank God she had half a dozen eggs.

He pulled the ingredients out and set to work with the cutting board, frying pan and a silent, solemn promise to equip her kitchen better. Starting with a decent set of knives.

He held up an old, dull one. "This is where it all starts. I recommend high carbon, stainless steel. It's the best of both worlds. Carbon is tough and has a great edge. Stainless steel keeps it from rusting and taking care of it is a lot less effort."

"Good to know. Can I do anything besides an emergency run to the kitchen gadget store?" she asked.

"Set the table and stay back."

Not that he couldn't work with her underfoot. The Gallatin Room kitchen was always swarming with people, a well-choreographed cauldron of activity, but experience had taught him how to tune everything out. He'd only ever been unsuccessful at doing that when Gianna was around.

He glanced at her in that oddly sexy oversize robe and felt his blood heat like butter in a frying pan. Now that he'd explored the curves under her quirky outfit, if she got any closer to him, resisting her would annihilate his concentration.

Fifteen minutes later they sat at her dinette just big enough for two and ate toast, cheese omelets and coffee. Gianna took a bite and made a sexy little sound of appreciation, not unlike something he'd coaxed from her in bed.

"This is so good, Shane."

"You sound surprised."

"Not at you. Just that it was possible from my survival rations." She chewed another bite. "Mmm. I can only imagine what you could whip up after a trip to the market."

Which reminded him… The reason they were here and not at his place was because she had an early day.

"So, you're up before God," he said. "What's on your agenda today?"

"I have to start my Christmas shopping."

"Really? By yourself?"

"Unlike the great and powerful Shane Roarke I don't have minions to do it for me."

"That's a shame."

"No kidding."

"Want some help?" He wasn't a fan of shopping but he was becoming a fan of Gianna's. He wanted to hang out with her even if that involved poking through stores and carrying bags. "I could be your minion."

"Singular?" Her auburn eyebrow lifted slightly. "By definition doesn't minion mean more than one?"

"How about if I chauffeur? Then it would be me and the car."

"Oh, gosh, I forgot. What with us— After we— Well, you know." She looked at him, blushing like crazy. "My car died last night."

He'd never heard sex described as us, we and you know, but definitely understood how it could push everything else from one's mind.

"Since you don't have wheels, that's even more reason to let me come along. I'll make a phone call and have the local garage bring your car back from the dead while you take care of Christmas." Sipping coffee, he watched her mull it over. "Gianna?"

"Hmm?"

"Don't think it to death. Just say yes. It's a good offer."

"It's an outstanding offer and I'd be all kinds of crazy to turn it down. Thank you, Shane." She stood and leaned over the small table to kiss his cheek. "My hero."

Right now, maybe. For as long as she didn't know the identity of his father. And there was no reason she should, even if he actually found out who his mother was. Right now all he knew was her first name. Grace.

A problem for another day. At this moment Gianna was looking at him as if he had wings and a halo. It felt really good and he didn't want that to change. Keeping his secret was the best way to do that.

Gianna was rocking a pretty awesome post-sex, post-breakfast glow while she waited for Shane to pick her up. She was scouting out Real Vintage Cowboy, the shop below her apartment, which was where they'd agreed to meet after he went home to shower and change.

There was a Christmas tree in the window decorated with ornaments made out of clothespins fashioned into reindeer, beads strung together into snowflakes, crystal dangles from old lamps and tin Santas and sleighs. Meandering the main aisle, she admired a saddle lovingly repaired and polished, a turn-of-the-century, repainted Singer sewing machine and a milk can holding a lamp as an example of how it could be used as an end table.

Everything looked beautiful to her this morning. She was happy. Being with Shane was magic and something about eating breakfast together was more intimate than sex. Her world was bright with possibilities and she believed with every fiber of her being that it really was the most wonderful time of the year.

Catherine Clifton Overton was standing by the far wall, near the cash register. She saw Gianna and smiled. "Hey, tenant."

"Merry Christmas, landlady."

The woman she paid her rent to was a willowy brunette with the warmest, darkest chocolate-colored eyes Gianna had ever seen. She was wearing a turtleneck top that came down over her hips and a coordinating gauzy skirt that skimmed the top of her signature cowboy boots. A leather belt cinched her small waist and pulled the whole outfit together perfectly.

Gianna's style leaned more to black-black jeans, gray sweater, black boots, leftovers from her days in New York. Compared to her landlady she felt as if she was on the fashion police's most wanted list.

"So how's married life?" she asked.

"Absolutely perfect." Catherine had a dreamy expression

on her face as she glanced at the wedding and engagement rings on her left hand. "Cody makes me so happy."

"You're a lucky woman. I envy you." Gianna figured if she couldn't stop the stab of jealousy, it was best to be up-front about it. "He's a great guy."

At this point in her life she'd expected to have what Catherine did—a growing business and marriage to the man of her dreams. She was a failure on both counts. As she saw it, the lesson was to not have expectations. Take it one day at a time. And today she was going to be happy.

Just then the bell over the front door rang and in walked Shane Roarke.

"Speaking of great guys..." Catherine arched an eyebrow. "I wonder what he's looking for this time."

"He told me about checking out your store." Gianna waved at him and he started toward her across the long room.

The other woman lowered her voice. "He was browsing and we ended up talking. He had a lot of questions about Arthur Swinton and the last owner of this place."

"Jasper Fowler?" Gianna had heard about the crazy old man who had conspired with Swinton to steal money and ruin the Traub family. The two were currently in jail.

Catherine whispered. "Vintage items all have a story. Shane just might be a man who appreciates that."

That implied he had a story, but Gianna was more interested in admiring the man. More caught up in the way her heart skipped and her breath caught at the sight of him. The broad shoulders and long legs wrapped in designer jeans would make it easy to mistake him for a cowboy. This was Montana after all, a little off the beaten path for a celebrity chef.

He walked up beside her and smiled at Catherine. "Nice to see you again."

"Same here. Can I help you find something?"

"I just did."

Gianna shivered at the sparkle in his eyes when she met his gaze. "My car is being uncooperative, as usual. Shane volunteered to take me Christmas shopping."

"Really?" Catherine looked impressed. And curious. What woman wouldn't be? "Most guys would rather take a sharp stick in the eye."

"I guess I'm not most guys." He grinned at them.

"My husband could take lessons from you."

"Didn't you just tell me he's perfect?" Gianna said.

"In most ways," the other woman agreed. "But, like the average man, he's a little shopping-challenged."

"I never said I'd be good at it," Shane corrected. "Just promised to do the driving."

Catherine tapped her lip as she studied him. "Do you give cooking lessons? Maybe I could persuade you to teach my husband a couple easy recipes."

"I'm happy to help out." He looked at Gianna. "Speaking of helping, I made a phone call. The garage is working on fixing your car as we speak and it will be delivered back here today. They're going to leave the keys with you, Catherine, if we're not back. Is that okay?"

"Of course. And in the spirit of good deeds—" she looked from him to Gianna "—do you know about Presents for Patriots?"

"I've already signed up to volunteer," Gianna answered, knowing what was coming. "Most of The Gallatin Room employees have."

"I haven't heard about this," Shane said.

"That's because you're not an employee," she shot back. "You're the boss."

"What is it?"

"Last year," Catherine said, "people in town got together

and wrapped donated gifts for military personnel serving overseas who couldn't get home for Christmas."

Shane nodded approvingly. "Sounds like a terrific event."

"You should come by if you're not too busy," the other woman suggested.

"I will. Where?"

"The Rib Shack. It's D. J. Traub's pet project." Maybe it was from working around things that all had a story, but Catherine warmed to telling one. "His mother, Grace, died when he was just a boy and he had difficulty connecting with his dad. They reconciled before Doug Traub died, but because of what he went through, family is very important to him."

"Okay."

It was one word, but Gianna heard something in Shane's voice and looked at him. His easygoing, relaxed manner had disappeared and there was tension in his jaw.

Catherine didn't seem to notice. "D.J. feels that we're all part of the American family and the military fights to preserve that for us. Presents for Patriots is his way of giving back to them for all they do."

"A worthy cause." Shane looked down at her. "Are you ready to go?"

"Actually, yes. There's a lot to do and a limited amount of time to do it in. Yesterday I made a date to meet my mother and sister for a late lunch. You're welcome to join us if you have time."

"Then we should get started." Shane didn't accept or decline, but put his hand on her lower back, a courtly gesture except she could feel him urging her to leave. "Have a good day, Catherine."

"You, too." She smiled. "Or just grit your teeth and get through it."

As they headed for the door Gianna didn't feel ready

for this expedition at all. It was possible she'd imagined the shift in Shane's mood, but not likely. The contrast was too stark. He'd arrived and was his usual friendly, charming self. When the subject of volunteering came up, he'd turned dark and broody. What was up with that?

Envying Catherine Overton hadn't punctured her happy balloon, but an "aha" moment did the trick. She'd slept with this man less than twelve hours before but still didn't really know very much about him.

Shane's SUV was at the curb in front of Real Vintage Cowboy and he held the door open for her. She could feel his body language change as soon as they walked outside. He was more relaxed, which made her think whatever had brought on the mood was somehow connected to Catherine or the store. Gianna slid into the car and couldn't contain a small sigh of pleasure as her body connected with the butter-soft leather.

When he was in the driver's seat, engine on and purring, Shane said, "Where to?"

Gianna returned his smile and pulled the list out of her purse. "Mountain Bluebell Bakery. It's at the corner of Nugget and Main in Old Town. Just east of the Tottering Teapot and ROOTS."

"Got it."

He put the car in gear, then glanced over his left shoulder before easing out into the stream of light traffic. Only the drifts of snow still in the shade were evidence of last night's storm. The street was clear, the sky was blue and the bad vibe was behind them.

"So, on this shopping expedition, I'm surprised the Bakery is the first stop. You've got a sweet tooth all of a sudden? Need an energy boost so you can shop till you drop? Or is there something I need to know?"

"Only that you should be warned. This will probably be

the easiest shopping of the day. I'm ordering something to send to a friend in New York."

"Male or female?" he asked.

"What?" She looked at him, the chiseled profile that made her want to touch his face.

"Your friend in New York. Man or woman?"

His tone was just a little too casual and that made her happy. "Before I answer that, I have a question."

"Okay."

"Are you jealous?"

He glanced at her and before returning his gaze to the road, his eyes burned bright and hot. "No. Just making conversation."

She was pretty sure that was a lie and a little ball of pleasure bumped against her heart. "Then, in the spirit of conversation…my friend is a woman. Hannah Cummings. We were roommates before I moved back to Thunder Canyon. I'm trying to talk her into coming for a visit."

"Will you be here that long?"

"My plans are still up in the air." That was true. She still hadn't fine-tuned her Plan B. Before he could question her more, the bakery came into view. "There it is. Looks like there's a parking place out front."

"I see it."

"That's really lucky. Lizzie Traub opened it about a year ago and this place is always busy." She chattered away. "She got some great publicity when the former owner, who was going to make Corey and Erin Traub's wedding cake, closed the place and left town with people's deposits. Lizzie made their cake and saved the wedding day."

"Is Corey related to D.J.?"

"They're cousins," she answered. "Lizzie and Ethan weren't married then. She was his administrative assistant and relocated to Thunder Canyon from Midland, Texas. Her family's bakery was a landmark there for years until her father lost money and the bank repossessed it."

"How do you know all this?" There was no teasing in his voice, just awe. "Weren't you living in New York?"

She didn't like reminders of her failed life. "My mother and sister live here. They talk to me."

"I'll keep that in mind," he said, pulling to a stop in front of the shop.

They got out of the car, walked inside and were immediately surrounded by the sweet smells of chocolate and icing. Gianna could almost feel her pores absorbing the sugar and calories and couldn't find the will to care. Her mouth was watering and she wasn't even hungry.

One glass case was filled with muffins—blueberry, pumpkin spice, banana nut, chocolate chip and more. Another display had old-fashioned donuts and buttermilk bars. Yet another showed cupcakes and specialty cakes and a book filled with pictures from various events handled by Mountain Bluebell Bakery.

A tall, beautiful woman in her twenties with gray-green eyes and dark blond hair walked out of the back room. "Hi. I'm Lizzie Traub."

"Nice to meet you. Gianna Garrison," she said and held out her hand. "And this is Shane Roarke."

"The chef at The Gallatin Room. I never missed your show—*If You Can't Stand the Heat*. You really smoked the competition. Pun intended." Lizzie smiled.

"Thanks." He grinned at her, then looked around at the bakery's interior. "I defy anyone to be gloomy in here."

"I like bright colors and since I spend a lot of time working, it seemed wise."

The shop was cheerful and bright with signs advertising Wi-Fi and tables scattered over the floor. It was the kind of place where someone could come for an espresso and muffin, set up a laptop and stay for a while. There were café lights with blown glass shades swirling with orange, yellow and blue, a sampling of the color scheme. Three walls were painted a sunny yellow and the long one behind the counter was a rich, deep burnt umber. At waist level along each wall flowed an endless chain of mountain bluebells.

"I love what you've done with the place. I hear the guy who used to own it wasn't nice, not a bluebells-on-the-walls type," Gianna commented.

"Tell me about it." Lizzie looked at the flowers. "My friend Allaire Traub hand stenciled all of that. She's so talented and great with kids. She teaches art at the high school."

"You could hate someone like that if they weren't so nice," Gianna said.

"I know, right?" Lizzie looked from one to the other. "Can I help you with something?"

"My sister highly recommended you. Jackie Blake?"

"Right." Lizzie nodded. "Three kids—Griffin, Colin and Emily. All chocolate connoisseurs, although they love the Mountain Bluebell muffins, too."

"That sounds like my niece and nephews."

"Adorable children." She smiled at Shane, then said, "But I have to say that I'm feeling some pressure. Your Gallatin Room desserts are legendary."

He smiled. "I fill a completely different business niche. And from what I see, your product is amazing."

"Thanks." She looked at each of them. "So, what can I help you with?"

"I understand that you ship orders?"

Lizzie nodded. "Anything over fifty dollars is no charge for shipping and handling. And I guarantee it will get there fresh."

"That sounds perfect."

"Did you want to sample something?"

"More than you can possibly imagine, but I already know what I want." She pointed into the display case. "Red velvet cupcakes."

"For Christmas, I assume?" At her nod, Lizzie continued. "Maybe a reindeer or Santa on the icing? Like the ones in the case."

Gianna bent to look. "Very festive. Sold."

"Wow." Shane looked impressed. "A woman who knows her mind."

It took a few minutes to fill out an order form with her choice, the quantity and the address in New York. When there was a total, Gianna handed over her credit card, then signed the receipt.

"Thanks, Lizzie. That was quick and I'm crunched for time."

"You made it easy."

Shane laughed. "She told me this would be the easiest errand of the day."

"I'm glad she was right. Come back again."

"Definitely."

They walked back outside and Gianna pulled her list out of her purse, then checked off the first item. "That's one down. Now there's my mom and dad. Jackie and her husband and my nephews and niece. A little something for Bonnie. I'm thinking maybe the mall would be good, going for a variety of stores rather than a lot of separate stops. But I'm feeling a little guilty about monopolizing your time."

"You shouldn't," he said. "I don't mind."

"Do you need to do some shopping for your family?" She looked up at his dark aviator sunglasses that hid his eyes. It occurred to her again that she knew very little about him. He'd never said much about himself. "I'm assuming you weren't raised by wolves."

"My mom and dad live in Los Angeles."

"Any siblings?" she asked, noting the dark change in tone and the way his mouth tightened.

"A sister and brother." He started to take her elbow and lead her to the car. "Next stop New Town Mall."

There was something going on with him. That was twice in less than an hour that he'd gone weird on her. If there was a problem she needed to know now. Relationships that had gone on too long had taught her not to ignore signs of trouble.

She dug in her heels. "Wait, Shane."

"What's wrong?"

"That's what I want to know." She looked up at him, took a deep breath and said, "I know you're struggling with something today. What's going on? Is it us? Are you sorry about last night?"

Chapter Six

"God, no."

Shane was sorry about a lot of things and right at the top of the list was the man who'd fathered him. But he would never in a million years regret being with Gianna. It was wonderful. She was amazing.

Standing on the sidewalk outside the Mountain Bluebell Bakery he looked into her eyes. "Last night was the best. And now who's feeding whose ego—"

She smiled as intended, but there was still concern in her beautiful turquoisey eyes. "Then what is it?"

He really thought he'd done a pretty good job of hiding his feelings. First when Catherine Overton had mentioned D. J. Traub's mother. It was the first time he'd heard her name. Grace was his birth mother's name, too. And just now when Gianna had asked him about his family, he was reminded that he was here in Thunder Canyon to dig up information about who he was. That thought was quickly followed by a whole lot of guilt.

One thing he wasn't: a poker player. He'd taken risks—on the reality show that launched his career and in business, opening restaurants. But that was different from playing a game. He didn't know if he could bluff, but this was as good a time as any to find out.

"You can talk to me, Shane." Her gaze searched his and she must have seen something. "I'm going to get coffee from the bakery and we can sit on that bench in the sun."

He saw the one she meant, a wooden bench on the side of the bakery facing Nugget Way. "There's nothing to talk about. And that will cut into your shopping time."

"The mall can wait. Somehow it will get done. This is more important."

Shane had a feeling there wouldn't be any putting her off now. "I'll get the coffee."

"No. Let me. You make sure no one takes our seats." She put a reassuring hand on his arm before disappearing inside the shop.

As soon as he sat down by himself he missed her warm presence. His darkness was no match for all that bright red hair and innate sweetness. And now he was on the spot—the classic man in conflict. He didn't want to talk about what he was dealing with because not talking was the only way to keep his secret. But obviously it was affecting him since she'd noticed his mood shifts.

He felt like a disloyal, ungrateful jerk. Gavin and Christa Roarke had done nothing but love, nurture and encourage him. He couldn't imagine a better brother or sister than Ryan and Maggie. All of them had pushed him to do what he needed to and hoped he found peace of mind. Fat chance after hearing the name Grace. It was on his birth certificate, but so what? There were probably a lot of women in and around Thunder Canyon with that name, including D. J. Traub's mother.

Gianna appeared with "to-go" cups of coffee in her hands. She sat beside him and held one out. "Cream, no sugar."

"You remembered." From breakfast just a few hours ago. Seemed like forever.

"Of course I remembered. It's my job and the boss has mentioned that I'm pretty good at it."

"He's a guy who can spot talent when he sees it."

"Also a guy who tries to hide his feelings and can't." Her expression grew sympathetic and serious. "He's got something on his mind. I'd be happy to listen and help if I can."

Shane looked up and knew why Montana was called Big Sky country. It seemed bigger, bluer and more beautiful here in Thunder Canyon. The snow-capped mountains were towering and the scenery spectacular. But that wasn't all that made this a special spot.

He'd lived all over the country in some of the biggest and most sophisticated, cosmopolitan cities. As his name recognition grew and his career soared, he'd been asked to endorse worthy causes or donate large sums of money. But he'd never been invited to cook for military families or wrap presents to brighten Christmas for a lonely soldier overseas.

That had changed here; he was a part of this community. The people had a hands-on spirit of caring that he'd never experienced before and was grateful and humbled to be part of it now. He didn't want to do anything to put him on the outside again.

And then there was Gianna. He looked at her, the sun shining on the most beautiful hair he'd ever seen. He knew she was just as beautiful inside.

"Shane?"

Damned if he did; damned if he didn't. He'd start at the beginning and wing it. "I'm adopted."

"Okay." Her expression didn't change. "The last time I checked, that wasn't a crime."

If she only knew how close that comment came to the truth.

"No, I'm aware that my story isn't one that makes a prime-time, news-magazine segment. It was too normal."

"How do you mean?" She took a sip of her coffee and angled her body toward him, listening with intense concentration.

"My parents are, quite simply, remarkable people. They're both lawyers."

"Pretty demanding careers. And yet a child was so important to them, they moved heaven and earth to have you in their lives."

"They chose me." It's what he'd always been told and a part of him had always felt special. Not anymore. "And not just me. They adopted my brother and sister—Ryan and Maggie. Also lawyers like our folks."

One of her auburn eyebrows went up. "High achievers. I realize we're not talking genes and DNA here, but how did your parents feel about your career choice?"

He smiled. "The three Roarke kids were encouraged to study what they loved and follow their passion."

"Good advice and it seems to have worked out for all of you," she commented.

"Professionally. But personally?" He shook his head.

"How do you mean? Do you have multiple wives and families stashed in cities and towns all over the country?"

"Yeah." He grinned. "Because I have so much time to pull that off. Can't you see the tabloid headline? Celebrity chef cooks up dual life."

She smiled. "So, what is it?"

"I was restless. Moved around a lot opening restaurants in Los Angeles, New York and Seattle. When I started talking about Dallas, my mother was worried."

"Why?"

"She felt I was deliberately or subconsciously avoiding settling down. And maybe I needed to look at who I was. That's when she finally gave me all the information she'd received about my birth parents from the adoption agency."

"That's incredibly courageous of her."

"No kidding." He remembered his mother's face, hesitation and concern battling it out. "She told me to use it however I wanted. Do whatever was necessary to find peace and put down roots."

"And?"

"I realized that as happy and loving as my childhood was, I'd always had questions about why I am the way I am. I wanted to connect the dots."

"What did you do?" she asked.

"Hired a private investigator."

Her eyes widened and comprehension dawned. "Is that why you took the job at The Gallatin Room here in Thunder Canyon?"

"What makes you say that?"

"You said it yourself—successful restaurants all over the country. Executive chef is a prestigious position, but this isn't Paris, New York or San Francisco. At best, it's a lateral career step. You had other reasons for taking this job."

Smart girl. He'd have to tread carefully. "Yes. The investigation and search narrowed to this town, so I contacted Grant Clifton."

"The manager of Thunder Canyon Resort."

"Right. When the previous chef's contract was up, I let Grant know I'd be interested. He jumped at the chance."

"Didn't he wonder why? A famous guy like you coming here?"

"The subject came up. I just said I'd been going at warp speed for years and wanted to throttle back for a while."

"Obviously he believed you."

"Because it was true." Shane just hadn't realized until he'd said it to Grant. And talking about it out loud now made the whole thing seem underhanded. Fruit doesn't fall far from the tree, he thought. Still, it was a good thing he'd gone about this quietly, otherwise everyone would know about his biological connection to Arthur Swinton. "But I also had personal reasons."

"To find your parents," she said. "Any luck with that since you've been here?"

He leaned forward, elbows on his knees. He didn't want her to read his expression. "Recently I found some information about my father."

"Oh, Shane—" She put her hand on his arm. "That's great. Do you know who he is?"

"Yes."

"Have you contacted him?"

"No." He laughed and heard the bitterness in the sound but hoped she didn't.

"Is he still alive?"

"Yes." And in jail. That part was best kept to himself.

"You need to talk to him."

"Not sure that's the wisest course of action."

"But it's why you started down this road in the first place." Her voice gentled when she said, "Are you worried that he'll reject you?"

That was the least of his concerns. Shane didn't want to risk *everyone else* rejecting him. The people in this town hated Arthur Swinton with the same passion that they loved being good neighbors. There was every reason to believe they would despise anyone related to their homegrown felon.

He finally met Gianna's gaze and saw the sincere desire to help shining there. She was easy to talk to, a good listener. A good friend. Maybe more than that. He didn't want to lose her by revealing what he suspected. He'd probably said too much already.

"It's complicated, Gianna."

"Of course it is. But, Shane, you're clearly not at peace the way things stand. Wouldn't it be better to get everything out in the open?"

That's what he'd thought before finding out his father was a criminal. "I'm not sure what to do with the information."

The sounds of laughter, women's and children's voices drifted to him just before he saw a large group of people round the corner. He glanced that way and the first person he recognized was D. J. Traub. They both worked at Thunder Canyon Resort restaurants so their paths crossed occasionally. They'd talked a few times.

And they both had mothers named Grace.

Gianna saw the exact moment when Shane's expression changed and he got that weird look on his face again. Before she had time to wonder what put it there, the two of them were surrounded by a big group of Traubs, Dax, D.J., their wives and three kids between them. Everyone was saying hello at once. Everyone, that is, but Shane, who stood a little apart. It was impossible to grow up in this town and not know these guys. Since she wasn't sure who Shane had met, she decided to make introductions.

"Shane Roarke, this is Dax Traub and his wife, Shandie."

"Nice to see you." Dax extended his hand.

He was a year older than his brother with dark hair and eyes, a brooding, James Dean type who oozed sex appeal.

His wife was tall, with shoulder-length blond hair cut into perfect layers.

"Dax owns a motorcycle shop here in town and Shandie works at the Clip 'n Curl," she explained.

"Nice to meet you," Shane said, cool and polite. He looked down when a little bundle of energy tripped over his shoe and nearly took a header. "Hey, buddy. You okay?"

Shandie steadied the little boy. "This is Max. Say hello to Mr. Roarke."

"Hi." The little guy had his father's dark hair and eyes. As soon as he dutifully said what was expected, he took off running down the sidewalk again.

Shandie called after him, "Slow down, Max."

Dax tugged on a young blond girl's pony tail. "This is our daughter, Kayla."

"Nice to meet you," the child said.

"The pleasure is mine, Kayla." Shane leveled all the considerable Roarke charm on her and a becoming pink stole into her cheeks.

"Sorry to be rude," a concerned Shandie said. "But I have to catch up with my son, the budding Olympic sprinter, and keep him out of trouble."

"I'll give you a hand, honey." Dax looked at Shane. "I'm sure we'll run into you again soon."

"We'll catch up with you, bro," D.J. said.

He was an inch or two shorter than his brother and not as dark. His brown hair had strands of sunlight running through it and his eyes were more chocolate than coal colored. "Shane and I have met, but I don't think you know my wife, Allaire."

The pretty, petite, blue-eyed blonde smiled. She had her hand on the shoulder of their little guy, who was quivering with the need to follow the other family and be with the kids.

"And this is our son, Alex." The proud mother smiled as she ruffled hair the same color as his father's.

"I'm four," the boy said. "Just like Max. People say I look big for four."

"I thought you were at least five and a half," Shane said seriously.

"There are days he makes me feel twice my age." D.J. shook his head.

"Mommy? Daddy? Can I go with Uncle Dax and Aunt Shandie?"

Allaire glanced up the street to the group gathered in front of a gift-shop window. "If you hurry."

"I'll run fast, like I'm already five." And he did.

"Dax?" D.J. called out and when his brother glanced over, he pointed to the boy running toward them. There was a nod of understanding and he settled a big hand on the small shoulder when Alex caught up and joined the merry little band.

Gianna glanced between them. "Is that a brother thing? Silent communication? Because my sister and I don't have that."

"Maybe because you're in different places in your lives," Allaire suggested. "Dax and D.J. both have four-year-olds and a protective streak as big as Montana."

Gianna knew it was a nice way of saying her sister Jackie was married with three kids. And she, Gianna, was a spinster with no prospects. Time to change the subject.

"So, Allaire, Lizzie was just singing your artistic praises. She said you hand-stenciled the flowers on the walls of her bakery."

"I did." The other woman smiled with pleasure.

"Beautiful job," Shane said. "I understand you're a high school art teacher."

"Yes. I wasn't cut out to be a starving artist." She looked

up at her husband. "And I'm not. Thanks to D.J.'s Rib Shack and my teaching job."

"What else do you like to work on?" Shane asked.

Gianna thought it was interesting that he was chatting up Allaire and hadn't said much to her husband. Probably the art connection. He had an interest in it judging by the collection she'd seen in his condo. The four of them moved closer to the building to let a mother with a baby in a stroller get by them on the sidewalk. The movement put Shane beside the other man.

"I really like portraits," Allaire answered. "But just for fun. I'm not very good at it. But it lets me indulge my people-watching tendency."

"She's way too modest about her amazing talent." D.J. slid an arm across her shoulders and looked at Shane. "So, how do you like Thunder Canyon?"

"Fine."

Along with the other couple, Gianna waited for him to elaborate. When he didn't, she put a teasing tone in her voice when she asked, "What happened to the poetic guy who said the scenery around here speaks to your soul?"

"If I was Shane," D.J. said with a knowing expression, "I'd never admit to that, either."

Gianna looked at Allaire and together they said, "Guy thing."

"Speaking of guys..." D.J. met her gaze, then glanced at her companion. "How's everything?"

Gianna knew he meant her love life. She'd gotten to know him since coming back to town. She'd applied for a job at the Rib Shack and he wasn't hiring, but steered her to The Gallatin Room. Then he'd taken her under his wing and become the big brother she'd always wanted.

"D.J." Allaire's voice had a scolding note to it. "Don't put her on the spot right now."

"Why?" His expression was clueless. "We talk."

"We do," she confirmed. "And I can tell you that everything is…" She'd ended up confessing to him her pathetic love life and all the time and energy she'd wasted in New York. D.J. wanted to know what was up with Shane and she wasn't going to talk about that in front of him. So she resorted to a girl's succinct fallback response. "Fine."

"You know…" Allaire glanced back and forth between the two men.

"What?" Gianna wasn't sure what was on her mind, but encouraged a change of subject.

"Speaking of people watching to indulge my artistic streak," the other woman said, "I've just noticed something."

"That I'm better looking than Ryan Reynolds?" D.J. said.

"No." She playfully punched him in the arm. "There's a very strong resemblance between you and Shane."

"Really?" Gianna studied them.

"Not the eyes." The other woman thoughtfully tapped her lip. "D.J.'s are brown and Shane's are strikingly blue. But the shape of the face is identical. And you both have a strong chin. So does Dax."

Gianna looked carefully at the two men standing side by side and saw what Allaire meant. She wondered why she'd never noticed before. Probably because she'd never seen them in the same room together, let alone side by side.

"You're right. I see it, too."

"They say everyone has a twin." D.J. pointed playfully at Shane. "Just don't pretend to be me and go changing the Rib Shack menu to snails and frog's legs."

Gianna snapped her fingers. "And you both make a living in the restaurant business. What a coincidence."

That's when she noticed Shane's weird look was back and even more intense. Not only that, he hadn't said a word since Allaire mentioned the strong resemblance. The face might resemble D.J.'s but it was not the face of the charm-ing, playful man who'd said her fleecy pants and ratty robe were cute. Was that only last night? Seemed so much longer.

Even this morning at breakfast he'd been carefree and gallant, offering to drive her wherever she wanted to go. His mood had changed when Catherine had mentioned Presents for Patriots. Then again when Gianna had asked him about shopping for his family. That led to the revelation about him being adopted and searching for his birth parents.

He took her arm. "We should probably get to the mall."

"That's where we're going," Allaire said.

D.J. looked down at his wife. "We should meet them for lunch. You can compare the shape of Dax's face to mine and Shane's."

"I wish I could. I already have lunch plans with my mother and sister. But maybe Shane—" She'd invited him to join her but he hadn't responded one way or the other. Now Gianna felt his hand tense. Even if she were free, it was clear he'd rather eat bugs than join them.

"I can't," he said. "I have a meeting with a vendor this afternoon."

"Too bad." The other woman slid her hand into her hus-band's.

"How about a rain check?" D.J. suggested.

"That would be great." Gianna figured like a typical man he hadn't noticed that Shane was quiet. But she'd bet every-thing she had that observant Allaire had sensed something. "See you guys soon."

"You're coming to Presents for Patriots?" D.J. asked.

"Wouldn't miss it. I'm all signed up," she said, but Shane remained quiet.

"Okay, then. Bye, you two," Allaire said before they strolled down the street in the same direction the rest of the family had gone.

Shane walked her to his SUV parked in front of the bakery and handed her inside. Then he came around to the driver's side and got in. "Do you still want to go to the mall?"

His tone said he hoped to get a rain check on that, too, and suddenly she lost the Christmas spirit.

"Shane, talk to me. What's bothering you so much?"

"I already told you. Just some family stuff."

"Come on. I'm not artistic like Allaire, but I observe people, too. I'd make a lousy waitress if I didn't notice things. You barely said a word to D.J. That's not like you. You're probably one of the friendliest, most charming men I've ever met. So, I ask again. What's wrong? And don't tell me nothing."

His hand tensed on the steering wheel and a muscle in the jaw so much like D.J.'s jumped. "It's complicated."

So, back to square one. He'd shut her down again. It didn't take Cupid to clue her in that she was beating her head against the wall. By definition, romance required two people to participate in order to achieve the desired result. Clearly she was the only one here doing the work.

At least it hadn't taken her very long to figure out that he had no intention of committing. And really, it was almost funny given her history of hanging on until all hope was gone.

She'd just set a personal record in the least amount of time it took her to lose a guy.

Chapter Seven

After asking Shane to take her home, Gianna hadn't had much to say. That technically wasn't true. She'd actually had a lot to say but kept it to herself since it was impossible to have a meaningful conversation with an obviously preoccupied man who would only tell her "it's complicated." Still, when the man said he would do something, he did it.

At Real Vintage Cowboy, Catherine Overton had her car keys. Per Shane's instructions, the car had a new battery and they'd dropped it off for her. Note to self: find out the cost and pay him back. She didn't want to owe him. On the other hand, at least she now had wheels, such as they were.

She never made it to the mall, but managed to get in a little Christmas shopping before it was time to meet her mother and sister at The Tottering Teapot. The customer base was primarily female and the restaurant was located in Old Town on Main Street near Pine, between the teenage hangout ROOTS and Mountain Bluebell Bakery. Not far from this morning's disaster with Shane.

She drove around for a while looking for a parking space because, of course, she was running late. The place did a brisk business but seemed more crowded than usual today. A lot of people were probably out Christmas shopping and stopped for lunch.

Gianna finally found a spot to park that felt like a mile up the block, then nearly jogged all the way to the entrance where the double, half-glass doors were covered with lace. She pushed her way inside and immediately the sweet scent of lighted candles surrounded her. She knew the fragrance was called Mistletoe and that made her think of kissing Shane. Thinking of him was like a sudden pinch to her heart so she tried not to.

A podium just inside the door had a sign that said "Please wait to be seated" but the hostess must have been leading another party because no one was there. Peeking into the dining room, she spotted her mother and sister already at a table.

"Because, of course, they have well-ordered lives with men who probably confide in them," she muttered to herself.

Without waiting for the hostess, she walked halfway through the restaurant. In addition to the menu of organic food, free-range chicken and grass-fed beef, everything about the place was female friendly. The tables were covered with lace tablecloths, no two the same. Food was served on thrift-store-bought, mismatched china. In deference to its name, there was an endless variety of teas, both herbal and otherwise. Normally this was Gianna's favorite restaurant, and catching up with her mother and sister was something she looked forward to. But not today.

Because getting grilled like a free-range chicken was really unappealing, Gianna pasted an everything's-just-peachy smile on her face just before sliding into the third of four chairs. The other held purses.

"Hi. Sorry I'm late. Took a while to find a place to park."

"Oh, sweetheart, don't worry about it. We haven't been here very long," her mother said.

Susan Garrison was in her early fifties and was walking, talking proof that fifty was truly the new forty. She was blond, with some chemical help at the Clip 'n Curl to cover just a sprinkling of gray. Her beautiful blue eyes had been passed on to both of her daughters.

Her sister, Jackie Blake, was about Gianna's height and had a trim figure even after three kids, but she'd inherited their mom's blond hair. There was no obvious link from either parent to Gianna's red shade and the family joke was that her father was the mailman. No one believed that since her parents only had eyes for each other.

"It seems like forever since we've done this," her sister said.

"Everyone is busy," Susan commented.

"No kidding." Gianna looked at her sister. "What's up with the kids?"

"Griffin wants to play basketball, but isn't he too short? Colin is in preschool, as you know, but he thinks he's such a big boy. Can you believe Em is two already? She's home with Frank. He doesn't have a firefighter shift for a couple of days and said I could use the break."

The brunette, twentysomething waitress brought a tray containing a china teapot filled with hot water and three cups, each with a mismatched saucer. Her name tag said "Flo." "Peppermint tea for three."

"I hope that's okay, Gianna. It's what you usually have," her mother explained.

"It's fine, Mom."

With the plastic tray under her arm, Flo pulled out her pad. "Are you ready to order?"

"I think so. I'll have the portobello mushroom sandwich and salad," Jackie said.

"Me, too." Susan folded her menu closed.

Gianna hadn't had a chance to look, but knew the choices pretty well. She usually ordered exactly like the other two but after the morning she'd had, her rebellious streak kicked in for unknown reasons.

She looked at the waitress. "Grass-fed beef burger and sweet potato fries."

"The fries are a new addition to the menu. Really yummy," Flo added. "I'll get it right out for you."

When they were alone, Susan poured hot water from the teapot into their cups. "So, how's work? What's new?"

Gianna knew the question was for her. Jackie was a stay-at-home mom and couldn't be more different from herself. She'd never had career ambitions or wanted to leave home and see the world. She married her high-school sweetheart shortly after graduation and their first child was born nine months later. Frank Blake was a county firefighter and they'd been married seven years and had two more children.

Gianna had a failed business, no romantic prospects and a junker car. She didn't really want to talk about any of it. "Work is fine."

"That's it?" Jackie asked.

"Pretty much."

"I want to hear about celebrity chef Shane Roarke." Her mother's blue eyes twinkled. "I watched *If You Can't Stand the Heat.* He's a hottie and that has nothing to do with cooking over a steaming stove."

"Mom," Gianna scolded. "What would Dad say?"

It was a deflection because she really didn't think her

carefree act would hold up to scrutiny if she was forced to talk about her boss.

"Your father would say there's nothing wrong with looking as long as I come home to him."

"Frank would agree with that." Her sister looked thoughtful. "This isn't the first time I've noticed that he and Dad are a lot alike."

Susan took a cautious sip of the hot tea, then set the cup on the saucer. "They're both good men. Solid. Stable. Dependable. It's what eased my worries a little bit when you insisted on getting married so young."

"It all worked out for the best," Jackie said.

And then some. It was everything Gianna wanted. Up until this morning she'd been sure Shane was cut from the same cloth as the other two men, but now she didn't know what to think. His behavior had changed so suddenly. Where he was concerned, her emotions were all over the map. One minute she was angry, the next worried about whatever was so "complicated."

"Are you okay, honey?"

"Hmm?" Gianna had zoned out and it took a couple of seconds to realize her mother was speaking to her. "Sorry, Mom. I'm fine. Just tired."

"Any particular reason?"

"No. Just that time of the year when we're all busy."

It wouldn't do any good to tell them that she'd lost sleep because of playing in the snow last night with Shane, then he drove her home and made love to her. Her head was still spinning from the speed at which everything had changed.

She looked at her sister. "What's going on with you?"

"Things are good. The kids aren't sick and I hope we make it through the holidays with everyone healthy." She crossed her fingers for luck. "Griffin is in the Christmas pageant at his school. Colin's preschool is going to the hospital to sing carols for the patients. I'm the room mother in both of their classes and responsible for the holiday parties. I love doing it, but when Emily is old enough for school, I'm not sure how I can spread myself that thin."

"You need minions." Gianna remembered talking about that with Shane and wondered how long casual conversation would set off reminders of him.

"She has minions," Susan said. "It's called family."

Jackie snapped her fingers. "That reminds me."

"What?" Gianna and her mother said at the same time.

Her sister grabbed her purse from the chair and pulled something from the side pocket. It was an oblong-shaped piece of cardstock and she handed one to each of them. "This is the Blake family Christmas card."

Gianna's heart pinched again in a different way as she looked at her sister's beautiful family. Handsome dark-haired Frank with four-year-old Colin on his lap. Beautiful Jackie holding Emily. She was wearing a sweet little red-velvet dress, white leggings and black-patent shoes. Griffin, seven and a half, stood just behind his parents, little arms trying to reach around their shoulders.

"Oh, sis—" Gianna's voice caught. "This is a fantastic picture."

"It really is, honey." Susan smiled fondly.

"Thanks." Her sister beamed. "It's a Christmas miracle. You have no idea the level of difficulty there is in getting a decent photo of three kids and two adults. No one is crying and by that I mean Frank and I. There are no spots on the clothes—at least none that show up."

Gianna laughed in spite of the fact that she was simultaneously rocking a case of jealousy and feelings of failure. She loved her sister very much and was so happy for her. But the picture she held in her hands was everything she'd ever wanted and thought by now she would have. She was thirty years old and had nothing to show for it except a string of broken dreams and long, unsuccessful relationships.

She wasn't sure Shane could be considered a relationship, but he was definitely the shortest. So it didn't make sense that what happened with him hurt so much more than all the others.

And it was going to get worse. She had to see him at work in a couple of hours.

Shane paced back and forth in the living room of his condo but today the fantastic mountain view and heavenly blue sky did nothing to fill up his soul. On the other hand, his mind was overflowing, mostly about how rude he'd been to Gianna that morning.

"I'm an idiot." An idiot who was talking to himself. "At the very least she just thinks I'm nuts. It's complicated? How does that explain anything?"

His cell phone rang and he plucked it from the case on his belt then checked the caller ID because he didn't want to talk to anyone unless absolutely necessary. This person was most definitely necessary.

He smiled and hit the talk button. "Hi, Mom."

"Shane. Is it really you? Not your voice mail?"

"Okay. I officially feel guilty."

She laughed. "Is this a bad time? Are you working? I don't want to interrupt—"

"You're not interrupting anything." Except him beating himself up. He had a little time before work. And facing Gianna. "I'm at home."

"Great." Christa Roarke's voice suited her. She was strong, sweet, tough and tender. A green-eyed brunette whose face showed the traumas and triumphs of life but remained beautiful. She practiced family law and after struggling to have a family of her own, it seemed appropriate.

"Is Dad okay?" Gavin Roarke was the strongest man he knew, but Shane always needed to check.

"Fine. Why?"

"Ryan and Maggie?" His siblings, lawyers like their parents. He'd wondered more than once if that's part of what made him question who he was. Though they were all adopted, he was the only one who didn't follow in their parents' footsteps, but took a completely different career path. He couldn't remember when he'd seriously begun to wonder why.

"Your brother and sister are fine." There was humor in her voice. "But the focus of your questions leads me to believe you think I called because of a family crisis."

"Did you?"

"Everyone here in L.A. is fine."

"Good." That left him the only family member in a mess. "What can I do for you, Mom?"

"I just haven't talked to you for a while." There was a slight hesitation before she added, "That comment was in no way meant to make you feel guilty."

He laughed. "If you say so."

"Maybe because it's the holidays and you're so far away, I've just been thinking a lot about you. Wondering how you are."

He stood beside the floor-to-ceiling windows and leaned a shoulder against the wall as he looked out. His mother was as transparent as the glass. She knew why he'd come to Thunder Canyon and was fishing for information. "I'm okay."

There was silence on the other end of the line for a few moments before she asked, "That's it? Just okay?"

"Yeah."

"This is why you're not an attorney like the rest of the

Roarkes. Practicing law frequently requires the use of words and apparently that's not your strength."

He grinned. "I communicate through food."

"That's all well and good. The culinary world loves you. The camera loves you. And I love you. But it's a mother's job to encourage her child to use words."

"It's a dirty job, I guess, but someone has to do it."

"And you know what an overachiever I can be," she said.

"What is it you're asking, Mom?"

"You just love to torture me, don't you?" She sighed. "Okay. You asked for it. Here comes the maternal cross-examination."

"I can hardly wait." A rustling sound on the line made him picture her sitting up straight in the chair, probably behind the desk in her office.

"Mr. Roarke, you've lived in Thunder Canyon, Montana, for nearly six months now. How is it going?"

He thought about the question and knew she was asking how the search for his birth parents was progressing. When he'd first stepped foot in the town something clicked into place inside him and it seemed crazy at the time. But the more he learned, the longer he stayed, the less crazy that feeling felt. Still, he wasn't ready to tell his family what was going on. So much of it was conjecture. Getting into her milieu, he only had half the facts to build a case.

So, Shane decided to use his words to go in a different direction. "When I made the decision to come here, I braced myself for a wilderness adventure."

"Survivor Montana?" she teased.

"Something like that." He studied the jagged snow-capped peaks with evergreen trees standing out in stark relief against the whiteness. "You can research anything on the internet, but there's no way to experience a place until you do it in person."

"There's a reverence in your voice, as if you're in church."

"Someone else said the same thing to me," he answered, thinking of Gianna. "And it feels like being in the presence of God sometimes. You can't know unless you see."

"And what do you know now, Shane?"

"I like this place. More than I thought." He pretended she wasn't asking about his search. "Thunder Canyon is small. Really small compared to anywhere I've ever lived."

"That could be a double-edged sword."

"People talk." He knew that and what he'd uncovered could give them a lot to talk about. "Around here everyone knows your business even if you haven't shared it with them. But that can also be a good thing. When there's a problem, they don't look the other way. They don't avoid getting involved or feel inconvenienced. Folks help each other out."

"And you like that?"

"Let me put it this way," he said. "I've donated money to charity and felt good about it, but was never personally touched by the cause. But it's different here. There's no comparison, no way to describe how good it feels to use your talent to make a difference. To be included in a cause bigger than yourself."

"Such as?"

"Just before Thanksgiving I prepared a dinner for the families of military members serving overseas. You could see the gratitude in their eyes, Mom. It was a fantastic feeling."

"Sounds wonderful."

"Of course I didn't do it alone. The staff at The Gallatin Room pitched in. Gianna was pretty amazing."

"Gianna?"

"Gianna Garrison. She's one of the waitresses who volunteered her time to serve that dinner." He pictured the sassy redhead with the beautiful smile that warmed him in dark places he hadn't even been aware of. "She worked her tail off and I never once saw her anything but considerate. Always laughing."

"Is she pretty?"

"What does that have to do with anything?"

"Humor me." There was a tone that said resistance was futile.

"She's very attractive." Such plain words to describe someone so bright, so special. And before his mother asked, he added, "A blue-eyed redhead."

"Hmm."

He wished he could see her expression. "What does that mean?"

"Nothing. Go on."

"That's it. I was finished."

"Hardly." Along with sweet and strong, his mother's voice could also be sarcastic. "There's a lot more you're not saying."

Mental note, he thought. Never play poker with this woman. But he added something that was completely true and also too simple to explain what he felt. "I like her."

"That does it. I really want to meet the new woman in your life."

"That's not how it is." At least not after the way he'd acted this morning. He probably blew it big time.

He just hadn't been able to pull off a casual act after Catherine Overton mentioned D.J.'s mother's name was Grace. If their mothers sharing a first name was the only coincidence, he could have laughed it off. But then Allaire Traub commented on his resemblance to Dax and D.J. She'd stopped short of calling it a family resemblance, but...

He and D.J. both had the food-service industry in common and every time he'd seen the other man there'd been a feeling. A shared sense of humor. A connection that Shane couldn't explain. Because they were brothers?

It *was* complicated. If he'd told Gianna all of his suspicions, she'd think he was crazy and call the shrink squad. Shane had heard the rumors of Swinton's unrequited love for Grace Traub, but everyone laughed it off as the raving of a lunatic. What if that was true? What if Arthur Swinton had slept with Dax and D.J.'s mother and he, Shane, was the result?

"Shane?"

His mother's voice yanked him out of the dark turn his thoughts had taken. "Sorry. What did you say?"

"I asked how it is with you and Gianna?"

It was nowhere because he'd pushed her away. Even a bad shrink would say it was because he didn't want to see the look of disgust in her eyes when she learned who his father was. Why would she not believe that an evil man's son didn't have evil in his DNA?

"I consider her a friend," he finally said.

"Hostile witness."

"Really, Mom?" He had to smile. "Now you're going all lawyer on me?"

"That's what you do when a witness holds back." She sighed. "But, it's all right. You're entitled to your secrets."

That word grated on him. He was learning the hard way that secrets could corrode the soul. Should he come clean with Gianna, give her the explanation? Maybe stop the blackness inside him from spreading? The risk was that everyone in town would find out. But maybe if he asked her to keep it to herself, it might be possible to control the flow of information even in a small town.

When he didn't comment, his mother continued, "Another reason I called is…what are your plans for Christmas?"

"I hadn't really thought that far ahead." What with everything else on his mind.

"It's a couple of weeks, so not really that far ahead. Will we see you for the holidays?" Her voice was carefully casual, an indication that seeing him meant a lot.

The truth was he missed his family. He'd never not been there for Christmas. No matter where he worked his heart was with the Roarkes—his parents and his siblings. Nothing he found out would ever change that.

"Of course I'll be there."

"Wonderful." There was a subtle sound of relief in her voice. "We'll look forward to seeing you, sweetheart."

"Same here, Mom."

"Hold on." There were muffled voices in the background, then she came back on the line. "I'm sorry, Shane. My next appointment is here."

"No problem, Mom. I have to get to work."

"Love you, son."

"Love you, too."

He clicked off and thought about the conversation. It didn't escape his notice that he no longer thought of Los Angeles as home. Something twisted in his chest when he opened the French door and walked out on the balcony to look at the big sky and mountains. The cold snapped through him and sliced inside.

He wasn't at all sure he would survive Montana unscathed. This place had become home and Gianna had become more important than he'd intended. It was entirely possible that he could be more lost now than when he'd first arrived in Thunder Canyon.

Chapter Eight

At work Gianna looked over the empty dining room, searching for anything out of place. Silverware was wrapped in cloth napkins and ready in a corner, out of the view of customers. Fresh linens and flower vases were on the tables along with lighted candles. She'd done everything ahead of time that could possibly be done and not compromise the quality and freshness of food.

The service business was always a delicate balance, not unlike navigating a relationship. Never give anyone a reason not to come back, but if a mistake was made, do whatever was necessary to make things right.

With all the prep work done, this would be a good time to grab a quick bite to eat. At lunch with her mother and sister she'd lost her appetite, but was starving now. The rest of the staff had already finished their pre-service meal and were gearing up for a busy night. A local company was having their Christmas party in the banquet room.

In the kitchen there was food left from the staff meal. She was just taking a bite when Shane walked in. This was the first time she'd seen him alone since he'd dropped her off at her apartment this morning. Not that she'd done anything wrong, or that she wanted to give him a reason to come back, but speaking of making things right... They did have to work together, at least for the time being.

There was a nanosecond of awkwardness between them before she finally said, "Hi. How are you?"

"Keeping my head above water." He shrugged. "How's the car?"

"Not getting any younger and still holding together with bubble gum and prayer." That produced a smile, which was good to see. "But running now, thanks to you. I left a check for the battery on the desk in your office."

"You didn't have to. I was happy to take care of it. And I'll be tearing up that check." She opened her mouth to protest, but he held up his hand. "No argument. Just say thank you."

"All right. Thank you. I appreciate it very much."

"You're welcome." He hesitated a moment. "So you saw your mother and sister?"

"Yes."

He moved closer, leaned a hip against the counter beside her and crossed his arms over his chest. The spicy scent of his cologne burrowed inside her and pushed every nerve into a spasm of need. If she hadn't been with him skin to skin maybe she could fight off this overwhelming feeling, but that wasn't the case. She had slept with him and there was no way to unremember the practically perfect way his body had felt against hers.

"How was lunch?" His gaze settled on hers.

Why was he suddenly so chatty? She'd take it as a good thing if the shadows weren't still in his eyes, just the way he'd looked outside of Mountain Bluebell Bakery. But her questions, even though asked with the intention of helping, hadn't helped either one of them.

She ran a finger around the edge of her plate. "It's always good to catch up with Jackie and my mom. They're busy getting ready for Christmas. Making plans."

"Apparently this is the day for it." He rubbed a hand across the back of his neck.

"Oh?" She took a bite of her food, although her appetite was missing in action again.

"My mother called."

"How was it?" He'd already opened that door by asking her the same question.

"Before or after she let me know I don't phone home often enough?"

"I can see how that would lead directly into holiday plans," she agreed.

"It did. And I'm going to Los Angeles."

"You're leaving?"

"For Christmas," he confirmed.

Even she had heard the shock and hurt in her voice. If only she were a computer and could backspace and delete those two words. She had no claim on him. Yes, he'd taken her to bed and she'd gone enthusiastically. But there was no reason to think it was more than fun. They'd gone into it with the understanding that one or both of them would be leaving town. Nothing serious.

Except somewhere in her subconscious she must have been thinking about spending the holiday with him. Otherwise she wouldn't feel like the rug had been yanked out from under her because he wouldn't be here for Christmas. The depth of her disappointment was a surprise, a very unwelcome one.

"Gianna—" He cupped her cheek in his palm. "Please don't look like that."

Obviously she wasn't very successfully hiding her disappointment. "I'm not looking any way. Not on purpose. You just surprised me. It's your first Christmas in Thunder Canyon and the way you talked—" She'd assumed when a place filled up your soul, it's where you'd want to be at the most wonderful time of the year. Apparently his soul was taken and this was proof that she had no claim on his heart. "I understand. They're your family."

"They are. And I love them." His gaze searched hers and he let out a long breath. "Look, I feel like a jerk—"

"No. Please don't. Of course you should be with your family. I didn't mean anything. I'm fine."

"You are fine." For just an instant as he caressed her cheek with his thumb, heat burned in his eyes. Then it was gone and the shadows returned. "And I acted like an idiot earlier. You deserve an explanation."

"That's not necessary—"

"I know it's not, but I want to tell you. I need to talk about this with someone. It's eating me up inside." There was a dark and dangerous expression on his face. He took her hand and led her away from the noise and bustle of the kitchen, into the pantry where he'd kissed her. He didn't look like he planned to kiss her now.

So she was right to be concerned about him. "What is it, Shane? Of course you can talk to me. I'm happy to listen."

"You might change your mind when I tell you what's going on."

"Be a Band-Aid."

"What?"

"Do it quick. Just spit it out."

He hesitated for a moment, then said, "Arthur Swinton is my biological father."

Gianna couldn't believe she'd heard him correctly. "What?"

"The man who embezzled from the city, disappeared with the money and was behind all the bad stuff that happened to the Traub family is my father."

"You're joking."

"If I was going to joke, it wouldn't be about that." He dragged his fingers through his hair. "The way everyone in town feels about that weasel makes him the last man on the planet I'd claim for a father unless it was true."

She stared at him. "Are you sure about this?"

"I have a DNA test confirming it to a ninety-nine percent certainty."

Her brain was spinning. "But don't you need a sample from him? I thought he was in jail."

"He is." Shane's gaze slid away for a moment. "I told you my mother gave me all the information she had on my birth parents? She also told me the adoption records were sealed and she didn't know what good it would do."

"Right."

"The private investigator said with everything on computers, now no records can be completely sealed. Nothing is hack-proof. My biological mother's first name and the first initial of her last name are on the birth certificate. It only has my father's initials. The guy I hired found the hospital and narrowed the search to Thunder Canyon. After tightening the parameters of age, names with those initials, then cross-referencing employment and personal interests, which included political ambitions, one name stood out."

"Arthur Swinton was on the town council for years," she remembered.

"He ran for mayor against Bo Clifton on a family-values platform." Bitterness hardened his eyes. "How hypocritical is that? Add being a fraud of a human being to his long list of sins."

Gianna was in shock. "I was in New York when that happened, but my mom told me what was going on. How did you get the DNA?"

"The P.I. visited him in jail. He made up something about being a journalist and doing a story on Thunder Canyon politicians. Swinton was only too happy to talk about how he was a victim of the Traubs. That they always hated him."

"And the investigator was able to get something to compare DNA?"

Shane nodded. "A soda can. He said it was easy and the guy never suspected anything."

"And the test is back?"

"I got a report just before Thanksgiving." His mouth twisted as if he'd eaten something bad. "*There's* something to be thankful for. Being the son of Thunder Canyon's most despised person."

"Oh, Shane—" Gianna suddenly got it. He was concerned that if anyone found out about this the whole town would turn against him, making him an outcast in the place he'd come to love. And the worst part was that he could be right. Some great person she was to talk to. She couldn't think of anything helpful to say.

"It will be okay." That was lame. So she put her hand on his arm.

"Careful." He pulled away from her touch. "You probably don't want to get too close to me."

"Don't be ridiculous. This doesn't change the good man you are." She met his gaze even as the struggle to wrap her mind around this raged inside her. "Did the investigator find out about your mother?"

"No." He slid his fingers into the pockets of his jeans. "But you've heard the rumors of Grace Traub and Arthur

Swinton. How he ranted and raved about them being a couple. Everyone in town thought he was just a wacko, but the name on my birth certificate is Grace S. Dax and D.J.'s mother's name was Grace."

"That doesn't prove anything."

"Not by itself. But you heard Allaire Traub. The resemblance—"

"Shane—" The ramifications of that rippled through her. "Do you think you're related to the Traubs?"

"I don't know. But that family has every reason to hate the man. He tried to destroy them, personally and professionally. How do you think they'd feel to find out he's my father and we could be half brothers? What does that information do to their mother's memory?"

He was so right. This *was* complicated and that word didn't even do it justice.

"Gianna?"

She looked up as the blond, thirtyish restaurant hostess poked her head in the door. "Hi, Ashley. What's up?"

"I just seated a party of four in your station."

"Thanks. I'll be right there." She looked at Shane. "I don't want to leave you like this—"

"It's okay." But there was nothing okay in the look on his face, or the tension coiled in his body. "We have a job to do."

She nodded, then slid off the stool and tossed her food in the trash. If only her thoughts could go with it. The fact was she needed time alone to let all this sink in. She wasn't sure how she felt, which was why Shane was justified in his concern. If this information got out, his reputation and standing in Thunder Canyon could be destroyed.

Shane wasn't sure if this was the smartest move, but he'd felt compelled to drop by D.J.'s Rib Shack. Both of their restaurants were on resort grounds and when business slowed at The Gallatin Room, he'd left the sous-chef in charge, with orders to call if there was an emergency.

It was possible he was jumping to conclusions about Grace Traub and Arthur Swinton. Somehow he couldn't think of the man as his dad. And he couldn't very well ask D.J. about what happened, so he wasn't sure what this visit would accomplish. Curiosity, maybe.

Now he stood in the doorway of the Rib Shack looking around. Really looking. He'd been in here before, but it all felt different now, given the things he'd learned. There were a few customers scattered around the large, open dining room in this primarily family restaurant. Booths lined the exterior with picnic-style tables and benches filling the center. The walls were covered with sepia-toned pictures of cowboys, ranches and a hand-painted mural depicting the town's history. He was surprised it didn't include a section with Arthur Swinton being led away in handcuffs.

That kind of thinking proved that this was a stupid idea. He started to leave then spotted D. J. Traub himself walking toward him. So much for a clean getaway.

"Shane. Hi." The other man held out his hand and gave him a firm handshake. "To what do I owe the pleasure of a visit from Thunder Canyon's celebrity chef?"

"Celebrity?" He shrugged. "I had an opportunity. I'm just a guy who's fearless with food."

"You just happened to be fearless on reality TV in front of millions of women. Thunder Canyon ladies are lucky to have you."

Shane couldn't suppress a grin at the good-natured teasing. "It's a dirty job, but someone has to do it and do it well."

"Modest, too. I can respect that." D.J.'s dark eyes glittered with amusement. "Do you have time for a beer?"

"Why not?" Actually he could think of a lot of reasons, but his curiosity was telling him to follow through on this.

"Follow me."

The other man led him to a quiet corner in the back of the restaurant where there was a table and two wooden barrel-backed chairs. He said something to one of the waitresses and she returned with a couple of frosty mugs of beer.

"Thanks, Jan," D.J. said to her. He looked across the small table at Shane. "So, how are things at The Gallatin Room?"

"Busy. Business is up compared to last year."

"That could have something to do with the famous and fearless chef running the place."

"Whatever." Shane took a sip of his beer. "It's all good."

He couldn't say the same for his personal life. Probably he didn't deserve it, but at least Gianna was speaking to him. If only he could forget the look in her eyes when he'd confessed about who his father was. He wouldn't have blamed her if she'd run screaming from the room.

"What about you?" he asked, glancing around. "How are things here?"

"The books look better than they have in a while. Grant Clifton says resort traffic is better than it's been in a while, so there's a direct connection. Part of the increase could be because Traub Oil Montana is gearing up, bringing jobs into the area."

"That means more families," Shane commented.

"Right. Since that's the Rib Shack demographic, we've been more in demand. I've been able to hire some people. Business is improving."

"Do you like it? Food service?"

D.J. nodded. "Yeah. I enjoy the chaos, seeing the customers having fun. How about you?"

"Can't imagine doing anything else. The complexity, creativity and everything you just said, too."

Their careers were in the same field and it felt good to

talk to someone who understood. They each filled a different niche under the Thunder Canyon Resort umbrella. Not for the first time he wondered if it was a coincidence or something in the genes.

Their thoughts must have been traveling a parallel path because D.J. said, "I'm glad our customer base is different."

"You mean because I get to serve romantic dinners to local lovers Forrest Traub and Angie Anderson? And budding couples like Ben Walters and Kay Bausch?"

"Ben and Kay?" One of D.J.'s dark eyebrows lifted in surprise.

"I understand it was a blind date." And now he was talking about people as if he was just like everyone else here in Thunder Canyon.

Gianna had told him about the older couple. She thought it was cute and he agreed. He also thought Gianna was pretty cute and so much more. He wasn't sure how he'd have come this far without her. She'd listened to him and he felt better after confiding in her. Although not if his revelation had cost him that connection with her. But that was something for later.

"Apparently Austin Anderson set up the two of them."

D.J. looked amused. "So you're saying your place is all about romance?"

"And you get what comes after. Families." Shane had meant it in a teasing way, but had an uncomfortable hollow feeling inside, a sense of loneliness he'd never felt before. That something was missing from his own life. "You're a lucky man, D.J. To have Allaire and your son."

"I've loved her for a long time." The other man toyed with his mug. "You know she was married to my brother Dax for a while."

"No, I didn't." Shane was surprised. The two brothers had looked like they were extraordinarily close and he'd envied the shared bond of growing up together. How could they maintain that when they had both loved the same woman?

"The look on your face says you've got a lot of questions about how we can still hang out." D.J. smiled. "It was a long time ago. They both knew it wasn't right and stayed friends. Things have a way of working out the way they're supposed to."

Shane wasn't so sure about that but hoped it proved true. He felt comfortable with this guy. Liked him. D.J. was honest, funny and could maintain a relationship with his brother, even though they'd been married to the same woman. That was extraordinarily open-minded. Maybe a friendship was possible, even if the truth of Shane's real father came out.

But it wasn't coming out now. He traced a finger through the condensation on the outside of his mug.

"So, do you think the Packers will make it to the Super Bowl?" D.J. must have sensed the need for a subject change.

"Not if the Forty-Niners have anything to say about it."

"Ah, a California guy loyal to the state's teams."

Shane shrugged. "I've moved around a lot. Seattle for a while. New York. Los Angeles is just where I grew up."

"But you could be persuaded to root for the Packers?"

"Maybe." He looked around the big room. "Is this where you hold the Presents for Patriots event?"

The other man nodded. "We've been collecting donations for a while now. Storing them in a back room here. Small electronics, toiletries, socks, candy. Baked goods are brought in the day when all the volunteers wrap and box it all up for shipping out."

"It's quite an undertaking."

"I'm privileged to do it. Family is precious," D.J. said,

suddenly serious and sincere. "No one knows that better than I do."

"Me, too." Catherine had mentioned that his mother died when he was young and there was a time that connecting with his dad was difficult. Shane loved his parents and would do anything for them, but he had different family issues.

"Our military men and women sacrifice so much every day," D.J. continued. "But even more this time of year. They give up holidays with their loved ones so that we can be safe and secure and enjoy ours. In some small way what we do says thanks for that."

Shane could see for himself that the other man felt deeply about family and roots. Would he understand why Shane needed to find out about his birth parents? Would D.J. have done the same thing if he'd been given up for adoption?

D.J. took a swallow of beer. "Wow, I can't believe it's been a year already."

"Since the last Presents for Patriots?"

"That. The holidays. Rose and Austin were married last year on Christmas Day." D.J. looked thoughtful. "It was a year ago that she was kidnapped."

"What?" Shane couldn't believe he'd heard right. Things like that didn't happen in Thunder Canyon.

"That's right. You weren't here then."

"She was kidnapped? By who?"

"Jasper Fowler."

The man who was linked to Arthur Swinton. It seemed as if everything bad that happened in this town could be traced back to his father. "What happened?"

"Rose works in public relations for the mayor and was helping clean out paperwork from the previous administration. She found evidence of Swinton's embezzling money from the city council and a link to Fowler as an accomplice."

Shane's stomach knotted. "I heard about that."

"Common knowledge," D.J. agreed. "But everyone thought Swinton had died in jail. Turned out he faked a heart attack and with inside help he escaped. He and Fowler conspired to ruin my business and launder the stolen money through The Tattered Saddle."

"Which is now Real Vintage Cowboy." Shane was concentrating on not reacting as if any of this concerned him personally.

"Right. Rose decided to pay Fowler a visit and ask him about what she found. It never occurred to her that the man could be dangerous. But she was wrong. He was desperate and crazy and took her at gunpoint."

"But she got away." That was stating the obvious but he couldn't manage much more than that.

"Smart girl." There was a dark satisfaction in D.J.'s eyes. "She managed to call Austin and leave the cell line open while she talked to the old man about where he was taking her. They were intercepted by her brother Jackson and Austin. I think a couple more of her brothers showed up, too, and then the cops. Fowler gave up Swinton and he was re-arrested. He won't be getting out of jail anytime soon."

"That's quite a story."

D.J. shook his head. "It really ticks me off that the rumor linking my mother to Swinton refuses to go away."

"I can understand that." If Shane could make his own connection to the man go away he'd do it in a nanosecond.

"Swinton is corrupt. A convicted criminal."

Anger and resentment twisted together in D.J.'s expression along with distaste and revulsion. Shane hoped it wasn't a preview of what he could expect. If he had it to do over again, he'd refuse to take the information his mother gave him. It came under the heading of be careful what you wish for. Or let sleeping dogs lie. When you went out of your way to connect the dots, you might not like the picture that emerged.

"I can't believe people would think my mother could be involved with someone like that," D.J. continued. "No way Grace Traub would associate with him. Actually it would have been before she married my dad. She'd have been Grace Smith then. She'd never have gone out with Swinton."

Shane went cold inside as the dots connected. If she'd only gone out with him, Shane thought, he and D.J. wouldn't be sitting here talking. Under the table his hands curled into fists. All the puzzle pieces fell into place and explained his resemblance to the other man. Only a DNA test would prove it to a ninety-nine percent certainty, but Grace S. was his mother's name. Smith was such a common last name that the P.I. wouldn't be able to pin down his mother's identity for certain. Evidence from his own search was piling up, though.

Shane was convinced that Dax and D. J. Traub were his half brothers.

Chapter Nine

Gianna stood in the shadows off to the side in The Gallatin Room. The customers at her tables were enjoying various courses of their meals. At the moment there was nothing for her to do and it was nice to take a breather. Interrupting every five seconds to ask if they needed anything was as bad as ignoring them.

Especially when there was romance in this room. Candles still flickered on pristine white tablecloths and there was a quiet hum of conversation and laughter. *She* didn't feel much like laughing as she watched Shane performing the public relations part of his job.

The information about who his father was had overshadowed her disappointment that he wouldn't be here for Christmas. What he'd talked to her about a little while ago was shocking enough, and then he'd disappeared. He was back now looking even more troubled.

He frequently schmoozed with the customers, moving

from table to table, meeting and greeting, using his natural charm and enjoying the connection. He was doing that now, but something was off. There was tension on his face in spite of the smile, and something like shock in his eyes. Each encounter was brief and smacked of duty, not the usual friendly and relaxed way he interacted. The lines of his body looked tight, as if he might snap.

Bonnie moved beside her and let out a long breath. "It's been so busy. I haven't had a chance to talk."

"Tell me about it." She smiled at her friend, then glanced at Shane. "How's everything with you?"

"Jim and I broke up."

"Bon—" Gianna gave her a quick hug. "I'm sorry. What happened?"

"He wasn't that into me." She tried to look spunky, but the disappointment leaked through. "I'm swearing off men. It's time to go back to college. No distractions."

"College is good. But don't back yourself into a corner with grand declarations about no relationships." If anyone could sympathize it was Gianna. "You really thought he was the one."

"Isn't it a rule or a law of physics or something that you can't be in love by yourself?"

"It's definitely more fun with two."

Her friend's gaze wandered to their boss, who was on his way back to the kitchen. "What's with Shane tonight?"

Gianna had to decide how to answer that question. She'd seen romances here at work burn bright and hot then fizzle and get awkward. The ones involved always thought they were discreet and keeping things under the radar. But when people worked as closely together as they did in food service, secrets were hard to keep. Although she'd managed. She hadn't said anything about sleeping with the boss, and wondered if her friend had noticed a change in anything.

"You think he's different tonight?"

"Not at the start of my shift," Bonnie said carefully.

"Then when?"

"The last hour or so. I've put in requests from customers, nothing out of the ordinary because he insists on one hundred percent satisfaction. But he's had to redo several meals, like his mind is on something else. One guy asked for no mango, not even a garnish on the plate. Shane put on the mango. Fortunately I noticed and fixed it."

"That's so unlike him," Gianna said.

"Tell me about it. His mind is somewhere else and the rest of him is on autopilot. I had to tell him about the mistake. He's always encouraged us to do that. It's one of the things I like best, that he's not a prima donna. But this time he practically bit my head off. He was gone for a while and came back different."

Gianna had noticed that, too. "Do you know where he went?"

"No. He's not in the habit of confiding in me."

Gianna couldn't say the same, except about where he'd gone, but when he walked back in the kitchen, he looked like a shell-shocked soldier on the battlefield.

"Don't be too hard on him." She looked at her petite, brown-eyed friend. "He's going through some stuff."

"So am I. Isn't everyone?" Bonnie dragged her fingers through her pixie haircut. "But it's not okay to bring it to work."

"We need to cut him some slack. He's dealing with more than a broken relationship."

Her friend's eyes widened into an "aha" expression. "Is there something you'd like to tell me?"

"Such as?"

"For starters how do you know so much about him? Like

what could he be dealing with other than cooking a filet to the customer's exact specifications?"

"Oh, you know—"

How could she? Who could possibly guess that he was Arthur Swinton's son?

And Gianna was torn. Part of her really wanted to talk to someone about her conflicted feelings and Bonnie was her best friend. But this information had the potential to ruin Shane's life.

"No, I don't know." Bonnie stared at her, waiting. "What's going on with you and Shane?"

"That's a good question." Maybe she could share just a little. "Remember when you called in sick?"

"Right, the Swiss travel delegation was here."

"I told you he invited me to his place and cooked dinner to thank me for efficiently filling in."

"More like working your butt off." Interest sparkled in her friend's eyes. "Yeah, I remember you thought it got awkward at the end."

"It did until…"

Did she say that out loud?

Bonnie's raised eyebrow told her she had. "Until he saved his moves for the pantry?"

Gianna's cheeks burned and she was grateful for the romantic lighting that hid her reaction. "You saw?"

"You didn't just ask me that. Of course I saw. Not much goes on in a restaurant kitchen that doesn't get seen by someone." There was nothing but teasing and the concern of a friend in her tone. "So give. I want details."

Gianna sighed. "It was maybe the best kiss of my entire life."

"In the pantry? He couldn't have picked somewhere—I don't know—with ambience?"

"That's what I said. He promised to make it up to me

because the first kiss didn't happen on the balcony of his condo."

"He passed up moonlight and a view of the mountains for a closet at work?" Bonnie sounded shocked and appalled. "That's just wrong in so many ways."

"He made up for it."

"Did he now?"

"It's not what you think," Gianna protested.

"I think you slept with him."

"Okay. It is what you think, but— But we're just having fun. No expectations."

"No one expects to fall in love. It just happens." Sadness slid back into her friend's eyes.

"It's not going to happen to me. Been there, done that. Not again." But caring about him was different, wasn't it? She hoped so because she couldn't help caring.

"Look, I know you, G. You don't have to pretend with me. You're not the type to take advantage of a situation. You pull your own weight and work harder than anyone because it's who you are." Her smile was sincere. "But if he hurts you, I'll make him sorry even if it costs me my job."

"Thanks, Bon." Gianna meant that from the bottom of her heart.

Her friend glanced at her tables. "I have to clear salads. Then hope the real Shane is back in control."

"Thanks for listening."

"Anytime."

"And Bonnie?"

"Right." She grinned. "I'll keep it to myself."

Gianna wasn't sure whether or not she felt better. And right now it didn't matter. She was here to work. Her shift was nearly over; the hostess wasn't seating any more customers. It was time to take care of her last few tables for the evening.

Gianna checked in with the diners and brought whatever was needed. With a little time on her hands, she walked back in the kitchen. Shane was the only one there, standing with his back against the stainless-steel counter, his dark eyebrows drawn together. This was not a man thinking happy thoughts.

"Shane?"

He looked up. "Hmm?"

"What's wrong?" She held up a hand when he opened his mouth, body language signaling a denial. "Don't waste your breath. It's obvious something is bothering you. I'm not the only one who noticed."

"I don't want to talk about it."

"Where did you go before?" she asked, trying to draw him out.

"What part of 'I don't want to talk about it' did you not understand?"

She blinked up at him. "Okay. It's just that you look upset. I wanted to help."

He drew in a deep breath. "Sorry. I didn't mean to snap. It's just—I can't do this now."

He stared at her long and hard before he simply turned and walked out the back door of the restaurant. Gianna started to go after him then stopped. She had to finish up her shift, but she hated the delay. Her heart ached for him because he had the look of a man who desperately needed to get something off his chest.

What more could there be? He'd already confessed who his father was. The disclosure had really rocked her and at the time, she wasn't sure how she felt. But she did now. Her feelings about him hadn't changed. He was a good man, the same man she couldn't wait to see every day at work.

The one she'd hoped for so long would notice her. Now

that he had, she couldn't walk away. No matter what else had happened between them, she considered him a friend.

Letting him brood alone wasn't an option.

After leaving work, Gianna drove the short distance to Shane's condo. She rode the elevator to his floor and stepped out when the doors opened. For so many reasons it was tempting to step right back in. She was more tired than she ever remembered being in her life. It had been a very long day. She could hardly believe that only twenty-four hours ago they'd walked in the snow and he'd kissed her. The battery in her car rolled over, died and Shane drove her home.

Then he'd made love to her—thorough, sweet love.

It had been only this morning they'd had breakfast in her apartment and were intimate, carefree. He'd been relaxed, funny and sweet. Rumpled in the best possible, sexiest way. The thought made her stomach shimmy like it had when the elevator whisked her up to his floor.

The expression on his face when he'd left work a little while ago was so different from this morning. It was a lot like his expression outside the bakery when Allaire commented on his resemblance to Dax and D.J. It was similar, but worse somehow.

And she had to know he was all right.

"Here goes nothing." She squared her shoulders, marched down the hall and rang his bell.

It wasn't answered right away and she was about to push the button again. She was prepared to pitch a tent in the hall if necessary because she had to see him face-to-face. Fortunately he finally opened the door.

"Hi." She lifted her hand in a small wave.

The only way to describe him was ragged. That seemed contradictory since his designer jeans were impeccable so it was more about attitude. His eyes were shadowed and his white cotton shirt untucked. His mouth was tight and the muscle in his jaw jerked. He had a tumbler in his hand with about two fingers of what looked like Scotch in it.

"I'm not very good company, Gianna."

"I'm not here to be entertained."

"Why did you come?"

"You look like a man in desperate need of a hug."

Nothing about him was welcoming, but she stood her ground. For some reason he'd confided things to her. His family might know, too, but they weren't here and she was. Whether he knew it or not, he needed someone and she was it.

"Can I come in?"

He rested his forearm on the doorjamb. "If you were smart, you'd turn around right now. I'm trouble. When it all blows up, you don't want to be close to me."

The devil of it was she *did* want to be close to him. That wasn't something she seemed to be able to change, even though there was every indication this wouldn't end well.

"I'll risk it. Tell me what happened, Shane. Where did you go tonight?"

Blue eyes, dark and assessing, stared into hers for several moments. "You're not going to leave, are you?"

"No."

Reluctantly, he stepped aside to let her in. "Do you want a drink?"

"What are you having?"

"Scotch."

Did she know her liquor or what? Tending bar part-time did that to a girl. "I'll pass."

She followed him into the living room. Unlike the last time here, she wasn't preoccupied with the expensive artwork and spectacular view. Her only concern was Shane.

She watched his shoulders shift restlessly as he stood by the big windows and stared out at the lights on the ski slope.

She moved behind him and put her hand on his arm and felt the muscles tense. "Let's sit."

He nodded and they walked to the couch, then sat side by side, close enough that their thighs brushed. She felt heat and awareness burn through her, but pushed it away. This wasn't about that.

"So, tell me," she said simply.

"I went to see D.J. at the Rib Shack."

"And?"

"We talked."

"Really? You didn't just stare at each other and grunt?" She tried to lighten the mood.

"We joked around." He rested his elbows on his knees, the tumbler of Scotch held loosely in his fingers. "He told me Dax and Allaire used to be married."

"I'd heard that."

"And yet they've managed to work through the past and still be close. Maybe because of the blood connection."

"Possible. Although a lot of siblings don't speak to each other over a lot less than that."

He lifted a shoulder. "Then he told me about what happened a year ago. How Jasper Fowler kidnapped Rose Traub. How everyone thought Swinton was dead."

"Yeah. You can take the girl out of Thunder Canyon, but you can't take Thunder Canyon out of the girl. My mom clued me in. It was pretty sensational."

He met her gaze. "Then he said something that makes me pretty sure his mother is also mine."

Shocked, she stared at him, the misery on his face. "What?"

"Her maiden name was Smith. Grace S. is the name on my birth certificate." His eyes were bleak. "D.J. said there's no way, but I'm almost certain she had an affair with Arthur Swinton and I'm the result."

"Think about this, Shane." She struggled to pull her whirling thoughts together and form a rational statement in order to help him. "Grace Smith is a common name. Is it possible you're jumping to conclusions?"

"Of course. Anything is possible. But the private investigator narrowed down the search criteria and the population of Thunder Canyon isn't that big. It was even smaller all those years ago. When you factor in the strong resemblance between me and the Traubs, that narrows the odds."

Gianna stared at him, trying to make sense of all this. "An affair?"

He nodded. "The whole Traub family believes Arthur Swinton fantasized about their mom, that not having her drove him crazy. To the point where all he could think about was getting even with them."

The implications of that sank in. "If she had his baby, that would challenge every belief they've ever had about their family. And they have the highest possible regard for their mother and her memory."

"I know." His tone was hard, tortured. "It would be so much easier if they were jerks. But I like them, Gianna, all of them. It feels as if we could be good friends, under other circumstances. If I'm right about this, I've got brothers. Another family. You can't have too much, right?" He tried to smile, but it just didn't work.

"Some people would argue that, but I'm not one of them." She blew out a long breath. "What are you going to do about this?"

"There's the question." He dragged his fingers through his hair. "Information like this could tear them apart after they worked hard to be close. I could tell them about my suspicions and they'll hate my guts, destroy any possible connection I might have had with them."

"Or?"

"Keep it to myself."

"And let it tear you apart instead?" Her heart cried out against that. It was an impossible choice.

He looked down, then met her gaze. "How can I trash their mother's memory? Especially at Christmastime?"

"No matter when they hear, news like this will rock their world," she pointed out. "They have a right to know that you might be a brother."

"I don't know if I can do that to them."

"Then you'd have to continue living a lie." Gianna put her hand on his forearm, feeling the warmth of his skin beneath the material of his shirt. It wasn't clear why, but she needed the connection to say what she had to say. "Hiding the truth is just wrong. Take it from me. I lied to you."

There was a spark of heat in his eyes for just a second, then it disappeared. "How big a lie can it be?"

"Not in the same league as keeping information about who you are from Dax and D.J. But I haven't been completely honest, either."

"About what?"

She looked down, not quite able to meet his eyes. "I did have a travel business in New York, but I lost it. Between people booking trips online and the recession costing them jobs and not traveling at all, I couldn't make a go of it. I lost everything."

"I'm sorry, Gianna."

"I'm thirty years old and have to start over, figure out what I want to be when I grow up. Do you have any idea how humiliating it is to have to move home with your parents?"

"You could have told me the truth."

"Saying I was only in town for a short time was just a

way to save face." He hadn't been sure about his long-term plans and it never occurred to her that things between them could get serious. So, here they were. "It was still a lie and I can tell you that I didn't particularly like living with it."

He looked at her for several moments, then his mouth twitched and he started to laugh.

That was unexpected and hit a nerve. "I bared my soul just now. I'm glad you think it's so funny."

"Sweet Gianna." He kissed her softly. Just a brush of his lips that was more promise than passion. "If anyone had told me that I could laugh at anything tonight I'd have said they were crazy."

"Happy to help."

"You have. More than you know." His mouth curved up again. "And you're right. Your lie of omission is nowhere near as bad as my mess." He took her hand in his. "But no one else could have coaxed a smile out of me. I'm glad you're here."

"I hope you still feel that way because I have to say what I think."

"And that is?" His fingers tensed around hers.

"You have to tell Dax and D.J. If you were in their situation, wouldn't you want to know you have a brother?"

"Yes, but—"

"Okay. Whatever their reaction, they have a right to know about this. Otherwise you're forcing them to live a lie, too."

"You have a point." For several moments he looked thoughtful. "Assuming I tell D.J., I wouldn't want to drop that on him until after Presents for Patriots. It's a big event and he's got to be under a lot of stress. That's more important. This secret has waited all these years—it can wait a little longer."

She put her head on his shoulder. "You're a good man, Shane Roarke."

"I'm glad you think so."

She was glad he couldn't see her face, guess how she felt inside. Her stomach was bouncing like a skier who took a tumble down the slope. Just because she believed what she said didn't mean she wasn't scared for him.

This could all go so badly and she would be to blame for convincing him to do it.

Chapter Ten

On Monday night the restaurant was closed so Gianna accepted her mother's invitation to dinner with the whole family. She parked at the curb and saw her sister's minivan already in the driveway.

This was her first holiday at home in a couple of years because she hadn't been able to afford the trip. Her parents knew now about her business failing and money problems, but at the time she'd been too proud to let on. She sat in the car, looking at the Christmas lights lining the roof of the house where she'd grown up. They didn't flash off and on, or do anything high-tech like change color. It was just happy and solid and stable.

Traditional.

The tree stood in the living-room window with white lights and ornaments, some of them made by Gianna and Jackie in school. Lights in the shape of candy canes lined the yard. Santa with sleigh and reindeer stood on the snow in the center.

Tears filled her eyes. She'd missed everyone so much and was looking forward to Christmas with her family. If only Shane was going to be here it would be perfect.

She brushed the moisture from her cheeks, got out of the car, and walked to the front door with the holiday wreath made of ribbons and pine cones.

After knocking, she let herself in. "Hello?"

Her mother walked down the long wooden floor of the entryway and hugged her. "I'm so glad you could make it, sweetheart."

"Me, too, Mom." Breathing in the scent of pine, she looked at the living room on the right and formal dining on the left. The table was covered with a red tablecloth and set for seven and a high chair. There was a poinsettia in the center with Santa Claus candles in brass holders on either side of it. "The house looks great. So festive. And I think I smell a roast?"

"Your nose is right on. Just put your things on the sofa," Susan said, pointing to the hunter-green, floral love seat by the Christmas tree. "Everyone's in the family room. The men are watching Monday Night Football."

"Okay."

Gianna did as directed, then joined the group in the room that always felt like the heart of the home. The kitchen with granite countertops and island opened to the family room with its overstuffed corner group and flat-screen TV.

Ed Garrison was lifting the roast out of the oven. He was tall and trim, with light hair that hid some of the silver streaking it. He had a distinguished look that could have him reading the nightly news on TV if he wasn't the most popular math teacher at Thunder Canyon High. Her mother worked part-time in a gift shop in Old Town and loved it.

The two of them were partners in life and tonight in the kitchen. They were working together to get the roast out of the oven, make mashed potatoes and gravy. She saw her dad's randy touch on her mom's rear. The playful way she pushed his hand away followed by a kiss on his cheek and a look filled with promise for later.

Jackie was following toddler Emily to make sure she only looked and didn't break any of the Christmas decorations. Her husband, Frank, was on the floor with the two boys, wrestling and tickling. The loud and loving scene made Gianna smile.

It also made her ache with missing Shane.

Jackie turned and spotted her in the doorway. "Look who's here."

The children stopped laughing and shrieking to look at her, then they jumped up and started shouting. "Auntie G!"

"Hi, guys." She went down on one knee and braced for impact as the two boys threw themselves into her arms.

Emily followed moments later, doing her best imitation of her older brothers. "Annie G!"

"Hey, baby girl."

She kissed each of them in order of age. Griffin, the dark-haired firstborn. Then Colin, with his lighter hair and sensitive soul. Finally, little Em, her legs and cheeks not as chubby as six months ago when Gianna had come back home.

She met her brother-in-law's gaze over the heads of his children. "Hi, Frank."

"Hey, G." He grinned. "I can't tell you how grateful I am that reinforcements have arrived."

"Are they wearing you out?"

He was a big guy, over six feet, with dark hair and eyes. Hunky and husky. All that firefighter training equipped him for all kinds of emergencies. If anyone could handle this group, it was Frank Blake.

He stood and grinned. "If I could bottle all their energy and sell it, I'd be a billionaire."

"No kidding." She looked at the three still hanging on her. "How are you guys?"

"Hungry," Griff said.

"Me, too," Colin chimed in.

"How's school?" she asked.

"I like recess best."

"Me, too," the little brother added.

The older boy scoffed. "You go to baby school. It's recess all the time."

"Nuh uh." The middle child shot a glare at his older brother. "You're a baby."

Emily held out her arms. "Up."

While their mother tried to referee, Gianna happily obliged her niece and held the little girl close. She breathed in the mingled scents of shampoo and cookies. "I could just eat you up, Em."

Jackie separated her boys. "Go watch the game with your dad."

"But, Mo-om—" Griff stopped when he got the look.

Gianna recognized it and knew her sister had learned from their mother. She wondered whether or not she'd do it, too, if she had kids. Her thoughts went to Shane and her heart ached for him again. So much had happened since he'd cooked for her at his place. He was trying to come to terms with everything he'd learned about himself and the consequences for others if it was revealed.

Now she understood the brooding expression she'd noticed in his eyes, the conflict about family and where he fit in. She'd never experienced that and hoped for the bazillionth time that her advice was sound.

"Dinner's ready," her mother called out.

Those words sent Jackie into field-commander mode. She and Frank rounded up the kids for hand washing then asked Gianna to put Em in the high chair already in the dining room. Like an intricately choreographed ballet, the adults worked together getting children and food to the table at the same time.

Griffin started to take some mashed potatoes and got another look when Jackie said, "Prayer first. Why don't you say it, sweetie?"

He nodded, then bowed his head and linked his fingers. "Thanks, God, for all the food. And for Mommy and Daddy, Grammy and Granddad and Auntie G." He looked at his parents then added reluctantly, "And for Colin and Em. Is that okay?"

"Good job, son."

"That's exactly what I would have said, Griffie." Gianna was surprised the words got past the unexpected logjam of emotion in her throat.

The next few minutes were a flurry of passing dishes, filling plates and making sure everyone had what they needed.

Her mother looked around the table and said, "Okay, everyone, enjoy."

"And if you don't," her father added, "keep it to yourself."

"So, Auntie G.," Jackie took a bite of mashed potatoes and gravy. "I saw Lizzie Traub at the bakery today. She said you and Shane Roarke were in a couple of days ago. Together."

That brought her up short. She'd forgotten how something like that could spread in a small town. Since coming home she hadn't done a thing that was gossip worthy. Until now. "That's right. I wanted to send something to my roommate in New York."

"At lunch you didn't tell us you were seeing him," her sister added.

At lunch Gianna wasn't sure about that herself. She still wasn't sure what they were, but had to tell them something. "I've gotten to know him recently. We're friends."

"Do you like him?" her mother asked.

"Of course. He's great to work for. Funny and charming."

"Mom and I and every female under seventy-five here in Thunder Canyon think he's drop-dead gorgeous," Jackie added. "What's not to like?"

Frank gave her a teasing look, clearly not threatened. "Should I be jealous?"

"If you'd like," his wife said, sass in her voice. "And I'm glad you even thought to be after all these years and three kids."

"Tell me, Gia—" Her father set his fork on his plate as he looked at her. "Do I need to ask him what his intentions are?"

As much as she wanted to know the answer to that question, she shuddered at the thought. "Please, Dad, I'm begging you not to do that."

"There's the reaction I was going for. My work here is done."

"Ed Garrison, you're going straight to hell," her mother scolded.

"Grammy said a bad word." Griffin's expression was angelic and superior because he wasn't the one in trouble.

Gianna was grateful for the diversion, and conversation for the rest of the meal was about other things. She could just listen, laugh, be with loved ones and distracted from worrying about Shane.

Later, after her sister's family had hustled home because of school the next day, Gianna was alone with her mother.

Her father was dozing on the couch in front of the TV. She wanted to hear again about her parents' first meeting.

"Mom? When did you know that Dad was 'the one'?" She was standing by the sink, a dish towel in one hand, wineglass in the other and braced for the personal questions that would follow about Shane. It was worth the risk given how confused she was.

Susan glanced at her husband and smiled lovingly. "I knew almost from the moment we met."

"Really?"

"Yes. There was attraction, of course." Her face went soft and sort of dreamy. "I still remember exactly how it felt. We were in a room full of people at a friend's wedding reception, but he was the only one I saw. And I stopped looking right then."

"It was that way for Jackie and Frank, too? In high school?"

Her mother nodded. "I worried some about them getting married right after graduation because they were so young. But I didn't try to stop her."

"Because of you and Dad?"

"Yes." Concern put creases in her mother's forehead. "Is there something with you and Shane?"

"No. Yes—" The first time she'd met him there'd been a room full of busboys, waitstaff and restaurant employees when Grant Clifton introduced them to the new chef. She'd felt the "wow" thing her mother just described. "Maybe."

Susan took the glass from her and put it in the cupboard. "Sweetheart, I know you've had disappointments. But you'll know when it's right."

"I guess."

Disappointment was a word designed to sugarcoat her catastrophe of a love life. She realized now that time invested didn't make a man less selfish or more right for her. She envied her sister and mother, getting it right the first time.

She wanted a solid relationship like her parents had. She wanted a guy like her brother-in-law. Six months ago she'd met Shane and had a crush on him from afar. Now she knew him, a man who thought of others first. The kind of man who would let the explosive information about who he really was eat him up inside rather than make trouble for the family he believed was his, one that had already been through a lot.

She'd felt that certain something the first time she saw him but…how could she trust her judgment after so much failure?

And more important, could Shane put the missing parts of himself together and find the peace he needed to settle down? That question might be answered after Presents for Patriots tomorrow night. He'd decided to talk to D.J. about his suspicions when the event was over.

Gianna looked around the Rib Shack's main dining room and hardly recognized it. The same historical town mural and sepia-toned pictures were on the walls, but all the tables usually scattered around in the center of the room had been pushed together for work space. People crowded around them and had an assembly line going. At several workstations, volunteers wrapped small electronics and toiletries in red, green, silver and gold Christmas paper, then passed it down for whoever was doing the ribbon.

Piles of presents waited for a volunteer to pick them up for delivery to where brown shipping boxes waited to be filled, addressed and stacked for transport.

Everyone who'd signed up for the event performed a function that utilized their talents as much as possible and her job was to circulate with hors d'oeuvres. She moved back and forth from where the volunteers were working and D.J.'s kitchen, where Shane was deftly balancing an assembly of ingredients, cooking and keeping things warm.

She pushed through the kitchen's double doors where he was working. "How's it going?"

"Good."

Stainless-steel bowls were in front of him, one with a tomato mixture, the other looked like cheese. Trays of sliced, toasted French bread marched up the long counter.

"Are you holding up okay?"

His expression was hooded but tension in his body said he knew she wasn't talking about food preparation, but what was coming after. "I'm made of stern stuff."

"Yes, you are." The only problem was some of that same stuff made up D.J. and Dax Traub. They didn't know yet that their world was going to turn upside down. She hated this and could only imagine how Shane felt. Stiff upper lip. "Everyone is raving about those little pastry things."

One corner of his mouth turned up. "It's a new recipe."

"Talk about a spectacular debut." Chalk up one good thing. "I'll just refill my tray. Hang in there."

She saw him nod and the way the muscle in his cheek moved. He was strung pretty tight and there was nothing to do but wait until this event was over.

After refilling her tray with napkins and food, she moved back out into the big room. The high ceiling held in the hum of voices and laughter. In one corner, the Thunder Canyon radio station was broadcasting Christmas music and live updates from the affair. On the opposite side of the room a TV reporter from a local affiliate was interviewing D. J. Traub, who looked happy, excited and intense. That was probably a family trait because she saw a lot of it in Shane.

She stopped at a table where Angie Anderson and Forrest Traub were working together. Holding out the tray, she said, "Care for a snack?"

"Wow, those look good. What is it?" Angie looked up from the MP3 player and paper she was lining up.

"Crab puffs."

Forrest put a piece of tape on the seam to hold the paper together. He shifted his weight to take the strain off his leg, still healing from the wound he'd sustained in Afghanistan. Better than anyone in the room, this former soldier understood what presents would mean to service personnel stationed in a foreign land at Christmas. He met her gaze and there was a twinkle in his light brown eyes. "You could just leave that whole tray right here if you want."

Angie laughed. "That's the spirit. Pig out for Patriots."

"I have to keep up my strength in order to help out my brothers in arms," he defended.

"Uh-huh. You're a giver, Forrest Traub." Angie put several of the puffs on a napkin. "Thanks, Gianna."

"You're welcome. And, Forrest?" She grinned at the former soldier. "If there are any of these babies left over, they're yours. I'll do my best."

He saluted. "If I wasn't already head over heels in love with Angie…"

"But you are," she reminded him, her voice teasing.

"I definitely am." He met her gaze and there was absolute sincerity in his own.

Gianna sighed as she moved to the next table. Antonia and Clay Traub were doing ribbon duty. She was surprised to see them. "Hey, what are you two doing here?"

Antonia pushed a long, wavy strand of brown hair behind her ear. Green eyes glowed with good humor, but looked a little tired around the edges. "What you really want to know is what have we done with the kids."

"No," Gianna said. "What I really want to know is how

you can possibly look so beautiful and *slim* after giving birth less than two months ago."

Clay gazed at his wife and the love there was clear for everyone to see. A boyishly handsome man with brown eyes, he'd been raising his own six-month-old son when he rented a room at Wright's Way, Antonia's boarding house, when she was in the third trimester of pregnancy. Her plan was to be a single mom, but they fell for each other and got married. Now they were mom *and* dad to two babies.

"She's an amazing mother," Clay said, then kissed his wife's cheek, "and an even more amazing woman."

"And that's my secret," she said, sending the love right back to her husband. "A man who thinks everything I do is perfect."

Gianna held back a sigh. "Okay. Now I want to know what you've done with the kids."

"It's a wonderful invention called grandparents." Clay laughed. "My folks are here from Rust Creek and will stay on through the holidays."

"Ellie and Bob are really good with the babies," Antonia gushed.

"They should be," Clay told her, "after having so many kids of their own."

"Maybe they should hire out," Gianna said, giving them some crab puffs.

If she had babies, her folks would be there for her. They were fantastic grandparents to Jackie's kids but it was looking like that would be it for Susan and Ed Garrison, thanks to the failure of their older daughter to provide any. Envy seemed to be Gianna's new best friend these days. She was jealous of everyone. Everywhere she turned people were deliriously happy and sappy with romance. Was she the only person in the room who had the love carrot dangling in front of her just out of reach?

She moved past more tables where she saw her landlady and husband, Cody Overton. After that came Joss and Jason Traub, who had renovated and updated The Hitching Post. They'd pretended to be a couple and ended up falling in love. Gianna was pretending to be full of holiday spirit but was falling into a funk.

Envy was nothing given the fact that she just wanted to be with Shane. But when she looked at the road ahead for her, all she could see were speed bumps. His biological parents were like a cloud hanging over him and he might not stay in Thunder Canyon.

She had a few hors d'oeuvres left on the tray when she stopped at the place where Dax and D. J. Traub were filling the brown packing boxes with gifts and sealing them with heavy duty tape. Apparently D.J. had finished his interview. Both men straightened and towered over her.

"Hungry?" she asked.

Dax took a napkin and popped one of the seafood-filled pastries into his mouth. "Mmm. What is this?"

"Crab puff," she said without much enthusiasm.

"Good," Dax said after chewing and swallowing. He took another. "Have you been scarfing these down?"

"No. Why?"

"Because you are what you eat and you look crabby."

"He meant thoughtful," D.J. said, glaring at his brother. "Maybe preoccupied. Or pensive."

"No." Dax folded his arms over his chest. "I meant crabby. Where's your Christmas spirit? What's up, G?"

The words yanked Gianna out of her funk with an almost audible snap. She was selfish, shallow and self-centered. These two brothers had no idea that their world was about to tilt. That when the evening ended everything they believed about their mother would be changed forever and not in a good way.

She didn't want to talk about what was bugging her. "Speaking of Christmas, it's only about two weeks away. Will these boxes get to Afghanistan in time?"

"The Air Force National Guard is on Operation Santa Claus," D.J. explained. "They've got transport aircraft standing by to take everything, and staff in place to get it distributed by Christmas."

"Thank goodness," she said.

D.J.'s expression was curious. "Nice try, G. But you didn't answer the question. How come your Christmas spirit is missing in action?"

She forced herself to look them in the eyes. "We're here to do our part to make Christmas merrier for the men and women halfway around the world who are protecting our freedom. Please don't make me feel as shallow as a cookie sheet and admit out loud, here of all places, that I'm feeling sorry for myself."

"Is there a guy involved?" D.J. took the last of the hors d'oeuvres on her tray.

Of course he'd go there. Since she'd been working at the resort restaurant, she'd stopped in the Rib Shack from time to time and D.J. took her under his wing. She'd confessed her pathetic and unfortunate relationship history and his advice was to pick better guys. Talking to him had helped, but now she wished she hadn't. She wasn't sure he wouldn't see through whatever lie she pitched him.

"Oh, you know—"

"The classic non-answer," he said nodding. "That's okay. It's not necessary for me to know details. But you don't have a big brother so I'll do the honors and beat him up for you if necessary."

Oh, God, don't say that, she prayed. She didn't want Shane hit. Not for her and especially not by the man who was his half brother.

"I appreciate the offer, D.J., but I can take care of my-self." At that moment she saw Shane nearby with a tray of bruscetta. Her heart boomeranged in her chest as he took out his reality TV smile and worked everyone over with it. She wasn't immune.

Dax's voice penetrated her haze with a comment that sounded as if he'd just remembered. "You and Shane were out shopping together."

"That's right." D.J. followed her gaze. "You and Shane? What's up, G?"

Good question. One she didn't want to answer. So she asked the first thing that popped into her mind. "What do you think of him?"

The brothers stared at each other for several moments, then Dax said, "His crab puffs are really good."

"Better than the ribs here at the shack?" D.J. challenged.

"Tomato, tomahto." Dax shrugged. "Just saying…"

"Seriously?" Gianna was aware that she was pushing, but this was important. The answer could make a big dif-ference in how they received the news he planned to give them. "You do know I wasn't talking about his cooking skill, right?"

"Well," Dax mused, "he's stepped up every time some-one asked him to pitch in. Thunder Canyon is lucky to have a celebrity who's also not a jerk."

"That's true," she said. "He spent his day off making all the hors d'oeuvres. And tonight The Gallatin Room only took a few reservations from people staying here at the re-sort so that the staff would be free to volunteer for your event. Shane figured most everyone from town would be here and not going out to dinner, anyway."

Dax nodded his approval. "Above and beyond the call of duty."

"I hate to admit my brother is right about anything." D.J.

grinned. "But Shane's willingness to be a part of this town goes a long way toward earning my loyalty. He and I have talked some and he seems like a great guy."

"He is. Really, really is."

Gianna knew her tone was more enthusiastic than necessary when the brothers exchanged a questioning look. This felt a lot like watching an air-disaster movie where she wanted to shout, "Don't get on the plane!"

There was nothing she could do and that was frustrating when she wanted so badly to help everyone involved because she liked, respected and cared about all of them. Shane was going to drop a very big bomb on this family tonight and she didn't want Dax and D. J. Traub to hate him for it.

Chapter Eleven

Gianna had left the Rib Shack a while ago after giving Shane a kiss and hug that went on so long he'd hated to let her go. She'd offered to stay, but this was something he had to do alone. He'd given her the key to his condo when she said sleeping wasn't likely until she knew what happened, and he was grateful to her yet again. If he was being honest, he wasn't sure how he'd have gotten this far without her.

Shane took his place in a line of volunteers who passed the brown cardboard boxes filled with presents into trucks for the next part of the journey to soldiers overseas. After that he pitched in with D.J. and a half dozen other men to move tables and chairs, put the Rib Shack's main dining room back the way it was before being taken over by patriotic holiday elves. At least he was doing something good while killing time waiting to do something not so good.

D.J. inspected the room after he and Shane moved the last table and settled the two chairs on either side. He nodded with satisfaction and announced, "Okay, everyone, I think that does it. Thanks for all your help. I literally could not have done this without you."

Shane watched D.J. shake hands with the men who left through the restaurant doors that led to the public parking lot just outside, which was nearly empty now. He locked up and wearily rubbed the back of his neck.

D.J. turned and seemed to realize he wasn't alone. He looked tired. "Shane— Sorry—I'll unlock the doors if you're going this way."

He was going to hell, but not through those doors. The Rib Shack had a rear entrance just like The Gallatin Room. "No. I'll head out through your kitchen, if that's okay."

"No problem. Would you like a beer? I could sure use one. And a little company would be welcome if you're not too tired."

"I'm used to these hours. Kind of goes with a food-service career," he said. "A beer sounds good."

"Follow me." The other man turned and led the way.

As they walked toward the kitchen, D.J. detoured into the bar and came out with two longnecks. He handed one to Shane, then continued to the back of the restaurant, turning off lights as he went.

He pushed through the double doors and glanced around. Shane knew that look, the one a chef used to make sure there's nothing out of place. To make sure heat sources are shut down, food put away, everything clean. Shane had been the last one in here and followed the other man's gaze.

The long, stainless-steel counter was spotless. Mixing bowls were nested and stacked on shelves. Recently washed pots and pans hung on overhead racks and different size knives back where he'd found them. After doing his volunteer part with the food, Shane had made sure this room was locked down.

"Looks good in here, too. Thanks." D.J. twisted the cap off his beer, then held it out for a toast. "Another successful Presents for Patriots. Here's to pulling it off."

"A job well done, thanks to you." Shane tapped the other man's bottle with his own.

"By the way," D.J. said, "my brother liked the crab puffs."

He's my brother, too, Shane thought. *And so are you.*

He hated this. They were good guys and he was tempted to walk away now, keeping the scandal to himself. But he couldn't fault Gianna's point. If the situation were reversed, he'd want to know. It was the right thing to do.

The timing couldn't be worse, just before Christmas, but there would never be a good time. This wasn't something he wanted overheard and indiscriminately spread around town.

Shane leaned back against the stainless-steel counter and took a long drink of beer. After drawing in a deep breath, he said, "D.J., there's something I need to talk to you about."

"Gianna." The other man nodded knowingly.

"What?"

"I saw the way you two looked at each other tonight."

"Excuse me?"

"My wife is a teacher, as you know. She's educating me in the touchy-feely stuff." He took a drink from his bottle, then leaned back against the cold cook top across from Shane. "Don't tell her I said this, but she's right."

"About?"

"If you watch body language, two people are having a conversation without words. Couple's shorthand, Allaire calls it."

"But Gianna and I aren't a couple."

"That's what all the guys say before they are."

"In my case it's true," Shane protested.

He thought about the sexy redhead constantly and she starred in his dreams. When he wasn't with her, he felt hollow inside and that had never happened to him before. The night he'd spent in her bed was seared in his memory, but he was the son of the town villain. He was pretty sure that was a deal breaker.

D.J. studied him. "Just so you know, I'm Gianna's honorary big brother and I offered to beat you up."

The words were teasing, the sort of banter Shane and his own brother did. Under the circumstances, he hadn't expected to smile, but he did. That only made him angrier about what he had to do.

"Did she take you up on it?" he asked, putting it off just a little longer.

"No. She said she could take care of herself."

"And there's nothing to take care of because we're not a couple."

Since coming to Thunder Canyon, Shane had been careful to not get involved, what with all the baggage he had. Gianna, with her sweetness and light, had made him forget just long enough to slip up. He'd only suggested dinner because it couldn't go anywhere. They were both leaving. But she hadn't been completely honest about going back to New York and he couldn't be sorry. If she'd told him the complete truth, he might have passed up the chance to know her and what a loss that would have been.

"Just don't hurt her," D.J. warned. "I'd really rather not have to hit you."

That was going to change. If only Shane could change who he was. He was doing his level best to keep his feelings in check so he wouldn't have hurting Gianna on his conscience along with deceiving everyone in town who'd welcomed him.

And it was time to quit stalling and say what he had to.

"D.J., there's something I need to tell you—"

The other man's eyes narrowed. "You're looking pretty serious. Did someone die?"

Not yet, but what he was going to say would be the death of something. "I came to Thunder Canyon for a reason—"

"Old news. There was a job opening."

Shane figured the best way to break this was to connect the dots from the beginning. "You said to me last week that Thunder Canyon was lucky to have me, but it's not about luck. I'd been researching this town. When I heard the executive chef position would be available, I contacted Grant Clifton to let him know I was interested. He jumped at the chance after a visit to my Seattle restaurant. Career-wise, coming here wasn't the best move. For me it was about getting answers."

"What are the questions?" D.J. tensed.

"As an infant I was given up for adoption. My adoptive family lives in Los Angeles. Mom and Dad are attorneys. Maggie and Ryan, my sister and brother are also adopted, and also lawyers." He set his half-empty beer bottle on the counter beside him. "I always knew I was loved, but still felt different from them."

"So you're looking for your birth parents." D.J. skipped steps and cut to the chase. "But why Thunder Canyon? This is a small town and pretty far off the beaten path."

"About a year ago my mother gave me all the information she'd received from the social worker at the adoption agency in Montana. I hired a private investigator who narrowed the search parameters to this town."

"Montana is a long way to go for a baby."

"I guess they wanted me to be far removed from the past." Shane shrugged. "My mother loves me enough to let me do what I need to do."

"And you needed to come here."

"I wanted to get some information on my own and the

kind of questions I had wouldn't get answers on a long weekend."

"So you took the job and positioned yourself to gain trust." D.J. finished his beer and still looked anything but relaxed. "Did you find what you were looking for?"

"I know who my father is, but it's not what I was looking for."

"You wouldn't have started this conversation if you didn't want me to know, too."

"I'd rather no one knew but it's not that simple." Shane dragged his fingers through his hair. Again he remembered what Gianna had said. Be a Band-Aid. Do it quick. "The P.I. managed to get a DNA sample and tests were run proving that Arthur Swinton is my biological father."

D.J.'s mouth dropped open, but no words came out. It took several moments for the information to sink in before he finally said, "He's in jail where he belongs."

"I understand why you feel that way." Shane didn't know what else to say except, "I'm sorry for what he did to you."

D.J. shook his head. "Not your apology to make. This is unexpected, I'll admit. But you're not responsible for his actions."

He figured D.J. continued to be in shock. That was the only reason he was still standing there and hadn't abruptly walked out. What Shane had to say next would probably do the trick.

"I found my mother, too. The name on my birth certificate says Grace S. I'm convinced the 'S' is for Smith."

"That's my mother's name, too." D.J.'s dark eyes narrowed angrily. The information sank in too fast for his mind not to have been moving in that direction. "But what you're implying can't be true."

"It is."

"No way. That would mean my mother slept with Arthur

Swinton and that's impossible. She would never have been with a man like that."

"I'm not making this up. Remember what Allaire said about the resemblance between us?"

"It's bull." D.J. slammed his empty beer bottle on the counter and glared. "What's this really about? Money? Is this a shakedown? You want me to pay so you don't spread dirty lies about my mother?"

"I don't need your money." Shane understood the surprise, shock and resulting anger, that his nerves were strung too tight. But he was treading on thin ice, suggesting Shane was like Arthur Swinton. "My family is wealthy and I've made a fortune on my own. That's not what this is about. We're brothers—"

"Get out." D.J. took a step closer. "I don't want to hear another word."

Shane started to argue, wanted to settle this, but he could see by the other man's expression that he'd shut down. He wouldn't listen to reason. Or anything else, for that matter.

"You can throw me out, but it won't change anything." Shane met his gaze, then headed for the back exit.

D.J. followed. "Don't even think about repeating this crap. I won't have my mother's memory and reputation ruined by a pack of lies."

"I don't lie," Shane said quietly. "And if I wanted everyone to know, I would have said something a couple of hours ago in the dining room when the whole town was there."

"I have no idea what sick game you're playing, but I want no part of it." D.J. opened the back door. "Now get out."

Shane nodded and stepped outside. The door shut instantly and he heard the dead bolt slam home. Cold and dark surrounded him.

When this journey of self-discovery started, he'd believed the truth would enlighten him. The real truth was that he'd never felt colder or more in the dark.

As the saying went, one picture was worth a thousand words and the instant Gianna saw Shane's face, she knew that was true. Things with D.J. hadn't gone well.

She'd been pacing in front of the spectacular windows looking out on the ski slope, snow-covered hills and lights but all she could think about was Shane, all alone while doing the hardest thing he'd ever done. As soon as she heard the condo door open, she rushed to meet him in the entryway. He looked tired, defeated. His mouth pulled tight and there was tension in his jaw.

Gianna asked anyway, "How'd it go?"

"Could have been better."

"He didn't take it well."

"How would you interpret getting thrown out of the Rib Shack?"

"Oh, Shane—"

She moved close and put her arms around him. He resisted for half a second, as if he didn't deserve her comfort, then pulled her tighter against him. He buried his face in her neck, breathed in the scent of her hair and held on as if he never wanted to let her go.

"I don't know, Gia—"

He'd never called her that before. He'd always used her full name. Something about the nickname got to her, intimate in a way sharing the pleasure of their bodies hadn't been. Her heart squeezed painfully in a way *it* never had before, and felt as if she'd stepped over the edge into feelings deeper and more profound than she'd ever known.

But she couldn't think about that now. She was simply grateful that he didn't seem angry at her for convincing him to tell D.J. they were half brothers. She hoped that didn't change.

Gianna slipped her arm through his. "Let's go sit in the living room."

He nodded and let her lead him over to the couch. On the coffee table there was a tumbler with two shots of Scotch in it waiting for him.

He kissed her softly and said, "Thank you."

"Anytime." And she sincerely meant that.

With a weary sigh he took the glass and tossed back half the liquor, closing his eyes as it burned all the way to his belly. "I needed that."

Gianna sat on the couch and looked up at him. "What did he say?"

"That it was a lie and I must be trying to shake the family down for money."

She shook her head. "He was just lashing out. This really came out of the blue for him. When it sinks in he'll realize that you don't need the money."

"That's what I told him. More or less." He drank the rest of the Scotch, then sat beside her, close enough that their arms touched and thighs brushed.

"I wouldn't hold it against him, Shane. Anyone would have reacted that way."

"Agreed. That wasn't a surprise. I expected it."

"But you're still upset." It wasn't a question. One look at his face had confirmed his inner turmoil.

"Yeah, I'm upset." He dragged his fingers through his hair. "The thing is… I like him, Gia. And Dax. The whole extended family. We could have been good friends. But now—" The look on his face was tormented. "I have a better chance of opening a restaurant on Mars."

He hadn't expected to be this troubled, she realized. The Traubs hadn't been in his life until a few months ago. But like the town of Thunder Canyon, he'd connected with the family in a way friendship didn't completely explain.

She cared deeply for this man and wished there was a simple, easy way to make his pain disappear. But the only weapon she had was words. Maybe talking it through would help. And she had to know...

"Are you upset with me for pushing you to say something to D.J.?"

"You didn't push me. No one could if I wasn't leaning in that direction in the first place. I'm stubborn that way." He linked his fingers with hers. "And I don't think I could ever be upset with you. I didn't say it before, but I'm glad you're here."

"There's nowhere else I'd be." She leaned her head on his shoulder.

"But," he said, "I can't help thinking that it would be better if I'd just left things alone. Not disturbed the ghosts of the past."

"For what it's worth, I don't think the Traubs are the type to run away from a problem. Seems to me they face things head-on, in a proactive way. Like you did tonight." She looked up at him, the strong profile, determined set of the jaw. "It occurs to me that besides the strong resemblance, that head-on thing is a trait you have in common with them."

"Did you just pay me a compliment?"

"That was my intent, yes." She rubbed her thumb over his. "The point is, and I do have one, regardless of the fall-out from all of this, the truth is always best."

"I'm not so sure about that." His voice was soft, sad, with a touch of self-loathing.

She thought carefully about what to say next. "How about looking at this another way."

"I'll take anything I can get."

"Okay, here goes. You already know Arthur is your father."

"Unfortunately, yes."

"This is where I argue that you need an attitude adjustment."

"Oh?"

Gianna knew if she looked at him, one dark eyebrow would be lifted. "Think about it. Whatever combination of DNA made you the way you are is something I'm grateful for. You're a good man. If not, the people of Thunder Canyon would not have embraced you so completely. They're funny that way. And you're awfully pretty to look at."

He laughed, the desired reaction, and hopefully that eased some of his tension. After several moments he sighed. "But the things my father did. He messed with people's lives, stole money. Conspired to commit God knows what kind of felonies."

"All part of the public record. But—" She met his gaze. "You're wondering about bad traits you might have inherited. If you had criminal tendencies, they'd probably have surfaced by now. Have you ever had a run-in with the law?"

"Just a couple of speeding tickets."

"That's so small-time," she scoffed. "And proves my point. The tests confirmed that he's your father. But the evidence is circumstantial that Grace Traub was your mother. Is it possible she's not? That she and Arthur never had a relationship and he is crazy just like everyone thinks?"

"Anything's possible," Shane admitted. "My parents told me everything they know and my mother turned over all the information she has. Grace died years ago. The only way to prove something like that would be a DNA test for Dax, D.J. and me. They'd never agree."

Gianna knew he was right. Grace was gone and couldn't confirm or deny. Dax and D.J.'s father had died, too, so there was no way to even find out if he knew anything. Obviously their children were all in the dark about the past. There must be another way to get the truth besides DNA testing. She just couldn't stand the idea of Shane not being able to know for sure and put this to rest.

If he was the type to let it drop, he never would have undertaken this journey in the first place. If it wasn't so important for him to find the peace to settle down, his mother wouldn't have given him her blessing for the journey that led him to where he was now. Gianna was afraid that not knowing for sure about his biological mother would cost him the piece of himself that he would need to have a life. And that gave her an idea.

"There's someone you haven't talked to yet about this. He might have the answers you're looking for."

Shane's body tensed, the muscle in his arm flexed. "I've talked to everyone I can think of. Who could possibly be left?"

"Your biological father."

"You're joking."

"No. I'm completely serious. Think about it. He's the only key player still alive. The only one who can tell you what really happened."

"But everyone says he's crazy. Delusional. A nut case. And even if he wasn't, there's the whole issue of not being truthful and less than an upstanding citizen."

"He did some bad things," she admitted. "But the Traubs are the most vocal about him being crazy. I think that's about them not wanting to believe their mother could ever have hooked up with a man like Swinton. What if they're wrong? You owe it to yourself to find out the truth."

"Even if I decided to go see him, what makes you think he'd tell me the truth? How could I know for sure whether or not to believe anything that comes out of his mouth?"

"Face-to-face you'd probably get a sense of whether or not he's delusional. The rest…" She shrugged. "I can't see that you've got a choice, Shane. It's the only thing left."

He thought about it for a long time. Finally he looked at her and said, "You're right about me being the type to face problems head-on. Whether or not I find out anything, no one can say I didn't at least try."

Gianna knew he meant himself. He didn't want to look back and hate himself for leaving even one stone unturned.

"I guess we're going to the jail," she said.

He lifted one eyebrow. "What's this 'we' stuff?"

"You don't think I'm letting you go alone, do you?"

There was a fiercely rebellious expression on his face. "This is my problem. More important, I don't want you in a place like that. Yes, I'm going alone."

"Wrong. I'll be there with you."

"I won't allow it," he said.

"At the risk of sounding childish…" She lifted her chin. "You're not the boss of me."

"Actually, I am," he reminded her.

"Only at work. This is different." It was personal.

Her track record proved that when things got personal she was the queen of perseverance.

Chapter Twelve

Shane wasn't sure what he'd expected of the county correctional facility half a day's drive from Thunder Canyon. Even at the holidays, or maybe because it was closing in on Christmas, this place was grim. No decorative lights on the outside. Not a Santa, sleigh, or reindeer in sight. Just a series of buildings enclosed by high concrete walls and law-enforcement personnel dressed in navy pants with contrasting light blue shirts.

With Gianna beside him they walked from the parking lot, then stopped at a guard station to show identification and declare their purpose for being there. Visiting was all Shane said and the guard directed them to the visitor center where they followed signs to a room with scratched tables and battered chairs. There was a surveillance camera mounted on the wall and a big window allowed guards to monitor everything that went on.

A few people were there talking to inmates wearing orange jumpsuits. A sad-looking artificial Christmas tree with a handful of red and green ornaments and tacky gold garland stood in the corner. This was where they'd been instructed to wait while someone went to get Arthur Swinton.

Shane walked to an empty table with three chairs in the farthest corner of the room. Gianna sat beside him and glanced around, blue eyes wide, looking curious and a little apprehensive.

"Scared?" he asked.

"No. You're here."

In spite of this surreal situation, he felt himself smile. "As good as I am with a knife in the kitchen, I'm not sure my skill set would be of much help in a jail riot."

"You've been watching too many prison shows on TV. I don't think this is that kind of place. It's not maximum security." She looked around at the dingy, institutional-green walls. "But we're not in Thunder Canyon anymore."

"I tried to talk you out of this. Are you sorry you came?"

She shook her head and slid her hand into his beneath the table. "Not even a little."

"That makes one of us." He listened to the low murmur of voices and glanced at the two prisoners with multiple tattoos, each talking to a wife or girlfriend. There was a hardness in the eyes, a toughness in the posture and he didn't doubt for a second that either or both could *lead* a prison uprising. These felons were his father's peer group and social contacts.

"I'd rather be anywhere else," he said. "If only I were cooking a five-course meal for a thousand pompous and pretentious food critics who don't know marjoram from parsley. That sounds like a warm and happy good time compared to this."

"Which is why I couldn't let you come here alone."

As much as he'd wanted to protect her from this toxic

environment, Shane was grateful for the stubborn streak that made her dig in and defy him. "Thank you. I appreciate it very much..."

Then the door opened and a uniformed guard walked in with an inmate wearing the same orange jumpsuit that would make it difficult to blend into a nonprison population should Arthur Swinton escape again. Shane's stomach knotted as he studied the prisoner.

His father.

The man was shorter and less significant than he'd expected, slightly built with gray hair. He was probably around sixty, but looked much older.

Since he and Gianna were the only other visitors without an inmate, the man walked over to them and sat down on the other side of the table. His blue eyes were sharp with suspicion.

"Are you Arthur Swinton?" Shane asked.

"Yeah. Do I know you?"

"We've never met. I'm Shane Roarke."

Gianna held out her hand. "Gianna Garrison."

He ignored it. "What do you want?"

"I'm here to ask you some questions."

He sniffed dismissively. "Another reporter. I don't—"

"It's not like that." Shane knew Swinton was referring to the private investigator's cover story when he'd posed as a journalist to get a DNA sample. "Actually I'm a chef in The Gallatin Room at the Thunder Canyon Resort. Gianna is a server there."

He was aware that she hadn't said anything since introducing herself, but knew she was studying both of them, comparing. Searching for a family resemblance. As far as Shane was concerned they looked nothing alike.

"What do you want?" Swinton asked again. The introductions hadn't done anything but deepen his distrust.

"I'd like to know about you and Grace Smith—you might know her as Grace Traub."

"She'll always be Grace Smith to me." Something that sounded a lot like sorrow took the sharp edge out of his voice. "What about her?"

"Obviously you knew her?"

"Yeah."

"Did you date her?"

"Yeah."

This was like pulling teeth, Shane thought, feeling frustration expand in his gut. Just then Gianna squeezed his hand, as if she knew what was going on inside him. It kept him focused. Allowed him to see that self-preservation was instinctive in a place like this. In navigating the criminal-justice system, offenders learned not to trust or give up anything that might incriminate them.

"There's no reason you should believe me," Shane assured him, "but I'm not here to do you any harm. I just want information about the past."

"Me and Grace."

"That's right." He stared hard into blue eyes that seemed familiar. "Were the two of you close?"

"You're asking if I slept with her. Not that it's any of your business or anyone else's. No one believed it then, why should you now?" The man was nothing if not direct. There was a vacant look on his face, as if he were remembering something from a long time ago. And apparently he wanted to tell his story because he added, "I slept with her, but it wasn't just sex. Grace is the only woman I've ever loved."

The guy had no idea who he was. As far as Shane could see, he had no reason to lie about that, but the admission profoundly shocked him. Probably because every time Swinton's name came up in Thunder Canyon it was in a negative context painting him as a heartless, unprincipled nut case who was incapable of deep feeling.

"Why did you break if off?" Shane asked.

"Of course I'm the bad guy." That was an ironic comment since he was the one in prison, but Swinton's gray eyebrows pulled together. "Who told you I did?"

"No one. I just—" Shane figured he was a heartless nut job.

"Gracie broke up with me. I tried to get her to reconsider, but she swore it was over." He took a deep, shuddering breath. "Her folks didn't like me much and Doug Traub was interested in her. They thought he walked on water."

So far the man hadn't said anything that convinced him Grace was his mother.

"She started going out with Doug?" Shane prodded.

"Not right away. At least not that I knew. I tried to see her, but her folks wouldn't tell me where she was."

When Gianna's hand tightened on his, Shane looked at her and knew they were thinking the same thing. Had she been sent away to hide a pregnancy? "She left town?"

"Yeah."

"But she came back."

"About six months later," he confirmed.

"Did she tell you why she went away?" His heart was pounding.

"Hell, no. She wouldn't even look at me, let alone be caught in a conversation."

Out of guilt? Shane wondered. Did her parents pressure her to keep quiet? Because it was sure looking like she was pregnant with Swinton's baby and didn't tell him.

"What did you do?"

"I kept trying to call her, see her, tell her I loved her. Then it was all over Thunder Canyon that she was dating Doug Traub. Next thing I knew she was engaged to him."

His hands clenched into fists on the table, right beside the word "hell" carved on the top. "She was making a mistake and I couldn't get past her father or Traub to make her see what she was doing."

Shane could feel the man's pain and didn't know what to say. This part of the story was history. "She married him."

"Yes." Swinton snapped out the single word. It was rife with bitterness, and sadness etched lines in his craggy face. "Then she died. So damn young. I hated that I didn't get time with her. The Traubs had her all to themselves. I never got to tell her I'll always love her. Never got to say goodbye."

"Mr. Swinton—" When Gianna finally spoke up, her voice was gentle. "Is that why you were trying to ruin the Traubs? To get even because you were shut out?"

"They had everything. I had nothing. It kept eating at me."

"But they're Grace's children."

He looked down, miserable and unhappy. "She'd hate me for it and I'm sorry for that." He looked sorry. "Grief does crazy things to a man. I was desperate for a way to get out from under it."

Shane studied the man. He looked alternately sad, angry and lonely, but not crazy. Loving a woman who didn't return his feelings had started him down a path of bitterness that led to a series of crimes that were all about revenge against the family he blamed for a lifetime of unhappiness. But he wasn't the only one with a black mark.

Grace Smith never told this man that she was pregnant with his child. Shane couldn't help wondering if knowing would have made a difference.

Swinton shook his head sadly. "I thought being left out in the cold was bad, but it's nothing compared to not having Gracie on this earth at all. Now I've got no one."

When Gianna squeezed his hand, Shane looked at her

and saw a slight nod. He knew what she was saying and agreed. "It's not entirely true that you have no family."

The suspicion ever present in the man's expression now turned to bitterness. "What are you talking about?"

"I'm your son. Yours and Grace's."

Blue eyes narrowed and turned angry. "If this is some scheme to get money out of me, you can just shove it—"

"No." Shane held up his hands in a take-it-down-a-notch gesture. Why was it that everyone accused him of a scam when his only goal was to get at the truth? "I had a DNA test."

"You didn't get a sample from me."

"Yeah, I did. Remember that reporter who came to see you?" There was a slight nod along with an expression that said he was wondering how Shane could know that. "He's a private investigator. I hired him to get a sample from you. The test results show to a ninety-nine percent certainty that you're my biological father."

"Is this some kind of sick joke, because I don't think it's funny."

"Tell me about it. You're in jail. I have restaurants in big cities across the country. This is not the kind of thing that would help my business. What possible good would making up this connection do me? My reputation could be ruined. The fact is that you *are* my father."

After several moments the old man's expression softened as the truth of the words sank in. "You're my son? Mine and Gracie's?"

"That's what I believe, yes."

"I have a son?" He stared across the table and didn't look quite so old and broken. "I can't believe it. I have a son."

Gianna looked at Shane, then his father. "You're not physically alike, but the eyes are the same, in shape, color and intensity."

"I didn't know she was pregnant. So that's why she went away. This is amazing. I don't know what to say. You're a part of me and Grace." He started to reach for Shane's hand, then stopped. "I don't know what to do. What's right. Sorry. I can hardly wrap my head around all of this."

Shane understood exactly what he was saying because he'd just confirmed the worst. He was the son of the man who was serving time in jail for crimes against Thunder Canyon and the Traub family.

His family, although they would reject that.

What the hell was he going to do?

"Shane, say *something*. You're starting to scare me."

Truthfully, the dark expression on his face had scared Gianna twenty miles ago, when they'd driven away from the jail. Now his chronic silence had her approaching frantic. She glanced at him, then turned the radio volume down.

He kept his eyes on the long, straight road. Most of the snow had melted, but there were still pockets of white where tree trunks and bushes shaded and protected it from direct sunlight. His hands gripped the wheel so tightly, she expected it to snap any second.

"I don't have anything to say."

"That's impossible. You just met your birth father for the first time." She didn't add that it was in jail, but knew he was thinking it, too. "I'm not buying the fact that you've got nothing."

"What do you want to hear?"

Stubborn, exasperating man. If she were bigger and he wasn't so tall, broad and muscular, she'd shake him.

"I don't have a script for you." She studied his profile, the lean cheek and stubborn jaw. There must be feelings, impressions—*something*—rolling around in his head. From the look of his expression, the thoughts were pretty dark. "Tell me what you're thinking."

"It's a nice day for a drive."

She sighed and shook her head. "Don't make me hurt you."

"So, you do have a script. Or a list of acceptable subjects."

"Not so much that as a specific topic," she said. Maybe questions would draw him out. "What did you think of him?"

"Arthur?"

Okay. He wasn't going to call the man dad. "Yes. Arthur."

"He's pretty intense."

So are you, she wanted to say, but decided he wasn't in the mood for a DNA characteristics comparison spreadsheet. It might get him to open up if she shared her impressions.

"I sort of expected him to look, I don't know, edgier somehow. More convict tough. Kind of like a hardened criminal."

"He's an old man." That sounded like he agreed with her and there was the tiniest bit of pity in his tone.

"Did it seem to you like he was telling the truth?"

"You mean do I think he's crazy?" Shane glanced at her. "No. He's a lot of things, but crazy isn't one of them."

"So you believe he and Grace were involved? That she left Thunder Canyon to give birth?"

He nodded without meeting her gaze. "Yeah, I do. I'm all but certain that Grace Smith Traub was my mother."

She was glad he knew the truth, but it also made her sad. After all his efforts to find his birth parents now he'd discovered his father in jail and his mother had died. It all seemed like a cruel twist of fate.

"So you'll never have a chance to know her."

"Not face-to-face."

She knew what he was saying. Grace had died when they were pretty young, but her sons, his half brothers, could share memories of their mother. "You could talk to Dax and D.J. about her."

"Not likely." He pulled off the road when a service station, convenience store and diner came into view. "I'm going to get gas. Are you hungry?"

Not really, but it was way past lunch and both of them needed food. "I could eat."

He nodded and parked by one of the pumps, then fueled up. Gianna watched his face as he worked and knew by the shadows swirling in his eyes that the surface of his feelings hadn't even been scratched yet. When he opened the driver's-side door and got in, cold air came with him and she shivered, but that was more about the emotional morning than winter in Montana.

He started the car and drove around the building and parked in front of the Pit Stop Diner. The windows were painted with snowflakes, a Christmas tree and other traditional signs of the season, with a big "Happy Holidays" in the middle. There weren't any cars in the parking lot, so it was no surprise when they walked in to find the place empty.

A thirtyish waitress wearing jeans, a Santa Claus sweatshirt and jingle bell earrings greeted them. Her name tag read Jamee. "Merry Christmas, folks. Sit anywhere."

"Thanks." Gianna picked a booth by the window and sat on the red plastic bench seat. The menus were tucked behind the salt and pepper shakers and the napkin holder. "May I have a cup of tea, please?"

"Sure thing." Jamee stared at Shane as if she were trying to place him, then there was a glimmer of recognition. "Wow. You're Shane Roarke."

"Guilty as charged."

"Wait till I tell Carl." She cocked a thumb toward the counter with swivel stools and the kitchen beyond. "He's the cook here. No pressure, huh?"

Shane smiled and only someone who knew him could tell his effortless charm was missing in action and his heart wasn't in it. "I'm sure the food is great."

She took a pencil from behind her ear and held a pad. "What are you doing all the way out here in the middle of nowhere?"

There wasn't much around except the jail compound they'd been to and Gianna was pretty sure he wouldn't want to share that he'd just visited his father there. She was at a loss with an answer, but Shane handled it with ease.

"I'm working at Thunder Canyon Resort, The Gallatin Room. I wanted to take a drive, clear my head." He looked across the table. "Gianna works with me and kept me company for some sightseeing."

"Not a lot to look at, but I'm glad you stopped in. I'm a big fan. Never missed an episode of *If You Can't Stand the Heat*." Jamee was gushing now and who could blame her? Of all the diners in all the world, a celebrity had just walked into hers. "I voted for you every week."

"I appreciate that."

"You're a lot better looking in person."

"Thanks." The brooding expression was back and pretty easy to read. He was thinking that probably his looks came from his mother because of the strong resemblance to Dax and D. J. Traub. "I think I'll just have a burger. Medium."

"That comes with fries."

"Fine," he said.

"Me, too, and a cup of tea." Gianna grabbed a couple of napkins from the container and put one in her lap.

"Coming right up."

She watched the waitress disappear through a swinging door, then met Shane's gaze. There was doubt, questions and confusion in his eyes and her heart ached for him. She wished she could wave a magic wand and take it all away.

"What are you thinking?" she asked.

His mouth tightened and anger took over his features. "How could she not tell him she was pregnant with his child?"

"I don't know." Gianna knew the "she" in question was Grace. "She was probably scared. It sounds like her parents were strict and controlling."

"It was wrong."

"I can't argue with you there. Arthur had a right to know. Just like Dax and D.J. have a right to know they have a half brother."

"To share memories of their mother with?" His tone was mocking. "That's not going to happen. D.J. made himself pretty clear. They don't want anything to do with me. My very existence puts a big bad ding in her perfect reputation and their memories."

She wasn't so sure he was wrong about that. "Who knew Arthur Swinton would turn out to be the injured party in all this?"

"Injured?" The single word was spoken in a soft, scornful voice. "That implies something he could recuperate from. She ripped his heart out and he never recovered. He fell in love and it ruined his life."

Just then the waitress brought their burgers and fries and set the plates down. "I'll get your hot tea right out. Anything to drink for you?" she asked Shane.

"Not unless you've got something stronger than coffee."

"Sorry." Jamee looked it. "Anything else?"

A miracle, Gianna thought. All she said was, "This is fine."

Her stomach was in knots and there was no way she'd get this or anything else down. Shane was slipping away. She could feel it and there was nothing she could do to stop it.

Leaving her food untouched, she stared across the table. "Shane, look at it from Dax and D.J.'s point of view. This has rocked your world and you always knew you were adopted. The Traubs are just finding out their mother had secrets. Give them time to process what's going on. You, too. Now you know what happened. You'll come to terms with the past."

"There's nothing to come to terms with." He shrugged. "I found out what I wanted to know. It's over."

That sounded so final. As if he was finished with a part of his life, the part that included her.

"What are you going to do?" she asked.

"It's the holidays. I need to see my family. The one that actually *does* want me around," he clarified. "I'm going to Los Angeles."

She had a bad feeling about this. Just the way he said it made her want to put a finer point on his plans. December 25th was a little over a week away and he was making a trip sound imminent. "For Christmas?"

He shook his head. "As soon as I can get a flight out."

"But that's earlier than you planned." Duh, stating the obvious.

He shook his head. "I never should have started any of this in the first place. If I just go away quietly, the Traubs can get on with their lives and Grace's memory will be preserved."

"But it's not the truth. She was human. She had flaws and made mistakes. That doesn't mean she was a bad person and they shouldn't love her. Or you."

He went on as if he hadn't heard her. "D.J. is the only one who knows. He probably didn't say anything to the rest of them because he didn't believe me, anyway. It's time for me to move on. Like you said, I found out what I came here for."

But was that all he'd found? What about her? What about the two of them? Neither of those were questions she could ask. Instead she said, "What about the restaurant?"

"The sous-chef can take over for me. I've trained her. No one is irreplaceable."

He was wrong about that. He couldn't be replaced in her heart. And that's when she knew she'd fallen in love with him. It was implied when she'd told him there was nowhere else she'd rather be than with him, even meeting his father for the first time in jail. And no matter that he denied it, she was pretty sure he blamed her for convincing him to tell D.J. the truth. The look on his face said he wouldn't forgive her, either.

She'd wasted years on relationships that were wrong and not long at all on one that she'd thought was right, only to find out it was one-sided. He'd connected the dots of who he was and his contract at The Gallatin Room was almost up. So, he had no reason to stay and every reason to go back to Los Angeles.

Somehow it was no comfort that she hadn't put in a lot of time falling for him. Fate had a way of evening the score and she was going to spend the rest of her life missing him.

Chapter Thirteen

In her apartment after work, Gianna took her cup of tea and walked over to the tiny Christmas tree on a table in front of her window. She'd changed out of her work clothes and put on fleece pajama bottoms and a red Henley top for warmth. It was a schleppy outfit, but what did it matter? No one was coming, and by no one she meant Shane. He was either in Los Angeles or on his way.

Between her regular time off and The Gallatin Room's Monday closure she hadn't seen him for a couple of days. Tonight when she'd gone to work Bonnie had broken the news that Shane told the staff he was leaving for the holidays. It felt as if he'd whipped her heart with a wire whisk. The rest of the staff thought he'd be back to work after New Year's, but Gianna knew better.

He was gone for good.

The last couple of days had given her a sad and painful preview of how life without Shane would feel. It was as if someone turned off a light inside her and not even holiday decorations could power it back up.

"The most wonderful time of the year, my backside," she mumbled to herself.

She set her steaming mug on the table where the tree stood and looked at the assembled presents. The packages for her family were arranged on the floor, too big to fit underneath in the traditional spot. Only one was small enough and the tag had Shane's name on it.

She picked up the square box wrapped in gold foil paper with red holly berries. She'd spent a long time getting the three-dimensional red bow just right. That investment of energy was nothing compared to how she'd agonized over what to buy for the man who had everything. Aftershave was a cliché. He didn't wear neckties—also a cliché. Nothing too personal—even though they'd made love and things didn't get much more personal than that. Her body ached with the memories of that magic night, doomed to be a single, life-changing event.

Of course she hadn't known that when picking out his present. It couldn't be too expensive, mostly because her budget would only stretch so far. But still the gift had to mean something.

She looked at the box holding the blue wool neck scarf that matched his eyes. "It means I'm an idiot."

He was gone and she should give this to charity so someone could use it.

Then she realized she *was* the charity case who could use it. "For a horrible warning to never fall in love again."

A knock on the door startled her because it was late and she wasn't expecting anyone. Her family would have called. No one would just drop in unless it was someone who knew her schedule. Someone like Shane.

Her heart started to pound and she walked to the door,

then peeked out the window beside it. He was there on the landing and the light that had gone dark inside her blazed brightly again. He was here; he hadn't left town. He was...

What? Her hands shook as she looked at the box she was still holding. How quickly the horrible warning was forgotten. But, she realized, the warning was too late, anyway, since she was already in love with him.

She opened the door and the outside cold made her shiver. His coat was open and his hands were in the pockets. He could really use a scarf to keep him warm.

"Shane. What are you doing here?"

His gaze dropped to her fleece pants and long-sleeved shirt. Maybe it was wishful thinking, but his eyes seemed to go intense for just a moment while lingering on her chest. "I saw your light was still on."

"I thought you'd left town. That's what they told me at the restaurant." Could he tell how hurt she was?

"I had a flight out tonight," he admitted. "I actually made it all the way to the airport, but it felt wrong."

"Define 'it.'"

"Can I come in? Would that be all right?"

No, it wasn't all right. This was like grinding his heel into her already broken heart, but closing the door in his face wasn't an option. And it was too cold to stand here.

She pulled the door wide. "Come in."

"Thanks. I won't stay long."

As he moved past her the air stirred with the spicy masculine scent of his skin and she knew forever wouldn't be long enough for him to stay. But she had no illusions about that wish coming true.

She closed the door and said, "I'm just having some tea. Would you like a cup?"

"No."

She picked up her mug and sat on the sofa, leaving room for him beside her. "So, why are you here?"

"I just wanted to talk to—" He stopped, then slid into the space next to her without taking off his coat. "We're friends, Gianna."

"I thought so." Even she could hear the hurt in her voice.

"I've been an ass and having a lot on my mind is no excuse. I thought going to L.A. would help me sort things out. Then I got to the airport and couldn't go. I've sort of gotten used to talking to you and it was unprofessional to leave the restaurant on short notice."

"What about D.J.?"

"So far I haven't heard anything from him. If there's any fallout from what I said, I'll be here to face it. I'm not hiding."

She nodded approval. "There are no more secrets and that's the way it should be. It's a good plan, Shane."

"It feels good." He met her gaze. "And I don't think I ever told you just how much I appreciate your support through everything. You didn't just listen. You were there for me."

She saw the light dim in his eyes and knew he was talking about that day at the jail. The day his father found out he had a son and the woman he'd loved all his life had kept that from him.

Friendship wasn't nearly enough for her, she thought, but it looked like that was all he was offering and she'd take what she could get. She stared at him to memorize the shape of his nose, the stubborn line of his jaw, the exact shade of blue in his eyes.

"I couldn't let you go to the jail alone," she said. "It's not what friends do."

He looked like he wanted to say something to that, but shook his head and let it go. "Anyway, I had another reason for stopping by."

She felt something quiver inside her and knew it was hope stirring. If she could slap it around and discourage the emotion she would, but that was hard when hope had a life of its own.

"Oh?"

"Yeah. I know you want to travel."

"It was a dream." She was surprised he remembered. "I was always told to study what you love in school. Do what you love in your job. I was good at business and marketing and wanted to see the world. A travel agency seemed like a perfect fit." She shrugged. "It was just a cruel twist of fate that I never got to go anywhere."

"Well, it's not the world, but I'd like to take you to L.A. for Christmas. You've been supportive of me through this weird, crazy, biological-parent journey and I'd very much like you to meet my real family."

"I'm sure they're wonderful people. How could they not be? They raised you and you're a very good man. I wish I could…"

He frowned. "I hear a but."

She squeezed the mug in her hands tightly. "This is my first Christmas with my family in a couple of years. I couldn't afford the trip from New York. I was trying to keep my business afloat and after I lost it, jobs were hard to find. Keeping a roof over my head was important and the city is a pricey place to live. I didn't have the money."

"You couldn't foresee what a toll the recession would take. A lot of businesses didn't make it. Not your fault."

She met his gaze and realized talking to him about her career disaster didn't embarrass her. Even though he was so phenomenally successful, he'd never made her feel less because she didn't hit it big. She appreciated that. "Anyway, this Christmas is all about reconnecting with my folks, my sister, my nephews and niece."

"I understand the importance of family in a very profound way." He was quiet for several moments, thinking. "I'm also not a man who gracefully takes no for an answer."

"Oh?"

"If so, I wouldn't have annihilated my reality show cooking competition by making an edible dish out of beef jerky, kidney beans and wine."

"Eww." She stared at him. "You're joking."

"Only about the jerky." He grinned. "Not about giving up easily. How about a compromise? You have Christmas Eve with your family. I'll take you to L.A. on Christmas day to meet mine."

She didn't like the idea of him being alone for any part of the holiday. "Do you have anywhere to go on the 24th?"

"No, but that's okay." He shrugged. "I'll manage."

"That's just wrong." She couldn't hold back the words. "I'm sure there's room for one more at the Garrisons."

"I wouldn't want to impose," he said.

"My family would love to meet you."

"I'd like to meet them. On one condition," he said. "Come with me to the west coast on Christmas. You've been an incredible friend, more than I deserve. Let me thank you for all you've done. I only want to hear a yes."

And she wanted to hear him say he loved her, but that wasn't going to happen. He was only interested in friendship and she understood why, because she'd been there when he met Arthur Swinton. Love ruined the man's life and Shane wasn't going to let that happen to him.

Where was a horrible warning when you really needed it? If she was smart, she'd tell him no. But she wasn't smart because she couldn't say it. She didn't want the light inside to go out sooner than necessary. Whatever time she had with him she would take, if only to store up memories for when she was alone.

"You win, but then you always do. I'd love to go to Los Angeles with you."

After following Gianna's directions, Shane pulled the car to a stop at the curb in front of her parents' house at the appointed time on Christmas Eve. Her gifts were in the backseat next to a pile that he'd brought. He'd quizzed her about the kids' ages, likes and dislikes, then shopped so he didn't come empty-handed.

He was in a great mood. To her knowledge, in the days since he'd postponed his trip to Los Angeles, he hadn't heard anything from D. J. Traub. Shane hadn't told her how he felt about it and she wasn't going to ask tonight. He wasn't brooding anymore and that was good enough for her.

Gianna removed her seat belt. "Do your brother or sister have any kids?"

"No."

"Can I assume that your career hasn't afforded you the opportunity to spend time with children?"

"That's an accurate assumption." There was a big dose of amusement in his tone.

"Then I have to ask, are you sure you really want to go in there? I love them with every fiber of my being, but they're loud. Probably sugar and any number of chemical food dyes have amped up their normally high energy level. The night before Santa Claus comes there's only peace on earth when they fall into an involuntary, exhausted sleep."

"Are you trying to scare me?" He opened his car door, and the overhead light illuminated his wry expression.

"Just keeping it real in case you want to beat a hasty retreat." She pointed to the driveway. "See that minivan? It means they're already here and waiting to pounce."

"Then let's go join the party."

"Don't say I didn't warn you." She got out of the car then retrieved her presents from the back.

Arms loaded with gifts, they walked to the front door and Shane managed to ring the bell with his elbow. Moments later it was opened and Griffin stood there.

"Auntie G is here," he announced in an exceptionally loud voice.

"Hi, Griff. You know," she teased, "I think there are some people a few streets over who didn't hear you."

"You're funny." He gave Shane a long, assessing look. "Is he your friend?"

She winced at the word, but probably her mother had told him that. "Yes. This is Shane Roarke. My boss. Shane, this is Griffin, my nephew."

"Nice to meet you, Griffin."

"You're the cook?"

"Chef," she corrected.

"What's the difference? Does he cook food?"

"Yes," Shane answered.

"My dad is a good cook. So is Grammy."

"We're coming in now, Griffie." She kissed the top of his head on the way to pile gifts under the living-room tree. "It smells good in here. Turkey, yum."

Griffin stared at the exquisitely wrapped boxes Shane put beside hers. "Did you bring me something?"

"Griffin, it's rude to ask that," she scolded.

"But I wanna know. How am I gonna know if I don't ask? Mommy says it's good to ask questions."

"Your mom is right," Shane said. "And the answer is yes, I did bring you something."

The boy grinned. "Can I open it now?"

"Let's go talk to Grammy and find out what the plan is."

"Okay." He grabbed Shane's hand. "I'll show you where she is."

"Lead the way." Shane whispered in her ear. "Retail bribery works every time."

When they walked into the combination kitchen/family room, the boy stopped. "Auntie G is here and Shane brought us presents. Can we open 'em, Grammy?"

Colin left his fire truck and toy firefighter figures on the rug in front of the TV and ran over to give her a hug. "Hi, Auntie G."

Right behind him was Emily, trying to keep up on her short, pudgy legs, saying, "Annie G!"

Gianna grabbed her up and spread kisses over her cheek until the little girl giggled. "Hey, baby girl. You smell like sugar cookies."

"Cookie." She held up her sticky, crumb-covered hands for inspection. Then she spotted Shane, who grinned at her. Apparently his charm translated to women of all ages because the normally shy-of-strangers child held out her arms to him. "Pick me up."

Jackie rushed over. "You don't have to take her. With those dirty hands she'll ruin your sweater."

It looked like cashmere, a cream color that wouldn't hold up well to grubby hands, Gianna thought. "This is my sister and her husband, Frank."

The two men shook hands, then she introduced her parents. "Shane Roarke, Susan and Ed Garrison."

Her father shook his hand and her mother smiled. "We're so glad you could join us for dinner, Shane."

"Thank you for including me."

"Any friend of my daughter's…" Her father had no idea how that touched a nerve.

Gianna decided for tonight she was not going to let that word get to her. "I smell mulled wine."

"On the stove." Her dad raised his voice to be heard over Emily's wailing.

"Pick me up!" Apparently oblivious to the fact that she was up, the little girl kept holding her arms out to Shane.

"Dirty hands don't scare me. Obviously it's early childhood training for a career in the food-service industry." He took the child who pointed into the family room. "I guess we're going that way."

While Em chattered to him in a language only a two-year-old could understand, he carried her to the pile of toys on the family-room floor. When he set her down, she grabbed a ragged plastic doll with all the clothes removed and pointed to the face.

"Eye," he said.

"Eye," Em repeated.

Gianna watched as he patiently played the naming-the-limbs game until the boys moved in to get his attention. Frank tried to run interference, but apparently two grown men were no match for three small children. The toys were forgotten in favor of wrestling, tickling and roughhousing. Shane easily went from instigator to casualty, alternately taking one of the boys on his back to letting them tackle him. Jackie and her dad tried to play referee, but no one was listening to them.

Her mother handed Gianna a glass of wine. "He's even better-looking than on TV."

"Am I the only one on the planet who never saw that show?" She was remembering the woman in the middle-of-nowhere diner who'd recognized him. The man playing with her nephews and niece was much different from the shell-shocked one who had just found his birth father.

"Apparently you are," Susan said. "He's a wizard with food and if I weren't so secure in my cooking skills, having a world-famous chef to dinner could be just a little bit intimidating."

"Your turkey is the best, Mom."

"You have to say that, sweetheart, but I appreciate the sentiment."

"It's the absolute truth."

"You were looking pensive just now." Her mother studied her face. "What are you thinking?"

"Just that Shane looks really happy and relaxed."

Susan glanced at the rowdy group with Shane in the center of it. "If that's noteworthy, it would seem he's lately been just the opposite."

This wasn't her story to tell so Gianna gave the heavily edited version. "He's had a lot on his mind lately, but I think the weight has finally lifted from his shoulders." When one of the boys climbed on his back, she laughed. "He's got Colin there now."

"Yes, he does. Also noteworthy is that the kids took to him right away." Susan was using her mother's-seal-of-approval voice. "They have a finely tuned BS—bad stuff—meter and can see through phoniness instantly."

Gianna could read through the lines and the same thought had already crossed her mind. He would make a wonderful father. Tears burned her eyes because no matter how determined she was to put the "friend thing" out of her mind, it would take a Christmas miracle to pull that off.

She ached to be more than that because he was everything she'd ever wanted.

"I like your family." Shane braked at a stoplight a few minutes after leaving the crazy, wonderful Christmas chaos at the Garrison house.

"I do, too," she said. "My mother thinks you're better-looking in person than on TV."

"Good to know." He was feeling a little reflective. "They make me miss my family."

"You'll be seeing them tomorrow."

"As will you."

He glanced at her in the passenger seat, streetlights making her red hair glow. God, he wanted her. In every way. How could he ever have considered leaving her at Christmas?

"Speaking of that," she said, "what time are you picking me up to go to the airport tomorrow?"

"Are you packed?"

"Are you kidding? This is me. I've been packed for a couple days. All ready except for the last-minute things."

That's all he needed to hear. "Then I'm not picking you up."

"Okay." She slid a puzzled glance across the leather console between them. "Do you want me to come by your place?"

"That won't be necessary."

She frowned. "If you changed your mind about me going with you—"

"Just the opposite." He accelerated when the light turned green and passed the street for her place. "Technically I won't need to pick you up because I'm taking you home with me tonight. We can get your things tomorrow on the way to the airport."

It was quiet on the passenger side for so long that he looked over. Gianna was staring at him.

Maybe he'd blown his chance with her after all, but every part of him fought against that. It couldn't be too late. "Do you want me to take you home now?"

"No," she said emphatically. "It's just that I'm confused. You pulled back— I thought— You said we're friends."

"About that—" It felt like he'd been in a fog for months,

a haze that just now cleared. "After seeing Arthur, I guess I went a little crazy. Like father, like son."

"It's called processing the information," she defended.

Loyalty and support were two of his favorite things about her. "In my case it was more about going to the bad place and moving in for a while." He looked over and saw her watching him intently. "I started ticking off the things about me that are like him, none of them good."

"Shane, he has positive qualities. And you didn't get all your DNA from him. You didn't know Grace, but look at her children. They're all good men. Salt of the earth."

"I know. I've thought a lot about everything and had to work it through. Just because he buckled under the weight of disappointment doesn't mean I will."

"That's right," she agreed. "He's not a bad man, I don't think. Just one who lost his way."

"So did I. For a while." Almost to his place, he took her hand while keeping his other on the steering wheel. "Now I've got my head on straight."

She squeezed his fingers. "I'm glad."

He pulled the car into the parking garage and guided it into his space. After getting out, he went to the passenger side and opened Gianna's door, then held out his hand. "Do you mind if we unload the gifts in the morning?"

He'd missed her more than he thought possible and was in kind of a hurry to get her inside. Besides, he had a lot to make up for.

"I don't mind at all." Her expressive eyes hid nothing and promised everything.

She took his breath away.

They went into the elevator and pushed the button for his floor, then walked down the hall to his place where he unlocked the door and led her inside.

"Alone at last," he said, taking her face in his hands. "You're cold."

"Not for long. And my mom gave me something." She reached into her pocket and pulled out a red-ribbon-trimmed sprig. "Mistletoe. Sometimes a girl has to take matters into her own hands."

She held it up as high as she could to get it over their heads. He took it from her and did the job as she slid her arms around his neck.

Need exploded through him as she touched her mouth to his, then pushed at his jacket, trying to get it off. In a frenzy of kissing and wanting he dropped the mistletoe because he needed both hands. They tugged at buttons and closures until coats and keys were on the floor and the raspy sound of their breathing filled the entryway. He could hardly wait to have her, but not here, not up against the wall.

Shane swept her into his arms and laughed at her shriek of surprise. "You know it's Christmas Eve and Santa won't bring presents until you're in bed."

She grinned. "Then what are you waiting for?"

"Not a damn thing."

He carried her to his room where they undressed each other then fell on the mattress in a tangle of arms, legs and laughter. He hadn't realized how lonely the past six months had been until Gianna. Or how much he didn't want to be just friends with her.

He concentrated on her pleasure, touching her breasts, finding the place on her thigh that made her breath come faster, kissing a certain spot near her ear that made her moan. And he couldn't hold back any longer. He entered her and brought her to the peak where she cried out with satisfaction. A heartbeat or two behind her, his release came sooner than he would have liked.

But they had all night.

He pulled her against him and felt her hand on his chest. "You're the reason I didn't go to Los Angeles sooner."

"Me?" Her voice was a little breathless, a little sleepy.

"I couldn't leave you on Christmas." Or any other time, he added to himself.

"Merry Christmas, Shane." She snuggled into him and relaxed, quickly falling asleep in his arms.

"And to all a good night," he whispered, kissing her forehead.

The journey he'd started in June had brought him to an unexpected place and the future was still unsettled. He wasn't sure where he and Gianna went from here because Thunder Canyon wasn't big enough for him and the half brothers who wanted nothing to do with him.

Chapter Fourteen

Gianna stretched sleepily and touched something that felt a lot like a man's broad back. That didn't happen often in her world so she opened one eye and grinned from ear to ear. *Merry Christmas to me,* she thought. Memories of loving Shane the night before warmed her everywhere. He hadn't said he loved her, but he hadn't turned his back. Metaphorically speaking, since she was loving the view of his very real, very wide shoulders.

"I can feel you looking at me." Shane's voice was raspy with sleep and tinged with amusement.

"How did you know?"

"Like I said—I can feel it." He rolled over and pulled her against him, resting his chin on her hair. "Merry Christmas."

"Merry Christmas, Shane." She snuggled her cheek on his chest and caught a glimpse of his digital clock on the nightstand. "Holy cow. We have to get moving. There's a plane to catch and I bet you're not packed. All my stuff is at my apartment and I have to do an overhaul—hair, makeup, just the right outfit—before flying to Los Angeles."

"Why? You're beautiful."

"Thank you." The compliment made her glow from head to toe, but a look for meeting his folks didn't happen without some effort. "But your family will be there."

"Yeah." He laughed. "What with Christmas dinner being at their house and all."

"Right. And I can't meet them for the first time looking like I just rolled out of your bed."

"Why not?" He tipped her chin up and their gazes locked. "I like you right where you are."

"Shane—"

"Okay." He kissed the tip of her nose. "But let's have coffee. We've got time. Weather's good. I've been watching the forecast all week. Flights will be on time. We'll be having Christmas dinner in L.A."

"And I have to look fabulous."

He rolled out of bed and picked up his jeans, then slid them on. "You need to stop worrying so much."

"And you need to start worrying just a little more."

Gianna got up and grabbed his long-sleeved white shirt. She was feeling a little shy, even though last night he'd seen every inch of her naked. The soft cotton was like wrapping herself in the scent of him and came down to midthigh. She buttoned it as she followed him to the kitchen.

Resting her elbows on the granite countertop, she watched him put warm water in a state-of-the-art coffee-maker that had more bells and whistles than her car. He ground up beans then added them to the disposable filter before pushing some of those bells and whistles. Several moments later the thing started to sizzle and spit.

He turned toward her. "It won't be long now."

"Okay."

She'd have said okay to anything. The sight of his bare chest and the dusting of hair that narrowed down his belly to the vee where his jeans were unbuttoned absolutely mesmerized her. Tingles danced up and down her spine and for a second she thought there was a tune involved. Then she realized it was the doorbell.

"Are you expecting someone?"

"No. It's probably whoever is manning the front desk."

"On Christmas?"

"It's part of the job, like bringing my car to the restaurant." He shrugged. "Someone might have dropped off a package and the front desk is delivering. I'll be right back."

Gianna listened to the front door open then heard a very loud, "Surprise! Merry Christmas!"

Shane's voice drifted to her as he said, "Mom. Dad. Wow. Ryan and Maggie, too."

His family was here? *Now?* Gianna's heart started pounding as she frantically looked around for an escape route. There wasn't a cupboard big enough in the kitchen to hide her and no way to make it to the bedroom without being seen. She was pretty sure Shane didn't have an apron as he wasn't an apron-wearing sort of guy. It was just a case of being royally up doo-doo creek. This was like the bad dream where you somehow ended up in the mall ladies' room naked to the waist with no choice except to suck it up and walk out, knowing humiliation would happen no matter how much you pretended otherwise.

It would just be worse the longer she stayed put so, head held high, she moved just into the kitchen doorway, visible from the living room where the Roarke family stood. It was clear they all saw her because suddenly everyone went silent.

"Merry Christmas," she said, forcing cheerfulness into her voice.

"You must be Gianna Garrison." An attractive older woman with a stylish brunette bob separated from the group. "Shane said you were a blue-eyed redhead."

She touched a tousled curl by her cheek. "Guilty."

The woman, who had to be his mother, laughed. "He said you were friends."

Shane moved beside her, his expression sheepish and apologetic. "It was an ambush phone call, I was under oath and she was cross-examining me."

"He gets that a lot." The older man, obviously his father, had silver hair, very distinguished-looking. "I'm Gavin Roarke."

"My dad," Shane confirmed. "This is my mom, Christa. That's my little brother, Ryan and baby sister, Maggie."

"Hi." Gianna smiled as confidently as possible at the tall, good-looking guy with brown hair and eyes. His sister was wearing a navy knit hat pulled over long blond hair that spilled down her back.

"Are you surprised?" Maggie asked.

"Yes. Now, what are you guys doing here?"

"Your mother wanted to be with you for Christmas," Gavin explained.

"What part of me flying out for dinner did you not understand?"

"It's a mom thing." Christa's shrug was apologetic. "I miss the days when you guys were kids and ripped into presents first thing. You're all grown up so the best we could do is surprise you and be here in the morning."

"So you took a red eye?" Shane asked, shock and pleasure mixing in his voice.

"Yes," Gavin said. "Your brother and sister haven't stopped whining about it yet."

"But I'd do it all again just to see the look on your face. And everything," Ryan said, sliding a glance at Gianna's bare legs and feet, then grinning at his older brother's obvious discomfort. There was no way his family didn't know they'd slept together.

"I can't believe we actually pulled off this surprise," Maggie said. "It's nice to meet you, Gianna."

"Likewise." She was trying to hide behind Shane. "I usually look so much better than this."

"You look fine," Christa said and sounded like she meant it sincerely. "Attractive doesn't do her justice, Shane."

"Attractive was the best you could do?" Gianna didn't know whether to be flattered or not.

Looking down, Shane met her gaze. "Again, under oath."

"Don't pay any attention to him," his mother scoffed. "You're stunning. And all my children will tell you that I don't say anything I don't mean."

"It's true. She doesn't suck up," Ryan agreed. "So, about last night—"

"There's coffee in the kitchen." Shane cocked his thumb toward the room behind them. "I'm going to put on a shirt."

"Preferably not this one." As they laughed, Gianna sidled in the direction of the master bedroom and after going into the hallway, she turned and ran.

She grabbed her things from the floor where Shane had tossed her sweater and jeans last night. It seemed the arms and legs were pulled inside out. That happened when someone was in a big hurry to get your clothes off. Quickly she put them back on while Shane dressed.

"I can't believe this is happening. I just said I didn't want to meet your family looking like I rolled out of your bed. It's official. I'm being punished because I did just roll out of your bed." She turned a pleading look on him. "Tell me there's a back way out."

"Sorry." He moved in front of her and cupped her face in his palms. "They love you."

"We barely met. And I do mean barely what with wearing nothing but your shirt. There's no way they like me."

"They do. I know them and there was nothing but approval. Now let's have coffee."

When they returned, only his parents were there. Shane glanced at them, surprised. "So much for being together this morning. Ryan couldn't wait ten minutes to start checking out Thunder Canyon women."

"He does have a talent for that," his mother said, fondness and exasperation swirling in her eyes. "Although I do wish he'd find the right one and settle down. But, no. He and Maggie are using your guest rooms for a cat nap. They've been up all night."

"So have you guys," Shane pointed out.

"And worth it. But those two…" Christa shook her head sympathetically. "Rookies. It doesn't matter that you're all grown up, your father and I remember being up all night with babies. We've still got it, don't we, Gavin?"

He put his arm around her shoulders. "We do, indeed."

His mother's eyes were suspiciously bright. "'Tis the season to be with the ones you love."

"Yes, it is." Shane walked over and kissed her cheek. "Can I buy you a cup of coffee?"

"Sounds heavenly."

When they were settled around the table in the kitchen, his mother said, "So, you seem much more relaxed than you did last time we talked."

"Yeah." Shane picked up his steaming mug. "I found my biological mother and father."

Gavin exchanged a glance with his wife before asking, "Do you want to talk about it?"

"Of course. You're my parents." He took a deep breath

and said, "Grace Smith died a long time ago, when her sons were pretty young."

"You have brothers." It wasn't a question and Christa's tone was carefully neutral.

"Yes. But they're not happy about it. My birth father's name is Arthur Swinton and he did some bad things, to them and the town. He's in prison."

"Oh, my—" Christa shook her head. "You tease me about having a gift for words, but at this moment I'm at a complete loss."

"It's really complicated," Gianna said. "Grace was pregnant with Shane and didn't tell Arthur. He was so in love with her and couldn't accept that she loved another man. It made him a little crazy."

The other woman studied her son. "How do you feel about all that?"

"I had a rough time in the beginning," he admitted. "I've come to love this town and finding out you're the son of public enemy number one was hard." He set his coffee down and took Gianna's hand. "But I got lucky. My *friend* talked me through it."

"I'm glad Shane has you," his mother said.

"Me, too. No one should have to go through something like that alone."

Shane squeezed her fingers. "I've been thinking, Mom. Since there are four lawyers in the family, maybe something can be done for Arthur."

That surprised Gianna. He hadn't said anything to her, but she approved. The man wasn't a danger to society. His was a crime of revenge and it was over now.

"We can look into his case," Gavin said. "There might be mitigating circumstances to bring before a judge when he's up for parole. If he can return the money he took while on the city council there could be a reduced sentence. Time off for good behavior."

"Thanks. You guys are—" Shane's voice caught. "I got really lucky when you picked me."

"We're the lucky ones," his mother said. "We loved you the moment we laid eyes on you, so tiny and sweet. Instantly I felt as if you were meant for us. All I ever wanted was for you to be happy. I hope that everything you found out will help you to find serenity and stop searching. Stop running."

"I have." He met Gianna's gaze, but his own was impossible to read.

She had no idea what he meant, but if she'd helped him find peace, that would have to be good enough.

"That was the best Christmas dinner ever." Maggie Roarke leaned back in her chair and groaned dramatically. "I've never been so full in my life."

Gianna glanced around Shane's dining-room table, set for six. He sat at one end, she at the other, sort of host and hostess. His parents, Maggie and Ryan were on either side, facing each other. The big windows made the majestic, snow-covered mountains an extension of the room and gave them a spectacular view.

"I'm glad you liked the food, little sister." Shane sipped his chardonnay. "When you drop in on a guy, you take potluck."

"Then we should drop in every weekend," his mother said. "That beef Wellington is, without a doubt, the best thing I've ever had."

He'd never looked so pleased and personally satisfied at work. "If I hadn't been able to pillage stuff from the restaurant it would have been grilled cheese."

"Right," his brother scoffed. "So speaks the cooking genius who won *If You Can't Stand the Heat* by putting together a little something with lima beans, honey and tofu."

"You're exaggerating."

"Maybe just a little," Ryan admitted. "I don't think even you could make something edible out of that."

"Never underestimate the palate appeal of tofu," Shane said.

Gianna loved watching him banter with his family and was very happy to be included in the group. She'd been looking forward to the trip to L.A., but didn't mind that the plans were altered. This was one of the best holidays ever. Her financial position hadn't changed, but she was rich in so many other ways.

Definitely there'd been recent ups and downs, but today had been perfect, if you didn't count meeting the Roarkes wearing nothing but Shane's shirt. While his family napped, he'd driven her home to clean up, then they'd stopped by The Gallatin Room to get what he needed for dinner. Judging by the satisfied groans all around, he was a smashing success.

His mother looked out the window and sighed. "I can see why your voice was full of reverence when you told me about Thunder Canyon. It certainly is beautiful. God's country."

"Amen," her husband said.

Gianna couldn't agree more. She'd come home with her tail between her legs, feeling like a failure, but somehow this place had healed her soul. Her heart was in jeopardy, but maybe life was always a trade-off.

"It makes you hardly notice that your place has no Christmas decorations," Maggie said. "Next year."

"Maybe." Shane's tone was noncommittal.

"I'm going to earn my keep and clear the table." Gianna stood and started stacking plates.

"I'll help you."

When his mother started to stand, Shane stopped her. "No, you don't."

"I'm not a guest," she protested.

"Tomorrow you can help. But you were up all night getting here. That buys you a pass on doing dishes. All of you," he said, looking at each of them in turn.

"He just wants to be alone with Gianna," Ryan teased. "If you can't stand the heat…"

Shane lifted one eyebrow at his brother. "Can you blame me?"

"No."

Gianna blushed. Ryan grinned. Shane glared.

While Shane stacked plates at the other end of the table, she carried hers to the kitchen. Behind her she heard his mother say, "You two make a good team."

Gianna thought so, but what did she know. Her judgment was questionable. She was the one who'd wasted so much time on the wrong guys. After setting dishes in the sink, she turned to go back for the rest, but Shane was right behind her.

"I'll get the food," he said, turning back the way he'd come.

That was her prompt to rinse and arrange the plates and silverware in the dishwasher. By the time she'd finished, he was putting leftovers in the refrigerator, beside the pumpkin chiffon pie he'd "borrowed" from the restaurant freezer, from the stock he'd made for the restaurant's holiday menu.

"Do you want to wait to serve dessert?" she asked.

"Good idea."

They assembled small plates and forks. He got coffee ready but didn't push the "on" button. Then they looked at each other.

"Christmas is almost over," he said.

"I know. At the same time I'm relieved, it kind of makes me sad."

"Did you get everything you wanted?"

"I love the perfume," she said, not really answering.

His question made her think and not about the gift he'd given her. There was only one thing that could possibly make this day perfect and it couldn't be bought in a store. She just wanted to hear that he cared.

"How about you?" she countered. "Did you get everything?"

"Almost." He rubbed the back of his neck. "It's silly, I guess. And unrealistic given the circumstances. But I'd hoped to talk to D.J. and Dax. It's not that I'm looking to be embraced as a brother. I'm not asking for a kidney or bone marrow transplant."

"But?"

"I like them." He shrugged. "It was natural. I'm going to miss the friendship."

"That could still happen. Your paths are bound to cross if you stay in Thunder Canyon." She still didn't know what his long-term plans were.

"What about you?" The question turned the conversation away from him, his goals. "Is traveling still what you want?"

What she wanted had certainly changed since she'd returned to her hometown. She'd thought she was confused and lost then, but the feeling had multiplied a hundred fold. There was only one point she was clear on.

Gianna looked up at him. "In the last six months I've found out that Thunder Canyon is in my blood. I was so anxious to get away, but now I can't imagine being gone forever. I saw this place through your eyes and fell in love with it all over again." She left out the part about falling in love with him at the same time.

"I know what you mean."

"So, I'm going to put my business degree to work as soon as I figure out what business *will* work."

He nodded and a dark expression settled on his face. "There's something I have to say."

Gianna didn't like the sound of that. It was the male version of "we have to talk" and it was never about anything good. But she'd wasted a lot of time on relationships that didn't work. If this "thing" with them was heading over a cliff, it would be best to find out now. Knowing wouldn't stop the hurt, but… She couldn't really think of an upside to knowing. Best get it over with.

"Okay. What's on your mind?"

"You and I," he started. "And the Traubs. There are a lot of them here in town. Based on D.J.'s reaction, when he tells the rest of the family about who I am. They're not going to like me much either. You know I care about you, but—"

She held up her hand. "Don't say it. I hate that word."

"Gianna—" He shook his head. "You want to make a life here. If you get hooked up with me that could get awkward and I'd do anything to keep you from being hurt."

"Really? You're actually saying that this town isn't big enough for both of you?"

"I know it sounds like something from a bad Western, but yeah, I am. And there's only one way to keep you out of it."

"You don't have to protect me."

"I can't help it where you're concerned."

He was talking about walking away. He was willing to give up a place that had touched his soul. But this wasn't a decision that just affected him and she should get a say in it.

"Look," she said, "It's not—"

"Shane?" His father was standing in the doorway and neither of them had noticed.

"Yeah, Dad?"

"There's someone at your front door. A young man. He says he'd like to speak with you."

Shane straightened away from the counter looking as surprised as she felt. "That's odd. I wasn't expecting anyone. Did he say what it's about or give you his name?"

Gavin shook his head. "He only said that he needed a few minutes of your time."

"Okay. I'll see what he wants."

Gianna had a bad feeling. This was like getting a phone call in the middle of the night. Someone stopping by unannounced this late on Christmas just felt weird. And that's why she walked to the door with Shane. He wasn't the only one who couldn't help going into protective mode. When she saw who was standing there, she slipped her hand into his.

"Hello, Dax. Merry Christmas."

"Shane. Same to you." If Dax Traub was surprised at the two of them together, he didn't show it.

"What can I do for you?"

"I have a favor to ask."

"What?" Shane's voice was neutral, but the rest of him tensed.

"I'd like to talk to you."

"My family is in from L.A."

"Sorry to interrupt your Christmas." Dax glanced into the room behind them. "Here isn't what I had in mind, anyway. Can you meet me at the Rib Shack? It won't take long."

The bad stuff didn't usually take very long to say. Shane's peace-on-earth expression disappeared, replaced by the intensity he'd worn like armor for the past six months. And Gianna couldn't blame him.

The two men stared at each other for several moments while Shane thought it over. Finally he said, "I'll meet you there. Is now okay?"

Dax nodded. "Thanks, Shane."

Gianna watched him walk down the hall to the elevator and her bad feeling got bigger. "Don't go, Shane. Whatever he has to say can wait until tomorrow when it's not Christmas."

"I want to get this over with. The sooner, the better."

Never would be better as far as Gianna was concerned.

Chapter Fifteen

On the short drive to the Rib Shack, Shane kept picturing Gianna's face, the stubborn tilt of her chin, the way her full mouth pulled tight with anger. He couldn't help thinking she was beautiful when she was angry. First, she'd been revving up to talk him out of leaving town, when he'd told her that things would be awkward with the Traubs.

They'd lived in Thunder Canyon for a long time. He was the newcomer who'd had ulterior motives and was the son of their enemy. It was a stigma that would stick; it would rub off on Gianna and her family. She'd found her way back and knew what she wanted. He wouldn't jeopardize that for her, which was why he had to do the right thing and go quietly.

He loved her too much to ruin her life by being in it.

Second, he'd had to talk her out of coming with him for this conversation with Dax. She would take his side against the Traubs. It's just the way she was and he couldn't let her do it. What finally convinced her to stay put was when he asked her to watch over his family. With her they were in good hands. And now it was time for the showdown.

The Rib Shack parking lot had a few cars, but it looked pretty quiet this late on Christmas. Holiday hours were posted inside for the guests staying at the resort, but he knew the restaurant was closed to the public now. He parked by the outside entrance; it would make for a quick exit.

"Best get this over with," he muttered.

"This" being the portion of the holiday entertainment where he was run out of town. He was stubborn enough to tell them to shove it, but for Gianna's sake he would listen politely then walk away. He wouldn't ask her to choose between the town and family she loved.

But, he'd learned something from his biological mother. Grace Smith Traub had shown him that the greatest love of all is letting someone go to give them a better life.

He walked through the parking lot as snowflakes started to fall and his breath made clouds in front of his face. As he opened the door and went inside the restaurant, the sounds of talking, laughter and children playing drifted to him. It pierced the loneliness that pressed heavily on his heart.

In the Rib Shack's main dining room, tables were pushed together to accommodate a large group—all of them Traubs as far as he could tell. He recognized Jason, who'd come from Texas to settle here. Clay, Antonia and their little ones were next to him. Forrest Traub and Angie Anderson sat so close together you couldn't see space between them. There were a couple more guys he didn't recognize, but they were Traubs, what with that strong family-resemblance thing.

As he moved farther into the room, conversation around the table stopped and everyone looked at him. When Dax angled his head, D.J. and Clay stood up, as if it was a strategy agreed on ahead of time. The three of them moved to meet him.

Dax slid his fingertips into the pockets of his jeans. "Thanks for coming, Shane."

"No problem. Looks like the gang's all here," he said.

"Not everyone could make it." Clay glanced over his shoulder at the group. "But there were too many to fit in anyone's house. D.J. volunteered the Shack for Christmas dinner."

Shane looked at the man in question who still hadn't said anything. The last time he'd been here, D.J. had thrown him out.

"We've got some things to say. Let's sit over there where it's quiet," Dax suggested, pointing to a far corner. "Otherwise the kids will drive you crazy."

That was a kind of crazy Shane wanted, but had given up hope he would ever have. Without a word, he followed the other men to the table all by itself in the big room. He had a feeling this wasn't so much about quiet as it was about protecting the women and children from the ugliness of the past, the flaw in him that was all about who his father was.

After the four of them took seats around the table, Dax looked at his cousin Clay, a look that said "get ready." "Some information has come to our attention."

Shane knew Clay was from Rust Creek where another branch of the family lived. He had the same Traub features—tall, muscular, dark hair and brown eyes. He was a little younger than the other two men and more boyish-looking. Although not now with intensity darkening his eyes and tension in his face.

Dax nodded at him. "Tell Shane what you told us."

"When I was a little kid…" Clay blew out a breath, then continued. "I overheard my parents arguing about Aunt Grace and Uncle Doug, Dax and D.J.'s parents. My mom just didn't understand how Grace could give away her own child then act as if he'd never existed. She was angry that

Uncle Doug didn't support her through it. Dad said that his brother would have had a hard time raising a child that wasn't his, but that ticked Mom off even more. She said Doug should have been man enough to put that aside for the sake of the baby, the child of the woman he loved." He shrugged at his cousins. "I only remembered recently. But when I was clear about the memory, I knew Dax and D.J. had a brother out there somewhere."

"Me." Shane looked at each man.

Dax nodded. "Clay wasn't sure whether or not to say anything to D.J. and me. Obviously that wasn't our father's finest hour."

"Or our mother's," D.J. added.

His brother nodded darkly. "We had a get-together last night for Christmas Eve and were talking about why the two sides of the family have been estranged all these years. Clay told us what he remembered. Then D.J. mentioned the conversation with you."

Shane looked at the man who looked so much like him. "The one where I told him about your mother and Arthur Swinton having an affair."

He waited for the explosion, but the two men didn't say a word. They looked shell-shocked and he realized the revelations were too recent. They needed time to take it all in.

"Look, I didn't come to Thunder Canyon to make trouble, just to find my birth parents. I did that. I'm sorry it involves your mother. I get that you don't want to believe it. But that doesn't change—"

Clay held up a hand. "D.J. told us what he said to you, but if you could cut him some slack… Just put yourself in his place. He had no reason to believe you. His mom died when he was a kid and his dad wasn't likely to bring up the subject." He rubbed a hand across the back of his neck. "But my parents knew Grace Smith had a baby and gave him up for adoption. They confirmed everything and it's why the two families had a falling out all those years ago."

"I didn't know any of this," D.J. confirmed. "Then you tell me my mother had a thing with Arthur Swinton. I thought you were lying and I couldn't figure out why you'd do that."

Shane figured he'd have felt the same if someone came to him with a wild story like this. All he could do now was reassure them. "I'm not looking for anything but the facts. If you want, we can do DNA tests to prove the truth once and for all."

"No." D.J. shook his head. "As soon as I calmed down, I realized all the evidence was right in front of me. Our personalities clicked. Similar sense of humor. I felt an almost instant connection."

"Then there was the strong resemblance that Allaire saw," Dax said.

His brother nodded. "We bonded right away, without even knowing the family link. It struck a chord that felt true. Then Clay tied everything together with what he remembered and we talked to Uncle Bob and Aunt Ellie, who confirmed his memory and everything else. We don't have any doubts."

Maybe not about being brothers, Shane realized. But there was still the fact of his father. He met their gazes, but this had to be said. "I know how you feel about Arthur Swinton."

The statement hung in the air and he knew they were filling in the blanks. His father was a criminal. But Gianna was right about him. "There's no reason you should believe this, but Arthur isn't a bad man. He loved our mother. Still does."

"You saw him in jail?" D.J. looked surprised.

"Yeah. He didn't know about me. She never said anything about being pregnant. No one should be too hard on her. Think about it. She was just a teenager. Scared. Under pressure from her family. I'm not judging and you shouldn't, either. No one's perfect and she was just doing what she thought was right for her family."

"I hear you," Dax said. "But it will take some time to work this through."

Shane nodded. "And I'm not saying Arthur deserves forgiveness, but he's a broken man. When she turned her back on him, he went off the deep end. He only saw that you all had her and he was left out in the cold."

"I'm not sure I can ever forgive him. He put me, my family and this town through a lot," D.J. said quietly.

Shane nodded. "I'd never tell you what to do, it's just that—"

"You're not like him," D.J. finished. "He couldn't handle what life threw at him, but it's not in the DNA."

"Pretty much." Shane was grateful he didn't have to make the case, that they got it. "I couldn't have said it better."

"It's a brother thing, I guess." D.J. stood and held out his hand. "I'm sorry for what I said."

"You mean the part where you threw me out of here?" Shane teased.

"That, too. I realized that in your shoes I'd have come looking for who I was. I'm sorry I was so hard on you."

"Forget it." Shane stood and took the other man's hand.

"Welcome to the family." D.J. pulled him into a quick bro hug.

Then it was Dax's turn. "Better late than never."

"Can't argue with that."

Shane remembered his dismissive comment to Gianna that you couldn't have too much family and knew now he was right about that. "This is a pretty good Christmas present."

"You're not getting mushy, are you?" D.J. joked.

"Of course not. You couldn't handle it."

And just like that they slipped into the teasing, macho banter thing that brothers did. It finally felt as if the last loose piece inside him clicked into place.

"Come on over and join the family," Dax said, indicating the gathering on the other side of the room.

"Can I get a rain check?" Shane asked. "Gianna is waiting for me—"

"I knew it," D.J. said. "There's something between you two, isn't there?"

"You're not matchmaking, are you?" Shane answered without answering.

"I don't have to. It's too late for that."

Shane just grinned at his brothers. The only thing that could keep him from joining the family group was Gianna. She'd been with him almost every step of the way. Even tonight she hadn't wanted him to be alone meeting his brothers and he wouldn't leave her alone any longer.

He had some things to say to her.

When she wasn't pacing, Gianna stood in front of the tall windows in Shane's living room, staring outside. It was a serene view most of the time, but not now. His family was watching a Christmas movie in the media room and had asked her to join them, but she couldn't sit still.

She shouldn't have let him go alone. D.J. was her friend. Maybe she could have been a bridge, helped the Traubs understand why he'd quietly gathered information instead of walking into their lives with guns blazing.

"Gianna?"

She turned and saw his mother. "Mrs. Roarke—"

"Please call me Christa. We're going to be seeing a lot of each other." There was a twinkle in her eyes.

Just a guess, but it seemed as if his mother was thinking there was something serious going on between her and Shane. It was serious, all right, but not in a good way. After learning that love had destroyed his father, it wasn't likely Shane would give it a try.

If Dax hadn't interrupted them, he would have told her he was leaving and they were over before even really getting started. Any second she expected Shane would come back and do just that. It was about protecting himself as well as her, but that didn't take the hurt away.

"Please tell me what's going on," Christa said.

"I'm not sure what you mean." That was lame and Gianna knew it. The woman was an attorney, for God's sake. Like she couldn't tell when someone was stalling?

"All right. I'll put a finer point on it. A man comes to see my son and he leaves. Now you're about to wear a hole in the floor from pacing." The woman's eyes narrowed on her. "Is he in some kind of trouble?"

"No." Probably not. She didn't think any punches were being thrown. All of them were too civilized for that, right? Except the information Shane had uncovered challenged all the Traubs' beliefs about their mother.

"Then why did he leave?" Christa asked.

Gianna didn't know what to do. This was Shane's journey, his story to tell, and should be done his way.

"He just went to the Rib Shack. It's a restaurant at Thunder Canyon Resort where they serve—ribs." She was babbling. And stalling.

"Imagine that." The woman gave her a "mom look," the expression specially designed to intimidate anyone under the age of forty.

"They're really good ribs," she said, all confidence leaking out of her voice. "A special sauce. Secret recipe."

"Uh-huh." Christa moved closer and there was understanding in her eyes. "Look, sweetheart, it's clear that you're trying to protect him and as his mother, I'm all for that. But if he needs help we need to go to him—"

At that moment the front door opened and closed, and Shane walked into the room. "Hi."

"You're back." Duh.

Gianna studied him and thank goodness he looked all right. No bruises or blood, but his expression gave no clue about what had happened.

"Shane, what's going on?" Christa asked. "Why did you disappear with that man?"

"Don't worry, Mom. Everything's fine. I'll tell you all about it later."

His mother studied him for several moments and seemed to see what she needed to. "You look all right. I'd know if you weren't. When you're ready to talk I'll be watching that hilarious Christmas movie about the little boy and the gun."

"Okay, Mom." When she started to walk away he said, "I love you."

She smiled. "I love you, too, son."

When she was gone, Shane said to Gianna, "We need to talk. Privately."

"Okay, but first—"

Without another word he took her arm and steered her to the French door. After opening it, he linked his fingers with hers, then led her outside.

"It's snowing," she said, blinking away the flakes that drifted into her eyes when she looked up at the sky.

"A white Christmas. That makes this an almost perfect day." He took off his jacket and dragged it around her shoulders. "There's just one more thing."

Perfect day? Not from her perspective. "What happened with Dax and D.J.?"

"I found my brothers," he said simply.

"That's not a news flash. What did they say?"

"That they're my brothers. If Ryan were here he'd say, 'What am I? Chopped liver?' The thing is, I love him, my whole family. I'd do anything for them."

"They feel the same about you." His mother had been this close to going to the Rib Shack to do battle with whoever might be hurting him.

"That's what makes it so hard to explain why getting to know the brothers who share my blood was so important." He dragged his hand through his hair. "I feel as if I've found the missing part of myself. But that implies that Mom, Dad, Ryan and Maggie aren't enough. And that's just not true."

"I think they understand. After all, your mother started this search. She knew you needed to find yourself."

"And I did."

"So, I guess Dax and D.J. had a change of heart and believed you?"

"Yeah. They're still reeling from the whole thing, but they welcomed me to the family."

"That means the Traubs and the Roarkes are all related, too."

"One big happy family. No one shut out," he said thoughtfully. "Like Arthur."

"I know. Thinking about that makes me sad for him."

"That's his cross to bear, but I can't hate him for it. My mother was a good woman, only trying to do the right thing for everyone. I believe that she loved me and wanted me in a place where I'd have a fresh start, no black mark to start life with. As for Arthur…" He was thoughtful for a moment. "He just loved too deeply a woman he could never have." He held the sides of his jacket together under her chin. "Now that I finally know who I am, I understand things about myself."

"Like what?"

"I've been running from life, but no more. When I

couldn't get on that plane it had nothing to do with the restaurant or a holiday plan. It was because of you. Through every important step on this journey of self-discovery I wasn't alone because you wouldn't let me be."

"It just wasn't right."

"Leaving you meant choosing to be alone and I couldn't do it."

He smiled down at her, then put his arm around her shoulders and held her close. Side by side they stared at the lights on the ski lift in the mountains.

"It was right here that I fell in love with Thunder Canyon." He met her gaze. "And right here where I fell in love with you."

She hadn't dared to hope and wasn't quite sure she'd heard right. "You fell in love with me? Right here?"

"Yes."

"But you didn't even kiss me that night," she reminded him.

"I was running then. How could I commit or ask you to when I didn't understand who I was? Now I know I'm a man who feels passionately, like my father. Except my story will have a happy ending because I don't intend to let you get away."

She rested her cheek on his chest, feeling the strong, steady beat of his heart, a rhythm that matched her own. "I assume you have a plan?"

"I do. First I want you to marry me."

She lifted her head and stared up at him. "I thought you were leaving Thunder Canyon."

"I want to put down roots here. Make this home base. I want you to be my partner in business and in life. With your experience and support, I believe together we can build a ridiculously successful restaurant empire and an even better marriage."

"Oh, Shane, I can't believe it—" Emotion choked off her words for a moment. "I didn't think it was possible to be so happy."

"I've never wanted anything as passionately as I want you, to have a family with you." He took her hands into his. "If I wasn't so dense I'd have bought you a ring, but we'll fix that as soon as the jewelry store opens tomorrow. Right now I just want you to say yes. I need to hear you say it because loving you is food to my soul."

"Yes. Yes. Yes. I love you so much." She threw her arms around his neck. "This is the best Christmas present ever. And you're right. This makes it an absolutely perfect day. Because 'tis the season of love."

He held her as if he'd never let her go. "That means every day for the rest of our lives will be like Christmas."

"And no mistletoe required. All I need is you."

* * * * *

A VERY SPECIAL DELIVERY

BRENDA HARLEN

This book is dedicated to my husband, Neill, an only child who gained two brothers (in-law) when we married.

Thanks for being a wonderful husband and the best father our boys could possibly have. XO

Chapter One

When she woke up the morning of November first staring at water stains on a stippled ceiling, Julie Marlowe wondered if she was having a bad dream. Then she remembered that uncomfortable twinges in her lower back had forced her to take a break on her journey home the day before, and the closest available accommodations had been at the Sleep Tite Motor Inn.

She managed to roll her pregnant body off the sagging mattress and swing her feet over the edge. The bathroom's tile floor was cold beneath her feet, and the trickle of spray that came out of the shower head wasn't much warmer. She washed quickly, then dried herself with the threadbare but clean towels on the rack. She had another long day of travel ahead of her, so she dressed comfortably in a pair of chocolate-colored leggings and a loose tunic-style top. Then she slipped her feet into the cowboy boots she'd bought "just because" when she'd been in Texas.

Seven months earlier, she'd had a lot of reasons for wanting to leave Springfield. But after traveling eight thousand miles through twenty-seven states and sleeping in countless hotel rooms, she was more than ready to go home.

She missed her family, her friends and the comfortable and predictable routines of her life. She even missed her father, despite the fact that he could be more than a little stubborn and overbearing on occasion. The only person she could honestly say that she didn't miss was Elliott Davis Winchester the Third—her former fiancé.

Julie had told her parents that she needed some time and some space to think about her future after ending her engagement. Lucinda and Reginald hadn't understood why she needed to go—and how could she expect that they would when there was so much she hadn't told them?—but they'd been supportive. They'd always been unflinching in their support and unwavering in their love, even when she screwed up.

When she left Springfield, Julie was determined to ensure that she didn't screw up again.

She felt a nudge beneath her rib, and smiled as she rubbed a hand over her belly. "You weren't a mistake, baby," she soothed. "Maybe I didn't plan for you at this point in my life, but I know that you're the best thing that ever happened to me, and I promise to be the best mommy that I can."

The baby kicked again, clearly unconvinced.

Julie couldn't blame her for being skeptical. Truthfully, she had more than a few doubts of her own. She and Elliott had talked about having children and neither wanted to wait too long after the wedding before starting a family, but she hadn't known she was pregnant when she gave him back his ring and left town.

After a quick visit to the doctor confirmed that she was going to have a baby, she wasn't even tempted to change her course. Though she'd known Elliott for two years—and had been engaged to him for six months—she'd suddenly realized that she didn't really know him at all. What she did know was that he wasn't the kind of a man she wanted to marry, and he certainly wasn't the kind of man that she wanted as a father for her baby.

Of course, that didn't change the fact that he *was* the father of her baby, but she hadn't been ready to deal with that reality in the moment. Maybe she'd been running away, but over the past few months she'd accepted that she couldn't run forever. In fact, in her current condition, she couldn't run at all anymore. The best she could manage was a waddle.

And she was ready to waddle home.

Lukas Garrett snagged a tiny box of candy from the orange bowl on the front desk—the remnants of the pile of Halloween candy from the day before—and emptied the contents into his mouth.

Karen, the veterinarian clinic receptionist and office manager, shook her head as he chewed the crunchy candy. "Please tell me that's not your lunch."

He swallowed before dutifully answering, "That's not my lunch."

"Lukas," she chided.

"Really," he assured her. "This is just the appetizer. I've got a sandwich in the fridge."

"PB & J?"

"Just PB today." He reached for another box of candy and had his hand slapped away.

"You need a good woman to take care of you."

It was a familiar refrain and he responded as he usually did. "You're a good woman and you take care of me."

"You need a wife," she clarified.

"Just say the word."

Karen, accustomed to his flirtatious teasing, shook her head.

"Go eat your sandwich," she directed. "As pathetic as it is, I'm sure it has slightly more nutritional value than candy."

"I'm waiting to have lunch after I finish with the morning appointments." He glanced at the clock on the wall, frowned. "I thought for sure Mrs. Cammalleri would be here with Snowball by now."

"She called to reschedule," Karen told him. "She didn't want to leave the house in this weather."

"What weather?" Luke turned to the window, then blinked in surprise at the swirling white flakes that were all that was visible through the glass. "When did it start snowing?"

"About an hour ago," Karen told him. "While you were ensuring that Raphael would never again be controlled by his most basic animal urges."

He moved closer to the window. "Did the forecast call for this?"

She nodded. "Twelve to fifteen inches."

He frowned. "How does global warming result in early season snowstorms?"

"We live in a Snowbelt," she reminded him. "And the current catchphrase is 'climate change.'"

"I'd prefer a climate change that included warm sun and sandy beaches."

"So book a vacation."

"I've been thinking about it," he admitted. And while an island getaway held a certain appeal, he had no desire to go on a holiday alone. Nor was he interested in venturing out solo with the goal of finding an anonymous female someone to share a few days of sun, sand and sex. That kind of thing had lost its appeal for Luke before he'd graduated college.

"Well, another thing you should think about is closing up early," Karen suggested. "Mrs. Cammalleri was your last scheduled appointment and the way the snow's already falling hard and fast, if we don't get out of here soon, we might not get out of here at all."

"The clinic's open until three on Fridays," he reminded her. "So I'll stay until then, but you go ahead."

"Are you sure you don't mind?"

"Of course not. There's no need for both of us to stay, and you've got a longer drive home than I do."

Karen was already tidying up her desk, straightening a pile of files, aligning the stapler with the edge of her desk calendar, putting the pens in the cup.

Luke took advantage of her distraction to snag another box of candy. "If this keeps up, the kids will be building snowmen tomorrow."

"Hard to believe they were trick-or-treating just last night, isn't it?"

"Yeah." He couldn't help but smile as he thought about his almost five-year-old nephews, Quinn and Shane, who had dressed up as SpongeBob and Patrick. Their baby sister, Pippa, was too young to go door-to-door, but even she'd been decked out in a pumpkin costume with a smiling jack-o'-lantern face on the front and a hat with stem and leaves.

His eldest niece—his brother Jackson's twelve-year-old daughter, Ava—had skipped the candy-grabbing ritual in favor of a Halloween party with some friends at the community center. And Jack had chaperoned. Luke wasn't at all surprised that his brother, who had earned quite the reputation as a heartbreaker in his youth, was a slightly overprotective father. The surprising part had been finding out that he was a father at all—especially to the daughter of the woman who had been Luke's best friend since fifth grade.

He was still surprised, and a little annoyed, that Kelly Cooper had managed to keep her weekend rendezvous with Jack a secret for more than twelve years. It was only when she'd moved back to Pinehurst with her daughter at the end of the

summer that Luke had learned that his brother was Ava's father and that his designation as "Uncle Luke" was more than
an honorary title. He still wasn't sure that he'd completely
forgiven her for keeping that secret for so long, but he was
genuinely thrilled that Kelly and Jack were together now and
making plans for an early December wedding.

"From carving pumpkins to throwing snowballs in the
blink of an eye," Karen noted as she turned to retrieve her
coat and purse from the cabinet behind her desk—then muttered a curse under her breath as she nearly tripped over Einstein, Luke's seven-month-old beagle puppy.

He'd been one of a litter of eight born to a severely mal-
nourished and exhausted female who had been abandoned
on the side of the road. A passerby had found the animal and
taken her to the veterinarian clinic. The mother hadn't sur-
vived the birth, and Luke had been determined to ensure that
her efforts to give life to her pups weren't in vain.

Thankfully, Karen had stepped up to help, and between
the two of them, they'd made sure that the puppies were fed
and nurtured and loved—and then they'd given them to good
homes. But Luke had always known that he would keep one,
and Einstein was the one he'd chosen. And he loved the crazy
animal, even if he wasn't exactly the genius of his namesake.

When the puppies were first born and required almost
constant care, it made sense for them to be at the clinic. Luke
also believed it would help with their socialization, getting
them accustomed to being around people and other animals,
and so he'd continued the practice with Einstein long after his
brothers and sisters had gone to other homes. Unfortunately,
one of Einstein's favorite places in the clinic was wherever
he could find Karen's feet.

"I swear that animal is trying to kill me." But despite the
annoyance in her tone, she bent to rub his head, giving him

an extra scratch behind his left ear because she knew that was his favorite spot.

"Only if he could love you to death," Luke assured her.

She shook her head as she made her way to the door. "You should go home, too," she said again. "No one's going to come out in this weather."

As it turned out, she was right. Aside from Raphael's owner who came to pick him up, the front door didn't open and the phone didn't ring. So promptly at three o'clock, Luke locked up the clinic and headed out to his truck with Einstein.

Of course, this was the puppy's first exposure to snow, and when he stepped out onto the deck and found himself buried up to his chest in the cold, white fluff, he was not very happy. He whined and jumped, trying desperately to get away from it. And when he couldn't escape it, he decided to attack it. He barked and pranced around, clearly under the impression that he was winning the battle.

Luke couldn't help but chuckle at his antics. The animal would probably play in the snow for hours if he let him, so he finally picked up the pup and carried him to the truck. He sat him on the floor of the passenger side and let the heater blow warm air on him while Luke cleared the thick layer of snow off of his windows.

Luckily he'd found an old hat and a pair of gloves in his office, and he was grateful for both. The unexpected snow-fall might have been fun for Einstein, but driving through it was a completely different story, even with all-wheel drive. The snow had been falling steadily and quickly and the plows hadn't yet been around, so he knew the roads would probably be slick—a fact that was proven when he fishtailed a little as he pulled out of the clinic's driveway and onto the street.

Warm and dry once again, Einstein hopped up onto the passenger seat and pressed his nose against the window, his breath fogging up the glass. When Luke finally turned onto

Terrace Drive, the pup barked excitedly, three quick little yips. The snow was still falling with no indication that it would let up anytime soon, and he was as happy as Einstein to know that they were almost home.

The cold had come after the snow, so the first layer of flakes had melted on the road, then frozen. Now there was a dangerous layer of ice beneath everything else, and Luke suspected the tow trucks would be working late into the night. It would be too easy to slide off the road and into a ditch in these conditions—as someone had apparently done right in front of his house.

Julie clenched the steering wheel with both hands and bit down on her bottom lip to hold back the scream of frustration that threatened to burst from her throat. A quick detour through Pinehurst to meet with a friend of her brother's from law school had seemed like a great idea when she'd called and made the appointment a few hours earlier, but that was before the snow started.

Still, she'd no intention of being dissuaded by some light flurries. Except that those light flurries had quickly escalated into an actual blizzard. Weather reports on the radio had warned people to avoid unnecessary travel. Since Julie had been on the highway between Syracuse and Pinehurst at the time and pulling off to the side of the road in order to be buried in snow didn't seem like a particularly appealing option, she decided her travel was necessary.

And she'd almost made it. According to her GPS, she was less than three miles from Jackson Garrett's office—but it might as well have been thirty. There was no way she could walk, not in her condition and not in this weather.

Tears of frustration filled her eyes, blurred her vision. She let her head fall forward, then jolted back again when the horn sounded. Great—not only had she driven into a ditch, she'd just drawn attention to the fact by alerting anyone who happened to be passing by. She didn't know if she was more relieved or apprehensive when she realized that no one seemed to be anywhere in the vicinity.

She was sure she'd seen houses not too far back. In fact, she specifically remembered a sprawling ranch-style with a trio of grinning jack-o'-lanterns on the wide front porch, because she'd noted that it wouldn't be too long before those pumpkins were completely blanketed by snow.

She closed her eyes and silently cursed Mother Nature. Okay, maybe she had to accept responsibility for the fact that she'd been driving through a blizzard with no snow tires— but who the heck would have thought that she'd need snow tires on the first day of November?

She felt a spasm in her lower back in conjunction with a ripple of pain that tightened her whole belly. Julie splayed a hand over her tummy, silently trying to reassure her baby that everything was okay. But as the first tears spilled onto her cheeks, she had to admit—if only to herself—that she didn't know if it was. She didn't know how being stuck in a ditch in the middle of nowhere during a freak snowstorm could possibly be "okay."

She drew in a deep breath and tried to get the tears under control. She didn't usually blubber, but the pregnancy hormones running rampant through her system had been seriously messing with her emotional equilibrium. Wiping the trails of moisture from her cheeks, she tried to look on the bright side.

She knew she wasn't lost. She wasn't exactly sure where she was, but she'd followed the directions of her GPS so she wasn't actually in the middle of nowhere. She was in Pinehurst, New York. An even brighter side was found when she pulled her cell phone out of her purse and confirmed that her battery was charged and she had a signal. Further proof that she wasn't in the middle of nowhere.

Confident that she would be able to get some roadside assistance, Julie leaned over to open the glove box to get the number and gasped as pain ripped across her back. Gritting her teeth, she blew out a slow, unsteady breath and prayed that it was just a spasm. That the jolt of sliding into the ditch had pulled a muscle in her back.

On the other hand, it could be a sign that she was in labor. And right now, that was *not* a scenario she wanted to consider.

"Please, baby—" she rubbed a hand over her belly "—don't do this now. You've got a couple more weeks to hang out right where you are, and I'm not even close to being ready for you yet."

Moving more carefully this time, she reached for the folio that contained her vehicle ownership and warranty information and—most important—her automobile association card. Hopefully there wasn't any damage to her car and as soon as it was pulled out of the ditch, she could be on her way again.

Except that when she dialed the toll-free number on the card, she got a recorded message informing her that all of the operators were currently busy assisting other customers and to please hold the line if she wanted to maintain her call priority. She disconnected. It would probably be easier—and quicker—for her to find the number of a local company and make a direct call. Or maybe, if she was really lucky, a Good Samaritan with a big truck conveniently equipped with tow cables would drive down this road and stop to help.

A flash of color caught the corner of her eye and she turned her head to see a truck drive past, then pull into a driveway she hadn't even noticed was less than ten feet from where she was stranded. The vehicle stopped, the driver's side door opened and then a gust of wind swirled the thick snow around, obliterating her view.

She thought she heard something that sounded like a dog barking, but the sound quickly faded away.

Then there was a knock on her window, and her heart leaped into her throat. Not thirty seconds earlier, she'd been praying that a Good Samaritan would come to her rescue, and now someone was at her door. But how was she supposed to know if he had stopped to offer help—or if his intentions were less honorable?

Her breath was coming faster now, and the windows were fogging up, making it even harder to see. All she could tell was that he was tall, broad-shouldered and wearing a dark cap on his head. He was big. The road was mostly deserted. She was helpless.

No, she wasn't. She had her cell phone. She held it up, to show him that she was in contact with the outside world, then rolled down her window a few inches. A gust of cold air blasted through the scant opening, making her gasp.

"Are you okay, ma'am?"

Ma'am? The unexpectedness of the formal address in combination with the evident concern in his tone reassured her, at least a little. She lifted her gaze to his face, and her heart jolted again. But this time she knew the physiological response had nothing to do with fear—it was a sign of purely female appreciation for a truly spectacular male.

The knit cap was tugged low on his forehead so she couldn't see what color his hair was, but below dark brows, his eyes were the exact same shade of blue-green as the aquamarine gemstone ring her parents had given to her for her twenty-first birthday. His nose was just a little off-center, his cheekbones sharp, his jaw square. He had a strong face, undeniably masculine and incredibly handsome. His voice was low and soothing, and when he spoke again, she found her gaze riveted on the movement of his lips.

"Ma'am?" he said again.

"I'm okay. I'm just waiting for a tow truck."

He frowned. "I'm not sure how long you'll have to wait. I managed to squeeze through just as the police were putting up barriers to restrict access to Main Street."

"What does that mean?"

"It means that the primary road through town is shut down."

She sighed. "Any chance you have tow cables in your truck?"

He shook his head. "Sorry."

She gasped as another stab of pain slashed through her.

"You *are* hurt," he decided. "Let me call an ambulance."

She shook her head. "I'm not hurt. I think...I'm in labor."

Chapter Two

"Labor? As in having a baby?" Luke couldn't quite get his head around what she was saying. Not until he noticed that her hand was splayed on her belly.

Her very round belly.

How had he *not* noticed that she was pregnant?

Probably because his most immediate concern, when he'd spotted the vehicle in the ditch, was that the driver might be injured, maybe even unconscious. He hadn't given a passing thought to the driver's gender. And then, when she'd rolled down the window, he'd been absolutely spellbound by her wide and wary blue-gray eyes.

But now, with his attention focused on the bump beneath her shirt, the words that had seemed undecipherable suddenly made sense. "You're pregnant."

Her brows lifted in response to his not-so-astute observation. "Yes, I'm pregnant," she confirmed.

She was also a pretty young thing—emphasis on the

young. Early twenties, he guessed, with clear, flawless skin, high cheekbones, a patrician nose and lips that were surprisingly full and temptingly shaped.

He felt the subtle buzz through his veins, acknowledged it. He'd experienced the stir of attraction often enough in the past to recognize it for what it was—and to know that, under the circumstances, it was completely inappropriate.

Young, beautiful *and pregnant,* he reminded himself.

"Actually, I don't think it is labor," she said now. "I'm probably just overreacting to the situation."

But he wasn't quite ready to disregard the possibility. "When are you due?"

"November fifteenth."

Only two weeks ahead of schedule. He remembered his sister-in-law, Georgia, telling him that she'd been two weeks early with Pippa, so the timing didn't seem to be any real cause for concern. Of course, Georgia had also been in the hospital. The fact that this woman was stuck in a ditch and nowhere near a medical facility might be a bit of an issue.

He took a moment to clear his head and organize his thoughts, and saw her wince again.

"Are you having contractions?"

"No," she said quickly, and just a little desperately. "Just… twinges."

Apparently she didn't want to be in labor any more than he wanted her to be in labor, but that didn't mean she wasn't.

"I think I should call 911 to try to get an ambulance out here and get you to the hospital."

"It's probably just false labor."

"Have you been through this before?"

"No," she admitted. "This is my first. But I've read a ton of books on pregnancy and childbirth, and I'm pretty sure what I'm experiencing are just Braxton Hicks contractions."

He wasn't convinced, but he also wasn't going to waste

any more time arguing with her. Not with the snow blowing around the way it was and the condition of the roads rapidly getting worse. He pulled out his phone and dialed.

"911. Please state the nature of your emergency."

He recognized the dispatcher's voice immediately, and his lips instinctively curved as he recalled a long-ago summer when he and the emergency operator had been, at least for a little while, more than friends. "Hey, Yolanda, it's Luke Garrett. I was wondering if you could send an ambulance out to my place."

"What happened?" The clinical detachment in her tone gave way to concern. "Are you hurt?"

"No, it's not me. I'm with a young woman—"

He glanced at her, his brows raised in silent question.

"Julie Marlowe," she told him.

"—whose car went into the ditch beside my house."

"Is she injured?"

"She says no, but she's pregnant, two weeks from her due date and experiencing what might be contractions."

"Twinges," the expectant mother reminded him through the window.

"She insists that they're twinges," Luke said, if only to reassure her that he was listening. "But they're sharp enough that she gasps for breath when they come."

"Can I talk to her?"

He tapped on the window, and Julie lowered the glass a few more inches to take the device from him. Because she was inside the car with the window still mostly closed, he could only decipher snippets of their conversation, but he got the impression that Yolanda was asking more detailed questions about the progress of her pregnancy, possible complications and if there were any other indications of labor.

A few minutes later, Julie passed the phone back to him.

"If I thought I could get an ambulance through to you, I'd

be sending one," Yolanda told Luke. "But the police have completely shut down Main Street in both directions."

"But emergency vehicles should be able to get through."

"If they weren't all out on other calls," she agreed. "And the reality is that an expectant mother with no injuries in the early stages of labor, as Julie seems to think she might be, is not an emergency."

"What if the situation changes?"

"If the situation changes, call me back. Maybe by then the roads will be plowed and reopened and we can get her to the hospital."

"You don't sound too optimistic," he noted.

"The storm dumped a lot of snow fast and there's no sign that it's going to stop any time soon. The roads are a mess and emergency crews are tapped."

He bit back a sigh of frustration. "What if the baby doesn't want to wait that long?"

"Then you'll handle it," she said, and quickly gave him some basic instructions. "And don't worry—I reassured the expectant mom that Doctor Garrett has done this countless times before."

"Please tell me you're joking."

"I'm not." There was no hint of apology in her tone. "The woman needed reassurance, and I gave it to her."

And although her statement was technically true, she'd neglected to mention that the majority of the births he'd been involved with had been canine or feline in nature. He had absolutely no experience bringing human babies into the world.

Luke stared at Julie, who gasped as another contraction hit her. "You better get an ambulance here as soon as possible."

Julie was still mulling over the information the dispatcher had given her when she saw her Good Samaritan—who was apparently also a doctor—tuck his phone back into the pocket of his jacket.

"Let's get you up to the house where it's warm and dry."

She wished that staying in the car was a viable option. She was more than a little uneasy about going into a stranger's home, but her feet and her hands were already numb and she had to clench her teeth together to keep them from chattering. She took some comfort from the fact that the emergency operator knew her name and location.

She rolled up the window—no point in letting the inside of the car fill up with snow—and unlocked the door.

As soon as she did, he opened it for her, then offered his other hand to help her out. He must have noticed the iciness of her fingers even through his gloves, because before she'd stepped onto the ground, he'd taken them off his hands and put them on hers. They were toasty warm inside, and she nearly whimpered with gratitude.

He walked sideways up the side of the ditch, holding on to both of her hands to help her do the same. Unfortunately the boots that she'd so happily put on her feet when she set out that morning had smooth leather soles, not exactly conducive to gaining traction on a snowy incline. She slipped a few times and no doubt would have fallen if not for his support. When she finally made it to level ground, he picked her up—scooping her off her feet as if she weighed nothing—and carried her to the passenger side of his truck. She was too startled to protest, and all too conscious of the extra twenty-nine pounds that she was carrying—and now *he* was carrying. But when he settled her gently on the seat, he didn't even seem winded.

He drove up the laneway, parked beside the house. When he inserted his key into the lock, she heard a cacophony of excited barking from the other side of the door.

"You have dogs?"

"Just one." Her rescuer shook his head as the frantic yips continued. "We just got home. I let him out of the truck at the end of the driveway when I saw your vehicle, and he raced ahead to the house to come in through the doggy door, as he always does. And every day when I put my key in the lock, he acts as if it's been days rather than minutes since he last saw me."

"They don't have much of a concept of time, do they?"

"Except for dinnertime," he noted dryly. "He never forgets that one."

He opened the door and gestured for her to enter. But before Julie could take a step forward, there was a tri-colored whirlwind of fur and energy weaving between her feet.

"Einstein, sit."

The dog immediately plopped his butt on the snow-covered porch right beside her boots and looked up with shiny, dark eyes, and his master scooped him up to give her a clear path through the door.

"Oh, he's just a little guy. And absolutely the cutest thing I've ever seen."

"He's cute," the doctor agreed. "And he hasn't met anyone he doesn't immediately love, but sometimes he's too stubborn for his own good."

She slipped her boots off inside the door, and when he put the puppy down again, it immediately attacked her toes with an enthusiastic tongue and gentle nips of his little teeth.

"Einstein, no!"

The pup dropped his head and looked up, his eyes filled with so much hurt and remorse, Julie couldn't help but laugh.

The doctor looked at her with a slightly embarrassed shrug. "He's got some kind of foot fetish. I'm not having a lot of luck in trying to curb it."

"No worries, my feet are too numb to feel much, anyway."

"Come on." He took her arm and guided her down the hall

and into what she guessed was a family room. The floor was a dark glossy hardwood and the walls were painted a rich hunter-green, set off by the wide white trim and cove moldings. There was a chocolate leather sectional and a matching armchair facing a gorgeous stone fireplace flanked by tall, narrow windows. The lamps on the mission-style side tables were already illuminated, but as he stepped through the wide, arched doorway, he hit another switch on the wall and flames came to life in the firebox.

"You should warm up quickly in here," he told her. "I converted to gas a few years ago. As much as I love the smell of a real wood fire, I prefer the convenience of having heat and flame at the flick of a switch."

"You have a beautiful home," Julie told him. And, it seemed to her, a big home, making her wonder if he had a wife and kids to help fill it. She hadn't seen a ring on his finger, but she knew that didn't prove anything.

"I like it," he said easily.

She moved closer to the fireplace, drawn by the flickering flames and the tempting warmth. "Do you live here alone?"

"Me and Daphne and Einstein," he clarified.

She was reassured by this revelation that she wouldn't actually be alone with a stranger. "Daphne's your...wife?"

"No."

He responded quickly—so quickly she couldn't help but smile. The immediate and predictable denial was that of a perennial bachelor with absolutely no desire to change his status.

"Daphne's a three-year-old blue Burmese, and not very sociable. Unlike Einstein, you'll only see her if she decides you're worthy of her presence."

Which meant that they *were* alone—except for a cat and a dog. But he was a doctor, and the emergency operator had vouched for him, and she had to stop being wary of everyone just because her experience with Elliott had caused her to doubt her own judgment. "It's a big house for one man and two pets," she noted.

"Believe me, it felt a lot smaller when I had to share it with two brothers."

"You grew up here?"

He nodded. "Born and raised and lived my whole life in Pinehurst, in this house. Well, I wasn't actually born in this house—my mother wanted to do things more traditionally and give birth in the hospital."

"That was my plan, too," she admitted.

"Sliding into a ditch and going into labor during an unexpected snowstorm was a spur-of-the-moment decision?" he teased.

"I'm not in labor," she said again. "My baby isn't due for another two weeks and first babies are almost never early."

"Almost isn't the same as never," he told her, and pushed the oversize leather chair closer to the fire so that she could sit down.

When she lowered herself into the seat, he sat cross-legged on the floor facing her and lifted her feet into his lap. "Your feet are like ice," he noted.

She was startled by the boldness of the move and felt as if she should protest—but only until he started to rub her toes between his hands, then she closed her eyes and nearly moaned with pleasure.

In fact, she probably did make some kind of noise, because Einstein bounded over, eager to play with her feet, too. But one sharp look from his master had him curling up on the rug in front of the fire.

"Don't you own winter boots or a proper coat?" the doctor asked her.

"Of course I do, but it wasn't snowing when I started out this morning."

"Started out from where?"

"Cleveland," she admitted.

"Then you obviously did a lot of driving today."

"About seven hours."

"Heading back to Boston?"

She eyed him warily. "What makes you think I'm going to Boston?"

"I saw the Massachusetts plates on your car, and there's just a hint of a Boston accent in your voice."

"I wasn't planning on going any further than Pinehurst today," she said, deliberately not confirming nor denying his assumption. Then, because she'd rather be asking questions than answering them, she said, "Is Luke short for Lukas?"

"It is." He set down the first foot and picked up the second one.

"I've been researching baby names," Julie told him. "Lukas means bringer of light."

And she thought the name suited him, not just because he'd rescued her—bringing her hope if not necessarily light—but because it was strong and masculine.

"Have you narrowed down your choices?"

She nodded.

"Any hints?"

She shook her head, then gasped when the pain ripped through her again.

Luke released her foot and laid his hands on the curve of her belly. She tried to remember everything she'd read about Braxton Hicks and how to distinguish those false contractions from real labor, but in the moment, she was lucky she remembered to breathe through the pain.

After what seemed like forever, the tightness across her belly finally eased.

"Twinge?" Though his tone was deliberately light, she saw the concern in his eyes.

"Yeah." She drew in a deep breath, released it slowly.

"I'm going to put the puppy in the laundry room, just so that he's out of the way in case things start to happen." Then he took the dog away, returning a few minutes later with an armful of blankets and towels and a plastic bin filled with medical supplies. He covered the leather chaise with a thick flannel sheet, then folded a blanket over the foot of it.

"Is there anyone you should call?" the doctor asked. "Anyone who's going to worry about where you are?"

She shook her head. Her parents wouldn't know that she'd been caught in this storm because they hadn't known about her intention to detour through the Snowbelt on her way home.

"Husband? Boyfriend?" he prompted.

"No." She could see the direction he was going with his questions, and she was almost grateful when her body spasmed with pain again. It was easier to focus on the contraction—whether false or real—than on the reasons why her relationship with her baby's father had fallen apart.

She was gripping the armrests of the chair, but noticed that he was looking at his watch, counting the seconds. She panted softly and tried to think of something—anything—but the pain that ripped through her. The books she'd read talked about focal points, how to use a picture or some other item to evoke pleasant memories and a feeling of peace. Right now, all she had was Luke Garrett, but his warm gaze and steady tone—proof of his presence and reassurance that she wasn't entirely alone—somehow made the pain bearable.

"Ninety seconds," he said. "And I'd guess less than five minutes since the last one."

"It doesn't look like my baby's going to wait for a hospital, does it?"

"I'd say not," he agreed. "Did you take prenatal classes?"

"No."

"Your doctor didn't recommend it?"

"I've been traveling a lot over the past few months, so I didn't have a chance."

"Traveling where?"

"Pretty much everywhere."

"Work or pleasure?"

"Both."

She knew it sounded as if she was being evasive, and maybe she was, but it wasn't in her nature to share personal information with someone she didn't know and whom she probably wouldn't ever see again when the roads were finally cleared and her car was pulled out of the ditch.

"I'm just making conversation," he told her. "I thought it might take your mind off of the contractions."

"I was counting on an epidural to do that," she admitted.

His lips curved. "Well, it's good that you have a sense of humor, because an epidural isn't really an option right now."

She liked his smile. It was warm and genuine, and it made her think that everything was going to be okay. "I knew it was too much to hope that you rented a spare bedroom to a local anesthesiologist."

He took her hand, linked their fingers together and gave hers a reassuring squeeze.

"I'm scared," she admitted.

"You're doing great."

"I don't just mean about giving birth," she told him. "I mean about being a parent."

"Let's concentrate on the giving birth part for now," he suggested.

She sucked in another breath and gritted her teeth so that she didn't embarrass herself by whimpering. Or screaming. The pain was unlike anything she'd ever experienced, and she knew it would continue to worsen before it got better.

"Breathe," Luke said, and she realized that she wasn't

doing so. She released the air she was holding in her lungs in short, shallow pants. "That's it."

"Okay," she said when the contraction had finally eased.

"Two minutes," he announced, not very happily.

She could understand his concern. Her contractions—and she knew now that they were definitely contractions—were coming harder and faster. The idea of giving birth outside of a hospital was absolutely terrifying, but somehow, with Luke beside her, she felt confident that she would get through it. More importantly, she felt that her baby would get through it.

"Should I get undressed now?"

It wasn't the first time he'd had a woman say those words to him, but it was the first time they'd come at Luke completely out of the blue.

And apparently Julie realized that her casual statement might be misinterpreted, because her cheeks flooded with color. "So that you can examine me," she clarified.

Examine her. Right. She was an expectant mother and he was the doctor who was helping to deliver her baby. Of course she would expect him to examine her.

He mentally recalled the brief instructions he'd been given by the 911 operator. Thankfully the human birthing process wasn't very different from that of other mammals, but Luke felt more than a little guilty that Julie was offering to strip down for him because she thought he was an MD.

It should have been simple enough to think like a doctor. But he couldn't forget the quick punch of desire he'd felt when his eyes had first locked with hers. Before he'd realized that she was eight and a half months pregnant. Still, the fact that she was about to give birth didn't make her any less attractive, although he would have hoped that this tangible evidence of her involvement with another man should have cooled his ardor.

But the combination of her beauty and spirit appealed to something in him. She'd found herself in a tough situation, but she was dealing with it. Sure, she was scared. Under the circumstances, who wouldn't be? But she'd demonstrated a willingness to face that fear head-on, and he had to respect that courage and determination. And when he looked into those blue-gray eyes, he wanted to take up his sword to fight all of her battles for her. Not that she would appreciate his efforts—most women preferred to fight their own battles nowadays, but the desire to honor and protect was deeply ingrained in his DNA.

He wasn't interested in anything beyond that, though. Sure, he liked women and enjoyed their company, but he wasn't looking to tie himself to any one woman for the long term. His brothers had both lucked out and found partners with whom they wanted to share the rest of their lives, and he was happy for them, but he didn't see himself as the marrying kind. Certainly he'd never met a woman who made him think in terms of forever.

Which was just one more reason that he had no business thinking about Julie Marlowe at all. She might be beautiful and sexy but she was also on the verge of becoming a mother—no way would she be interested in a fling, and no way was he interested in anything else.

So he gave her privacy to strip down—and his plush robe to wrap around herself. He was trying to think about this situation as a doctor would—clinically and impartially. But how was he supposed to be impartial when she had those beautiful winter-sky eyes and those sweetly curved lips, sexy shoulders and sexy feet? And despite the baby bump, she had some very appealing curves, too.

When he returned to the family room, he was relieved to see that she was wearing the robe he'd left for her so she wasn't entirely naked beneath the thin sheet she'd pulled up over herself. But she still looked vulnerable and scared, and every last shred of objectivity flew out the window.

She was panting—blowing out short puffs of air that warned him he'd missed another contraction. "I thought I had a pretty good threshold for pain," she told him. "I was wrong."

He knelt at the end of the chaise, and felt perspiration beginning to bead on his brow. She was the one trying to push a baby out of her body, and he was sweating at the thought of watching her do it. But when he folded back the sheet and saw the top of the baby's head, everything else was forgotten.

"The baby's already crowning," he told her.

"Does that mean I can start to push?"

"Whenever you're ready."

He talked her through the contractions, telling her when to push and when to pant, trying to ensure that her body was able to adjust to each stage and rest when possible.

Of course, it was called labor for a reason, and although it was progressing quickly, he knew it wasn't painless. Her hands were fisted in the sheet, and he covered one with his own, gave it a reassuring squeeze. "It won't be too much longer now."

"Promise?"

He looked up and saw that her stormy eyes were filled with tears and worry. "I promise."

As she pushed through the next contraction, the head slowly emerged. The soft, indignant cry that accompanied the baby's emergence from the birth canal confirmed that its lungs were working just fine.

"You're doing great," he told Julie. "Just—"

He didn't even have a chance to finish his sentence before the baby slid completely out and into his hands.

Chapter Three

Luke stared in awe at the wet, wrinkled infant that was somehow the most beautiful creature he'd ever seen. And when the baby looked at him with big blue eyes wide with innocence and wonder, he fell just a little bit in love with the little guy.

He wiped the baby's face carefully with a clean, soft towel to ensure that his nose and mouth were clear of fluid. Then he wrapped him, still attached by the cord, in a blanket and laid him on his mother's chest.

"And there he is," he told her.

Julie blinked, as if startled by this statement. *"He?"*

"You have a beautiful, healthy baby boy," he confirmed. "Born at 4:58 pm on November first."

"A boy," she echoed softly, her lips curving just a little. "My baby boy."

Tears filled her eyes, then spilled onto her cheeks. She wiped at them impatiently with the back of her hand.

"I'm sorry. I'm not usually so emotional."

"It's been an emotional day," Luke said, feeling a little choked up himself.

It took her a few minutes to get her tears under control before she spoke again, and when she did, she surprised him by saying, "I thought he'd be a girl. I *wanted* a girl." After a moment she continued. "I don't even feel guilty admitting it now. Because looking down at him, I know that I couldn't possibly love him any more if he had been a she. All that matters is that he's mine."

"Why did you want a girl?" he asked curiously.

"I guess I thought it would be easier to raise a girl, since I was once one myself. I don't know anything about little boys. Or big boys." She glanced up at him and offered a wry smile. "And personal experience has proven that I don't understand the male gender at all."

"Are you disappointed that he's a he?"

She shook her head. "No. I'm not disappointed at all. He's…perfect."

"That he is."

"I never expected to feel so much. I look at him, and my heart practically overflows with love." But she managed to lift her gaze from the baby to look at Luke now. "Thank you, Dr. Garrett."

He didn't know how to respond to her gratitude, especially when he felt as if *he* should be thanking *her*. Because in his entire life, he had honestly never experienced anything more incredible than helping to bring Julie's beautiful baby boy into the world.

What he'd told her earlier was true—the hard part was all hers. And he couldn't help but be awed by the strength and determination and courage she'd shown in face of the challenge. He felt honored and privileged to have been a part of the experience, to have been the very first person to hold the brand-new life in his hands.

By the time he'd cut the cord and delivered the placenta, Julie had put the baby to her breast and was already nursing. And Luke finally let himself exhale a silent sigh of relief.

He tidied up, gathering the used sheets and towels, then left mother and child alone while he stepped away to call Yolanda to let her know that an ambulance was no longer a priority. She offered hearty congratulations and a smug "I knew you could handle one little baby" then signed off to deal with other matters.

After putting a load of laundry in the washing machine, Luke fed Einstein, then realized that his stomach was growling, too. And if he was hungry, he imagined that Julie was even more so. He put some soup on the stove to heat, then peeked into the family room again.

"How are you feeling now?"

"Exhausted," she admitted. "And ecstatic. I don't know how I can ever repay you for everything you've done."

"I'm just glad I was here to help."

She smiled at that. "And if an ambulance could have got through the storm, you would have shipped me off to the hospital in a heartbeat."

"Absolutely," he agreed without hesitation.

"Since I am still here, there is something I wanted to ask you."

"Sure."

"What do you think of the name Caden?" She looked at him expectantly, trying to gauge his reaction.

"What does it mean?" he asked.

"Fighter or battle."

He nodded. "I like it."

She smiled down at the baby before lifting her eyes to

meet his again. "Then let me formally introduce you to Caden Lukas Marlowe."

She saw surprise flicker in his eyes, then pleasure. He offered his finger to the baby, and Caden wrapped his tiny fist around it, holding on tight. "That's a lot of name for such a little guy," he noted.

"You don't mind the 'Lukas' part?"

"Why would I mind?"

She shrugged. "I wanted him to have a small part of the man who helped bring him into the world. I know we probably won't ever see you again after we leave Pinehurst, but I don't want to forget—and I don't want Caden to forget—everything you've done."

"You're not planning to go anywhere just yet, are you?"

"Not just yet," she assured him. "But I figured you'd want to get us out of here as soon as the roads are clear."

Of course, she couldn't go anywhere until her car was pulled out of the ditch and any necessary repairs were made, but she didn't expect her Good Samaritan to put them up for the duration.

He shrugged. "As you noted, it's a big house for one person and two pets."

She wasn't entirely sure what he was suggesting. Was he really offering to let them stay with him? And even if he was, she could hardly stay in the home of a man she'd just met. No matter that she already felt more comfortable with him than with the man she'd planned to marry.

Before she could ask, she heard the sound of footsteps stomping on the porch. Despite the fact that the roads were still closed, Lukas didn't seem at all surprised to have a visitor—or that the visitor, after a brisk knock, proceeded to open the door and walk right into the house.

Einstein had been released from the laundry room and cautiously introduced to the baby. Since then, he hadn't left Julie's side. But he obviously heard the stomping, too, because he raced across the room and down the hall to the foyer, barking and dancing the whole way.

The sharp barks startled the baby, and Caden responded with an indignant wail of his own. Julie murmured reassuringly and snuggled him closer to her chest, and by the time the visitor had made his way down the hall to the family room, he was settled again.

"This is a friend of mine," Lukas told her, gesturing to the tall, dark-haired man beside him. "Cameron Turcotte." Then to Cameron he said, "This is Julie Marlowe and Caden."

"Are the roads clear now?" Julie asked him. She assumed that they must be if he was able to get through, although she couldn't begin to fathom why he would have chosen to visit a friend in the middle of a snowstorm.

"The plows are out in full force, but it's going to take a while," he told her. "Main Street is technically still shut down, but I knew the officer posted at the barricade and told him that I had to get through to deal with a medical emergency."

"Are you a doctor, too?" Julie asked him.

Cameron's brows lifted. "Too?"

"Yolanda wanted to reassure Julie that she was in capable hands with Doctor Garrett," Lukas told his friend.

The other man chuckled.

"Why do I feel as if I'm missing something?" Julie asked warily.

"The only thing that matters is that you and your baby are okay," Cameron said. "And since I was on my way home from the hospital, Luke asked if I could stop by to check on both of you. With your permission, of course."

She looked questioningly at Lukas. "I don't understand. You said everything was okay. Is something—"

"Nothing's wrong," he said, answering her question before

she could finish asking it. "But you may have misunderstood my qualifications."

She frowned. "What do you mean?"

"I'm a DVM, not an MD," he told her.

It only took her a few seconds to decipher the acronym, and when she did, her jaw dropped.

"My baby was delivered by a *vet?*"

Lukas nodded.

Julie was stunned.

And mortified.

Dr. Garrett wasn't a qualified medical doctor—he was an animal doctor.

She drew in a deep breath and tried to accept the reality of the situation. And the truth was, neither of them had had any other choice. She'd been stranded in his house in a blizzard with no one else around to help. Her options had been simple: accept his assistance or try to deliver her baby on her own. And, in his defense, he hadn't claimed to be a doctor— it was the 911 operator who had offered that information.

And she'd grasped at it with both hands. It wasn't how she'd wanted to deliver her baby but knowing that she had no chance of getting to a hospital, she'd considered herself lucky that her car had gone into the ditch by a doctor's house. Proving once again that she had a tendency to see what she wanted to see.

"I didn't intend to deceive you," Lukas said to her now. "But you seemed to find comfort in believing that I was a medical doctor, and I didn't want to cause you undue stress by correcting that impression."

And she'd willingly stripped out of her clothes because a doctor—especially an obstetrician—was accustomed to his patients doing that. Glancing at the veterinarian who had delivered her baby, she didn't doubt that he was accustomed to women stripping for him, too, although probably not in a clinical setting.

"So." She cleared her throat. "How many babies have you delivered?"

"One," he admitted.

"And it looks to me like he did a pretty good job for a first-timer," Cameron—*Doctor* Turcotte—commented.

"But I think we'd both feel better if Cameron checked Caden over, just to make sure I didn't miscount his toes or something."

She could smile at that, because she'd already counted his fingers and toes herself.

"And you might want some numbers—weight and length, for example—to put in his baby book," Cameron said.

"I guess 'tiny' is somewhat vague," she admitted, relinquishing the swaddled infant to the doctor.

He measured Caden's length and the circumference of his head, then he used a kitchen scale to weigh the baby.

"Not as tiny as I thought," he said, handing the infant back to his mother. "Just about seven and a half pounds and twenty inches. A pretty good size for thirty-eight weeks. You obviously took good care of yourself throughout your pregnancy."

"I tried to exercise regularly and eat healthy," she said, then felt compelled to confess, "but I sometimes gave in to insatiable cravings for French fries and gravy."

"Well, I don't think those French fries and gravy did any harm to you or your baby," Cameron assured her.

He opened a backpack she hadn't seen him carry in. "Newborn diapers and wipes," he said, pulling out a bunch of sample packs. "Some receiving blankets and baby gowns."

"Thank you," Julie said. "I've got a few outfits and sleepers in the trunk of my car, just because I wandered through a baby store the other day, but I didn't think I'd be needing diapers just yet."

"Well, there should be enough here to hold you for a couple of days, until you can get out—or send Luke out—to stock up on supplies." Then he said to his friend, "You did a good job—for someone who doesn't specialize in obstetrics."

Lukas narrowed his gaze in response to Cameron's grin, but he only said, "Julie did all the work."

"Knowing you, I don't doubt that's true," the doctor teased. "Now I'm going to get home to my wife and kids, while I still can. If the storm doesn't blow over, you might be snowed in for the whole weekend," he warned Julie. "But if you have any questions or concerns, please call."

"I'm sorry."

They were Luke's first words to Julie when he returned to the family room after seeing Cameron to the door.

"I'm not," she told him. "I'm grateful."

He sat down across from her. "You're not even a little bit mad?"

She shook her head. "I'm a little embarrassed. Okay, more than a little," she admitted. "But the truth is, I couldn't have done it without out you."

"It was an incredible experience for me, too."

"Could you do one more thing for me, though?"

"What's that?"

"Not tell anyone that you got me naked within an hour of meeting me."

"Not even my brothers?"

"No one," she said firmly.

He chuckled. "Okay, I won't tell anyone. But speaking of telling—was there anyone you wanted to call? Or have you already posted newborn photos from your phone on Facebook or Twitter?"

She shook her head. "I don't do the social media thing."

His brows lifted. "Do you do the telephone thing?"

"Of course, but I don't think any of my friends or family is expecting to hear any news about a baby just yet."

"He's only a couple weeks ahead of his due date," Lukas reminded her.

Which was true. It was also true that no one was expecting any birth announcement because no one had known that she was pregnant. Not even her parents, because it wasn't the type of news Julie wanted to tell them over the phone. She'd wanted to talk to her mother in person, to share her joy—and her fears—with the one person she was sure would understand everything she was feeling. But she'd been traveling for work for the past seven months and hadn't had a chance to go home. In fact, no one aside from her boss at The Grayson Gallery knew, and it wasn't Evangeline's voice that Julie wanted to hear right now—it was her mother's.

But more than she wanted to hear Lucinda's voice, she wanted to see her, to feel the warmth of her arms around her. Julie wondered at the irony of the realization that never had she more craved the comfort of her own mother than after becoming a mother herself.

"I guess I need to figure out a way to get home."

"You're not going anywhere until this storm passes," Lukas pointed out to her.

Watching the snow swirl outside the window, she couldn't dispute the point.

She'd hoped to be home before the weekend. She'd only taken this detour through Pinehurst to discuss some issues with the lawyer her brother had recommended. Of course, she hadn't admitted to Daniel that she was the one in need of legal advice, because he would have demanded to know what the issues were and insisted that he could handle whatever needed to be handled.

Instead, she'd told him that she had a friend in New York State—because she hadn't been too far away at the time and heading in that direction, suddenly aware that she couldn't go home until she had answers to some of the questions that had plagued her over the past several months—who was looking for a family law attorney and wondered if he had any contacts in the area.

"I guess you're stuck with us for a little bit longer, then," Julie finally said to Lukas.

"It's a big enough house that we won't be tripping over one another," he assured her.

"When the snow stops, I'll have my car towed and make arrangements for someone to come and get me."

"I already called Bruce Conacher—he owns the local garage and offers roadside assistance—to tell him that your car was in the ditch. He's put you on the list but warned me that there are at least a dozen vehicles ahead of yours."

"I'm not sure if that makes me feel better or worse—knowing that I wasn't the only one who slid off the road in that storm."

"You definitely weren't the only one," he assured her. "And I'm sure there will be more before the night is over. But on the bright side, the storm hasn't knocked out the power lines."

She shuddered at the thought.

"It's past dinnertime," he pointed out. "Are you hungry?"

"Starving," she admitted.

"How does soup and a grilled cheese sandwich sound?"

"It sounds wonderful," she said.

Luke headed back to the kitchen where he'd left the soup simmering. He ladled it into bowls, then flipped the grilled cheese out of the frying pan and onto the cutting board. He sliced each sandwich neatly in half, then transferred them to the plates he had ready. He carried the soup and sandwiches to the table, then went to the drawer for cutlery.

"It smells delicious," Julie said, coming into the room with Caden carefully tucked in the crook of one arm.

"Of course it does—you're starving," he reminded her.

She smiled at that, drawing his attention to the sweet curve of her lips.

He felt his blood pulse in his veins and silently cursed his body for suddenly waking up at the most inappropriate time. Because yes, he was in the company of a beautiful woman, but that beautiful woman had just given birth. Not to mention the fact that she was in his home only because there was a blizzard raging outside. There were a lot of reasons his libido should be in deep hibernation, a lot of reasons that feeling any hint of attraction to Julie Marlowe was wrong.

But after six months of self-imposed celibacy, his hormones apparently didn't care to be reasoned with. Not that he'd made a conscious decision to give up sex—he just hadn't met anyone that he wanted to be with. At least not longer than one night, and he was tired of that scene. He was looking for more than a casual hookup.

He could blame his brothers for that. Until recently, he hadn't wanted anything more than the casual relationships he'd always enjoyed with amiable members of the opposite sex. And then he'd started spending time with Matt and Georgia, and Jack and Kelly, and he'd realized that he envied what each of them had found. He'd even had moments when he found himself thinking that he'd like to share his life with someone who mattered, someone who would be there through the trials and tribulations.

But he figured those moments were just a phase. And the unexpected feelings stirred up by Julie Marlowe had to be another anomaly.

She was simply a stranger who had been stranded in a snowstorm. He'd opened up his home to her because it was what anyone would have done. And he'd helped deliver her baby because circumstances had given him no choice. The fact that his body was suddenly noticing that the new mom was, in fact, a very hot mama, only proved to Luke that no good deed went unpunished.

She moved toward the closest chair, and he pulled it away from the table for her. As she lowered herself onto the seat, he caught just a glimpse of shadowy cleavage in the deep V of the robe she wore before the lights flickered. Once. Twice.

Then everything went dark.

He heard Julie suck in a breath. Einstein, who had positioned himself at his master's feet as he was in the habit of doing whenever there was food in the vicinity, whimpered. Beyond that, there was no sound.

No hum of the refrigerator, no low rumbling drone of the furnace. Nothing.

And the silence was almost as unnerving as the darkness.

"So much for the power holding out," he commented, deliberately keeping his tone casual.

Thankfully, he had an emergency flashlight plugged into one of the outlets in the hall. It ran on rechargeable batteries and automatically turned on when the power went out, so the house wasn't completely pitch black. But it was pretty close.

While he waited for his eyes to adjust to the darkness, he reached for Julie's free hand, found it curled into a fist on top of the table. He covered it with his own, squeezed gently.

He heard the distant howl of the wind outside, a sound even more ominous than the silence. Julie heard it, too, and shivered.

"I've got some candles by the stove," he told her. "I'm just going to get them so we can find our food."

He found half a dozen utility candles in the drawer, set a couple of them in their metal cups on the counter and lit the wicks. The scratch of the head against the rough paper was loud in a room suddenly void of all other sound. He lit a couple more and carried them to the table.

They were purely functional—a little bit of illumination so that they could see what they were eating. And yet, there was something about dining over candlelight—even if the meal was nothing more than soup and sandwiches and the lighting was necessity rather than mood—that infused the scene with a romantic ambiance he did not want to be feeling. But somehow the simple dishes and everyday glassware looked elegant in candlelight. And when he glanced across the table, he couldn't help but notice that Julie looked even more beautiful.

"Dig in before it gets cold," he advised.

She dipped her spoon into the bowl, and brought it up to her mouth. Before her lips parted to sample the soup, they curved upward and her gaze shifted to him. "Chicken and Stars?"

"So?" he said, just a little defensively.

"So it's an unusual choice for a grown man," she said.

"It's my niece's favorite."

"How old is your niece?"

"I have two nieces," he told her. "Two nieces and two nephews. Matt's daughter, Pippa, is only a baby. Jack's daughter, Ava, is twelve going on twenty."

Her brows drew together, creating a slight furrow between them. "Is Jack short for Jackson?"

"Yeah," he admitted. "Why?"

"Your brother is Jackson Garrett?"

Now it was his turn to frown. "You know Jack?"

"Actually, he's the reason I came to Pinehurst," she admitted.

Luke carefully set his spoon down in his bowl, the few mouthfuls he'd consumed settling like a lead weight in the pit of his stomach. "Please tell me that he isn't the father of your baby."

Chapter Four

"What?" Julie lifted her head to look at him, her blue-gray eyes wide. "No. Oh, my God, no! I've never even met the man."

Luke exhaled a long, slow breath. "Okay," he finally said. "So why were you coming to Pinehurst for a man you've never met?"

"Because my brother, Daniel, knows him. They went to law school together." She picked up half of her sandwich, nibbled on the corner. "Why would you ask if your brother was the father of my baby?"

"Because it was only a few months ago that I found out Ava—the niece who likes Chicken and Stars soup—was Jack's daughter."

"She's twelve and you only met her a few months ago?"

"No—I've actually known her since she was a baby," he clarified. "But I didn't know that my brother was her father."

"I'm having a little trouble following," she admitted.

"Ava's mother, Kelly, was one of my best friends growing up. When she was in college, she had a fling with some guy and got pregnant, but she never told me who that guy was."

Julie's gaze dropped to her bowl again. "She must have had her reasons."

"She had reasons," he acknowledged. "But I'm not sure anything can justify that kind of deception."

"Is your brother still as upset about it as you are?"

His smile was wry. "Is it that obvious?"

"There was a bit of an edge to your tone."

"I was—maybe still am—upset," he admitted. "I was the first person she told when she found out she was pregnant, because I was her best friend. When Ava was born, Kelly asked me to be the godfather, but she never told me that her baby was actually my niece."

"And you didn't even suspect the connection?"

"No, I didn't suspect anything. Because I didn't know that Jack and Kelly had been involved, however briefly."

"So why didn't your brother guess that the child she was carrying might be his?"

"Because he didn't know she was pregnant. Kelly made me promise not to tell anyone," he confided. "I thought she'd met someone when she was away to school, fallen for the wrong guy and ended up pregnant. So I promised, because I never suspected that her baby was my brother's baby."

"Why didn't she tell him that she was pregnant?" Julie asked curiously.

"I guess she was planning to tell him, but by the time she knew about the baby, he was engaged to someone else."

She winced. "That would hurt."

"Yeah." He could acknowledge that fact without accepting it as justification.

"How did his wife react to the news that he had a child with someone else?"

"She never knew. They were divorced more than five years ago," he told her. "And now Jack and Kelly are engaged."

"Apparently your brother has forgiven her for keeping their child a secret."

"It took him a while, but he did. And Ava is thrilled that she's finally going to have a mother *and* a father."

"In a perfect world, every child would have two parents who loved him or her and one another," she said.

Which told him absolutely nothing about her situation. Where was Caden's father? Was he part of their lives? Luke didn't think so, considering that she hadn't wanted to contact anyone to let them know that she was in labor, or even later to share the news that she'd had her baby.

"I feel fortunate that I grew up in that kind of home," he said, in the hope that offering information to Julie would encourage her to reciprocate.

But all she said was, "That is lucky."

And then, in what seemed an obvious attempt to change the topic of conversation, "How long do you think the power will be out?"

Or maybe she was genuinely worried. He heard the concern in her voice and wished he could reassure her, but he didn't want to give her false hope. "I don't know. I think it depends on what caused the outage."

"So it could be a while," she acknowledged.

"It could," he agreed. "But we've got the fireplace and lots of blankets, candles and flashlights, and a pantry full of canned goods. I promise—you might be bored, but you won't freeze, get lost in the halls or starve."

Her lips curved. "If nothing else, today has proven to me that there's no point in worrying about things I can't control."

He could tell that she was trying to stay upbeat, but he didn't blame her for being concerned. She was a first-time mother with a brand-new baby, trapped in a stranger's house without any power in the middle of a snowstorm.

"Speaking of starving," she said. "I think this little guy's getting hungry."

By the flickering light of the candles, he could see that the baby was opening and closing his mouth and starting to squirm a little despite being snugly swaddled in one of the receiving blankets Cameron had brought from the hospital.

"Just hold on a second," Luke said, and went down the hall to retrieve the emergency flashlight.

He came back with the light and guided Julie the short distance back to the family room.

"While you're taking care of Caden, I'll get some blankets and pillows," he told her.

"Okay."

It didn't take him more than a few minutes to gather what they would need, but he took some time to putter around upstairs, giving the new mom time to finish feeding her baby. He didn't know a lot about the nursing process. Matt's wife, Georgia, had only recently weaned Pippa, and while she'd been pretty casual about the whole thing, Lukas had always averted his gaze if he was around when she was breastfeeding the baby. Not that he was uncomfortable with the act of a mother nursing her child—he just didn't think he should be looking at his brother's wife's breasts.

Of course, the whole train of thought was one that should definitely—and quickly—be derailed. Because now he was thinking about Julie's breasts. And since there was no family connection between them, and therefore no intrinsic moral conflict, he couldn't seem to shift his thoughts in a different direction.

He changed out of his jeans and shirt and into a pair of pajama pants and a long-sleeved thermal shirt. Bedtime usually meant just stripping down to his boxers and crawling beneath the sheets of his king-size bed, but he didn't want to be too far away from Julie and Caden in case either of them needed anything through the night. Not to mention that it would probably get a little chilly in his bedroom if the power stayed out through the night.

He remembered that Julie was still wearing the robe he'd given to her earlier, and while it had served the purpose of providing some cover during the childbirth process, he didn't think she would be very comfortable sleeping in it. He rummaged through his drawers until he found a pair of sweatpants with a drawstring waist and a flannel shirt with buttons that ran all the way down the front so that it would be easier for her to—

Trying *not* to think about that, he reminded himself sternly.

Instead, he turned his attention to the storm. He could hear the wind howling outside and the brush of icy snowflakes battering against the windows. If it didn't stop snowing soon, it would take him forever to clear his driveway. And if the power stayed out, it would take even longer because his snowblower required an electric start.

The starter on the gas fireplace was electric, too, so he was grateful he'd turned it on when they'd first come in from the storm. The fire would keep the family room toasty warm, which wouldn't just make it more comfortable to sleep through the night but was absolutely essential for the newborn.

He gathered up the clothes for Julie—adding a thick pair of socks to the pile—and the blankets and pillows and carted everything down the stairs. Having lived in this house his whole life, he wasn't worried about missing a step or bumping into a wall, but he was worried about Einstein getting tangled up in his feet. However, the dog was conspicuously absent as Luke made his way down the stairs, causing him to wonder where the pint-size canine had disappeared to and what mischief he might be getting into.

He found the puppy curled up beside the sofa, close to Julie and Caden.

She was obviously exhausted after her busy—and traumatic—day, and she'd fallen asleep with the baby still nursing. The sight caused an unmistakable stirring in his groin, and Luke chastised himself for the inappropriate reaction. She was a stranger, in his home and at his mercy because of the storm. She'd just given birth to a baby, and he was ogling her as if she was a centerfold.

Except that he had never seen anything as beautiful as the sight of the baby's tiny mouth suckling at his mother's breast. The tiny knitted cap that Cameron had brought from the hospital had fallen off Caden's head, revealing the wisps of soft dark hair that covered his scalp. His tiny little hand was curled into a fist and resting against his mother's pale, smooth skin.

Luke tiptoed closer to set the bundle of clothes beside her on the couch. As he neared, Einstein lifted his head, his tail thumping quietly against the floor.

"Good boy," he whispered, patting the dog's head.

Then he unfolded one of the blankets and gently laid it over the lower half of her body, careful not to cover the baby. The little guy looked up at him, those big blue eyes wide and completely unconcerned. His mother didn't even stir.

Luke took another blanket and a pillow for himself and settled into a chair nearby, prepared for a very long night.

When Julie awoke in the morning, she found the bundle of clothes Lukas had left for her on the sofa. Though she had more than a few changes of clothes in the suitcases in the trunk of her car, she didn't want to trudge through the snow to retrieve them while wearing nothing more than her host's robe, so she gratefully donned the borrowed shirt and sweats.

He'd also put a few toiletries out on the counter of the powder room: hairbrush, new toothbrush and a tube of toothpaste, all of which she put to good use.

Her first clue that the power had been restored was that the light in the powder room came on when she automatically hit the switch. Her second was the tantalizing aroma of bacon that wafted from the kitchen as she made her way down the hall. Though her grumbling stomach urged her to follow the scent, she knew she needed to take care of her baby's hunger first. Because she had no doubt that Caden would be hungry, too.

She'd lost count of how many times he'd woken her in the night, his avid little mouth instinctively seeking her breast and the sustenance it provided. And while he never seemed to nurse for extended periods of time, he nursed frequently. The books she'd read offered reassurance that this was normal, but reading about it and living it were two entirely different scenarios. She understood now why new mothers were always exhausted—feeding a newborn was pretty much a full-time job.

Of course, she also realized that she wasn't really feeding him yet, and that the frequent nursing sessions were necessary to help her milk come in. Throughout her pregnancy, she'd gone back and forth on the breast versus bottle issue but, in the end, she was persuaded by all the benefits found in breast milk—not to mention the simplicity of the method.

"Something smells delicious," she told Lukas when she finally made her way into the kitchen.

"Hopefully better than the bread and jam you would have got if the power had still been out," he told her.

"Right now, even that sounds good," she told him.

"How do bacon, eggs and toast sound?"

"Even better."

"How are you doing this morning?"

"I'm a little sore," she admitted. "And tired."

"I don't imagine you got much sleep with Caden waking you up every couple of hours."

She winced at that. "Obviously he woke you up, too."

He shrugged. "I'm a light sleeper. Thankfully, I don't need a lot of sleep, so I feel pretty good. Of course, being able to make my morning pot of coffee helped a little."

"I gave up coffee six months ago," she admitted, just a little wistfully.

"So what can I get for you?" Lukas asked. "Juice? Milk?"

"Juice is great," she said, noting that there were already two glasses poured and at the table.

He gestured for her to help herself, then pointed to the carton of eggs on the counter. "Scrambled or fried?"

"Whichever is easier."

"Which do you prefer?"

"I like both," she assured him.

He shook his head as he cracked eggs into a bowl. "You're a pleaser, aren't you? The type of person who says yes even when she wants to say no, who goes out of her way to avoid conflicts or disagreements."

She laughed. "No one's ever accused me of that before," she told him. "But I do try not to be difficult—at least not until I've known someone more than twenty-four hours."

"So how do you like your eggs?" he prompted.

"Benedict," she told him.

He chuckled. "Okay. But since I don't have hollandaise sauce, what's your second choice?"

"Scrambled," she decided.

"That wasn't so hard now, was it?" He added a splash of milk to the bowl, then a sprinkle of salt and pepper and began to whisk the eggs.

"I'll let you know after I've tried the eggs."

He grinned as he poured the mixture into the frying pan.

"My brother and sister-in-law are going to stop by later today, as soon as Matt finishes clearing his driveway."

She moved closer to the window. "I can't believe it's still snowing out there."

"It's just light flurries now," he noted. "Nothing like what we had yesterday."

"Everything looks so pretty, covered in a pristine blanket of snow."

"Take a look out the back," he suggested. "It's not quite so pristine out there."

She carried Caden to the window at the back of the room, noted that the snow there had been thoroughly—almost desperately—trampled. And then she spotted the culprit. Einstein, Lukas's puppy, was racing around as if being chased by the hounds of hell. He had his nose down and was using it like a shovel to tunnel through the cold white stuff and then, when he'd pushed enough to form a mound, he'd attack it.

She chuckled. "What is he doing?"

"I have no idea," Lukas admitted. "*He* has no idea."

"It's his first snow," she guessed.

"Yeah. He's been out there for half an hour and every few minutes, he spins in a circle and barks at it."

"Pets are a lot like kids, aren't they?" she mused. "They give you a fresh perspective on things we so often take for granted."

"Some of them," he agreed. "Daphne's perspective is neither sociable nor very sunny."

She laughed again. "Considering I haven't seen more of her than a flick of her tail, I can't disagree with that."

"She ventured downstairs last night to sleep by the fire, but I'm sure it wasn't for company but only warmth."

"It was warm," Julie agreed. "I even threw the blanket off a couple of times in the night."

"I thought about turning the fire off, but until the power came back on, I was reluctant to lose our only source of heat."

"I really can't thank you enough," she said. "When I think about what could have happened if you hadn't come home and found me in the ditch last night—"

"There's no reason to think about anything like that," Lukas told her.

"Well, I'm grateful. I don't know anyone else who would have done everything that you've done—for me and Caden."

"If the people you know would have left a laboring mother trapped in a ditch, you need to meet new people."

She managed to smile at that. "Okay—most of my friends would have opened their doors under those circumstances, but I don't know that their hospitality would have outlasted the storm."

"Are you suggesting that I should throw you out into a snow bank now?"

"Well, maybe you could wait until after you've fed me breakfast," she suggested.

He set a plate in front of her, then reached for Caden.

Julie transferred the baby to him without any protest or hesitation. After all, this man had helped bring her son into the world. And even if that hadn't been her choice at the time, she couldn't fault his competence—and she couldn't forget the expression of awe and wonder on his face as he'd gazed down at her newborn baby. Or the sense of absolute rightness that she'd felt in the moment that he'd placed the tiny, naked body in her arms so that he could cut the cord.

It was as if that act had somehow forged a bond between them—two strangers brought together by circumstances neither of them could ever have foreseen.

"He really is tiny, isn't he?" Lukas said, settling the sleeping baby into the crook of his arm. "I'll bet he doesn't weigh half as much as Einstein."

"You wouldn't say he was tiny if you'd had to push him out of your body," Julie told him, and dug into her eggs.

He winced at the thought as he picked up his own plate to take it to the table. "You're probably right about that."

She nibbled at a slice of crisp bacon and hummed with pleasure as the salty, smoky flavor flooded her taste buds. "Why is it that the foods that are so bad for you always taste so good?"

"I never really thought about it," he said, scooping up a forkful of eggs.

"You wouldn't."

"What's that supposed to mean?"

"You're a guy. You don't have to count calories or worry about fat content or carbs."

He shrugged as he chewed. "I pretty much eat what I want to eat."

"For the past several months, I have, too," she admitted. "I figured a pregnant woman should be allowed some latitude. Of course, I'll probably regret it when those extra ten pounds keep me in maternity clothes for another couple of months."

"You don't look as if you're carrying ten extra pounds," he told her.

"Right now it's more like twenty."

"Then you were too skinny before."

She picked up another slice of bacon. "No one ever accused me of being skinny, either," she assured him.

He studied her from across the table for a minute before he asked, "Why would you want to be?"

It wasn't a question anyone had ever asked her before. All of her friends—everyone she knew—wanted to be thinner, prettier, richer. It was every American woman's dream. Wasn't it?

"I've never understood why women obsess so much about their bodies," Lukas continued.

"Yeah, because men never judge us on the basis of our appearance," she said dryly.

He didn't deny it. "A pretty face and an appealing figure usually catch our attention," he admitted. "But men are simple creatures. We're not looking for perfection—we're just looking for a woman who's willing to get naked with us."

Her brows lifted. "Really?"

"Pretty much."

"I'll be sure to share that insight with my friends when we're sweating through Zumba classes."

He grinned. "We also like women who aren't afraid to shake their stuff."

Julie couldn't help smiling at the predictably male response. And as she finished her breakfast, she found herself marveling over the fact that she'd known Lukas for such a short period of time but somehow felt comfortable and at ease with him.

At home in Springfield, she knew a lot of people through her job at The Grayson Gallery and through her association with Elliot. As a result, she felt as if she had a certain image to uphold. She would never pop out for a quart of milk unless her hair was neat and her makeup immaculate. She rarely wore blue jeans and the only gym shoes she owned were exclusively for use in the gym.

Now she was wearing borrowed clothes that didn't fit, her hair was in a haphazard ponytail and her face was bare of makeup. And maybe it was because Lukas had held her hand as she sweated through labor and childbirth, but he seemed unaffected by the absence of mascara on her lashes and he honestly didn't seem to care who she was. He'd come to her aid simply because that was the kind of man he was, with no ulterior motive or hidden agenda. It wasn't just a surprising but a liberating revelation.

As was the fact that when he talked to her, he actually

seemed to listen to what she was saying—even if they were having a nonsensical conversation about carb counting or Zumba classes. He was charming and funny and genuine, and she'd never known anyone quite like him.

And whenever he smiled at her, she felt a subtle clenching low in her belly that made her just a little bit uneasy. Not because she worried that he would do or say anything inappropriate, but because she was worried that her response to him was inappropriate.

The last time she'd had sex was probably the night that Caden was conceived. In the eight and half months since then, she'd hardly thought about it—she certainly hadn't missed it. So why was she thinking about it now?

Was this flood of hormones through her system simply a side effect of the birth experience? Or was it connected to the sexy man who had rescued her from a blizzard and delivered her baby?

If she'd met Lukas Garrett in a different time and place— and if she wasn't the new mother of a beautiful baby boy— she would probably strike up a conversation, flirt with him a little, see if there was any evidence that the sizzle she felt was reciprocated.

But it wasn't a different time or place, and Caden was her priority. She didn't have the leisure or the energy for any kind of romantic complications.

As she pushed away from the table to carry her empty plate to the sink, she couldn't help but feel just a little bit disappointed by the fact.

Chapter Five

The window by the sink overlooked the driveway, and as she glanced outside, she realized that she'd been so focused on the snow earlier she hadn't noticed that it was cleared.

"How did you have time to shovel your driveway already?" she asked.

"I didn't. Jon Quinlan came by first thing this morning with his plow."

"Is he a neighbor?"

"Not exactly."

It was an evasive response from a man who had impressed her as being anything but, and it piqued her curiosity. "Then what is he—exactly?"

"He owns a landscaping and yard maintenance company."

"So why didn't you just say that you hire someone to clear it?"

"Because I didn't hire him," he admitted. "And he won't let me pay him."

"He must not have a very successful business if he works for free." She returned to the table and took the baby again.

"That's what I keep telling him, but Jon thinks he owes me. His daughter has a poodle-mix named Sparky. A few years back, Sparky had a hernia, but Jon had just been laid off from his job and didn't have the money for the surgery."

"But you did the surgery, anyway," she guessed.

He lifted one shoulder. "I couldn't let the animal suffer."

And in that moment, she realized it was true. Someone else might have turned the man away, but Lukas Garrett couldn't. It simply wasn't in him to do nothing when he could help. She also realized that he wasn't comfortable talking about what he'd done because he didn't think it was a big deal.

So instead of commenting on his generosity, she asked, "What kind of pet does Mrs. Kurchik have?"

He was visibly startled by her question—so she tapped a finger to the label that advertised "Mrs. Kurchik's Peach Jam" on the jar.

He shrugged again. "An aging basset hound and a battle-scarred tabby cat."

"The joys of living and working in a small town?"

"Pinehurst isn't nearly as small as it used to be, but the population growth hasn't affected the sense of community," he told her.

Before she could comment further, she heard something that sounded like a thud from behind the door to the laundry room. "What was that?"

"Einstein," he admitted. "He can come in and out through the doggy door, but I closed the inside door so that he doesn't race in and track snow through the house."

She frowned as another thump sounded. "Is he...knocking?"

He laughed. "Maybe he does think that's what he's doing. It's certainly a better explanation than that he likes to bang his head against the door." He pushed away from the table. "I'd better go dry his paws and let him in before he gives himself brain damage—if it's not already too late."

While Lukas was dealing with the dog, Julie decided to give her parents a call. She bypassed the handset on the table for her cell phone. Not just because she didn't want her host to incur long-distance charges for the call but because she didn't know how to explain a stranger's name and number showing up on her parents' call display. It was easier all around to call from her cell, as she was in the habit of doing.

When she heard her mother's voice on the other end of the line, her throat tightened and her eyes filled with tears.

"Hello?" Lucinda said again when Julie was unable to respond. Then, confirming that her mother had checked the display, "Julie—is that you?"

She cleared her throat. "Yes, it's me. Hi, Mom."

"Is everything okay?"

"Of course," she said. "I think the connection just cut out for a second."

"I'm so pleased to hear from you. I was going to call from the car on the way to the airport, but I wasn't sure of your schedule."

"You're going to the airport?"

"We're on our way to Melbourne." Lucinda practically sang out the announcement. "Your dad booked the tickets for our thirty-fifth anniversary."

Julie wondered for a minute if she'd somehow overlooked the milestone because of everything going on in her own life, but she knew that she hadn't. "Your anniversary isn't until the end of the month."

"But Reg wanted us to be there for our anniversary," her mother explained. "To celebrate thirty-five years together at the place we met."

Julie knew the story, of course. Her mother had been an

American student studying in Melbourne, her father had been on vacation after his first year of law school, and they'd met at a café near Brighton Beach.

"We always said we would go back some day, but we never did. After we got married, we got so busy with other things. Your father was building his career, and I was focused on raising four children."

"You sound really excited about this," Julie said, wishing that she could share her mother's enthusiasm. For the past several months, she'd been looking forward to going home. Now her return was almost imminent, but her parents weren't even going to be there. And she was more than a little apprehensive about the prospect of returning to Massachusetts—and facing Elliott—while they were away.

"We both are," Lucinda told her. "It's been a long time since we've been on vacation together, just the two of us."

"Then it's definitely long overdue," she agreed with false cheerfulness. "When will you be home?"

"December seventh."

"You're going for more than a month?"

"Thirty-five days—one for each year we've been together."

Which, Julie had to admit, was an incredibly romantic gesture on her father's part. And it was incredibly selfish of her to be upset because her parents were leaving the country rather than hanging around at home to welcome the grandchild they didn't know they had.

"That's…wonderful," she finally said.

"You'll be home by then, too, won't you?" Lucinda asked her.

"I'll be home by then," Julie promised, gently tracing the curve of her baby's cheek with her fingertip. "With a surprise for you."

"For me?" Lucinda sounded delighted.

"For both you and Dad."

"I can't wait," her mother said. "Although honestly, it's enough to know that you're finally coming home. We've missed you, baby."

She felt the sting of tears in the back of her eyes. "I've missed you, too. All of you."

"You're doing okay, though?" Lucinda prompted.

"I'm doing better than okay," Julie assured her. "I needed the time away, to figure some things out, but I'm looking forward to coming home." And it was true, even if the thought of seeing her former fiancé tied her stomach into knots.

"Where are you now?"

"In Upstate New York."

"I saw on the news that there's a big storm moving in that direction. You make sure you keep an eye on it," her mother advised.

Julie had to smile. "I'll do that."

"Oh, your father's tapping his watch," Lucinda said regretfully. "I have to run."

"Okay. Give my love to Dad. And have a fabulous time."

After Einstein was dry, Lukas carried him into the kitchen to ensure that he didn't try to jump all over their guests. Except that when he opened the laundry room door, he found Julie's chair was empty and both mother and son were gone.

His heart gave a little jolt—an instinctive response that he didn't want to think about too deeply—but settled again when he heard her voice in the family room. At first he thought she was talking to Caden, but as he finished tidying up the dishes from breakfast—not an easy task with the dog tucked under his arm—he realized that she was on the phone. Though he wasn't trying to listen to her conversation, he couldn't help but hear bits and pieces of it. She sounded cheerful and upbeat, so he was surprised—and distressed—to enter the family room after she'd ended the call and see tears on her cheeks.

From the time they were kids, his brothers had always teased him about his protective instincts. He never liked to see anyone or anything hurting. It was one of the reasons he'd become a vet—to help heal injured creatures. It still broke his heart when he couldn't save one of them, and it still brought him to his knees whenever he saw a woman in tears.

"Julie?" He crouched down beside the sofa, setting Einstein on the floor by his feet. "Is everything okay?"

She wiped at the wet streaks on her cheeks, but the tears continued to fall. "I'm sorry."

"Don't apologize," he said. "Just tell me what I can do to help."

She offered a wobbly smile but shook her head. "Nothing. I'm just being a big baby."

Which he didn't believe for a minute. "Do you want to tell me about the phone call?"

"My mom," she admitted. "I guess, now that I'm a mom, too, I really wanted to hear her voice and to tell her that I would be home in a few days. I haven't seen them in a while— my fault, because I was working out of town—and I just found out that she and my dad are going to Australia for a month."

He frowned. "They couldn't postpone their trip to see you and meet their new grandson?"

"They probably could—and they would."

"But?" he prompted.

"But it's their thirty-fifth anniversary and the trip was a surprise for my mom from my dad, a journey back to the place they first met."

"You didn't tell them that you had the baby, did you?"

"No," she admitted.

"Will there be anyone else at home when you get there?"

She shook her head. "My youngest brother, Ethan, is at school in Washington. He won't be home until Christmas break. Daniel lives in Boston and Kevin in New Haven."

"Are you going to tell them about Caden?"

"I can't tell them before I tell my parents," she said matter-of-factly.

"What about..." He wanted to ask about Caden's father, but he let the words fade away. He was undeniably curious, but he had no right to ask. They had been brought together by circumstances beyond anyone's control, and he didn't want to make her uncomfortable by pressing for information she didn't want to give.

She looked up at him, waiting for him to finish his question. She seemed to tense, as if she anticipated what he was going to ask and didn't want to answer. But instead he only said, "What do your brothers do?"

"Daniel's a corporate attorney, Kevin's the producer of a talk radio station and Ethan is still trying to figure out what he wants to be when he grows up."

"How old is he?"

"Twenty-seven," she admitted.

"You're the youngest."

"Is that a statement or a question?"

"It's a guess," he admitted. "But you don't look like you're even close to thirty."

"I'm the youngest," she confirmed, but didn't actually tell him how old she was.

"And the only girl."

She nodded.

"How was that—growing up with three older brothers?"

"Most of the time it was great," she said, then one corner of her mouth quirked upward in a half smile. "Except when it wasn't."

Being one of three brothers himself, he knew what she meant.

"Any of them married? Kids?"

"Just Kevin. He and Brooke recently celebrated their second anniversary, and they're expecting their first child in March."

"So Caden is the first grandchild for your parents?"

She nodded.

He frowned. "That's a pretty big milestone for most people."

She just nodded again.

He sensed that there was something she wasn't telling him, something she didn't want to tell him. And although he knew it wasn't any of his business—after all, they were only strangers whose paths would never have crossed if not for an unexpected snowstorm—he couldn't help but comment. "I know Caden came a couple of weeks early, but I wouldn't have thought they'd make plans to go anywhere when you were so close to your due date."

She finally lifted her gaze to meet his. "They wouldn't have—if they'd known I was pregnant."

He couldn't quite get his head around what she was saying. "Are you telling me that you managed to keep your pregnancy a secret from your family for the better part of nine months?"

"I didn't intend to keep it a secret," she admitted. "I wanted to tell them. But when I first left town, I didn't know I was pregnant."

"When did you know?"

"A few days later. And then, I didn't know *how* to tell them. It didn't seem like the kind of news I should share over the phone, and I was sure I would see them soon. But my job kept me so busy, I never had a chance to go home."

"You haven't been home in nine months?"

"Actually, it's more like seven months—since April," she admitted.

"And that kind of extended absence isn't unusual?"

"It was an extraordinary career opportunity," she explained. "As an art curator at The Grayson Gallery, I was invited to travel to select galleries around the United States with Evangeline Grayson's private collection of impressionist and post-impressionist art."

"Has it been that long since you've seen Caden's father, too?" Luke asked.

"Caden doesn't have a father," she said coolly.

His brows lifted. "I might not have any kids of my own, but I'm pretty sure I understand the basics of reproduction."

"Then you know that donating sperm doesn't make a man a father."

He didn't believe that her child had been conceived through intrauterine insemination. She seemed too young to have chosen that route—and too defensive. Which suggested that the story of Caden's father was a little more complicated than she wanted him to know.

And while he had a lot more questions, he accepted that she had no obligation to tell him anything. He also suspected that if he pushed for answers, she might lie, and he'd rather wait until she trusted him enough to tell him the truth.

So all he said was, "I just got a message from Bruce. He's towed your car, but he won't have a chance to look at it until Monday at the earliest."

"Monday?" she echoed, obviously disappointed.

He shrugged. "He's going to be busy the rest of the day hauling cars out of ditches, and he doesn't work on Sundays."

"I guess I should make some kind of arrangements, then."

"Arrangements for what?" he asked.

"Transportation to a hotel."

"We don't have a hotel in Pinehurst," he told her. "There are a few bed-and-breakfasts, and one roadside motel on the outskirts of town, but no hotel."

She frowned at that. "I guess I could try the motel."

"Why would you want to try somewhere else when there's plenty of room for both you and Caden here?"

She was shaking her head even before he finished speaking.

"Why not?" he challenged.

"Because we've imposed on you too much already."

"It's not an imposition."

"How is having a stranger and her newborn baby in your home *not* an imposition?"

"Because I want you to stay," he told her honestly. "At least until the weather clears and your car is fixed."

He didn't need to point out that there was no one waiting for her at home, as her response confirmed.

"I feel like I should decline your invitation, but considering that my options are extremely limited right now, I'll say thank you instead."

"You're welcome. I made up the bed in the first room at the top of the stairs," he told her. "It has a private en-suite bathroom, so you don't have to worry about sharing one."

"Does it have a shower?"

"As a matter of fact, it does."

"Because I would really appreciate being able to... Oh, no."

"What's wrong?"

"My suitcases are in the trunk of my car, and my car's on its way to Bruce's Body Shop."

"Your suitcases are already upstairs in the spare bedroom."

"They are?"

He shrugged. "You mentioned that you'd been travelling, so I figured you'd have some essentials with you. I got your luggage out of the trunk this morning."

"Thank you," she said sincerely. "After a shower and some clean clothes, I just might feel human again."

The guest room was bathed in natural light that poured through the pair of tall narrow windows. The double bed was covered in a beautiful sage-green comforter in a rich suede-like fabric. The dressers had strong but simple lines and were made of light-colored wood, and—as promised—her suitcases were on top of the blanket chest at the foot of the bed. The overall effect of the room was both warm and welcoming, and Julie wanted nothing as much as she wanted to fall into the bed and sleep for several hours.

Actually, that wasn't entirely true. As much as she wanted sleep, she wanted a shower even more. She opened the biggest suitcase and found her robe, then dug around for the toiletry bag with her shampoo, body wash and feminine hygiene products. Thankfully, she'd thought to stock up a few weeks earlier, because she wouldn't want to have to ask Lukas to make a trip to the pharmacy for her. On the other hand, the man had willingly stepped in to deliver her baby, so there probably wasn't much that fazed him.

The en-suite bathroom not only had a glass-walled shower with an adjustable showerhead but a separate soaker tub. For just a few seconds, Julie imagined herself sinking into a tub filled to the rim with frothy, scented bubbles, but she didn't want to chance taking a bath without checking with a doctor first. She also didn't want to leave Lukas with Caden for too long. Her host seemed comfortable and easy with the baby and she appreciated his willingness to help with him, but her son was her responsibility and a quick shower would have to suffice.

The towels on the rack were the same sage color as the spread in the bedroom, and thick and fluffy. There were apothecary jars filled with cotton swabs and cotton balls on the granite countertop and an assortment of decorative soaps in a basket on the apron of the tub.

She reached into the shower to turn on the faucet, then quickly stripped out of her clothes. When she stepped under the spray, the warm, pulsing water felt so good she nearly whimpered with relief. She poured a handful of body wash into her hand, then slicked it over her skin. She'd always figured that they called it *labor* because it wasn't a walk in the park, but she hadn't expected it to be such sweaty work. In retrospect, however, she was grateful that the process had gone so smoothly.

Since she'd learned of her pregnancy, Julie had been focused on doing everything she could to take care of herself and her unborn child. Everything she'd done over the past eight months had been with the goal of giving birth to a healthy baby.

Of course, she hadn't planned to give birth on a stranger's family-room couch, but when the only alternative was the frigid interior of a ditched car, it was undoubtedly the better option.

She'd thought about the birthing process a lot in recent months, but she'd always imagined herself in a brightly lit and sterile hospital room with a team of doctors and nurses around her. She'd never considered a home birth. That was fine for other people, if they chose, but not for her. She wanted to be in a hospital with medical personnel and pain-numbing drugs and emergency equipment in case of any complications.

It had been scary, the realization that there were none of those supports available when she went into labor, and she was sincerely thankful that there had been no problems. She was even more thankful that Lukas had been there to deliver her baby. Yeah, the realization that he was a veterinarian and not a medical doctor had thrown her for a minute, but in the end, all that really mattered was that he'd helped bring Caden into the world, because there was no way she could have done it without him.

It wasn't just that he'd been there to catch the baby—his calm demeanor and patient reassurance had alleviated a lot of her doubts and fears so that the process wasn't quite as terrifying as it might otherwise have been. She hadn't planned on having anyone in the delivery room with her and had resigned herself to going through the process alone.

In the end, however, she didn't feel as if she'd been alone at all. Lukas Garrett might have been a stranger, but he'd been there for her. And now, after everything they'd shared, she really felt as if he was a friend—someone she could count on.

Trust didn't come easily to her, especially not since the incident with Elliot, but she trusted Lukas. Of course, she'd had no choice but to trust him when she was in the middle of labor. She couldn't get to the hospital and her baby refused to wait to be born. But with every look, every word and every touch, he'd been compassionate and gentle and reassuring. And when she'd finally pushed her baby out into the world, she'd been grateful not just that someone was there to receive him, but that it was Lukas.

She squirted shampoo into her hand, scrubbed it through her hair. Through the whole childbirth experience, she'd been so preoccupied with the process and trying not to panic that she hadn't thought about anything else. She'd barely even noticed her rescuer's impressive physical attributes—but she hadn't been nearly as preoccupied this morning.

A brand-new mother probably shouldn't be aware of the incredible sexiness of a well-built man, but she was still a woman, and Lukas Garrett was definitely a man. A man who made her blood hum and her skin tingle, and those were very definite warning signs that Julie should keep a safe distance from him.

She'd been hurt by Elliott. Not just by his actions and his words, but by the realization that she hadn't known her fiancé nearly as well as she'd thought she did. She'd seen only what she wanted to see, and she'd made the wrong choice. Again.

Her father—a baseball aficionado—was fond of the expression "three strikes and you're out." So after Julie's third strike in the romance department, she'd accepted that it was time to walk off the field. That was it—she was finished with dating and done with men.

Travelling across the country with Evangeline's collection, she'd had more than a few handsome men cross her path. But none of them had made her feel anything. She chatted, she flirted—it was part of the job, after all, to be sociable—but she didn't feel anything. In fact, she'd been certain that she wouldn't ever feel anything again, that what Elliott had done had left her numb inside.

She wasn't feeling numb now.

She knew that her body was flooded with hormones as a result of the pregnancy and childbirth processes. It was entirely possible that her physiological response had absolutely nothing to do with Lukas Garrett personally and everything to do with the fact that she had an overabundance of estrogen and progesterone zinging through her system that wanted to rendezvous with the testosterone in his.

Except that she hadn't had the same reaction to Cameron Turcotte. The other man was arguably just as handsome as the veterinarian, but her pulse hadn't even fluttered when he'd walked into the room. Of course, he'd also worn a wide gold band on the third finger of his left hand, so maybe her hormones weren't completely indiscriminate, after all. Or maybe it was the emotional connection that had been forged through the sharing of the childbirth experience with Lukas that was stirring her up inside.

Whatever the reason, it was a complication she didn't need or want. Thankfully, this awareness or attraction or whatever she was feeling wouldn't be an issue for long. As soon as Bruce checked over her car and deemed it road-worthy, she would be on her way back to Springfield and would probably never see Lukas Garrett again.

With that thought, she flicked off the tap and reached for a towel. Every inch of her skin felt hypersensitive, almost achy, as she rubbed the thick terry cloth over her body. It had been a long time since anyone had touched her—since she'd even thought about a man's hands on her. But she was thinking about it now. And wanting.

Muttering an oath of frustration, she wrapped the robe around herself and knotted the belt at her waist. Her hair was dripping wet, and she'd forgotten to get her hair dryer out of the suitcase, so she strode back into the bedroom to retrieve it—and let out a startled gasp.

Chapter Six

Luke didn't realize Julie had finished in the shower until he heard her gasp.

"Sorry." His apology was immediate and sincere. "I didn't hear the water shut off, and I didn't expect you to finish in the shower so quickly." Which was true, even if it didn't begin to explain his presence in her bedroom.

She tugged on the lapel of her robe, no doubt to close the open V that he couldn't help but notice dipped low between her breasts. "What are you doing in here?"

"I found something in the attic that I thought you could use."

She glanced at Caden, lying on his back in the middle of the bed, as if to reassure herself that he hadn't been abandoned or neglected. "What is it?"

"Come and have a look," he invited, and stepped aside so that she could see.

Her gaze shifted, her eyes went wide. "Oh. Wow."

Her instinctive response obliterated any lingering doubts about his impulsive gesture.

She took one step forward, then another. She knelt beside the cherry wood cradle, her lips curving as she ran a hand over the smooth, glossy wood. "This is…beautiful."

"It's old," he admitted.

"Timeless," she whispered, almost reverently. Then looked up at him. "Was it yours?"

He nodded. "But it was Jack's before it was mine, and Matt's before that."

She trailed a finger down one of the spindles. "I've never seen anything like it."

"It was handmade by Rob Turcotte—Cam's father. He was a really good friend of my dad's—and an incredibly talented carpenter. He made it as a gift to my parents when my mom was expecting Matt."

Luke was babbling, but he couldn't seem to stop himself. Because he hoped that conversation would help focus his attention on something—*anything*—but the sexy curves of the woman in front of him.

He knew that he should look away, but he seemed to be suffering a momentary disconnect between his eyes and his brain. Or maybe he was simply a red-blooded man facing a beautiful, mostly naked woman. Looking at her now, he never would have guessed that she'd given birth just about eighteen hours earlier.

Her skin was rosy from the shower, and droplets of water glistened on her skin. The short silky robe belted at her waist did nothing to hide her distinctly feminine shape, and the hem skimmed just above her knees, drawing attention to her long, sexy legs.

His gaze skimmed upward again, and he couldn't help but notice that her wet hair tumbled over her shoulders, dripping onto her robe so that there were wet patches on the fabric just above her breasts. And when he realized that the nipples of those breasts were taut beneath the silky fabric, his mouth went completely dry and the blood in his head started to quickly migrate south.

He took a deliberate step back, a tactical retreat.

She cleared her throat, then gestured to the suitcases at the end of the bed. "I forgot my, um, hair dryer."

He nodded. "Clothes," he said, his voice sounding strangled. "You might want some clothes, too."

Her cheeks flushed prettily. "Yeah."

"I'll get out of your way," he said, and hurried out of the room.

After Julie's hair was dried and she was dressed in a pair of yoga pants and a tunic-style top, she fed Caden again before carrying him back downstairs to the family room. Apparently Lukas had found more than a cradle in the attic, because he was now in the process of putting together something that looked like a playpen.

"This doesn't have any sentimental value," he said, when she entered the room. "It's just old. And it probably doesn't comply with current safety guidelines, but since Caden isn't rolling around yet, it should suffice if you want to put him down for a few minutes without having to worry about Einstein climbing over him."

She eyed the structure dubiously as she settled back on the sofa. Although Lukas's puppy had actually shown incredible restraint around the baby so far, she wasn't convinced that the well-spaced spindles would keep him out. "Are you sure Einstein can't squeeze through those bars?"

"I'm sure," Lukas said. "He's tried three times already and he keeps getting his head stuck."

"Oh, the poor thing." She rubbed behind the puppy's ears,

and his whole back end wagged happily in response to the attention.

"The 'poor thing' should have learned after the first try," Lukas grumbled.

"Isn't perseverance a virtue?"

"What you think of as perseverance others might consider stubbornness or stupidity," he said, with a stern look at the puppy.

Einstein, obviously sensing his master's disapproval, dropped his head and looked up at him with sad eyes.

Julie had to bite down on her lip to hold back a smile. "I think he's a lot smarter than you give him credit for."

Before he could respond to that, the back door slammed, and she heard a female voice say, "Snowsuits and boots off." The command was followed by the rustle of outerwear being shed and the thump of boots hitting the floor, then footsteps pounded.

Lukas winced. "It sounds like Matt may have brought the whole family," he warned.

She was afraid to ask what "the whole family" entailed, but the first part of the answer was apparent when two dark-haired boys raced into the room. They were similarly dressed in jeans and hooded sweatshirts, one red and the other blue, and Einstein raced to greet them, dancing around their legs.

"Where is he?" The one in red pushed ahead. "I wanna see him."

"Me, too," his brother chimed in.

Lukas stood in front of Julie—a human barrier between the new mom and the eager twins—and held up his hands. "Slow down, boys."

"But we wanna see the baby," red shirt entreated. "We don't have a boy baby at our house."

"We just gots a girl," blue shirt said.

"You *have* a girl," an authoritative female voice said from the doorway.

The boy in red tilted his head to peek around Lukas. "Her name's Pippa," he told Julie. "She's our sister."

"And who are you?" she asked him.

Now that the boys weren't barreling full-speed ahead, Lukas stepped aside so that they could talk to Julie—and see the baby.

"I'm Quinn." He nudged his brother closer. "This is Shane."

"And I'm their mother." The other woman set an overflowing laundry basket on the floor beside the sofa. "Georgia."

Her smile was warm and genuine, and Julie found herself responding easily. "Julie Marlowe. And this is Caden."

"Oh—he's absolutely gorgeous," Georgia said, crouching down for a closer look.

"Speaking of gorgeous—where is Pippa?" Lukas asked.

Georgia slapped a hand to her forehead. "I knew I was forgetting something."

Julie actually felt her heart skip a beat. Had she really—

Then the boys giggled.

"You didn't forget her," Quinn assured his mother. "She's with Daddy."

"We gots a new daddy," Shane told Julie. "'Cuz our first daddy went to heaven."

Julie didn't have a clue how to respond to that, so she was relieved when Georgia spoke up.

"There are some more things in the van," she told Lukas. "And the boys insisted on bringing Finn and Fred, too, so I'm sure Matt would appreciate a hand."

"I've got two I can lend him," he said, and headed out to do that.

"Who are Finn and Fred?" Julie wondered.

"Our puppies!" Quinn announced.

"From the same litter as Einstein," Georgia elaborated.

"The local softhearted vet was stuck with eight orphaned puppies, and somehow convinced his brother to take two of them."

"What's a orphan?" Shane wanted to know.

"*An* orphan is someone who doesn't have a mommy or a daddy," his mother explained.

"How was he born if he didn't have a mommy?"

Georgia forced a smile. "Can we save this conversation for home? We came here to meet Julie and her baby, remember?"

Shane nodded. "He's even smaller than Pippa."

"She was about the same size as Caden when she was born," Georgia told him. "Although it's probably hard to remember that now."

"I never heard of the name Caden," Quinn told Julie. "But we gotsa Cain in our kinnergarden class."

"He eats glue," Shane informed her solemnly.

Julie had to chuckle at that. "Well, hopefully I'll teach Caden not to do that before it's time for him to go to school."

The boys crowded closer to get a better view of the baby. Caden looked back at them, his big blue eyes wide. For a whole minute, neither of the twins moved, they just watched intently.

Finally Quinn's gaze shifted to Julie. "Does he do *anything?*"

"Not really," she admitted. "Right now, he eats a lot and sleeps a lot."

"Does he poop a lot, too?" the boy wanted to know. "'Cuz Pippa does."

Julie found herself laughing again. "Well, he hasn't done a lot of that yet, but he was only born yesterday."

She saw movement in the doorway, and glanced over just as Lukas walked back in. Two seconds later, she realized that it wasn't Lukas, after all, but a man who looked so much like him, he had to be his brother. And the baby on his hip—an adorable little girl dressed in pink overalls with tiny pink sneakers on her feet—had to be Pippa.

"There's my girl," Georgia said.

Pippa smiled widely, showing four tiny pearly white teeth, and held her arms out to her mother.

"She is gorgeous," Julie said.

"That's because she looks just like her mama," Matt said, touching a hand to his wife's shoulder.

"Another unbiased opinion," she said dryly.

He just grinned. "I'm Matt," he said, offering his hand to Julie. "The *real* Dr. Garrett."

"Not that he has much more experience than Lukas when it comes to delivering babies," Georgia said.

"I did an obstetrics rotation in med school," he pointed out.

"How many years ago was that?" his wife challenged.

"More than I'm willing to admit."

"Well, according to Dr. Turcotte, Lukas did just fine," Julie told him.

"Lukas had the easy part," Matt told her.

"I'm not sure how easy it was to keep me from going into full-scale panic when I realized I wasn't going to make it to the hospital to have my baby," she admitted. "But he did it."

"Those Garretts know how to get what they want," Georgia told her.

"That we do." Her husband's admission was accompanied by a quick grin.

"I wanna play outside," Quinn said. "In the snow."

"Me, too," Shane said.

"That sounds like a terrific idea," their mother agreed. "Especially if Daddy and Uncle Lukas go with you."

Both boys turned to Matt. "Yeah, Daddy. *Pleeease.*"

He looked at Georgia, his brows lifted. "Trying to get rid of me?"

"Just so that Julie and I can share labor stories and talk about babies and breasts and—"

"I'll go play with the boys," he said.

"Yay!" They raced out of the room with as much energy and enthusiasm as they'd raced into it.

Matt dropped a kiss on the top of his wife's head and walked out of the room.

"I'm so sorry," Georgia apologized when they were gone. "I really tried to entice the boys to stay at home with Ava—Jack and Kelly's daughter—but even though they absolutely adore their cousin, they didn't want any part of that today."

"I'm glad you brought them," Julie assured her. "They're fabulous kids."

"Most days," Georgia acknowledged with a weary smile.

"And Matt—does he always do what you tell him to?"

"Usually." The other woman grinned. "Of course, it helps that it's usually what he wants to do, anyway. And he loves spending time with the kids—it gives him an excuse to act like a kid himself."

"Do you mind if I ask you another question?"

"Ask away."

"How did you manage two of them? I feel as if I didn't sleep at all last night, and Caden's only one baby."

"I wasn't on my own when the twins were born. Their dad worked a lot of long hours, but it seriously helped me get through the day just knowing that I could pass one or both of them off to him when he got home. So if you have any kind of support network, I would strongly recommend you utilize it."

"I'll keep that in mind," Julie said.

She was relieved that Georgia hadn't asked about Caden's father. She didn't want to lie but she didn't know any of these people well enough to tell them the truth. Still, she knew that she needed to tell someone, which made her think again about the appointment she'd missed with Jackson Garrett.

Since her reasons for wanting to consult with a lawyer hadn't changed, she should reschedule that appointment. Except now that her brother's friend was also the brother of the man who had delivered her baby, the situation was a little more complicated, making her doubt whether she should confide in him or find different legal counsel.

"Another thing to keep in mind is that it will get easier," Georgia told her. "It will take a while, but you and Caden will establish rhythms and routines, you'll start to anticipate his needs and adjust your schedule accordingly."

"Fingers crossed," Julie said.

"And when things get really crazy and you want to out-scream your screaming baby, just try to remember that incredible feeling of love and joy that filled your heart when he was first placed in your arms."

"I still feel that," Julie admitted. "Every time I look at him."

"Savor it," Georgia advised.

"What aren't you telling me?"

The other woman hesitated, then shrugged. "Pippa went through a colicky stage, which was pretty much pure hell for about three months."

Julie looked at the smiling, cooing baby. "Neither of you looks any the worse for wear."

"Not now," Georgia agreed.

"You have a beautiful family."

"I'm a lucky woman—although it took me a while to get settled here in Pinehurst and realize how very lucky."

"You're not from here?"

Georgia shook her head. "I moved from New York City last February."

"That's a major change—not with respect to geography so much as lifestyle, I would think."

"You'd be right. But I needed to make a major change.

Phillip, my first husband, passed away when I was pregnant with Pippa, and I found it more than a little overwhelming to be on my own with two toddlers and another baby on the way. So when my mother invited me to move in with her, it seemed like a perfect solution." She smiled wryly. "And it was until four months later when she moved to Montana."

"Why Montana?"

"She fell in love with a cowboy." Georgia smiled. "Which was great for her but a little unsettling for me, since I'd moved here to be closer to her. And then Matt moved in next door to me."

"That's how you met?"

She nodded. "And three months later, we got married."

"Fast work," Julie mused.

"On his part or mine?"

"I guess you'd have to tell me."

Georgia chuckled. "I wasn't looking for happily-ever-after. I wasn't even looking for a relationship. I had my hands more than full enough with three kids, but Matt found a way to be there, to fit in, to be everything I never knew I needed. How could I not fall head over heels in love?"

Julie didn't envy the other woman her happiness. Georgia had obviously traveled a difficult road to get to where she was at. But she did wonder what it would be like to fall head over heels in love and to know, as Georgia obviously did, that she was loved the same way in return.

Julie had never experienced that depth of emotion. She'd had intense crushes and serious infatuations, all of which had eventually faded or fizzled. She'd thought she was in love with Elliott—she never would have agreed to marry him otherwise—but she also would never have described herself as head over heels. Their affection for one another had grown over time, a result of common goals and shared interests. Which, in retrospect, seemed more like the foundation for a strong business partnership than a successful marriage. And then even that foundation had crumbled.

"Of course, the Garrett men are all charmers," Georgia continued. "Which might explain why Luke is the only one in Pinehurst who's still single. Is your baby's father in the picture?"

The question came at her so unexpectedly, Julie found herself shaking her head before she realized it.

"Good."

"Why is that good?" she asked curiously.

"Because of the vibes in the air between my brother-in-law and you."

"I think you're misinterpreting something."

"Am I?" the other woman mused.

She felt her cheeks flush. "I don't even know him."

"You don't have to know a man to be attracted to him," Georgia said matter-of-factly.

"I suppose not," she agreed.

"But I didn't mean to make you uncomfortable."

"You didn't. I'm not," Julie said. "I'm…confused."

Georgia smiled. "Yeah, I remember that feeling, too."

Julie didn't know what to say to that, so she was grateful that the other woman didn't seem to expect a response.

"But I didn't come over here to play matchmaker, only to bring a few things that you might be able to use for Caden."

"It looks like more than a few things," Julie noted, relieved by the change of topic.

"I had twins," Georgia reminded her. "Which means that I had to have two of everything, including infant car seats. I'm still using one for Pippa, but you're more than welcome to the other one. The base secures into your vehicle, and the carrier pops in and out, which is great for carting a baby around or even just as a place for him to sit while you're doing something else.

"When the twins were babies, I used to put them in their car seats on the floor in the bathroom while I was in the shower, because I was absolutely paranoid that something would happen if I didn't have my eyes on them every single minute."

Julie smiled at that. "Glad to know it's not just me."

"It's not just you. In fact, it's probably most new mothers."

"I just feel so completely unprepared. I thought I'd have more time to get ready. My own fault for listening to a friend who assured me that first babies never come early."

"They are more often late than early, but each baby comes in his own time," Georgia told her.

"It would have been nice if Caden had waited to come until after the storm had passed."

"But now you have an interesting story to tell when he asks about when and how he was born."

Julie would never forget the circumstances of her son's birth—or the connection that she now felt to the man who had helped deliver him. "There is that," she agreed.

"Mommy!" Clomping footsteps came through the kitchen, then a snow-covered bundle appeared in the doorway. Wrapped up as he was in the bulky snowsuit with a red hat pulled down to his eyes and a matching scarf wrapped around his throat, Julie couldn't tell if it was Quinn or Shane. But if she had to guess, she would say Quinn, since he seemed to be the more talkative and outgoing of the two brothers.

"Uncle Luke sent me in to get a carrot," he announced.

Georgia rose to her feet. "A carrot?"

"We made a snowman!"

"You look like a snowman," his mother told him.

The child giggled. "Shane 'n me made angels in the snow, too."

"Well, you're dripping all over Uncle Lukas's floor," Georgia chided. "So come back to the kitchen while I find you a carrot."

Since Caden was asleep again, Julie set him down in the playpen and followed them to the other room. "I think I want to see this snowman."

"It's out there." Quinn pointed a red, snow-covered mitten toward the back window.

Julie had made her share of snowmen as a kid, but even with the help of her older brothers, she'd never managed to put together anything of the scope or scale that the twins, along with their new daddy and uncle, had assembled.

It was a larger-than-life creation, with arms that reached up to the sky. There were mittens on its hands, a striped scarf around its throat, and a matching knitted hat on its head. The eyes were probably dark stones but they looked like coal and the mouth was made up of smaller stones curved into a lop-sided but undeniably happy grin.

But as impressive as the snowman was, it was Lukas, wrestling in the snow with his shy nephew, who captivated her.

Georgia joined her at the window.

"Isn't he awesome?" the little boy said.

Yes, he is, Julie thought, before she tore her attention from the flesh-and-blood man and shifted it to the one made of snow.

"I almost expect him to start dancing," she told Quinn.

"You'd need a magic hat for that," Georgia advised.

"Do we have a magic hat?" he asked hopefully.

"Nope. Just a carrot," the boy's mother said, and handed him the vegetable.

When Frosty's nose was in position, Matt decided that the boys' hard work had earned them big cups of hot chocolate with lots of marshmallows on top. Of course, this suggestion sent them racing back into the house to beg their mother to make it, which warned Luke that his brother wanted to talk to him without the twins overhearing their conversation.

A suspicion that was confirmed when Matt said, "So what's her story?"

There was no point in pretending he didn't know who the "her" was that his brother was asking about. "I don't know many of the details," he admitted. "She tends to skirt around personal questions."

And though his brother probably wasn't concerned with her financial status, Luke suspected that Julie came from a family with money. The car Bruce had towed out of the ditch was a late-model Audi A6 that he knew, from a trip to last year's auto show, was worth a pretty penny. The watch on her wrist was also pretty—and costly—and her clothes were likely designer. He wasn't familiar enough with any specific label to be able to identify what she was wearing, it was more in the way they fit, the quality of the fabrics and the cut. On the other hand, he suspected that Julie would look equally stylish dressed in an old potato sack.

"Did she say anything about the baby's father?" Matt pressed.

Luke shook his head.

"Did you ask?"

"Of course not."

"Why not?"

"Because I figured if she wanted me to know, she'd tell me."

"Aren't you curious?"

"Sure," he admitted. "But it's really none of my business."

"She's living under your roof."

"She was stranded in a storm." Luke felt compelled to point out the obvious. "I haven't put her on the title to the property."

"I know," his brother admitted. "Just…be careful."

"Careful of what?"

"Falling for her—and her baby."

He snorted. "I'm not the falling type."

"There's a first time for everything," Matt warned.

"No need to worry," he assured his brother. "She's not going to be here long enough for me to even lose my balance."

"It doesn't take long."

Of course, Matt would know. Seven years earlier, he'd accepted the daddy role not just easily but eagerly when he'd learned his girlfriend was pregnant—only to find out, three years after their wedding, that the child she'd given birth to wasn't his. And yet, that experience hadn't prevented him from falling all over again—this time for a young widow and her three children. Thankfully, that story had a much happier ending.

"And I've seen the way you look at her," Matt added.

He frowned at that. "How do I look at her?"

"The same way you used to look at the green mountain bike in the window of Beckett's Sporting Goods store when you were a kid."

Luke remembered that bike—and the quick thrill that had gone through him when he'd seen it in the family room with a big bow on it the morning of his twelfth birthday. A thrill not unlike what he felt whenever Julie walked into the room.

"She's a beautiful woman," he said, careful to keep his tone light.

"She is that," his brother agreed. "But there's something about her—a vulnerability that reminds me too much of the wounded strays you were always bringing home."

"First a bike, then a puppy—I wonder if Julie would appreciate either of those comparisons."

"I'm not worried about her. I'm worried about you."

"I'm thirty-four years old," he reminded Matt.

"And starting to think that it's time to settle down and have a family?"

"No." Luke shook his head. He was happy for both of his brothers, pleased that they were happy, but he didn't want what they had. Marriage and kids? Not anywhere on his radar.

At least not before he'd heard Caden's first indignant cry and looked into those wide, curious eyes trying to focus on a whole new world. In that moment there had maybe—just maybe—been the tiniest blip on Luke's radar. Not that he would ever admit as much to his brother.

"Right now, the only thing I'm thinking about is hot chocolate," he said, and turned to follow the path his nephews had taken back into the house.

Chapter Seven

"I really like your brother's family," Julie said to Lukas after Matt and Georgia had packed up their kids and puppies and gone.

"He definitely lucked out when he bought the house next door to Georgia," Luke agreed. "She's one in a million."

"He must be one in a million, too—a man willing to take on the responsibility of her three kids."

"Not just willing but eager," he admitted, remembering how he and Jack had both worried about their big brother's single-minded pursuit of the widowed mother of three. "Of course, Matt's always wanted a big family. And he couldn't love those kids any more if they were his own."

"You can see it in the way they are together—like all of the pieces just fit." She sounded just a little bit wistful.

"They do fit," he agreed. "But that doesn't mean it was easy."

She looked down at her baby, snuggled contentedly in

her arms. "That's what I want for Caden," she told him. "A real family."

Luke waited for the warning bells to start clanging inside of his head, but nothing happened. Okay, so maybe he was overreacting. After all, she hadn't been looking at him when she'd said it, but at the baby. There was no reason—aside from a possibly overinflated ego—to think that she imagined him anywhere in the picture of that family she wanted.

In fact, it was entirely possible that she wasn't thinking about him at all but the man who was her baby's father. Which, recalling his brother's warnings, seemed the perfect opportunity to ask about him.

"Maybe Caden's father wants the same thing," he suggested.

"I told you—Caden doesn't have a father."

Of course, he knew that wasn't true. He also knew that whatever had happened between the man and Julie didn't negate his parental rights and responsibilities. But she obviously wasn't ready to tell him anything about that relationship. Maybe he'd cheated on her—or maybe he'd been cheating *with* her. If the man already had a family with someone else, he wouldn't be in a position to give Julie the family she wanted for her son.

"Well, I'd say he's off to a good start, because he's got a great mother, anyway," he told her.

Her lips curved, but the smile didn't reach her eyes, and he suspected that she didn't trust he was willing to drop the subject of Caden's father. "I'm flattered you think so," she said. "But the truth is, I have absolutely no idea what I'm doing."

"Fake it till you make it."

"That's interesting advice."

"I'm an interesting guy," he said immodestly.

She looked at him now, her gaze speculative. "And far too charming for your own good," she decided.

"Since when is an excess of charm a bad thing?"

"When it's part of a package that includes a too-handsome face and a smile that makes a woman's knees weak."

There was no way he could not smile in response to that. "You think I'm handsome?"

"It's not an opinion but a fact," she told him.

"Do I make your knees weak?"

"Right now, I'm weak from hunger," she told him. "Breakfast was a long time ago and that chili your sister-in-law brought over smells fabulous."

His teasing smile faded. He was accustomed to being on his own and not having to think about anyone else, and it was only now he realized they'd skipped lunch. Which wasn't unusual for him, but probably wasn't advisable for a nursing mother.

"You should have said that you were hungry," he admonished. Then he shook his head. "No, you don't have to tell me—just help yourself to anything you want. And if there's something that you want that I don't have, let me know so I can get it for you."

She touched a hand to his arm, silencing his rambling apology.

"I'm not really starving," she assured him. "But that chili does smell good."

"I'll dish it up."

Julie decided to try Caden in the car seat/carrier that Georgia had brought over. When he was buckled in, she sat him across from her at the table while Lukas sliced a loaf of crusty bread to accompany the chili.

Conversation throughout the meal was casual and easy, and Julie began to relax again. She'd enjoyed the teasing banter they'd exchanged earlier, had felt comfortable with Lukas. And then she'd touched him—just a casual brush of her fingertips to his sleeve—but the sparks that had flown from the contact had unnerved her.

"Fiction or nonfiction?" he asked, pushing aside his now empty bowl.

"Sorry?"

"What do you like to read?"

"Almost anything," she told him. "But I'm not a fan of the horror genre. What about you?"

"Mostly nonfiction," he said. "Rock or country?"

"Alternative."

His brows lifted at her response. "Me, too," he admitted. "Romantic comedies or action flicks?"

"Depends on my mood."

"What are you in the mood for tonight? There's a Sandra Bullock, Hugh Grant movie on TV or we can choose something from my James Bond collection."

"You don't have to entertain me," she told him.

"I don't see how sliding a DVD into a player qualifies as me entertaining you."

"I just figured you had better things to do than hang out with me."

"I can't imagine anything better than spending a few hours in the company of a beautiful woman," he countered.

Julie was flattered—and tempted. Because as tired as she was, she was even more tired of being alone. For the past seven months, she'd moved from city to city, gallery to gallery. Yes, she'd routinely been introduced to new people, but at the end of each day, she'd gone back to an empty hotel room alone. She'd kept in touch with her family and friends, but the distance had been lonely.

Now the show was over, Evangeline's collection had been carefully packed up and shipped back to The Grayson Gallery, and Julie was officially on the three-month maternity leave that she'd negotiated with her employer. She didn't have to be "on" anymore, she didn't have to present a polished and professional image. What Lukas was offering her right now—the chance to sit and relax and tuck her feet up beneath her on the sofa—sounded too good to refuse. And she wasn't going to.

"Despite the blatantly inaccurate but much appreciated compliment, I would enjoy watching a movie with you," she told him.

"So what will it be? Rom-com or double-oh-seven?"

"Double-oh-seven," she said without hesitation. "I'm still feeling a little emotional and I don't know you well enough to want to bawl my eyes out in front of you twice in one day."

"You didn't bawl earlier," he denied. "You were just a little teary."

"That doesn't make me feel better," she told him.

"Okay—any particular Bond flick you want to see?"

"Do you have the latest one?"

"Is it your favorite?"

"I haven't actually seen it yet."

"Then that's what we'll watch." He stood up to carry their bowls to the dishwasher. "Did you, uh, want to nurse the baby before we start the movie?"

She glanced at the slim, white-gold watch on her wrist. He noticed that the elegant oval was ringed with diamonds and the name on the face said Cartier. "I probably should," she said in response to his question.

"I'll tidy up in here and make popcorn while you're doing that," he said.

"Popcorn? We just finished dinner."

"There's always room for popcorn," he insisted.

She frowned. "Isn't that Jell-O?"

"Sorry, I don't have any Jell-O."

She was shaking her head when she carried Caden out to the family room.

Luke puttered around in the kitchen for a while, putting

away the leftovers, loading the dishwasher, checking that both Einstein and Daphne had water in their respective dishes. The popcorn would only take a few minutes in the microwave but it would take Julie longer than that to nurse Caden.

When the popcorn was popped, he dumped it into a bowl and carried it, along with a can of cola for himself and a glass of water for Julie, to the family room.

"Can I ask you a question?"

"Sure," he agreed easily.

"Does being around a nursing mother make you uncomfortable?"

"No," he immediately responded, though his gaze shifted away. "I think it's one of the most incredible and beautiful things I've ever seen."

"Then why do you jump up and leave the room every time you think Caden's hungry?"

"Because I thought you might be uncomfortable, nursing in front of a stranger."

She shrugged. "My body stopped being my own when I got pregnant. And considering that you helped deliver my baby, it seems pointless to be self-conscious about baring a breast when you've seen much more intimate parts of me."

"Okay, then," he said, because his brain suddenly seemed incapable of generating a more articulate response.

"And it's your house," she reminded him. "So if I'm uncomfortable, I can go to my room. And if you're uncomfortable, you can send me to my room."

"Seeing you nurse your baby doesn't make me uncomfortable," he assured her. "This conversation, on the other hand…"

She laughed. "Okay—conversation over."

"Thank you," he said, and picked up the remote.

Luke wasn't surprised that Julie fell asleep before the end of the movie. What did surprise him was that when she did succumb to slumber, her head tipped toward him, then nestled against his shoulder.

He could smell the scent of her shampoo, and it reminded him of fruity drinks and tropical beaches. Her hair was soft and shiny and a thousand different shades of gold. Her skin was flawless and pale, her cheekbones high, her lashes long and thick. Her lips were exquisitely shaped, and temptingly full.

He felt a stirring low in his belly, tried to ignore it. She was an attractive woman so it wasn't unexpected that he would be attracted to her. But under the circumstances, it would be completely *in*appropriate to act on that attraction.

So though he was tempted to dip his head, to brush his lips over the sweet, soft curve of hers and wake her with a long, lingering kiss, he knew that he couldn't. She wasn't *his* sleeping beauty and he wasn't anyone's prince.

Even if, for just a minute, he wanted to be.

Luke loved all of his nieces and nephews, and he got a kick out of hanging out with the kids, but that was good enough for him. He had no desire to tie himself to one woman—who would want that when there were so many fascinating and interesting women to choose from?—and no concern about carrying on the family name—and why would he, when his brothers already had that covered? In fact, he couldn't remember the last time he'd been involved in a relationship that had lasted even six months. And that was okay, because he'd never seen himself as the type to settle down with a wife and a couple of kids.

But his mind had started moving in a different direction when he'd helped deliver Julie Marlowe's baby. There was something about the little boy that had taken a firm hold on his heart. Maybe it was the fact that his hands had been the first to hold the newborn infant, but whatever the reason, he felt as if there was a real connection between them.

Unfortunately, he knew that when Julie decided to go back to Massachusetts he'd probably never see her or Caden again. The prospect left him feeling strangely empty inside.

And it wasn't just the little guy that he would miss. Though he'd barely known Julie for twenty-four hours, they'd been through a lot together in that short period of time. He didn't know her well, but he knew that she was smart and strong and brave and spunky, and he knew that he wanted some time to get to know her better.

Whether it was fate or providence or luck, she wasn't going anywhere for at least a few days. Not while the snow was still falling and her vehicle was at Bruce's Body Shop. And maybe, by the time the storm passed and her car was fixed, she would want to stay a little longer.

Or maybe by then he'd be ready for them to go.

Okay, so he didn't think *that* was a likely scenario, but living with a woman and her baby was completely outside of his realm of experience so he wasn't going to assume anything.

The end credits rolled, and still she didn't stir. With sincere reluctance, he finally nudged her gently with his shoulder.

"Come on," he said. "I don't want to sleep in a chair again tonight."

Her eyelids flickered, then slowly lifted. It took a moment for her soft blue-gray gaze to focus, but the moment that it did, she pulled away from him. "I fell asleep," she realized. "I'm so sorry."

"No need to apologize to me." He lifted the baby from her arms, then helped Julie to her feet. "Although Daniel Craig would probably be upset to know that he put you to sleep."

"I *wish* Daniel Craig was here to put me to sleep."

He sighed and shook his head. "Runner-up again."

"Actually, you're better than Daniel Craig," she told him. "He's just a fantasy, but you're real. And you saved my baby."

He wasn't comfortable being thrust into the role of a hero.

Especially when anyone else would have done the same thing under the circumstances. So he ignored the latter part of her comment and said, "Come on." He nudged her toward the stairs. "Let's get you up to a real bed."

When they reached the guest room, he turned on the bedside lamp, then gently laid Caden down in the cradle.

"Do you have pajamas?" he asked Julie, who was already tugging back the covers on the bed.

"I'm too tired to get changed," she said.

He didn't argue with her. And when she'd crawled between the sheets, he moved over to the bed and dropped a chaste kiss on her forehead. "Sweet dreams."

"You, too," she said, her eyes already shut.

As Luke made his way to his own room down the hall, he suspected that he would be tossing and turning all night. Thinking about the woman down the hall, and wanting what he couldn't have.

When Julie awoke the next morning, she didn't remember if she'd dreamed, but she'd definitely slept better than the night before. She was still up countless times to nurse and change and cuddle with Caden, but she didn't have any trouble falling back to sleep in between. And Caden had slept well in the cradle—if not for any longer than three hours at a time.

After his morning feeding, Julie took another shower and changed into a clean pair of yoga pants and a wrap-style sweater. A quick glance at the clock revealed that it was after 8:00 a.m. She hadn't heard any activity from down the hall, and she wondered if Lukas was already up and about or if he was still sleeping.

As she started down the stairs, she noticed Einstein waiting for her at the bottom, dancing around in excited anticipation.

She bent to pat his head, and he fairly quivered with excitement. For an active and exuberant pup, he was surprisingly restrained around the baby, which she appreciated.

He raced down the hall, then back again. She didn't have any trouble interpreting his silent message, and she followed him to the kitchen.

"Pancakes okay?" Lukas said by way of greeting when she appeared in the doorway.

"Very okay," she said. "But you don't have to cook for me all the time."

He shrugged. "I was cooking for myself, anyway."

She settled Caden into his carrier as Lukas put a platter of food on the table. Along with a generous stack of fluffy pancakes was a pile of crisp bacon strips.

"You made bacon again?"

"You don't have to eat it if you don't want it," he told her.

"The problem is that I do want it," she admitted, and snagged a piece from the platter.

"Would you feel less guilty if I told you it was turkey bacon?"

"Yes." She bit into it. "Is it?"

"No, but I'll lie if it will make you feel better."

She took a couple more slices, then added a couple of pancakes to her plate. Lukas sat down with her and proceeded to slather his pancakes with butter and drench them with syrup.

They chatted while they ate. Lukas teased her with hints about what parts of the movie she'd missed when she'd fallen asleep the night before—although she was skeptical about his claim that James Bond had to battle a one-legged Gypsy bank robber and his buxom transgendered girlfriend. He made her smile and laugh, and he made her forget all the reasons that she'd run away from Springfield more than seven months earlier and appreciate the fact that she was with him here in Pinehurst now.

He was halfway through his stack of pancakes when a low hum sounded from across the room. "Sorry," he apologized, pushing his chair away from the table. "That's my pager."

He read the message on the display, then disappeared into his office, no doubt to make a call. Julie finished her breakfast, stealing another piece of bacon from the platter and chatted with Caden while she waited for Lukas to return.

When he came back to the table, he wasn't smiling. Without a word, he picked up his plate and scraped the contents into the garbage.

"Is everything okay?" she asked tentatively.

He shook his head. "No. I have to go see a patient."

"I didn't know vets made house calls."

"Sometimes." He grabbed his keys from the counter, and Einstein was immediately at his feet, tail wagging. Lukas shook his head. "Sorry, buddy. Not this time." When the puppy's ears dropped, he bent to give the dog a quick scratch.

"I'll be back soon," he said.

Julie wasn't sure if he was talking to her or the dog, and then he was gone.

Despite his promise to be back soon, Lukas was gone for most of the day. Julie wasn't concerned by his absence so much as she was concerned about him, because it was apparent that whatever had called him away from home on a Sunday morning had been serious.

Early afternoon, she made herself a peanut butter sandwich and washed it down with a glass of milk. After she'd fed and changed Caden, she sat him on her lap and read out loud to him from one of the picture books that Georgia had brought over.

The DVD was still in the player from the night before, so

Julie fast-forwarded to the part where she'd fallen asleep and watched the end of the movie.

When it was over, she fed Caden—again, and changed him—again. Then she laid him on a blanket on the floor for some "tummy time" because it was supposed to help develop upper body strength for crawling.

As soon as Einstein heard the key in the lock, he was racing toward the door, dancing and barking in excited anticipation of his master's return. Julie scooped Caden up from the floor and carried him to the hall to greet Lukas.

From the wide doorway, she could see that he was seated on the deacon's bench beside the closet, a takeout bag beside him and Einstein in his lap. His boots were still on his feet, there was a light dusting of fresh snow on his jacket, and though his eyes were closed, tension was evident in the clenched muscles of his jaw.

She took a quick step back, not wanting to intrude on what was obviously some private pain, and retreated to the family room again. She'd turned on the TV after the movie finished, more for the background noise than because she had any interest in the crime investigation show that was playing out on screen, but she settled back on the sofa now and feigned rapt attention.

A few minutes later, Lukas spoke from the doorway. "I picked up Chinese."

Caden, who had just started to drift off to sleep, woke up again. His eyes opened wide and immediately began searching for him. The realization that her son already recognized the man's voice was both startling and unnerving for Julie, but it was Lukas's avoidance of her gaze that worried her.

She followed him into the kitchen and put Caden in the portable car seat.

"I'm sorry," he said, still not looking at her. "I didn't think I'd be gone so long."

"I'm just a stranger passing through town," she reminded him lightly. "You don't have to clear your schedule with me."

He got plates from the cupboard, retrieved cutlery from the drawer. "I know. But I didn't even think about the fact that you were stranded here without a vehicle—"

"There wasn't anywhere I needed to go," she interjected gently.

He started to unpack the bag of food, still not looking at her. "I got spring rolls, chicken fried rice, orange beef—"

Julie deliberately stepped in front of him, so that he had no choice but to look at her. And when he did, the stark pain evident in his blue-green eyes hit her like a fist.

She took the foil container from his hands and set it aside. "Why don't you leave the food for a minute and tell me what happened?"

"It's not a story with a happy ending," he warned her.

"I kind of figured that."

He blew out a breath. "It was Mrs. Boychuk who called about her seven-year-old boxer." One side of his mouth kicked up in a half smile. "Sweet'ums.

"Even as a pup, the dog was built like a tank and with the proverbial face that only a mother could love, but to Mrs. Boychuk, he was Sweet'ums. Six months ago, he was diagnosed with osteosarcoma—bone cancer."

"What kind of treatment do you offer for that?"

"We don't have the ability to offer any treatment locally," he admitted. "So Mrs. Boychuk took him to a clinic in Syracuse for radiotherapy. The treatment seemed to be successful, at least initially, but a couple of months ago we found that the cancer had spread to his lungs."

And she could tell by the flat tone of his voice that there was nothing to be done at that point.

"She lost her husband to cancer three years ago—she didn't want to lose her companion, too. She refused to believe the diagnosis. But over the past couple of days, Sweet'ums really began to struggle with his breathing and yesterday he stopped showing any interest in food."

"She called you to put him down," Julie realized, her eyes filling with tears.

He nodded.

She swallowed around the lump in her throat. She wanted to say or do something to help ease his pain, but she felt completely helpless. He obviously cared about his animal patients and losing this one was tearing him up inside.

And although Julie didn't know Mrs. Boychuk or Sweet'ums, she felt as if she knew Lukas, and it hurt her to see him hurting. In the end, she went with her instincts, lifting her arms to wrap around his neck and holding him tight.

For a brief second, he went completely and utterly still, and she wondered if she'd overstepped the boundaries of their fledgling friendship. Then his arms came around her, too, and he hugged her tight. She felt a shudder run through him, an almost-physical release of the grief he was holding inside, and then the tension seemed to seep from his muscles.

After a long moment, he finally eased away.

"Are you okay now?" she asked gently.

"No," he admitted. "But I'm doing much better. Thanks."

And he impulsively touched his lips to hers.

She felt the jolt of the fleeting contact all the way down to her toes. And when he took a quick step back, she knew that he'd felt it, too.

She cleared her throat, focused her gaze on the takeout containers on the counter. "Orange beef?"

He nodded. "Are you hungry?"

"Always," she said, and forced a smile.

What she didn't admit was that she was suddenly craving something other than Chinese food. Because that teasing brush of his lips had triggered a hunger for more of Lukas Garrett's kisses.

Chapter Eight

Luke was at the clinic before eight o'clock Monday morning. Not surprisingly, Karen's vehicle was already in the parking lot. He hung his coat on a hook in the staff room/kitchenette, then traded his boots for shoes before heading out to the front to retrieve the files for his morning appointments.

When he opened the door to reception, he heard Karen lift the top off the jar of doggy treats that she kept on her desk. She frowned when he came around the corner and there was no dancing puppy at his feet.

"Where's Einstein?"

"He decided to stay at home today," Luke told her.

"*He* decided?"

"Yeah." He shook his head, still baffled by the animal's unusual behavior. "He seems to have assigned himself as the baby's protector and doesn't like to be too far away from him."

Her brows lifted. "Baby?"

"Sorry—I guess a lot of things happened on the weekend that you don't know about."

"I saw Sweet'ums's file on top of the stack this morning," she said, her voice quiet, her eyes filled with compassion.

He just nodded.

"But since that doesn't explain Einstein staying home with a baby, maybe you should fill me in."

He did—briefly summarizing the details of discovering Julie's car in the ditch and inviting the laboring mother into his house to help deliver her baby.

"That was Friday?" Karen asked.

He nodded.

"And this woman and her baby are still at your place?"

"Her car's at Bruce's shop," he pointed out. "What was I supposed to do—call a cab to take them to a bed-and-breakfast?"

"It sounds like you did more than enough," she told him. "I would have thought *she* might have called her baby's father to come and pick them up."

"I don't think he's in the picture," Lukas admitted.

Karen's brows rose again. "You don't *think?*"

"She hasn't volunteered very much information about her personal life."

"And that isn't waving an enormous red flag in your mind?"

Of course it was. Julie's reluctance to talk about Caden's father did give him cause for concern. But he wanted to give her the benefit of the doubt. He wanted to believe that she had legitimate reasons for the secrecy. And he hadn't demanded answers or explanations because he wanted her to trust him enough to tell him those reasons of her own volition.

If he thought about it, he might wonder why he wanted her to open to him, why it mattered so much to him. He'd only known her for three days. He barely knew her at all. But there was something about her that made him want to know her a whole lot better.

Part of that was the immediate and undeniable physical attraction he felt toward her. An attraction that hadn't dimmed when he'd realized she was pregnant nor even through the experience of childbirth. But he'd managed to downplay it—to convince himself that it didn't need to be a factor.

Of course, that was before he'd kissed her. Not that it had been much of a kiss. In fact, he would have argued that the brief contact barely met the most conservative definition of a kiss, except that he'd felt the impact of it in every cell of his body.

And if that wasn't reason enough to be wary, Karen had pointed out another: there was too much about Julie that he didn't know. He wasn't sure what to think about the fact that she'd never told her parents about her pregnancy. If she'd hidden the existence of her baby from them, had she also hidden it from her baby's father? This disconcerting possibility inevitably made him think about Jack, who hadn't learned about his daughter's existence until Ava was twelve years old.

And the effortless way that Caden had completely taken hold of Luke's heart made him remember that Matt had raised another man's son as his own for three years—until the child's biological father came back into the picture. Which wasn't something he should be worrying about after only three days with Julie and her son, except that after only three days, he already knew that he would miss them when they were gone.

He pushed those concerns aside when Megan Richmond came through the front door with her eighteen-month-old chocolate Lab. He loved his job and the familiar routines of his work. Not that the work was ever routine, but there were certain patterns and rhythms to his days at the clinic. The needs of the pets and the concerns of their owners were always his primary focus, but several times throughout the day on Monday, he found his attention drifting. He called home three times, just to see if Julie and Caden were doing okay, to ensure that Einstein wasn't being a bother, to inquire if there was anything they needed.

And when the last patient was gone from the clinic at the end of the day, he was the first one to head out, even before Drew—the animal tech—had finished wiping down the exam rooms.

He could smell the rich, savory scents of basil and garlic as soon as he walked through the door. Einstein came running when he tossed his keys on the counter, reassuring Lukas that the pup still did know who was his master, even if he'd chosen a mistress for today.

Then Luke looked up and saw Julie standing at the stove, and he felt an instinctive hum through his veins.

He was a decent cook. He didn't live on fast food the way some of his single friends did, but he did eat a lot of grilled cheese sandwiches in the winter and hamburgers in the summer—usually because, by the time he got home at the end of the day, he didn't have the energy or the imagination to make anything else. It was a pleasant change to walk in the door and have a meal waiting. And an even more pleasant change to find a beautiful woman in his kitchen.

"I didn't know what your after-work routine was and I didn't want to overcook the pasta, so I haven't put it in yet," she said.

"My after-work routine is to look in the fridge, then look in the freezer, then open a bottle of beer while I try to figure out what I want to eat."

She went to the fridge and retrieved a bottle of beer, twisted off the cap and handed it to him. "Tonight you're having chicken parmigiana and spaghetti with green salad and garlic bread. It will be on the table in fifteen minutes."

He grinned. "You just fulfilled a fantasy I never even knew I harbored."

"Do I want to know?" she asked cautiously.

"A sexy woman offering me a home-cooked meal at the end of a long day." He tipped the bottle to his lips, drank deeply.

She laughed at that as she used her thumb and finger to measure the pasta, then dropped it into the pot of boiling water. "If you think I'm sexy, you need to seriously reevaluate your standards."

As he swallowed another mouthful of beer, he realized that she wasn't being coy or fishing for compliments—she honestly believed what she was saying. "You really don't see it, do you?"

"See what?"

"How incredibly attractive you are."

"I had a baby three days ago," she reminded him.

"Yeah, I think I remember hearing something about that," he said dryly, and turned his attention to the infant securely strapped in the carrier on top of the table, where Julie could keep an eye on him—and vice versa.

"How was the little guy today?" he asked, tweaking Caden's toes through the velour sleeper. The baby kicked his legs instinctively in response to the touch, making Luke smile.

"Hungry. Sleepy. The usual." She lifted the lid of another pot, stirred the sauce that was simmering.

"Did you manage to get any rest?"

"A little." She stirred the pasta. "What did your day entail?"

"Along with the usual checkups and vaccinations, there was a calico with a mild respiratory infection, a diabetic Doberman, a Saint Bernard with a urinary tract obstruction and a ten-month old kitten whose owner was convinced she had a tumor in her belly."

She held her breath. "Not a tumor?"

"Not a tumor," he confirmed. "Pregnant."

Her lips curved. "So a better day than yesterday?"

"A much better day," he agreed.

"I'm glad."

"I also talked to Bruce Conacher today. He didn't have a number for you, so he called me."

"Is my car fixed?" she asked hopefully.

Luke shook his head. "Unfortunately, it's going to be out of commission for at least a few more days."

"Why?"

"You snapped the right front drive axle and Bruce has to wait on delivery from an out-of-town supplier. He was apologetic, but he doesn't do a lot of work on imports so he didn't have the part in stock or easy access to one."

She sighed. "Are you willing to put up with us for a few more days?"

"I told you, you can stay as long as you want," he reminded her. "And the few more days will only make your car drivable. If you want the damaged bumper and fender repaired, it will be a little bit longer than that."

"I guess, since my car's already at his shop, Bruce might as well fix everything that needs to be fixed."

"I'll let him know," Luke said. "And I promise—you'll be pleased with the results. He does good work."

She nodded. "Okay. Now wash up so we can eat."

He fed the animals first, then scrubbed his hands at the sink while she served up the meal. His brows drew together as he looked at the plate she set in front of him.

"You don't like Italian food?"

"What?"

"You're frowning," she noted.

"I love Italian food," he assured her. "But when you asked

if pasta was okay for dinner, I thought you'd cook some spaghetti and top it with canned sauce."

"This is canned sauce," she admitted. "You didn't have all the ingredients to make fresh, but I doctored it up a little bit."

"It doesn't look anything like what comes out of the can."

"I'll take that as a compliment."

"It was intended as one," he assured her. "I really didn't expect anything like this. You didn't have to go to so much trouble."

"It wasn't any trouble. I like to cook."

"Well, that's convenient because I like to eat."

"Then dig in."

So he did, and his taste buds nearly wept with joy. "This is really good."

"You didn't believe me when I said I could cook, did you?"

Truthfully, the luxury car, the diamonds at her ears and designer labels on her clothes had made him suspect that she was more accustomed to having someone cook for her than vice versa. "I didn't think you could cook like *this*," he admitted.

She smiled, choosing to be pleased by his obvious enjoyment of the meal rather than insulted by his skepticism. "Carla, my parents' housekeeper, was originally from Tuscany—although she would be the first to renounce this meal as American Italian and not *real* Italian."

The revelation about the housekeeper confirmed his suspicion about her privileged upbringing. And yet, she seemed perfectly at ease in his humble home, more than capable of looking after herself—and perfectly content to do so. "What is real Italian?"

"Simple recipes with quality seasonal ingredients," she said, then shrugged. "But I've always been partial to a good red sauce."

"This is definitely that," he agreed. After a few more bites, he couldn't resist asking, "What else did Carla teach you to make?"

"You'll have to wait until dinner tomorrow to find out."

The next night Julie made stuffed pork chops with garlic mashed potatoes and green beans. The night after that was broccoli and beef stir-fry with wild rice. On Thursday, it was chicken in a cream sauce with new potatoes and baby carrots.

"Did you want any more chicken?" she asked, when he set his knife and fork down on his empty plate.

"No, thanks." He rubbed a hand over his flat belly. "I couldn't eat another bite."

"You have to have room for dessert," she told him. "Caden napped a little bit longer than usual today, so I had time to make apple crisp."

"One of my favorites," he told her.

"And you've got French vanilla ice cream in the freezer to go with it."

"We never had dessert on a weeknight."

"Never?"

"Well, maybe a slice of birthday cake, if it happened to be someone's birthday."

"When is your birthday?"

"June twenty-second."

"I guess I won't be making a birthday cake anytime soon," she noted.

"When's yours?"

"March fifth."

"How old are you going to be?"

"That was a smooth segue," she told him. "If not exactly subtle."

He shrugged. "I've been trying to guesstimate, but I can't figure out if you're older than you look or younger than you seem."

"I'll be twenty-four on my next birthday," she admitted.

Which meant that she was only twenty-three now, eleven years younger than him. But so what? There were no age taboos with respect to friendship. And he really felt as if he and Julie were becoming friends. Or they would be if he could continue to ignore the way his pulse pounded and his blood hummed whenever he was near her.

"Apple crisp?" she prompted.

"Why not?"

She cut a generous square of the still-warm dessert and topped it with a scoop of ice cream.

"I am feeling seriously spoiled," he confessed, lifting his spoon toward his mouth. "I don't think I've ever eaten as well as I've eaten this past week."

"If you want to continue eating, you're going to have to make a trip to the grocery store," she said. "Since I'm going to be here for a while, I could make a list of some things that will help with the menu planning."

"Why don't you make that list and we can go out tonight?"

She seemed startled by the suggestion. "Tonight?"

"Sure. I figured, since you haven't been out of the house since you got here, you might enjoy a quick outing."

Her face lit up as if he'd given her a precious gift. "I would *love* to go out."

Julie had been so excited about the opportunity to get out of the house for a little while that she hadn't thought about the repercussions of going out with Lukas. What was intended to be a quick trip to the store ended up being an hour-long parade up and down the aisles as the local vet seemed to be acquainted with everyone in town—and everyone was curious about the unknown woman and baby who were in his company.

He was always polite and made a point of introducing her

to everyone who stopped to chat, but he didn't divulge any information about her aside from her name. After the third introduction, Julie realized that he was being deliberately secretive. When he put his hand on her back to nudge her along after a brief exchange of pleasantries with a bubbly blonde he'd introduced as Missy Walsh, the pieces started to come together.

"Why do you want people to think that we're together?"

"We are together," he said, deliberately misunderstanding her question.

Her gaze narrowed. "You know what I mean."

Before he could reply—and undoubtedly deny any complicity—they turned up the next aisle and crossed paths with someone else he knew. It was another woman, this one stunningly beautiful with long dark hair, warm golden eyes and a wide smile.

"Hey, stranger," she said, and touched her lips to his cheek in a way that confirmed they were anything but strangers. Her gaze shifted to take in Julie and Caden, then moved back to Lukas again. "I heard whispered speculation in aisle four about whether or not it was 'his baby,'—now I know who they were talking about."

He just shrugged. "People are always going to find something to talk about."

The brunette moved to take a closer look at Caden, then shook her head. "No way. He's much too cute to be your kid." She offered her hand to Julie. "I'm Kelly Cooper."

"Jack's fiancée," Lukas added, in case she hadn't made the connection.

"And one of Lukas's oldest friends," Kelly told her.

"It's nice to meet you," Julie said.

"Who was in aisle four?" Lukas asked.

"Tara Gallagher and Missy Walsh."

"Is there anything I can bribe you with to go back there and tell them that the baby is mine?"

Kelly shook her head. "It wouldn't matter. Not to Missy, anyway. I could say that you had a dozen kids by a dozen different mothers, and she would take that as hope she might bear the thirteenth." Then she turned to Julie. "Missy's been in love with Lukas since tenth grade, but he never gave her the time of day."

"Julie isn't interested in ancient history," Lukas said.

"It doesn't sound ancient to me," she couldn't resist teasing.

Kelly laughed. "I've got a lot more stories I could tell."

"And we've got to get to the produce department," Lukas said pointedly.

His friend rolled her eyes. "You could at least pretend to be subtle."

"Why?"

"To make a good impression on your houseguest."

"I'm trying to make a good impression—which is why I don't want her hanging around here to talk to you."

She poked her tongue out at him. Lukas kissed her cheek then started to push the cart away. Since Caden's carrier was attached to the cart, Julie automatically fell into step beside him. "It was nice meeting you," she said to Kelly.

"We'll finish our conversation another time," the other woman promised.

"I'll look forward to it."

After Julie had selected the fruits, vegetables and fresh herbs she wanted, they made their way to the checkout line. She always liked to have a list when she went to the grocery store, but she invariably added to the list as she shopped. She hadn't realized how much she'd added until Lukas was unloading the cart onto the checkout belt.

She tried to move past him, closer to the register so that

she would be in position to pay, but he deliberately blocked her path.

"I want to get this—"

He put a hand over hers as she reached into her purse. "We'll discuss this later."

"But—"

He dipped his head closer, his mouth hovering just a few inches above hers. "The gossip from aisle four just moved her cart into line behind us."

She lifted a brow. "What does that have to do with the price of free range chicken at the Saver Mart?"

"Nothing," he admitted. "But I wouldn't mind adding fuel to the speculative fires."

"You think she'd really believe that we're together?"

"Why not?"

To an outsider, it probably did look as if they were having an intimate conversation. Their heads were close and their voices pitched low so that only Julie and Lukas could know that they were arguing about who should pay the grocery bill. "Because I drove into town less than a week ago."

"Eight months after the brief but blistering hot affair we had when I was in Boston for a veterinary rehabilitation symposium."

His lips brushed the shell of her ear as he spoke, making her blood heat and her heart pound. It was an effort to focus her attention on their conversation, and she had to moisten her lips with the tip of her tongue before she could respond. "Were you really in Boston eight months ago?"

"Actually it was Baltimore," he admitted. "But Missy never had an aptitude for geography."

The clerk announced the total of their order and Lukas drew away to pull out his wallet. Julie's fingers tightened on the handle of the buggy as she exhaled a long, shaky breath.

She wanted to believe the flood of heat that made every

inch of her skin itch was nothing more than postpartum hormonal overload, but the more time she spent with Lukas, the more she was beginning to suspect otherwise.

She secured Caden's car seat into the truck while he loaded the grocery bags.

"I'm writing you a check when we get back to your place," she said, when he slid behind the wheel.

"We'll talk about it then," he said agreeably.

But she wasn't fooled for a minute. And since she knew he was going to give her grief about paying for a few groceries—even though she would be eating the food—she decided to give him some grief, too.

"I'm a little surprised that you'd be resistant to such an attractive woman."

He turned the key in the ignition. "Who?"

"Missy Walsh."

He pulled out of the parking lot and onto the road. "You don't know anything about the situation."

"I know that you're apparently afraid of a five-foot-tall curvy blonde in pink spandex."

"With good reason," he told her. "She adopted a kitten last year just so that she could make regular appointments to come into my clinic."

"You don't think it's possible that she just wanted a pet?"

"Within six months, she gave it away because she was allergic. Then she tried a dog—same problem."

"Maybe she's just a lonely woman who wants some company," she suggested.

"I told her to try a goldfish."

"And?"

"She brought the bowl in when the fish went belly up."

Julie couldn't help but laugh. "You're kidding?"

"I wish I was."

"Okay, that is a little strange," she admitted.

"The biggest problem is that she's really sweet," Lukas admitted. "She just tries too hard. She actually dated one of my friends for a while, and he really liked her at first. He said she was fun and interesting to talk to. But the more time they spent together, the more she assimilated his ideas and opinions. She liked everything he liked, wanted to do whatever he wanted to do, agreed with everything he said."

"I would think that's the kind of woman every man would love."

"Maybe for five minutes," he acknowledged. "After that, it would get pretty boring."

"So you've never gone out with her?"

"No. And I've never given her the slightest bit of encouragement. But that hasn't stopped Missy." He shook his head, obviously frustrated by the situation. "She came into the clinic a couple of weeks ago—coincidentally only a few days after Jack and Kelly got engaged—to ask my opinion about geckos."

"With one brother recently married and the other engaged, it's understandable that she might think you're ready for a committed relationship," Julie pointed out to him. And then she couldn't resist asking, "So why are you still single?"

"Never met the right woman, I guess."

"Really? That's your answer?"

"Or maybe I'm just not the marrying kind."

"That sounds like the response of a man who's been burned by love."

"It's the truth."

"How old are you?"

"Thirty-four."

She shifted in her seat so that she could see him more clearly. "Are you honestly telling me that you've never known a woman who made you think in terms of forever?"

"Not really."

"What does that mean?"

"Well, I did propose to someone once," he confided. "But she turned me down."

Which confirmed her "burned by love" theory but still didn't quite add up. "And that was it? One heartbreak and you gave up?"

"I wouldn't even call it a heartbreak," he admitted, turning into his driveway. "In retrospect, I'm not even sure I was in love with her, but I could imagine sharing my life with her."

"Now that's the foundation of a really romantic proposal."

Her dry tone made him smile. "My proposal was motivated by more practical considerations."

"And you wonder why she turned you down?"

He just shrugged.

"So if you weren't wildly in love, why did you want to marry her?"

"Because she was pregnant."

Her jaw dropped. "You have a child?"

"No," he said quickly. "It wasn't my baby."

"Oh." She thought about that for a minute. "Have you always had a hero complex—a desire to save the damsel in distress?"

He scowled. "I don't have a hero complex. She was a friend, and the baby's father was out of the picture, and I knew she was terrified by the thought of going through pregnancy and childbirth on her own.

"And," he confessed with a small smile, "for the few minutes that she took to consider my offer, I was absolutely terrified that she would say yes."

"I can understand why she would have been tempted," Julie admitted.

"Because I'm so tempting?" he teased.

"Because having a baby without a father is a scary prospect—even when it's the right thing to do."

"Right for whom?"

She didn't say anything, was afraid that she'd already said too much.

"Who were you thinking about when you decided to have your baby on your own?" he pressed. "Yourself or Caden?"

"Both of us."

Then she unbuckled her belt and reached for the door handle, a clear signal that the conversation was over.

Chapter Nine

Kelly tried not to worry. She knew that Lukas was a grown man, capable of making his own decisions and accepting the consequences of those decisions. But he was also her best friend and, as such, she was entitled to pry—just a little.

And wasn't it a lucky coincidence that she had an appointment to take Puss and Boots—the pair of kittens her daughter had insisted on adopting from Lukas a few weeks earlier—to the clinic for their sixteen-week immunizations the following Tuesday morning?

The vet gave them a quick once over, nodded approvingly. "They're doing well. Thriving."

"Does that mean they're getting fat?" she asked. "Because every time I turn around, Ava's giving them treats."

"They're not getting fat. But as long as they're eating the right amount of food, treats should be reserved for special occasions."

"Tell your niece that."

"I will," he promised.

"She won't listen," Kelly warned. "I told her that they had to have their own bed—which they do. And they still sleep with her."

"So long as she has no allergies and they aren't interfering with her sleep, it shouldn't be a concern. In fact, for these two—because they were orphaned at such a young age—that close physical contact could be one of the reasons that they're thriving. Love is as necessary as food, water and shelter to living creatures."

"Even you?" she asked.

He glanced up at her, his brows raised. "Where did *that* come from?"

"It's a simple question," she told him. "I can't help but admire the life you've built for yourself. You have a successful veterinarian practice, a fabulous house—but no one to go home to at the end of the day."

"I have Einstein and Daphne," he reminded her.

"And now you have Julie and Caden."

"They're not mine."

"But you want them to be," she guessed.

"What are you talking about?"

"I'm talking about you playing house with a beautiful woman and her brand-new baby."

"I'm not playing house."

"And I'm concerned about you falling for her," Kelly admitted. "For both of them."

"I'm not falling for her," he said.

She didn't believe that claim for a second. "I don't want you to get hurt, Lukas."

"Don't you have more important things to worry about—like your wedding?" he said pointedly.

She shook her head. "Ava's taken care of every single detail—I don't have to do anything but show up."

"You're letting your twelve-year-old daughter plan your wedding?"

"She's almost thirteen," Kelly reminded him. "And she had very strong opinions about what she wanted. Since Jacks and I really just want to make it legal, we decided to put Ava in charge of the details."

"And is everything on schedule?"

"Almost everything." She let out a long sigh. "I still don't have a dress."

"You know that Jack will be happy to marry you if you show up at the church in old jeans and a T-shirt."

"Yeah," she said, and smiled because she did know it was true.

The smile slipped as her stomach pitched. She sucked in a lungful of air, trying to fight against the unexpected wave of nausea. *Not now. Please not now.* Unfortunately, her body refused to listen to the mental pleas, and she bolted out of the exam room and to the washroom.

After she'd expelled the meager contents of her stomach—and heaved a few more times just to make sure there was nothing left inside—she flushed the toilet. Her hands were shaking as she dampened some paper towels and wiped her face. When she was reasonably certain that her legs would support her, she returned to the exam room, where Lukas was waiting with the kittens.

He handed her a bottle of water. "Morning sickness?"

"I don't know." She lowered herself onto the stool beside the exam table and unscrewed the cap from the bottle. "It might just be a touch of a stomach bug that's going around. Ava was home from school two days last week."

"Do you have any other flulike symptoms? Fever? Chills?"

"No," she admitted. "Just the nausea."

"Then I'd guess *pregnant* over *flu.*"

Kelly lifted the bottle to her lips, took a long swallow of

water. "Jacks and I both wanted to have another baby, and Ava has been asking for a brother or a sister almost since she could talk. But a baby in the abstract is a lot different than a flesh-and-blood child."

"You're scared," he realized.

"I'm almost thirty-four years old," she said. "The last time I had a baby I was twenty-one—too young and stupid to know that I should have been terrified."

"You're not alone this time," he reminded her.

"I know. I mean—assuming that there is a 'this time.'" She sighed. "He said that this is what he wanted—but what if it isn't? I know Jackson still thinks about everything he missed out on when Ava was a baby, and I understand that. But I don't know that he's truly ready for the reality of a baby."

"Is any parent ever truly ready?"

"Good point," she admitted. "Okay, on the way home I'll stop at the pharmacy and pick up a pregnancy test."

Lukas settled the kittens back in their carrier. "And you'll let me know?"

"If there's anything to know," she told him. "You'll be the first—*after* Jackson this time."

He grinned. "I can live with that."

While Kelly was at Lukas's clinic, Julie was at Jackson's law office.

After an extended delay waiting for parts that had be or-dered from an out-of-town supplier, Bruce had finished the repairs to her vehicle and delivered it to Lukas's driveway the previous afternoon. She'd been waiting to get her car back so she could continue her journey to Springfield, but with her parents out of the country, she wasn't really anxious to go home. Because going home meant facing Elliott, and she wasn't ready to do that just yet.

So when Lukas had assured her that she was welcome to

stay as long as she wanted, she found herself accepting his offer "for just a few more days." But she was grateful that having her car back afforded her the freedom to come and go as she pleased, because she was finally able to reschedule her appointment to see the lawyer.

She hadn't told Lukas about the appointment, although she couldn't have said why any more than she could have said why she felt as if she was going behind Lukas's back to meet with his brother. After all, Jackson Garrett was the reason she'd come to Pinehurst in the first place. It was just an odd twist of fate that his brother was the reason she'd stayed.

She was summoned into the office at precisely 11:15 a.m., and when she walked through the door, Jackson rose from the chair behind his desk.

"I've been trying to figure out why your name sounds familiar," he admitted, offering his hand. "But I don't think we've ever met."

"We haven't," she admitted. "I was looking for a family law attorney in the area and my brother, Dan, recommended you. He said you went to law school together."

"Dan Marlowe," he said, and smiled. "It is a small world, isn't it?"

"Smaller than I ever would have guessed," she agreed. "Because your brother Lukas delivered my baby."

"So this little guy is the one?" He crouched down to get a closer look at the sleeping infant. "Well, he doesn't look any the worse for wear."

"I feel very fortunate that your brother knew what he was doing—or at least how to fake it."

"Then you're not here to sue him for malpractice?" Jackson teased.

She managed a smile. "No. I just wanted some general information. At least, that's why I originally requested to see you."

"And now?"

"Now that Caden was born in New York State, I have some specific questions about registering his birth." She opened her purse, pulled out a checkbook. "How much do you need as a retainer?"

"I don't need a retainer at all if I'm only answering a few questions."

"I'd rather keep this official."

"The minute you walked through the door of my office, the rules governing solicitor-client privilege came into effect," he assured her. "I'm not going to repeat anything you say here to anyone—not even your brother or mine."

She dropped her gaze. "I feel a little disloyal," she admitted. "Talking to you instead of Lukas."

"If you need a rabies shot, my brother's your man. If you have legal questions, not so much."

She smiled again. "Fair enough. Okay, the first question is about the paperwork I have to fill out to register Caden's birth. Do I have to include his father's name?"

"Are you married to him?"

She shook her head. "No."

"Then there's no presumption of paternity," he told her. "He could sign an acknowledgment of paternity, in which case his personal information would be included on Caden's birth certificate, but if he isn't willing to do so, you would have to apply to the court to request a paternity test."

"What if I don't want him named on the birth certificate?"

He considered her question for a minute. "Your son's biological father has certain rights and responsibilities, regardless of what either of you wants," he finally said. "Has he indicated that he is unwilling to fulfill his responsibilities?"

She dropped her gaze to the sleeping baby. The beautiful baby who was the reason for everything she'd done since she'd learned of the tiny life growing inside her. The reason she was here now.

"He doesn't know about Caden," she admitted.

"I try not to make judgments," he told her. "Especially when I don't know the whole story."

"I appreciate that." And she knew it couldn't be easy for someone with his personal experience to remain objective. Lukas had told her about his fiancée keeping the existence of their child a secret for twelve years. But despite that history, they'd obviously worked things out and were together now.

Julie knew that she and Elliott would never work things out, because she would never forgive him for what he'd done—or herself for not taking control of her life sooner. And right now, she wanted to focus on her son, to be the best mother that she could be, and to keep him away from his father.

"But I can't give you legal advice specific to your situation if I don't know what that situation is," he told her. "So you're going to have to give me at least some of the details."

"I can do better than that." She reached into her purse again, this time pulling out a slim envelope of photographs. "I can show you."

When Julie looked at the calendar Saturday morning, she was surprised to realize it was the fifteenth of November. The month was already half over and her stay in Pinehurst had been extended from a few days to more than two weeks.

Even more surprising was the fact that she wasn't eager to leave. Part of her reluctance was because her parents were on the other side of the world, but another—maybe even bigger—part was that she enjoyed spending time with Lukas.

And she was starting to worry that she was enjoying this unexpected detour a little too much, and starting to seriously crush on the man who had delivered her baby. So when Lukas asked if she wanted to go over to Matt and Georgia's for a while after breakfast, she decided that was probably a good idea. Being around other people would help keep her focus off the man who occupied far too many of her thoughts.

She started questioning her decision when she stepped into the entranceway of Matt and Georgia's house and realized that the entire Garrett family was in attendance—adults, children and pets. Her reservations multiplied when Kelly said, "Don't take your coat off—we're kidnapping you."

Julie took an instinctive step back, holding Caden tight against her chest. "What?"

"Only for a couple of hours," Georgia said, her tone reassuring. "And you will thank us for it—I promise."

Her panicked gaze met Lukas's amused one. "Did you know about this?"

"Not until about two minutes ago," he assured her. "But I heartily approve of their plan."

"What is the plan?" she asked warily.

"A mini-spa retreat," Georgia said.

Wariness gave way to interest. "Really?"

Kelly grinned. "Massage, pedicure. A few hours of girl talk."

"No boys allowed," Jack's fiancée said firmly. "Not even baby boys."

"But—"

"No buts, either," Georgia said.

"I'm not sure about leaving Caden," Julie admitted. While she was undeniably tempted by the invitation, she couldn't help but think that abandoning her two-week-old baby into someone else's care made her a bad mother.

"Of course you're not," Georgia acknowledged. "It's the scariest thing in the world for a new mother to leave her baby for a few hours. But he'll be with Luke and Matt and Jack—they know what they're doing."

"Their hands will be full with the twins and two babies, three puppies and two kittens."

"Ava's here, too," Kelly reminded her.

Which made Julie feel a little better. Jackson and Kelly's daughter might be twelve, but she was mature for her age. She promised Julie that she had "tons of experience" looking after Pippa, and her easy confidence and obvious competence in handling the infant reassured the new mother.

But truthfully, Julie would never have even considered saying "yes" to the proposed outing if she didn't know that Lukas would be there, too. And she had pumped so that she'd have the option of giving Caden a bottle instead of nursing at Matt and Georgia's house, so she didn't have to worry about her baby going hungry if she wasn't around.

"You need this," Kelly told her. "And even if you don't think you do—*we* do."

Julie smiled at that.

"Everything is new and exciting now," Georgia told her. "But trust me, a few hours away from your baby to recharge your batteries will make you an even better mother."

"The new mother looked panicked at the thought of leaving her little guy for a couple of hours," Matt commented when the women had finally gone, leaving the men with the kids and a menagerie of pets.

"Maybe she was just panicked at the thought of leaving him with Lukas," Jack teased.

"I don't blame her," Luke said. "What do I know about babies?"

"A lot more now than a couple of weeks ago," Matt guessed.

"Which means you have more experience at this stage than I do," Jack admitted. "I never knew Ava when she was this young. In fact, I can't believe that she was ever this small."

"Next time around, you'll be there every step of the way," Matt said.

"The next time around is going to come sooner than either of us expected," Jack confided.

"Really?" Matt grinned. "Kelly's pregnant?"

"Due next summer—July twenty-seventh, to be exact."

"Congratulations," Luke said.

"It's hush-hush right now," Jack told them. "Because it's early days, but mostly because Kelly doesn't want to tell Ava until we're married."

"Yeah, you wouldn't want your twelve-year-old daughter to suspect you've had sex with her mother out of wedlock when your wedding isn't scheduled for another few weeks," Matt said dryly.

"We've had the talk," Jack said. "Ava knows all about the important role of the stork."

His brothers laughed.

"Seriously, though," Luke said. "You're good with Kelly's pregnancy?"

Jack nodded. "I'm thrilled. I think Kelly's a little apprehensive, because Ava's almost a teenager. But I know our daughter will be all for it. She desperately wants to be a big sister."

"She certainly enjoys being a big cousin," Matt commented. "She's great with the twins and Pippa. And she's jumped up to check on Caden every five minutes since he went down for his nap."

"Yeah—Luke's managed to limit his checks to every seven minutes," Jack said dryly.

He just shrugged.

"It's pretty obvious you've fallen for the kid," Matt said. "The question is—have you fallen for his mother, too?"

"I'm just helping her out," he said.

"By inviting her to move in with you?"

"She hasn't moved in," he denied. "She's only staying with me temporarily."

"Temporary is a couple of days," Jack said. "Julie's been sleeping in your bed for longer than that already."

"Jesus, Jack. She just had a baby two weeks ago—she's not sleeping in my bed."

His brother's brows lifted. "I was speaking figuratively. The house and everything in it is yours, including the guest room bed. Therefore, she's sleeping in your bed."

"But that was quite the vehement protest," Matt noted.

Luke glowered at him.

"She's a beautiful woman, you're both single and living in close quarters. You wouldn't be human if you hadn't thought about taking things to the next level."

"And what is the next level of friendship?"

Jack shook his head. "You can lie to yourself all you want, but you can't fool your brothers."

And, of course, they were right. Luke *was* attracted to Julie. But he had no intention of putting the moves on a woman who'd had a baby just two weeks earlier—he wasn't a completely insensitive idiot.

Unfortunately, her time in Pinehurst was limited. Exactly how limited, wasn't sure. He'd half expected her to start packing up when she got her vehicle back, and the fact that her parents were away had obviously been a factor in her decision to stay in Pinehurst a little bit longer. But how much longer? And would she stay long enough for him to figure out if there was any fire to go with the sparks he felt whenever he was around her?

"You can't fool Missy Walsh, either," Matt interjected.

"What does any of this have to do with Missy?" Luke demanded.

"I heard she was absolutely distraught after seeing you cuddling up to Julie in the grocery store," Jack told him.

"I wasn't cuddling up to her," Luke denied.

"It's not like Missy to get her facts wrong. At least not where you're concerned."

"I was purposely flirting with Julie," he admitted.

"Is it possible to accidentally flirt with a woman?" Matt wondered.

"Actually it is," Jack told him. "If flirtation is perceived but not intended."

Matt turned back to Luke. "But you were purposely flirting with Julie."

"I just wanted to give Missy something to think about."

"How is Missy?" Jack teased. "Has she got a new pet yet?"

"I'm glad you think it's funny. But at least I haven't come home and found her in my bed," Luke retorted.

His middle brother winced at the memory of what a former client had done to try to win his affection. As if that scenario wasn't awkward enough, Kelly had been with him when they found the naked woman in his condo.

"Not yet," Matt warned.

"I can't imagine her trying to break in when she knows Julie and Caden are there."

"So it's the new mom-and-baby security system," Jack concluded.

"Which might work with respect to Missy but has to put a damper on the rest of your love life."

"It would if he had one," Jack scoffed. "He hasn't even dated anyone since Sydney Dawes—and how long ago was that?"

More than six months, but Luke wasn't going to admit that. Instead, he just shrugged. "I got tired of going through the same routine with different women, and I decided I wasn't going to do it anymore."

"You've given up dating?"

"I've given up dating for the sake of dating," he clarified.

"You've finally realized that all those meaningless relationships were…meaningless?" Matt teased.

"Just because I'm not looking to hook myself up 'till death do us part' like you guys doesn't mean I don't want to meet someone different, someone who matters."

"How can you possibly know if someone's different unless you get to know her—by dating her?" Jack demanded.

"You ask her to move in with you," Matt said, not entirely tongue-in-cheek.

"Julie and Caden are only staying at my place for the short term," Luke reminded his brothers.

"You just keep telling yourself that, and maybe you'll even start to believe it," Jack said.

"Or maybe," Matt suggested, "you'll figure out that a real relationship isn't such a bad deal, after all."

Chapter Ten

When the women arrived at Gia's Salon & Spa, they were escorted to individual treatment rooms. Julie enjoyed a head and neck massage with warm oils and scented wraps that worked out knots she hadn't even known existed. After that, she rejoined Georgia and Kelly in the pedicure area. It was set up like a private living room, with the chairs arranged in a semicircle facing the fireplace. Flames were flickering in the hearth and soft music was piped through speakers in the ceiling.

Totally relaxed now, they talked about everything and anything—from recent movies and favorite books to local events and sports legends—which, Julie learned, included the three Garrett brothers.

When their toenails were painted and they were sitting around waiting for the polish to dry, Kelly looked at Julie and huffed out a breath. "Dammit," she said. "I like you."

"Thank you," Julie said cautiously.

The other woman smiled. "I didn't want to like you," she admitted. "Because I know that Lukas is falling for you and I'm afraid that you're going to break his heart."

Julie felt a jolt of something—surprise? alarm? hope?—in her chest in response to Kelly's words, but she shook her head. She didn't believe it, couldn't let herself believe it.

She was just beginning to acknowledge to herself that she had feelings for Lukas. And under different circumstances, she knew that she could easily fall for him. But circumstances weren't different. Maybe he was the right man, but this was definitely the wrong time. Her life was simply too complicated right now to even consider a personal relationship, no matter how much she might wish otherwise.

"I think you're misreading the situation."

"I don't think so," Kelly denied.

"Lukas has been incredibly kind but—"

The other woman snorted.

"He *is* kind," Georgia confirmed, shooting a look at her soon-to-be sister-in-law. "But I think Kelly's suggesting that his motives aren't quite so altruistic where you're concerned."

Julie shook her head. "He knows that I'm not staying in Pinehurst, that my life's in Springfield."

"Is it?"

The question surprised Julie. But then she realized that Kelly was right to challenge her statement, because in the two weeks that she'd been in Pinehurst, she'd barely thought about her former life at all. She certainly didn't miss it.

Yes, she missed her family. But they were still her family and always would be, regardless of where she made her home. On the other hand, she had no reason to consider making her home in Pinehurst. Her growing feelings for a sweet and sexy veterinarian aside, there was nothing for her here.

"It used to be," she finally said. "Although the truth is, I've been on the road working for the past seven months."

"What do you do?"

"I'm a curator at The Grayson Gallery in Springfield, but I've been traveling with a private collection since April."

"You haven't been home in all that time?" Georgia asked.

Julie shook her head.

"I'm thinking there's a better reason than an art show to stay away for so long," Kelly mused.

"A lot of reasons," she agreed. "Although I fully intended to be home before my baby was born."

"Except that Caden had other ideas."

"Or maybe it was fated that you would get stuck in Pinehurst," Georgia suggested.

Kelly frowned, obviously not pleased to consider that stronger forces might have factored into setting up the current situation.

"It wasn't fate," Julie denied. "It was simply the combination of no snow tires and a freak blizzard."

"The snow melted last week," Kelly pointed out.

"I just got my car back from Bruce on Monday." Which even she knew was a lame explanation, considering that it was now Saturday and she was still there, still without any firm plans to leave or any set date to do so.

"Monday," Kelly echoed in a considering tone. "So maybe Lukas isn't the only one who's falling?"

Julie sighed. "I'm *not* falling. But I will say that Lukas is handsome and kind, sexy and sweet. He's smart, funny, warm, compassionate and probably the most incredible man I've ever met."

"She's definitely falling," Georgia confirmed. "Can you believe it—all of the Garrett brothers finding true love in the same calendar year?"

Kelly shook her head. "You read too many romance novels."

The mother of three shrugged, unapologetic. "I like happy endings."

"And you got your very own when you married Matt."

"Actually, I like to think of the day I married Matt as a happy beginning," her friend clarified. "And speaking of weddings…"

Kelly sighed. "I know—I need a dress."

"Not that you should rush into anything," Georgia said. "After all, you still have three whole weeks before the wedding."

Julie's jaw dropped. "You're getting married in three weeks and you don't have a dress?"

"I've got the groom," Kelly said, just a little smugly.

"And an appointment at Belinda's Bridal in Syracuse next Saturday," Georgia told her.

"Why do I have to go all the way to Syracuse to go shopping?"

"Because your daughter found a beautiful strapless satin Alfred Sung gown in stock and in your size, and she begged and pleaded and somehow convinced the manager to hold it until next weekend."

"She just wants me to go strapless so that she can go strapless," Kelly muttered.

"Possibly," Georgia admitted. "But she showed me a photo of the dress she picked for you, and it's gorgeous."

The bride-to-be still didn't look convinced. "Any dress looks good on an airbrushed model in a glossy magazine."

"Next Saturday," Georgia said firmly.

Kelly wiggled her painted toes, then looked at Julie. "Can we kidnap you again next Saturday?"

Julie grinned. "For shopping? Anytime."

Only later did she realize that none of them—herself included—had questioned the assumption that she would still be in Pinehurst a week later.

* * *

Julie enjoyed her visit to the spa with Kelly and Georgia, but by the time she slid her "Fabulous Fuchsia" painted toes into her shoes, she was anxious to get back to Caden and Lukas. Not that she would dare admit as much to either of the women in her company.

When they arrived at Matt and Georgia's house, they found a much quieter scene than the one they'd escaped from a few hours earlier. Lukas was in the living room with Caden in his lap, watching a football game and explaining the set plays and terminology to the baby. When there was a stoppage in play, he told them that Matt was in the basement playing video games with the twins, Pippa was napping in her crib upstairs and Jack was in the kitchen working on a science project with Ava.

As the other women went off to track down their respective partners, Julie crossed to the sofa and scooped her baby into her arms. She breathed in his sweet baby scent and noisily kissed both of his cheeks. "There's my big guy."

"And still in one piece," Lukas said proudly.

"If I hadn't been absolutely certain, I never would have left him with you."

"Did you leave him with me?" he asked. "Because Ava seemed to think she was in charge."

She smiled at that. "Kelly says she's desperate for a baby brother or sister of her own."

"And in the meantime, she's been practicing with Pippa—and now Caden."

"Did either you or Ava have any problems?"

Lukas shook his head. "Aside from the fact that he did *not* want to take the bottle you left for him."

"I wondered about that. The books warn that when nursing mothers attempt to bottle-feed, their babies can suffer from nipple confusion…" She let the explanation trail off as she felt her cheeks flush. "Sorry, I spent the last few hours with two women who have been through the same thing, I wasn't thinking about the fact that you probably don't need to hear those kinds of details."

He just shrugged. "He screamed for a while—and let me tell you, that boy has a very healthy set of lungs—but when you didn't miraculously appear to give him what he wanted, his hunger won out."

"I guess that's a good thing," she said. "But it almost makes me feel superfluous."

"It was one bottle—you're not superfluous."

"I know I'm being silly. It's just that I really missed him. I had a fabulous time, but I missed him."

"You look like you had a good time. In fact, you look…" He trailed off, as if not quite sure how to complete the sentence.

"Rested and refreshed?" she suggested. "Kelly promised that I would be both when Gia was finished with me, and that's definitely how I feel."

"I was going to say beautiful," he admitted.

"Oh." There was something about the way he was looking at her, the intensity in his eyes that started her heart pounding just a little bit faster again.

"But you're always beautiful," he continued. "Even the first time I saw you—through the foggy window of your car—you took my breath away."

"Of course, that was before I got out from behind the wheel and you saw me waddle like a penguin behind the belly of a whale," she teased.

"You never waddled," he denied.

"I was eight and a half months pregnant," she reminded him.

"And beautiful."

He brushed his knuckles down her cheek, but it was her knees that went weak.

"And I've been thinking about kissing you since that first day." His words were as seductive as his touch, and the heat in his gaze held her mesmerized as he lowered his head, inching closer and closer until his lips hovered above hers.

"You have the most tempting mouth." He traced the outline of her lips with his fingertip. "Soft. Shapely. Sexy."

"Are you still thinking about it?" she asked, the question barely more than a whisper. "Or are you actually going to kiss me?"

Luke breached the tiny bit of distance that separated their mouths and lightly rubbed his lips against hers.

They were even softer than he'd suspected.

Even sweeter.

He kissed her again, another gentle caress—a question more than a statement. She sighed softly, her eyes drifting shut—the answer that he'd been seeking.

He nibbled on her mouth, savoring her texture and flavor. Her response was unhesitating. Her lips yielded, then parted, and her tongue dallied with his. They were barely touching—it was only their mouths that were linked, and the taste of her made him crave more. He slid an arm around her waist, to draw her closer, and finally remembered that she had a baby in her arms. And that they were standing in the middle of his brother's living room.

With sincere reluctance, he eased his mouth from hers.

She looked up at him, her eyes clouded with desire and confusion.

"That wasn't an actual kiss," he told her.

She blinked. "Then what was it?"

He wasn't sure how to answer that honestly without scaring her off. Because the truth was, it had been just enough of a taste to make him realize that he was starving for her, and that he wanted to feast not just on her mouth but on all her delicious parts.

"Let's call it…a prelude to a kiss," he decided.

"So am I ever going to get a real kiss?"

It was reassuring to know that she was experiencing at least some of the same attraction that was churning him up inside. Unfortunately now wasn't the time or the place to figure out how much.

"Yeah," he promised. "But not when I have to worry that we might be interrupted by either of my brothers, their significant others, kids or animals, or any combination of the same."

When they were home and Caden was fed and settled down for a nap, Julie went to the laundry room to take the clothes out of the dryer. She carried the basket into the family room, intending to fold while she watched TV, and froze in the doorway when she saw Lukas was already there.

He was reading a veterinarian periodical and didn't even look up when she entered the room. She exhaled an unsteady breath and sat down on the edge of the sofa, with the basket on the coffee table in front of her.

At Jackson and Kelly's house, when Lukas had been looking at her and talking about kissing her, all she'd been able to think about was how much she wanted the same thing. Now that her mind wasn't clouded by his nearness and her hormones weren't clamoring for action, she was having second thoughts. Mostly because what he'd called a prelude to a kiss was actually one of the best kisses she'd ever experienced in her entire life.

"I'm not going to jump you, Julie."

But she jumped when his voice broke the silence, knocking the basket off the table and spilling its contents all over the floor.

He immediately crossed the room, dropping to his knees beside her to help gather up the laundry.

"I'm sorry," he said. "I didn't mean to make you nervous."

She wanted to say that she wasn't, but since it would obviously be a lie, she remained silent.

"Although I have to admit I'm a little curious about why you're suddenly so on edge," he continued. "Is it because you're afraid I'm going to really kiss you? Or disappointed that I haven't already?"

"I'm not sure," she admitted, picking up scattered baby socks. "Maybe a little of both."

His smile was wry. "At least you're honest."

She scooped up the last sleeper and dropped it into the basket.

"Your pulse is racing," Luke noted, and touched his fingertip to the side of her neck, just beneath her ear.

Her skin felt singed by the touch, and her throat went dry. She lifted her gaze to his, and saw the desire in his eyes. She hadn't seen it when he looked at her before. Maybe she hadn't wanted to see it. But there was no denying it was there now.

"It's the way you look at me," she admitted. "You make my heart pound."

He took her palm and laid it against his chest, so she could feel that his heart was pounding, too. And then his head lowered toward her, and her breath caught in her lungs.

"Can I kiss you now, Julie?"

She wanted him to kiss her. She wanted to feel his lips against hers so desperately she ached, but she also knew that if he kissed her, everything would change. And she wasn't sure she wanted anything to change.

She genuinely liked Lukas. She enjoyed spending time with him, talking to him. She even enjoyed being with him when they didn't have anything to talk about, because the silence was never awkward or uncomfortable. She didn't want things to get awkward between them.

But as his lips hovered above hers, she couldn't deny that she wanted his kiss a lot more than she wanted the status quo.

His hands—those wide-palmed, strong, capable hands—cradled her face gently. He tilted her head back, adjusting the angle to deepen the kiss. He touched his tongue to the center of her top lip, a light, testing stroke. She met it with her own, a response and an invitation. He dipped inside her mouth, and the sweep of his tongue sent shockwaves of pleasure shooting down her spine, leaving her weak and quivering with need.

After what seemed like an eternity—and yet somehow nearly not long enough—he finally eased his mouth from hers. "That was a kiss," he told her.

She made no attempt to move out of his arms, because she wasn't sure her legs would support her. "Maybe we should have stopped with the prelude," she said, when she'd managed to catch her breath.

"I don't think that would have been possible."

"I don't want to start something we can't finish. You know I'm only going to be in town for a few more weeks."

"How could I possibly forget when you keep reminding me every time I turn around?"

"I just don't want to give you mixed signals."

He tipped her chin up, forcing her to meet his gaze. "Are you attracted to me, Julie?"

"Do you really have to ask?"

He grinned. "Then I can be satisfied with that."

She eyed him doubtfully. "Really?"

"I'm not going to push for more than you're ready to give."

"I'm grateful for that," she told him.

"And until you trust me enough to talk to me, I can't see a few kisses leading to anything more."

"I do trust you."

"And yet you haven't said a single word to me about Caden's father."

Well, that was a complete mood killer. Except that she knew it wasn't unreasonable for Luke to want at least some of the details. "Not because I don't trust you," she told him. "But because I don't want to talk about him."

"As I said, I'm not going to push for more than you're ready to give."

She understood why he would have questions, and maybe it was time to give him some answers. She sat back on the sofa and drew in a deep breath. "His name is Elliott Davis Winchester III. He works in public relations at the Springfield Medical Center but has aspirations of a career in politics. I've known him for two years—well, I guess closer to three now, although I haven't seen him since I gave him back his ring seven and a half months ago."

Luke had been reluctant to push for answers—probably because he suspected he might not like what he learned. Her words confirmed it. "You were engaged to him?"

She nodded.

He wasn't really shocked by the revelation. Julie didn't seem the type of woman to get pregnant as a result of a one-night stand. But a relationship, however long-term, was different than an engagement. An engagement was a promise to marry, a plan for forever. If Julie had been engaged to Caden's father, she'd obviously been in love with him. Maybe she still was.

He cleared his throat. "What happened?"

"I realized he wasn't the man I thought he was—and he definitely wasn't a man I wanted to marry."

"Have you been in touch with him, to tell him that you had the baby?"

She shook her head.

"Don't you think he has a right to know?"

"Of course, the biological father has all kinds of rights, doesn't he?"

Something in her tone alerted him to the possibility that there was more to her situation than a jilted lover not wanting to fight over custody of her child. "Tell me what happened, Julie. Because I can't imagine that you went from making wedding plans one minute to hiding out with your baby the next without a pretty good reason."

His patient tone succeeded in dimming the fiery light in her eyes. "He hit me."

Luke hadn't seen that coming, and he almost felt as if he'd been punched.

"We'd been out to a political fundraiser and Elliott had been busy working the room, drinking and chatting with everyone who was anyone, telling jokes and laughing and drinking. When we got back to his place, he poured another drink and wanted to rehash every word of every conversation he'd had, but I was tired and just wanted to go to bed. He accused me of not being supportive, I said that he seemed more interested in Johnny Walker's company than mine, and he backhanded me.

"He only hit me once," she said, and touched a fingertip to her cheek where there was a tiny white scar he'd never before noticed. "But it was with the hand that proudly displayed the Yale class ring, and that was enough for me. I left.

"There was a pattern of escalating behavior, of course, that I only recognized after the fact. But the slap was—for me—the final straw."

"What else did he do?" Luke asked the question through gritted teeth.

"Does it matter? I left him. It's over. Now I just want to forget."

"Yes, it matters," he insisted. "Because unless you tell somebody about what he did, he gets away with it."

"Most of the time he was very courteous and considerate," she finally said. "But sometimes, when he was drinking, he would become impatient, angry, aggressive."

"What did he do?" he asked again.

"He'd berate my opinions, belittle my feelings. Outwardly, he would be attentive and affectionate, but he'd hold my hand a little too tight, or his fingers would bite into my skin when he took my arm."

"Did he leave bruises?"

"Not really. He never really hurt me before the night I left. But…"

"But what?" he prompted.

"I guess I knew it was escalating toward that," she admitted. "I wasn't really scared of him, but I was uneasy. I think that's one of the reasons that I didn't want to set a wedding date, because I was waiting for something like that to happen so I could leave him."

"Why did you need a reason to leave?"

"Because until he actually hit me, he seemed like the perfect man. My parents knew him, respected him. And for the first time in my life, they approved of a man I was dating. When we got engaged, they were thrilled."

"Do you think they would be thrilled to know that he'd hit you?"

"Of course not," she immediately denied. "Neither of them has any tolerance for domestic abuse."

Luke didn't, either. He'd never understood how anyone could hurt someone they claimed to love—spouse, child, parent or even pet. But he knew that it happened far too often.

"I understand now why you don't want him to be part of Caden's life, but I don't understand why you didn't immediately go to the police and press charges," he said.

"It was my first instinct," she confided. "My cheek was still burning when I reached for the phone. Elliott saw what I was doing, and there was a quick flare of panic in his eyes... and then he smiled.

"And he warned me that if I called the police—if I told anyone at all—he would destroy my father's career."

Chapter Eleven

Luke knew it didn't matter if the man had the ability to follow through on his threat, what mattered was that Julie obviously believed he did.

"How was he going to do that?" he asked her now.

"My father's a judge—a superior court judge, actually, with a reputation for being strict and unyielding. He built his career on a foundation of ensuring everyone had equal access to justice and was treated equally by the law."

"And it didn't occur to you that he might be a little bit upset that you gave in to your abusive fiancé's blackmail?"

"It occurred to me that he'd be devastated if his career was ended and I could have saved it."

"What do you think he did that you needed to save it?"

She picked up a sleeper out of the basket and carefully began to fold it. "Can I refuse to answer that question on the grounds that it may incriminate me?"

"This isn't a court of law," he reminded her. "You don't have to tell me anything that you don't want to."

"I don't want you to think badly of me," she admitted.

"I don't think I could."

She put the sleeper down, reached for another. "I had a very privileged upbringing," she confided. "I had the luxury of a stable home and a loving family, but I didn't always make smart choices.

"In my junior year of high school, a bunch of kids were planning to go to Mexico for spring break. My parents weren't thrilled with the idea, but they agreed that I could go if I paid for it. After Christmas, I went shopping with a few friends and there was this gorgeous Kate Spade handbag that I just couldn't resist. Except that, after buying the bag, I realized that I was almost two hundred dollars short for the trip and my parents refused to loan me the money."

"Which made you furious," he guessed.

She nodded and kept folding. "Because it wasn't that they didn't have the money—it was the principle, they said. They'd agreed that I could go if I paid for it, and I said that I would."

"So you didn't get to go on the spring break trip," he concluded.

"No—I went. When I told Tomas, my boyfriend at the time, that I didn't have the money, he said that he would loan it to me and let me pay him back in a few months. It seemed like the perfect solution to me, except that when we were ready to leave Mexico, Tomas wanted me to carry some souvenirs back for him as repayment for the loan."

He could see where she was going with this story and he really didn't want to hear anymore. But it was like passing the scene of a motor vehicle collision—he didn't want to see the carnage, but he couldn't seem to look away.

"I was young and naive, but I wasn't stupid," Julie continued. "I told him to carry his own drugs and I would reimburse him the cost of the ticket when we got home."

"Nothing about that sounds scandalous to me."

"No, that's just background—the first really bad choice that I made. Of course, I promised myself that I'd learned my lesson. Then, about six months later, I met Randy Cosgrove."

She'd finished with the sleepers and moved on to diaper shirts. "Randy was another bad boy. His father was a minister and Randy was the stereotypical preacher's kid who went in the opposite direction of everything his family believed. He was dark and brooding and sexy—the type of guy that all fathers warn their daughters about."

He wasn't sure how much more he wanted to hear about her relationship with Randy, but he wasn't willing to interrupt now that she was finally talking to him.

"My father warned me. My mother warned me. My brothers warned me. But I didn't listen. I was so sure they were wrong about him, and even if they weren't, I didn't care. Because I had fun with Randy—he was defiant, sexy and exciting, and I was totally infatuated with him.

"One night Randy came by to take me for a drive in a friend's car he'd borrowed. It was a candy-apple-red 1965 Ford Mustang convertible and it was a starry night, and we drove around for nearly an hour with the top down and the music blaring. And then the cops showed up and arrested both of us for stealing the car."

"How old were you?"

"Seventeen."

"That must have been a scary experience for you."

"I was terrified. I don't know how long I was at the police station before my parents came—probably not more than a few hours—but it felt like forever. Then my dad and the arresting officer were in conference for what seemed like several more hours, and when they finally came out, we went home."

"The way you told the story to me, you didn't even know the car was stolen."

"I didn't," she assured him. "But I didn't ask any questions, either. Not even the name of the friend Randy supposedly borrowed the car from. Randy did six months in juvie, and I walked away.

"Elliott told me that he could prove my dad had pulled strings and called in favors to keep me out of jail, that I wasn't charged because I got deferential treatment. If that's true, if he has proof, it will completely undermine my father's assertion that everyone is equal under the law."

"If you were never charged, what kind of proof could he have?"

"I don't know," she admitted.

"Then maybe you should consider that he manufactured whatever so-called evidence he has."

"I wish I could believe that was true, but I never told Elliott about that…incident. Which means that he must have gotten the details from someone else. Someone who was there, at the police station, and who knows what happened behind the scenes."

"Have you talked to your father about this?"

She shook her head.

"Why not?"

"I couldn't. At first, I couldn't because I didn't want to face my parents after what Elliott had done. And then—" she blew out an unsteady breath "—I was afraid to ask him about it."

"Afraid that it might be true?" he guessed.

She nodded. "I didn't want to believe it. At the time, I was so relieved that I didn't have to be photographed and fingerprinted and go to court, that I didn't even question it. But later, I started to wonder how I'd managed to slip out of that sticky situation so easily.

"Elliott's allegation that my father pulled strings and called in favors would certainly answer that question. And after everything my parents had done for me, there was no way I could do anything that would risk my dad's reputation and career."

"Instead, you let Elliott get away with what he did to you?"

She winced at his blunt assessment, though it was true. "I chose to end my relationship with Elliott and walk away. It seemed like the easiest solution at the time. Of course, that was before I knew I was pregnant."

"And now?"

"Now…I don't know," she admitted. "Elliott has political ambitions, and a strict timetable in which he wants things to happen. And I honestly don't know how he'll react to his ex-fiancée showing up with his out-of-wedlock child.

"I know I have to tell him about the baby, but one of the reasons I didn't tell him when I first discovered that I was pregnant was that I was worried he would try to force a reconciliation. He would say it was for the sake of our baby, but it would really be for the sake of his career. In politics, married men are viewed as more trustworthy and reliable than unmarried men—add a baby to the mix, and he'd be laughing."

"Do you think he'd still try to get you back?"

"I don't know," she admitted.

"Would you go back to him?"

"No." Her response was unequivocal and without hesitation.

"I'm sorry."

"For what?"

"Asking you to talk about this."

"You didn't push me for more than I was ready to give," she reminded him.

"Okay, then I'm sorry that talking about this undid all the good of Gia's massage."

She managed a smile. "Well, at least my toes still look good."

There was a definite chill in the air on Monday, so Julie decided to put a roast in the oven for dinner. She peeled carrots and potatoes to go with it, and figured she would try her hand at Yorkshire pudding, too.

Sunday had been a quiet day. Despite the passionate kisses she and Lukas had shared on Saturday night and her heart-wrenching confessions afterward, there was no lingering awkwardness between them.

There were also no more kisses, and although she was undeniably disappointed, the rational part of her brain reassured her that it was a good thing. It was scary to think about how much he meant to her already, how quickly he'd become not just a good friend but an important part of her world. And she knew that if there were more kisses, if they took their relationship to the next level, it would only be that much more difficult for her to leave.

After the basic prep for dinner was done, she spent some time playing with Caden—talking nonsense to him and showing him blocks and squeaky toys. Then they had a nap together, lying on a blanket on the floor with Einstein. When Julie woke up, she noticed that even Daphne had joined them. And when she reached a tentative hand out, the cat not only endured her gentle scratching but actually purred in appreciation.

She had just checked the potatoes when Lukas called to say that he was leaving the office. Caden wasn't on any kind of schedule yet, but she liked to nurse him before Lukas got home. Despite his claim that he was okay with the nursing thing, and although she knew her breasts were functional rather than sexual, the sizzle she felt around Lukas was so completely sexually charged that she'd decided it was best to keep her clothes on whenever he was around.

After Caden was fed and his diaper changed, Julie put him in a clean sleeper. She was just fastening the snaps when she heard the crash.

She raced down the stairs with the baby in her arms just as the back door opened and Lukas walked in.

They stood on opposite sides of the room, staring at the scene. The roasting pan had been upended in the middle of the kitchen floor, meat juices were spreading over the ceramic tiles and Einstein was in the middle of all of it, joyfully wolfing down prime rib.

It took Luke all of two seconds to accurately assess the situation. "Einstein!"

The dog cowered, his ears flat, his belly against the floor. Which meant that he was pretty much marinating himself in beef juice.

Julie was silent for a long minute, trying to comprehend the carnage, then her blue-gray eyes filled with tears.

Luke's first instinct was to go to her, to put his arms around her and reassure her that it wasn't a catastrophe of major proportions. But he knew that if he took a single step in her direction, Einstein would jump up, vying for his attention, and splashing in the au jus. Instead, he moved toward the dog, trying not to step in the gravy. He scooped him up and held him at arm's length.

"Let me get him cleaned up first, then I'll come back to deal with that," he told Julie, nodding toward the remains of Einstein's feast.

Of course, bathing a wriggling puppy who didn't like to be bathed wasn't an easy task. Einstein kept trying to jump out of the laundry tub, which meant that Luke ended up as wet as the puppy, and every time he plunked the animal back down in the water, he howled so desperately and pitifully that Luke started to feel guilty for forcing the bath.

When he finally drained the tub and rubbed the dog down, Julie had cleaned up the kitchen.

"I hope you're not hungry," she said, when he came out of the laundry room. "Because that was dinner."

"For what it's worth, it smelled really good."

"It would have been delicious." She glared at the dog. "He didn't even savor it—he scarfed it down like it was a bowl of three-dollar kibble rather than thirty dollars worth of prime rib."

Luke tried to look in the bright side. "I was kind of in the mood for pizza, anyway."

She just stared at him. "Pizza?"

"What's wrong with pizza?" Aside from the fact that it wasn't prime rib, of course. But he wasn't going to bring that up again.

"Nothing," she finally decided. "As long as we can get it with pineapple and black olives."

"I'll go along with the pineapple and black olives if I can add bacon."

"Are you that determined to clog your arteries before you're forty?"

"My doctor isn't worried."

"Fine. Pineapple, black olives and bacon," she agreed.

"Speaking of doctors," Lukas said. "Weren't you supposed to take Caden for a checkup soon?"

"We have an appointment with Dr. Turcotte on Thursday afternoon."

"What time?"

"Two o'clock."

"Do you want me to go with you?"

She lifted a brow. "You don't think I can manage to take the baby to a doctor's appointment on my own?"

"I'm sure you can," he agreed. "But I usually book surgeries on Tuesday and Thursday afternoons, and it just so happens that I don't have anything scheduled for this Thursday. Besides, I'm kind of curious to see how much the little guy has grown."

"You're not worried that going to see my baby's doctor with me might send the wrong message?"

"Cameron isn't the type to jump to conclusions," he assured her.

"I wasn't thinking about him so much as any other patients who might be in the waiting room—particularly those of the female variety."

"They can jump to all the conclusions they want."

She smiled. "So it's true."

"What's true? Who have you been talking to?"

"Maybe I'm just observant."

His gaze narrowed. "Kelly."

"Perhaps," she allowed.

"What else did she tell you?"

"I'm not dishing on our girl talk to you."

"Then I'll ask Kelly."

"You do that," she said, her tone reflecting certainty that Kelly would keep her confidence.

"We go back a long way," he reminded her.

"You were the first friend she had when she came to Pinehurst in fifth grade and still her best friend," she said, repeating what Jack's fiancée had obviously told her. "And the woman you once proposed to."

He winced. "Apparently she had no problem dishing to you."

"She wanted me to understand what kind of man you are,"

Julie explained. "But I already knew, and I'd already figured out that she was the woman you told me about."

"When she told me that she was pregnant—I knew she was terrified. And I didn't want her to think that she had to go through it on her own."

"And you were in love with her."

He frowned at the matter-of-fact tone of her statement. "Maybe I thought I was," he allowed.

"Of course you were," she continued. "And why wouldn't you be? She's a beautiful woman, you obviously shared a lot of common interests and history."

He was surprised—and a little unnerved—by the accuracy of her insights. No one else had ever known the true depth of his feelings for his best friend. No one had ever guessed that the real reason he'd never fallen in love with any other woman was that he was in love with Kelly.

Then he'd realized that she was in love with his brother— and that truth wasn't just a blow to his ego but a dagger through his heart. Until he'd seen them together and saw the way they looked at one another. Even when they were both still hurt and angry, there was no denying the love between them—and he knew they'd both tried.

And that was when Luke had finally let go. Because he knew that he could feel hurt and betrayed, but he couldn't continue to pretend that he and Kelly had ever been anything more than friends.

"We did share a lot of things," he admitted to Julie. "But never more than a single kiss when we were in seventh grade."

She held up her hands. "None of my business."

"I just want to make it clear that I didn't have any kind of romantic history with my brother's fiancée."

"Aside from the fact that you were in love with her."

"Infatuated," he clarified, because he understood now that unrequited love wasn't really love at all. He'd spent too many years comparing all the other woman he met to the ideal of the one he held in his heart, and now that he'd finally let go of that ideal, a different woman had taken up residence in his heart.

"To-may-to, to-mah-to," she countered.

He frowned, feigning confusion. "I thought you said bacon, pineapple and black olives?"

She rolled her eyes. "Why don't you actually order it so that we get to eat sometime tonight?"

So he did.

The pizza was delivered within twenty minutes, but even when the delivery boy rang the bell, Einstein didn't move from the corner to which he'd been banished. In fact, he even stayed there the whole time that Luke and Julie were eating.

But when the pizza box was empty and pushed aside, the pup slowly inched across the floor on his belly until he was beside her chair. Even when Einstein dropped his chin onto her foot, Julie pretended she didn't see him. Einstein, devastated by this rejection, licked her toes.

"He's trying to apologize," Luke pointed out to her.

"Well, I don't accept his apology," she said.

But in contradiction to the harsh words, one hand reached down to scratch the top of his head, and Einstein's tail thumped against the floor.

She had every right to be furious with the animal still, but her soft heart couldn't hold out against the obviously contrite puppy. It seemed to Luke further proof that she fit into every aspect of his life, and with each day that passed, he couldn't help wondering if she might change her mind about passing through.

He'd dated a lot of women in his thirty-four years, and he wasn't sure how to interpret his growing feelings for Julie. Was it just proximity? Was it the shared experience of Caden's birth that had forged a bond between them? Or was it because his brothers had both fallen in love so recently that he was looking to fill some void in his own life?

He knew that was a distinct possibility, except that he'd never felt as if there was a void in his life. He'd always been happy—he had a job he loved, good friends, close family and pets that lavished him with affection.

Okay, so that might be a bit of an exaggeration where Daphne was concerned, but he knew the cat loved him, too. Or at least appreciated being fed every day, having a warm bed to sleep in and a clean litter box at her disposal.

But with Julie and Caden under his roof, even though they'd been there only a few weeks, he felt as if they belonged. Which wasn't something he should be thinking when she was planning to go back to Springfield soon.

He didn't know exactly when, but he was hoping he could convince her to stay at least until her parents came back from Australia.

"Ava called me at the clinic today," he told her.

She was immediately concerned. "Is something wrong with Puss or Boots?"

"No. She just wanted to know if I'm bringing a date to the wedding. Apparently she's trying to finalize the seating plan for Jack and Kelly's wedding and the numbers would work better if I had 'plus one.'"

"I'm sure Missy Walsh would clear her schedule for you," Julie teased.

"I was actually hoping you might be available."

"You want me to go with you to your brother's wedding?"

"Sure."

She looked wary. "That's a pretty monumental occasion."

"The second wedding in five months for the Garrett brothers," he confirmed.

"That's why you want me there," she realized. "As a barrier against all of the single women in Pinehurst who will be looking at you and dreaming of orange blossoms."

"I've never understood the connection between weddings and orange blossoms."

"They've played a part in wedding traditions tracing back to the ancient Greeks and Romans."

"So they're just a myth?"

She rolled her eyes. "They're a symbol."

"Of what?"

"Of innocence, fertility and everlasting love."

"That's a weighty responsibility for one flower."

"And they smell nice," she told him.

"They don't have any mystical powers, do they? Because apparently I have to wear one in the lapel of my tux."

"No mystical powers," she assured him. "You don't need to be afraid that you'll fall in love with the third woman who crosses your path after the sun sets."

"I'm not afraid of falling in love," he denied.

"Says the only Garrett brother who's never sweated in a tux waiting for his bride to walk down the aisle."

"I never used to think that I wanted what my brothers have."

"Why not?" she challenged.

"Maybe I just never found the right woman," he said, his tone deliberately casual. "Until you."

Chapter Twelve

Julie's eyes went wide, wary. "You don't even know me."

"I know that my life is better—richer and fuller—since you and Caden have been part of it," Luke told her. "I know that I look forward to coming home at the end of each day because you're here. And I'm hoping that you'll stay in Pinehurst at least until the wedding."

She sighed. "Does anyone ever say 'no' to you?"

"Do you want to say 'no'?"

"No," she admitted. "And that's the problem."

"You're going to have to explain how that's a problem."

"Because you're a good man, Lukas Garrett, and I've never fallen for a good man before."

Although she hadn't come right out and said that she'd fallen for him, he was happy enough to accept the implication.

"In fact, I've always had notoriously bad taste in men," she continued. "I thought that had changed when I met Elliott, but even then, it turned out that he wasn't a good man—I only thought he was."

"And you're afraid that you might be wrong about me?" he guessed.

"I'm afraid that I'm totally wrong *for* you."

"You're not," he insisted.

"I'm a twenty-three-year-old single mother who ran away from home without even telling her parents that she was pregnant."

"You had a lot of reasons for running, but now you've stopped."

"Have I? Or is the fact that I'm still here and not in Springfield proof that I'm still running?"

It was a question that Julie spent a lot of time thinking about over the next few days, and still the answer continued to elude her.

As she kept reminding Lukas, her home was in Springfield. So why wasn't she in any hurry to go home? Part of the reason for her reluctance was that if she went back to Massachusetts now, she'd be alone in the house she'd grown up in. Another part of the reason was apprehension. When she returned to Springfield, it was inevitable that she would cross paths with Elliott, and she wasn't yet ready for that to happen. She wasn't afraid of him—at least not physically. But she was afraid of what it would mean for Caden when Elliott learned that he had a child.

But the primary reason that she was still in Pinehurst was that it was where she wanted to be. Not just because it was a picturesque town in Upstate New York, but because it was where Lukas was.

Julie felt more comfortable in Lukas's home than she'd ever felt in Elliott's condo. Her former fiancé hadn't liked her to cook. He'd preferred that they go out to eat, to be seen at the best restaurants, to be seen with people who could advance his career ambitions.

She couldn't remember ever tucking her feet up beneath her on his couch and falling asleep while they watched TV. Because they didn't watch TV—they went to the theatre and museums and political fundraisers and charity events.

She hadn't realized how tiring it was to always be "on" until she finally had the opportunity to turn "off" and just relax. She could relax with Lukas—so long as she didn't think about the physical attraction that had her on edge.

His nearness made her weak, the slightest touch made her quiver, and even from across the room he could make her all hot and tingly with just a look. And the way he looked at her, she knew he felt the same way.

But he hadn't kissed her since that day she'd been kidnapped by Georgia and Kelly, and that was probably for the best. She was already more involved than was smart, and when she finally left Pinehurst, she knew that she'd be leaving a big part of her heart behind.

It was Sunday night, just four days before Thanksgiving, and Luke and Julie still hadn't reached a consensus with respect to their plans for the holiday.

"Kelly called today to tell me that she borrowed a highchair for Thanksgiving—one that has a reclining seat specifically designed for infants so that Caden can be at the table with everyone else."

"That was very thoughtful of her, but we're not going to be there for Thanksgiving."

"You and Caden were invited," he reminded her.

"Thanksgiving is a family holiday, and we're not family."

"Thanksgiving is a time to celebrate with those we care about," he countered. "Family *and* friends."

Apparently she didn't disagree with that, because she said nothing.

"And it's Caden's first Thanksgiving—so it should be special."

She lifted a brow. "Are you really using my child as a negotiating tool?"

He grinned. "Whatever works."

"Not that," she assured him.

"Okay, what if I said that my brothers and I haven't had a real Thanksgiving in a lot of years and I'd really like you and Caden to be there?"

"What do you mean, you haven't had a real Thanksgiving?"

"For the past few years, Matt, Jack and I have ordered pizza and chowed down on it while watching football on TV. This year, Georgia and Kelly have promised a traditional turkey dinner with all the trimmings," he explained. "And I'd really hate to miss out on that."

"There's no reason why you should," she assured him.

"I can't go if you don't go."

"Of course you can."

"And leave the two of you here?" He shook his head. "My mother raised me better than that."

The look she gave him confirmed that he'd finally played the trump card. But when she spoke, she said, "You often mention your parents in casual conversation, but you've never told me what happened to them."

"It's not a favorite topic of conversation," he admitted. "They were on a yacht that ran into a bad storm near Cape Horn. The boat capsized and everyone on board drowned."

"You lost them both at the same time?"

He nodded.

"I'm sorry," she said sincerely. "I can't even imagine how devastating that must have been."

"It was a shock for all of us," he agreed. "But I think it was the best way. Neither of them would have been happy without the other."

"They must have really loved one another."

"They did. They didn't always agree about everything, but there was never any doubt of their affection."

"Do you have any other family?"

"A couple of aunts and uncles and cousins on my father's side, but they're all in North Carolina, so we don't see them much."

"How long have your parents been gone?"

"Six years," he told her. "For the first three, I didn't make any changes around the house. I couldn't even rearrange the furniture. It was Jack who finally asked me one day if I was going to live in Mom and Dad's house forever.

"The house had been left to all three of us, but both Matt and Jack had already moved out, so I secured a mortgage on the property to buy them out. When I reminded my brother that it was my house now, Jack said he just wanted to be sure that *I* knew it, because every time he walked in the front door, he felt as if he was walking into their house still—right down to the ancient welcome mat inside the front door."

"Because part of you was still hoping they would come home," she guessed.

"That might have been a factor. And maybe I needed some time to accept that they wouldn't. But about six months after that conversation with Jack, I started a major renovation. It wasn't enough to tear down wallpaper and buy new towels for the bath—I knocked out walls, added another bathroom upstairs, updated the kitchen cabinets, refinished the hardwood."

"Converted the wood-burning fireplace to gas," she remembered.

He nodded. "Jack convinced me that the instant ambiance would help me get laid. And I can't believe I just said that out loud."

But she laughed. "I can't imagine you needed any help with that."

"That sounds like a compliment."

"A statement of fact," she noted. "You're an extremely handsome man—smart, sexy, charming. You've got a good heart, and a generous nature."

"And a soon-to-be sister-in-law who will give me no end of grief if I show up for Thanksgiving dinner without you and Caden."

Julie sighed. "You're also relentless."

"Does that mean you'll come for dinner?"

"If I do go, I can't go empty-handed," she protested. "I want to make a contribution to the meal."

"Kelly assured me that she and Georgia have everything covered."

"Even dessert?"

"Even dessert," he confirmed. "But if you want, we could take a couple bottles of wine."

"And flowers."

He wrinkled his nose. "For the main meal or dessert?"

She swatted his arm. "For the hostess."

"Okay," he relented. "We'll take wine and flowers."

He was right. Georgia and Kelly had everything covered. Roast turkey with pecan cornbread stuffing, buttermilk mashed potatoes, gravy, maple-glazed sweet potatoes, buttered corn, baby carrots, green beans with wild mushrooms, cauliflower gratin, tangy coleslaw and dinner rolls. Of course, everything looked so good that Julie couldn't let anything pass by without putting at least a small spoonful on her plate.

And everything was absolutely delicious. But even more than the meal, Julie found she genuinely enjoyed the interactions that took place around the table. There were often several conversations happening at the same time, bowls of food being passed in both directions and across the table, glasses clinking and cutlery clanging. It was, in her opinion, the most chaotic—and the most enjoyable—Thanksgiving dinner ever.

She was seated between Lukas and Caden and across from Quinn. The baby had sat contentedly in the borrowed highchair throughout most of the meal, but when Julie pushed her plate aside, she noticed that he was starting to fidget and rub his eyes. It was a sure sign that he was ready for a nap, and because he always fell asleep easier when he was being cuddled, she lifted him out of his chair.

Kelly and Georgia got up to start clearing away the leftovers and dishes to make room for dessert, so she passed the baby to Lukas in order to help.

She picked up the bowl that was mostly empty of buttermilk mashed potatoes and another with a few cauliflower florets and traces of cheese sauce, and headed toward the kitchen. But she couldn't resist turning back for one lingering look at the gorgeous man holding her baby. It wasn't just that he looked so comfortable with her son but that he looked so *right* with Caden in his arms.

Was it luck or fate that her car had slid into the ditch in front of his home? She didn't know, but she was grateful for whatever had brought him into her life. And she knew that her son was going to miss Lukas when she finally took him home to Springfield—maybe almost as much as she would.

Julie had just returned to the dining room when she heard Quinn say, "I was thinkin'."

The words made her smile, because the precocious twin had started a lot of conversations with the same preamble throughout the meal. Some of her favorite topics were the proposed marriage of his puppies, Finnigan and Frederick, with Ava's kittens, Puss and Boots, so that they could have "pup-tens"; having separate spaces for the boys and girls during carpet time at school so Shelby Baker couldn't sit beside him; and his confusion about why, if the glue at school was non-tot-sick (which Miss Lennon explained to him meant it wouldn't make kids sick) she worried about Cain eating it.

"What were you thinking?" Matt asked gamely.

As Julie gathered up a handful of cutlery, she waited to hear the child's response.

"There's lotsa mommies and daddies here."

"Sure," Matt agreed, a little cautiously.

"Me an' Shane an' Pippa have a mommy and daddy. And Uncle Jack and Auntie Kelly are Ava's mommy and daddy. But Caden only gots a mommy."

"Uncle Luke could be his daddy."

There was immediate and stunned silence, although Julie wasn't sure if it was the statement or the fact that Shane had spoken it that was the bigger surprise.

"Yeah," Quinn agreed, immediately onboard with that plan. "'Cuz he doesn't gots any kids."

"That's...an interesting idea," Lukas said. "But it isn't that simple."

"I know." Quinn nodded solemnly. "You'd hafta get married—like when Dr. Matt married Mommy so he could be our daddy."

"Yeah, it was all about you, kid," Jackson said dryly.

But Quinn's gaze was still focused on Lukas. "So—are you gonna do it?"

"I think we should focus on getting Uncle Jack to the altar before we start planning any more weddings," he replied cautiously.

"What's a altar?"

"It's where the wedding takes place," he explained.

"Uh-uh." Quinn shook his head. "Mommy and Daddy got married at the church."

As Lukas proceeded to explain that the altar was located inside the church, Julie felt a tug on her sleeve and saw Shane looking up at her. She was eager to make her escape to the kitchen, but she couldn't ignore the little boy's overture.

"Did you want something, sweetie?"

He shook his head. "We gots Legos."

She breathed a slow sigh of relief, confident this was a subject could handle. "I know. I saw you and Quinn playing with them earlier."

"When Caden gets big enuff, he can play Lego with us."

The offer, so unexpected and earnest, caused her throat to tighten. Or maybe it was regret that she knew they would be long gone from Pinehurst before her son was old enough to play anything with these adorable little boys.

"I know he would really like that," she said, because it was the truth.

"I like the blue blocks best," he told her.

"I like the yellow ones."

He offered her one of his shy smiles, and she made her escape with the handful of cutlery she held clutched tight in her fist and tears shimmering in her eyes.

Julie was quiet on the drive back to his house after dinner, and Luke didn't try to make conversation, either. He was thinking about the discussion Quinn and Shane had initiated, and wondering how it was that a couple of kids could so easily see what adults tried so hard to deny.

When they got home, Julie took Caden upstairs to feed and bathe him while Luke took care of feeding his pets.

Uncle Luke could be his daddy.

The words echoed in his head as he measured out food and filled bowls with water. They were words that, even a few weeks before, would have sent him into a panic. Because at that time, he hadn't been thinking about kids or a family.

But everything had changed when Julie and Caden came into his life. And now, instead of causing his chest to tighten with fear, those words filled his heart with hope.

He *could* be Caden's daddy. He *wanted* to be Caden's daddy. And he wanted Caden's mommy with a desperation that made him ache.

But over the past couple of weeks, he'd been careful to keep things light between them. He tried to remind himself that Julie was a guest in his home and he didn't want to make any overtures that might make her feel pressured or uncomfortable.

After the animals were fed, he went to the office to check his email. Then he played a few games of solitaire on the computer as he waited for Julie to come downstairs. Then he played a few more games and wondered if she'd fallen asleep with Caden or was avoiding him.

It was Einstein who alerted him to her arrival. The pup's keen sense of hearing always picked up the soft creak of the sixth step, and he raced out from under the desk to the bottom of the stairs.

"I thought maybe you'd fallen asleep," Luke said to her when she came into the family room.

She shook her head. "Unfortunately, Caden didn't want to, either. I think he was a little overstimulated today."

"Is this where I apologize for dragging you to the chaos that was Thanksgiving with the Garretts?"

"No. This is where I thank you for dragging us into the chaos." Then she touched her lips to his cheek. "Thank you."

"You really had a good time?"

"I really had a good time," she assured him. "Your family is wonderful."

He took her hand and led her over to the sofa, drawing her down beside him. "Even Quinn?"

"All of them," she confirmed with a smile.

"I wasn't sure if that was more awkward for you or for me," he admitted.

"I'd say for you—because I had an excuse to escape from the table."

And he suspected that she was thinking of making an escape now.

A suspicion that was confirmed when she said, "But his comment did make me wonder if we're giving people the wrong impression about us."

"What do you think is the wrong impression?"

"I think that the longer I stay the more awkward it's going to be when I go," she said, deliberately sidestepping his question.

"So what's your plan? Are you going to pack up now?"

"Do you want me to?"

He shook his head. "No. I don't want you to go," he said, and barely managed to hold back the word *ever*.

He let his fingertip follow the soft, full curve of her lower lip, felt it tremble in response to the slow caress, before he forced his hand to drop away.

The tip of her tongue swept along the same path as his finger, making her lip glisten temptingly. "Then we'll stay until December seventh, if you're sure it's okay."

December seventh was when her parents were due back from their cruise, and the date was now just a little more than two weeks away. It didn't seem like nearly enough time—but he would take whatever she was willing to give him.

"I'm sure. Besides, you promised to be my 'plus one' for the wedding," he reminded her.

"I know I did, but—"

"Ava's finished the seating plan," he said. "If you try to back out now, you'll have to face her wrath."

"I'm not backing out," she denied, though they both knew she'd been thinking about doing precisely that.

He tipped her chin up, forcing her to meet his gaze. "But you're still worried about 'people' getting the wrong impression."

She nodded.

"Then let's clarify the situation," he suggested, and covered her mouth with his.

It had been so long since he'd kissed her that Julie had forgotten how good he was at it. Of course, there didn't seem to be anything that Lukas Garrett wasn't good at, but kissing was definitely near the top of his list of talents.

He used just the right amount of pressure, so that his kiss was firm but not forceful. And he took his time. The man certainly knew how to draw out the pleasure until it seemed as if time was both endless and meaningless. His lips were masterful, his flavor potent, his kiss a leisurely and thorough seduction of all of her senses.

She was lost, drowning in sensation. He could have taken her anywhere, done anything, but he only continued to kiss her. In her admittedly limited experience, men raced around first base with their gaze already focused on second. Lukas didn't seem to be in a hurry to go anywhere.

And she didn't want to be anywhere but right where she was—in the moment with Lukas.

She lifted her arms to link them behind his neck, pressing closer to him. The soft curves of her body seemed to fit perfectly against the hard angles of his. He was so strong and solid, but when he was holding her, she didn't feel vulnerable, she felt…cherished.

His hands slid down her back, over her buttocks. He drew her closer, close enough that there was no doubt he was as thoroughly aroused as she was. Heat pulsed through her veins, pooled between her thighs. She wanted this man— she couldn't deny that any longer. But she couldn't afford to be reckless. She had a child to think about now—a four-week-old baby who had been fathered by another man. She had to be smart, rational, responsible. Unfortunately, that reprimand from her conscience did nothing to curb her desire.

Or was she just lonely? She'd been away from her family and her friends for so long, she wasn't sure how much of what she was feeling for Lukas was real and how much was simply a need for human contact. Except that being close to him now had her feeling all kinds of other things—none of which was lonely.

When he finally eased his mouth from hers, she touched her fingertips to lips still tingling from his kiss. "You're awfully good at that."

His lips curved in a slow, and undeniably smug, smile. "My father always told us that anything worth doing is worth doing right."

"Why do I think he probably wasn't expecting you would apply that advice to seducing women?"

"Do you think I could? Seduce you, I mean."

After that kiss, she didn't have the slightest doubt. "Just because you can doesn't mean you should."

"I realize that I'm probably a few steps ahead of you, that you probably haven't even thought about—"

"I've thought about it," she interrupted softly.

His gaze narrowed. "About what?"

"Making love with you."

He started to reach for her, then curled his fingers into his palms and thrust his hands into his pockets.

"You have?"

She nodded.

"So why are we talking instead of doing?"

"Because you scare me," she admitted.

He took an instinctive step back, his brow furrowed.

She immediately shook her head. "I'm not afraid that you'd

hurt me—not physically," she assured him. "But the way you make me feel—the intensity of it—absolutely terrifies me.

"When I'm with you, everything just seems right. But I don't understand how that's even possible. I've only known you a few weeks and there is nothing usual about the circumstances that brought us together. How can I trust that any of what I'm feeling is real?"

Luke didn't know how to respond, what to say to reassure her—or even if he should. She was right to be wary. He was wary, too. Neither of them could have anticipated what was happening between them. Neither could know where this path might lead. But he wanted to find out.

She'd been clear from the very beginning that she didn't plan on staying in Pinehurst beyond the short-term. Her family and her life were in Springfield. And even though he knew he could be setting himself up for heartbreak, he couldn't stop wanting to be with her, wanting to share every minute that she was in Pinehurst with her.

"I can't make you any promises or guarantees," he told her. "But I can tell you that the feelings you just described—I'm feeling them, too."

"You know I don't have a very good track record with men," she reminded him.

"It takes two people to make a relationship work."

"And I'm only going to be here another couple of weeks, so I can't let myself fall in love with you."

He wanted to smile at that. Though he was hardly an expert on the subject, he knew that falling in love wasn't a choice. He certainly hadn't chosen to fall in love with Julie, but he knew that he was more than halfway there.

Of course, admitting as much would only scare her more. So instead he said, "I'm not asking you to fall in love with me—just to let me make love with you."

She nibbled on her lower lip, something he'd realized that

she did when she was thinking. Unfortunately, the subconscious action deprived him of the ability to think. Instead, he wanted to cover her mouth with his own, to sink into the lush fullness of those lips again.

Then she drew in a deep breath and looked up at him, meeting his gaze evenly. "I guess those are terms I can live with."

His brows lifted. "You guess?"

She smiled. "Do you want to stand here and argue about my choice of words or do you want to take me upstairs?"

Before the words were completely out of her mouth, he swept her off her feet and into his arms.

Chapter Thirteen

Julie took a moment to glory in the thrill of being carried by a strong man. It was another new experience for her and a memory that she knew she would carry with her forever. As he made his way up the stairs, her heart pounded inside her chest and anticipation hummed in her veins. There wasn't any hesitation in her mind, no reservations in her heart.

But when he set her on her feet beside the bed, she felt the first subtle stirring of apprehension. When she realized that he'd already unfastened the buttons that ran down the front of her blouse—that he was undressing her—nerves jittered.

She hadn't thought about the "getting naked" part. It was a usual prerequisite to adult lovemaking, but it wasn't something that her lust-clouded mind had grasped when she'd suggested they come upstairs.

Then he pushed the blouse off of her shoulders and reached for the zipper at the back of her skirt. Except that there wasn't a zipper because it was a maternity skirt, complete with the stretchy panel in front because she wasn't yet able to squeeze into any of her pre-pregnancy clothes. But he quickly figured things out, and pushed the skirt over her hips until it pooled at her feet.

"My body isn't as toned or tight as it was a year ago," she said apologetically.

His hands skimmed from her shoulders to her knees, leisurely caressing her curves along the way. "You feel perfect to me."

She shook her head. "I'm not—"

"Shut up, Julie." The words were muttered against her mouth as he covered it with his own.

She wanted to make some sort of indignant reply, but she couldn't say anything while her lips were otherwise occupied kissing him back. And truthfully, kissing him was a much more pleasurable pastime than arguing with him. And when he kissed her and touched her, she couldn't think clearly enough to worry about the extra pounds. In fact, she couldn't think at all.

And when he pulled her closer, the turgid peaks of her nipples brushed against the hard wall of his chest, making her ache and yearn so that everything else was forgotten. His hands skimmed up her back, and down again. Lust surged through her veins, making her blood pound and her knees weak.

She slid her hands beneath the hem of his sweater, then upward, tracing over the ridges of his abdomen. His skin was warm and smooth, and his muscles quivered. The instinctive response emboldened her, and she let her hands explore further.

"Do you know what you're doing?" he asked, his voice strained.

"It's been a while," she admitted, with a small smile. "But I think I'm on the right track."

"You stay on that track and the train is going to start forging full-steam ahead."

She nibbled on his lower lip. "Is that a promise?"

"Yeah, it's a promise," he said. Then he captured her mouth, kissing her deeply, hungrily.

She pulled away from him to tug his sweater over his head, then reached for his belt. The rest of their clothes were dispensed with quickly, then he eased her back onto the bed. The press of his body against hers, the friction of bare skin against bare skin, was almost more than she could handle.

And then he cupped her breasts, his thumbs rubbing over the aching peaks, and she actually whimpered. When he replaced his hands with his mouth and laved her nipples with his tongue, she felt as if she might explode.

She arched beneath him, pressing closer so that his erection was nestled between her thighs.

"Somebody seems to be in a hurry," he mused.

"It's been a long time for me," she told him.

"Then let's not make you wait any longer."

"Condom?"

"Yeah, I'll take care of it," he assured her. "But first—I'm going to take care of you."

He kissed her then, deeply, hungrily and very thoroughly. Then his mouth moved across her jaw, down her throat. He nibbled her collarbone, licked the hollow between her breasts then kissed his way down to her navel, and lower. He nudged her thighs apart, and her breath backed up in her lungs.

Before she could decide if she wanted to say "Yes, please," or "No, thank you," his mouth was on her, stroking and sucking and licking, pushing her toward the highest pinnacle of pleasure. She fisted her hands in the sheets and bit down hard on her bottom lip as everything inside of her tightened, strained, and finally...shattered.

* * *

She was absolutely and stunningly beautiful.

Luke had meant it when he told her that he'd thought so from the very first, but never had Julie looked more beautiful than she did right now, with her cheeks flushed, her lips swollen from his kisses and those dreamy blue-gray eyes clouded with the aftereffects of passion.

But he wasn't nearly done with her yet.

He wanted to make love with her, slowly, patiently endlessly. And it would be making love. This wasn't sex—not on his part, anyway. Because he was in love with her. Not halfway in love or starting to fall, but one hundred percent head over heels. And for him, that changed everything.

Unfortunately, he knew it wasn't the same for her. She'd told him clearly and unequivocally that she wasn't going to fall in love with him. She was still intending to go back to Springfield on the seventh of December, with the expectation that he, of course, would stay in Pinehurst. Because this was where he lived, where his family, his career and his life were. But if she left—*when* she left—he knew that his heart would go with her.

And that was why this moment mattered so much. He wanted to touch her as no one had ever touched her before, so that when she was gone, she would always remember him. Their time together was already nearing its end, but he was determined to ensure that she enjoyed every minute of the two weeks that they had left together. Starting right now.

He worked his way back up her body, kissing and caressing every inch of her smooth, silky skin. He nipped her earlobe, nuzzled her throat, and his name slipped from her lips on a sigh. "Lukas."

He wanted to spend hours touching her, learning her pleasure points by listening to her soft gasps and throaty moans.

She had a lot of pleasure points, and discovering each and every one of them gave him an immense amount of pleasure.

But he was already rock-hard and aching for her. He sheathed himself with a condom and fought against the urge to lift up her hips and plunge into the sweet, wet heat at the apex of her thighs. Even if she hadn't warned him that it had been a long time for her, he knew it was her first time since giving birth, so he forced himself to go slow. He wasn't usually patient or restrained, but he focused his attention on both, easing into her a fraction of an inch at a time, giving her a chance to adjust and accept him.

Apparently he was taking too much time, because she suddenly planted her heels in the mattress and thrust her hips upward, taking him—all of him—fast and deep inside her. And that quickly, the last of his restraint snapped. She was so wet and tight around him, he feared for a minute that he would erupt like a teenager in the backseat at a drive-in.

But he drew in a deep breath and fisted his hands in the sheets, and when he had at least a semblance of control again, he began to move inside her. And she met him, stroke for stroke, in a synchronized rhythm that mated them together so perfectly he couldn't tell where he ended and she began.

Together they soared high and ever higher, until he captured her mouth and swallowed the cries that signaled her release even as his own rocketed through him.

Luke awoke alone in his bed. He'd heard Caden fussing in the night and then Julie had slipped out of his arms to attend to her child. He wasn't really surprised that she hadn't come back to his bed, but he was disappointed.

He grabbed a quick shower, shaved and headed down to the kitchen to make breakfast. To his surprise, Julie was already there, taking a pan of cinnamon buns out of the oven.

He crossed the room and nuzzled the back of her neck. "I'm not sure what smells better—you or breakfast."

"It's breakfast," she said, turning to face him. "And you have—"

"To kiss you," he said, and covered her mouth with his own.

Julie held herself immobile for the first three seconds, then her lips softened, and she responded to his kiss.

"Just because it's the morning after doesn't mean it has to be awkward," he said.

Her cheeks filled with color. "It's not the timing," she said quietly. "It's the fact that your brother's fiancée is sitting at the table."

He hadn't noticed Kelly when he walked in. He hadn't noticed anything but Julie. It didn't matter that they'd made love through the night—he only had to look at her to want her all over again.

"I brought over some leftovers from Thanksgiving dinner," Kelly said. "There's no way Jack and Ava and I will eat everything, and I'd hate to throw it out."

"Thanks," he said. "I'll think of you when I'm enjoying turkey sandwiches later. Now get out."

"Lukas!" Julie was shocked by his blunt—and undeniably rude—comment.

But his childhood friend simply pushed her chair away from the table and carried her empty coffee mug to the counter. "I'm going," she said. "I promised to take Ava shopping today, anyway."

But she looked worried as her gaze moved from Lukas to Julie and back again. Because he didn't want her expressing her concerns to Julie, who already had enough of her own, he kissed her cheek and steered her toward the door.

After he'd closed it behind Kelly, he turned to see Julie

spreading icing over the top of the warm pastry. "I kind of thought we would keep…this…between us," she said.

He went to the cupboard for a mug, poured himself a cup of the coffee she'd made. "I wasn't planning on any billboard advertising, but I don't keep secrets from my family."

She put two of the warm buns on a plate for him, took one for herself. She sat down beside Caden's carrier, tapped a fingertip to his nose, earning a wide, gummy smile.

"You're not worried that they'll disapprove?"

"No," he said simply. "I'm thirty-four years old—long past the age where I look to my big brothers for approval."

She poked at her cinnamon bun with a fork, peeling off layers of pastry. Luke had polished off one of the pastries and was halfway through the second before he realized that she hadn't taken a single bite.

"What else is on your mind?" he finally asked her.

She picked up her glass of juice, sipped. "Last night," she admitted. "It wasn't quite what I expected."

"Disappointed?" He didn't mind teasing her with the question because he knew very well that she had not been. "Because I promise you, I can do better."

"I wasn't disappointed," she said, and the color that flooded her cheeks confirmed it. "More like…overwhelmed."

"Why do you say that as if it's a bad thing?"

"Because I had no intention of getting involved with you. Because I thought—I'd hoped—the attraction was purely a hormonal thing."

"An itch that would go away once it was scratched?"

"I wouldn't have put it in such crude terms but, okay, yes."

"And now?"

She shook her head. "It's not just the way you made me feel last night. It's how you make me feel all the time. I've been happy here with you. Happier than I could have imagined."

He actually felt his heart swell inside his chest. "I'm glad," he said. "Because you make me happy, too. I care about you, Julie. You and Caden both."

Her eyes filled with tears. "I told you—I'm not going to let myself fall in love with you."

"I'm just asking you to give us a chance."

"A chance for what?"

He shrugged. "For whatever might happen."

"You make it sound so simple."

"I don't see any reason to complicate the situation unnecessarily."

"So you think we can keep this simple?" she asked hopefully.

"As simple as you want." He lied without compunction because he knew that the truth would send her back to Springfield before the words *I love you* were out of his mouth.

He couldn't have pinpointed when it happened. The revelation hadn't come to him like a bolt of lightning out of the sky, but he didn't doubt for a moment that it was true. What had started out as attraction had developed into affection that, over the past few weeks, had deepened and intensified. He loved her.

But he knew that even hinting at that would induce a panic. Instead, he gestured to her plate with his fork and said, "Are you going to eat that or dissect it?"

After breakfast, Lukas tidied up the kitchen while Julie nursed Caden and tried to convince herself that her relationship with the sexy veterinarian wasn't getting more complicated by the day.

When she'd put the baby down in the cradle, she checked her email and found a message from her parents. They'd been in regular contact over the past few weeks and their messages were always rich with details about excursions they'd taken, places they'd seen and people they'd met. In every word she read, Julie could tell that they were having a fabulous time, and she was happy for them. Because as much as she missed her family, she realized that she was happy, too. Being here with Lukas made her happy. Happier than she could ever remember being. So why did that scare her?

After things had gone so wrong with Elliott, she hadn't been able to imagine being with another man. How could she trust anyone when her judgment had been so wrong? Maybe she was confusing sex with love. Maybe her mind was still clouded from the incredible orgasms Lukas had given her the night before.

She wanted to believe that was the answer—that what she was feeling for him was lust and gratitude and nothing more. But she knew that what she was feeling was about so much more than the phenomenal lovemaking they'd shared. In fact, if she was being honest with herself, she would admit that she'd probably fallen in love with Lukas before he'd ever kissed her.

Yeah, she could tell him she wouldn't fall in love with him, but those words didn't actually give her power over her heart. And the fact was, she loved who he was and everything about him.

The past few weeks with him had been absolutely fabulous, but as much as she enjoyed being with him, she didn't belong here. She lived and worked in Springfield. And Evangeline was expecting her back at The Grayson Gallery at the beginning of February.

She didn't need to work, and she certainly wasn't working for the money. Being a part-time curator was never going to make her rich. True, there was a certain amount of prestige associated with her position, but that had never mattered to Julie. She'd taken the job because she'd needed the sense of purpose that it gave her, the independent identity. Something that separated her from Elliott, goals and ambitions that were entirely her own.

Except that, sometime during the past few months, those goals and ambitions had changed. Or maybe it was having Caden that changed everything. Now her career didn't matter to her nearly as much as being a good mother to her son. And she didn't want to go back to Springfield nearly as much as she wanted to stay with Lukas.

She'd never imagined herself living in a town like Pinehurst—but only because she'd never known that towns like it existed. She'd never thought of settling anywhere outside of Springfield because everything she needed and everyone she loved was there. Four years at college aside, she'd never lived anywhere else. She'd taken plenty of trips— educational jaunts to various destinations in Europe and Asia, vacations to sandy beaches in the Caribbean and exotic ports of call on the Mediterranean.

Her trip across the United States probably represented the most significant journey in her twenty-three years. Not just because she'd seen so much of the country and met so many interesting people, but because she'd learned so much about herself. And her favorite part of the journey was this unscheduled and extended layover in Pinehurst.

She felt as if she belonged here, in this town, with Lukas. She loved his house—the history and character of it; she adored Einstein—despite the prime rib incident; she was even starting to develop warm feelings toward Daphne— although she wasn't entirely sure the cat reciprocated. And she loved Lukas.

Her mind was still spinning with that realization when she walked into the bedroom and found him on her bed. He was lounging against a pile of pillows, reading a book. Or maybe just pretending to read while he waited for her, because as soon as she stepped through the doorway, he closed the cover and set the novel aside.

He rose to his feet and reached for her, drawing her into his arms and covering her lips in a slow, mind-numbing kiss.

"Are you okay? After last night, I mean."

Of course he would ask. And of course, the fact that he did made her heart go all soft and gooey. "Yes, I'm okay. Better than okay," she admitted.

"Good." He smiled and drew her closer.

"Lukas—" She tried to wriggle out of his embrace. "It's the middle of the day."

"And?"

"And I have to get dressed."

"Why would you bother putting clothes on when I'm just going to take them off of you again?" he asked logically.

Because she wasn't quite sure how to respond to that, she folded her arms over her chest. "Just because I let you seduce me last night, doesn't mean I'm going to get naked with you—"

With one quick tug, he had the belt of her robe unfastened. She sucked in a breath as the cool air caressed her bare skin, then released it on a sigh when he cupped her breasts in his palms.

"You were saying?" he prompted.

She didn't see any point in fighting with him when the truth was, she wanted the same thing he did. She reached for the hem of his sweatshirt. "I was saying that you have far too many clothes on."

"I can remedy that."

The night before Jack and Kelly's wedding, Matt and Luke decided to take their brother out for an impromptu bachelor party. In other words, wings and beer at DeMarco's.

"Tomorrow night's the big night," Matt said, pouring draught from the pitcher into three frosty mugs.

Jack's smile was wide as he accepted the first glass. "The biggest."

"Well, I guess I don't have to ask if you're having second thoughts."

"Not a one," his brother agreed.

"I'm glad," Lukas said. "Because I'm not sure whose side I'd be on if something went wrong."

"Nothing's going to go wrong," the groom-to-be said confidently. "In fact, for the first time in my life, I feel as if everything is exactly the way it should be."

"You're a lucky guy—she's an incredible woman."

"I know it."

"And though I wouldn't usually admit this, I think she's pretty lucky, too."

"Undoubtedly." Jack grinned again.

"It's a second trip down the aisle for Jack, and I've done it twice myself," Matt noted, turning to Luke. "When are you going to take your first?"

"When I find the woman who makes me believe that the first will also be the last," Lukas told them.

"You don't think you've already found her?" Jack prompted.

"Maybe I have."

"So why are you hesitating?"

"It's…complicated."

"It's always complicated," Jack noted.

"You mean because she has a child with another man?" Matt guessed.

"I don't want to go through what you went through," Lukas told him.

"It's not even close to being the same situation," his brother pointed out. "Lindsay lied to me. For three years, she let me believe that I was Liam's father. I don't think you're under any similar illusions about Caden."

He wasn't, of course. And the paternity of Julie's son wasn't an issue for him—except when he thought about what his brother had gone through. "And when Liam's father came back into the picture, you lost your wife and your child."

"Is that what you're afraid of?" Matt prompted. "That Julie will go back to Caden's father?"

"No. She's been clear about the fact that he's not part of her life anymore."

"But he could be part of Caden's," Jack reminded him.

Luke nodded.

"So what?" Matt challenged.

"So what?" he echoed.

"Maybe Caden's biological father will be part of his life," his brother acknowledged. "So what? I know it isn't an ideal situation, but at least you'd be with the woman you love."

"I never said I loved her," Luke said, just a little defensively.

"If you don't, then why are we even having this conversation?" Jack wanted to know.

"Okay—I do love Julie. And Caden. And the idea of being without either one of them…" He shook his head. "I don't even want to think about it."

Matt clapped a hand on his shoulder. "Then I guess you'd better convince her to stay."

Chapter Fourteen

While the Garrett brothers were drinking beer at DeMarco's, the women were eating chocolate fondue at Kelly's house. It was a girls' night in under the guise of a bachelorette party.

Ava hung out with them for a while, more for the chocolate than the conversation, and when she'd had her fill of both, she retreated to her room to study for a history test. Georgia had earlier sent the twins to the basement to play video games and since that was about as much privacy as they were going to get in a house full of kids, she took advantage of the moment to ask Julie, "So, how long have you been sleeping with Lukas?"

Julie paused with a chunk of chocolate-covered banana over her plate and glanced over at Jack's fiancée.

Kelly held up her hands. "I didn't tell her."

"She didn't tell me," Georgia confirmed, then turned to scowl at her soon-to-be sister-in-law. "You knew and didn't tell me?"

"Well, it's not as if I had a chance," Kelly admitted. "This is the first time I've seen you since Thanksgiving."

"So how did you know?" Julie asked Georgia.

"I'm not sure," the other woman admitted. "It wasn't anything obvious, but you seem…different. More relaxed and contented."

"One of the benefits of mind-blowing sex," Kelly agreed.

Georgia kept her gaze on Julie. "So…is it?"

She felt her cheeks flush, but she couldn't stop her lips from curving in a slow and very satisfied smile.

"That good, huh?"

"I don't know if it's hormones or Lukas," she admitted. "But I've never experienced anything like what I've experienced with him."

"So why are you not dancing on the ceiling?" Kelly asked.

"Because there are too many reasons why a relationship between us would never work."

"From where I'm sitting, I'd say that you already have a relationship," Georgia noted. "And it seems to be working just fine."

"I'm going back to Springfield after the wedding."

Kelly frowned. "Does Lukas know?"

"Of course he knows. We both knew, from the beginning, that this was only a temporary arrangement. My family, my job, my *life* are in Springfield." But the most important factor, from her perspective, was that Lukas hadn't asked her to stay.

"You're going back to work?" Georgia asked.

"I have to." Well, financially she didn't have to—she had a trust fund from her maternal grandmother and significant savings of her own that she didn't need to worry about where she'd find the money for rent, but she'd promised Evangeline that she would come back.

"When?" Kelly asked.

"In a couple of months."

"Who's going to look after Caden while you're working?"

"I haven't had a chance to make those arrangements just yet."

"When I was living in New York City, if you weren't on a waiting list before you were pregnant, you weren't going to get a spot in any reputable daycare before your child's third birthday," Georgia told her.

"Springfield isn't Manhattan."

"I did the single-working-mother thing," Kelly told her. "And I lucked out in finding an absolutely wonderful woman who looked after Ava while I was working. But I promise you, if I'd had any other choice, I would have done things differently, and I'd have spent every possible minute with my child."

"I don't have any other choice," Julie insisted.

The other woman's pithy one-word reply made her blink.

"If you think you don't have any other choice, it's because you don't want to see the opportunity that's right in front of you."

"Kelly," Georgia admonished. "Julie was always clear about her plans to go back to Springfield."

"Then she shouldn't have let Lukas fall in love with her."

"He's not in love with me," Julie denied.

Kelly scowled at her. "Do you really not see it?"

Julie refused to argue with the bride-to-be on the night before her wedding. "How did we get on this topic, anyway? Aren't we supposed to be celebrating one of your last nights as a single woman?"

Kelly stabbed a strawberry with her fondue fork, a little more viciously than necessary. "I just have one more question."

"Okay," Julie said cautiously.

"Do you feel *anything* for him?"

She couldn't lie, not to Kelly and Georgia, and not about this. "I feel *everything* for him."

Georgia's brows drew together. "Then why are you leaving?"

"Because he hasn't asked me to stay."

Kelly blew out a breath. "The man truly is an idiot."

"But even if he did," Julie said, "I wouldn't want to stay so that Lukas could take care of me and my son."

"No one's suggesting that," Georgia told her.

"You should stay here with Lukas because it's where you want to be," Kelly said. "Because he's who you want to be with."

Julie wondered if it could be that simple, because she had no doubt that it was true.

Later that night, when Julie and Lukas were snuggled together after lovemaking, he said, "I've been thinking about what Quinn said on Thanksgiving—about us getting married so that I can be Caden's father."

"He also said that Finn and Fred should marry Puss and Boots so that they could have 'pup-tens.'"

"I think the former idea is a little more valid and definitely worth considering," he insisted.

"I'm not surprised that you'd be thinking about marriage when your brother's getting married tomorrow. But to think about marrying a woman you've only known a few weeks is crazy."

"I am crazy about you, Julie."

Her heart felt as though it was going to leap right out of her chest. But someone needed to be rational, and it obviously wasn't going to be him. "This entire conversation is insane."

"I'm starting to get the hang of this daddy thing," he told her. "And if we got married, it would alleviate a lot of questions and speculation about Caden's paternity."

"Do you really think anyone would believe that story about the two of us having a torrid affair in the spring?"

He shrugged.

"And even if they did, that's hardly a valid reason to get married."

"Okay, how about the fact that I want to spend every day—and every night—for the rest of my life with you?"

Her heart leaped again, but she knew she couldn't accept his offer. He'd said that he was crazy about her, that he wanted to spend his life with her and be a father to her son, but he hadn't said anything about loving her.

"I'm flattered, Lukas," she said, because she was. "But when I gave Elliott back his ring, I promised myself that I wouldn't ever get married for the wrong reasons."

"And you don't think you could love me?" he guessed.

Julie didn't know how to answer that question. Because the truth was, it wasn't that she didn't think she could love him but that she already did.

Because Jackson had insisted on a short engagement and the church that Kelly wanted to get married in was booked for every Saturday into the following spring, they decided to have a midweek evening candlelight service. And when the bride and groom held hands and looked into one another's eyes to exchange their vows, it was one of the most beautiful and heartwarming ceremonies Julie had ever witnessed.

Of course, being at Jackson and Kelly's wedding got Julie thinking about her own aborted plans. She'd been so excited when Elliott proposed. As many young girls do, she'd dreamed about her wedding for a long time. She'd stockpiled bridal magazines, clipped out photos of dresses and flowers and cakes. Yet when Elliott put his ring on her finger, she'd never taken her planning to the next level. She hadn't gone dress shopping or visited floral shops or sampled wedding cakes.

And she had absolutely no regrets that the wedding had

never happened. Because even if Elliott had never raised a hand to her, he'd also never looked at her the way Jackson looked at Kelly. Or the way she looked right back at him.

Of course, Julie hadn't looked at Elliott that way, either. She'd loved who she thought he was and the life she'd envisioned for them together, but in the end, she'd had no difficulty walking away from him. There'd been no void in her life when she left him. In fact, she'd felt a sense of relief, a feeling of peace that she'd finally made the right choice. And that choice had, eventually, brought her to where she was today.

Glancing over at Lukas now, she saw that he was looking at her, and the warmth and affection in his gaze made her tingle all over. No one had ever looked at her the way he did; no one had ever made her feel the way he did.

But did he love her?

Despite Kelly's conviction that he did, Lukas had never said those words to Julie. And why would he put his heart on the line when she'd told him that she wasn't going to fall in love with him? Of course, she knew now that those words had been a lie even when she'd spoken them. But was she strong enough—brave enough—to trust in what they had together?

She thought about that question through the meal and the numerous toasts and speeches in honor of the happy couple. The first dance of the bride and groom was usually followed by the traditional father and bride dance. Instead, it was the groom who danced with his daughter. As they waltzed around the dance floor, Julie marveled at the fact that Jackson had only recently learned that he had a daughter—and now he was dancing with her at his wedding to her mother.

Her gaze shifted across the table to Lukas's other brother. Matt, always the doting father, was sitting beside Georgia with Pippa in his lap. Certainly no one would ever guess that he wasn't the biological father of the three kids he loved as if they were his own. Julie didn't have to wonder if Lukas could ever love Caden the same way—because she knew that he already did.

And it wasn't just Lukas—his whole family had accepted Julie and her son, easily and without question. Well, Kelly had had more than a few questions, but Julie understood that her inquiries were motivated by concern and affection. She was trying to protect Lukas, and Julie could appreciate and respect that kind of loyalty.

That was one of the reasons she could imagine herself living here, being part of this family, part of the community. Pinehurst would be a wonderful place to raise her son. In fact, Georgia had said one of the reasons she'd decided to move here with her family was to raise them in a smaller town with old-fashioned values. Looking at Georgia's adorable twins now, Julie remembered Shane's impulsive offer to share his building blocks with Caden, and she knew that she didn't want to take him away from here.

She wanted her son to know Quinn and Shane and Pippa. And although Ava was already mostly grown up, she absolutely adored Caden and Julie knew she wouldn't ever find a babysitter for him that she liked or trusted more. Maybe they wouldn't be related by blood, but spending time with Lukas's family had made her realize that family was about so much more than shared DNA. It was the bonds and connections that developed through mutual respect and affection, but the greatest connection was love.

Julie loved Lukas with her whole heart.

And that, she finally realized, was why she had to go back to Springfield.

When the dance floor was opened up to all of the other guests, Lukas came looking for her. The third song had barely begun when she saw him walking toward her, determination in every step. There was something incredibly sexy about a man with a purpose. Or maybe it was the glint in his eye that made everything inside her quiver.

He offered his hand to her. "Dance with me."

It was more of a demand than an invitation, but Julie didn't care. She just wanted to be in his arms. Ava, back at the table after her turn around the dance floor, willingly took Caden from her.

"Have I told you that you look absolutely spectacular tonight?" Lukas asked, as he drew her into his embrace.

She shook her head.

"Well, you do. When I saw you come down the stairs in that dress...you actually took my breath away."

She'd gone shopping for the occasion, because she knew she didn't have any appropriate wedding attire with her, and because she was always happy for an excuse to go shopping. The emerald-green wrap-style dress was both flattering and functional, with long, narrow sleeves and a full skirt that twirled above her knees.

He dipped his head and lowered his voice. "But as fabulous as you look in that dress, I can't wait to get you out of it."

The words sent a quick thrill through her veins. And as much as she wanted the same thing, she couldn't resist teasing, "You think you're going to get lucky tonight?"

He smiled, but his eyes were serious. "I think the luckiest day of my life was the day I met you."

"I feel the same way," she admitted.

"I realized something today, when Jack and Kelly exchanged their vows. For the first time in my life, I seriously envied my brother. And no—not because he was marrying Kelly, but because he was marrying the woman he loves. And because I know that they're going to be together forever, happily ever after.

"I want the same thing, Julie. I want to spend the rest of my life with you because you mean everything to me. But

I don't just want you—I want Caden, too. I want to be your husband and his father, and maybe, in the future, we could add another kid or two to the mix, but that doesn't matter to me nearly as much as being with you."

Her heart was pounding so hard inside her chest it actually ached. "Is that your idea of a proposal?"

"I've got the ring in my pocket," he told her. "And I'll get down on one knee right here and now if you want me to."

She shook her head. "No."

The last thing she wanted was the focus of all of Jack and Kelly's guests on them—especially when she couldn't give Lukas the answer he wanted.

"I'm hoping for a different response to the spending our lives together part," he prompted.

"I want to give you a different response," she admitted. "But I'm going back to Springfield. Tomorrow."

"What? Why?"

"To see Elliott."

Though the music continued, he stopped moving. "You're still in love with him."

"No." Her response was as vehement as it was immediate, because she didn't want Lukas to believe that for even half a second. "But I have to tell him about Caden. I've been putting it off, for reasons I'm not even sure I understand. But sometime during the past few days, I realized that I won't ever be able to move forward with my life until I know that the past is behind me." She held his gaze, not even trying to hide the depth of emotion she knew would be reflected in her eyes. "I want to move forward with my life—with you."

He took her hand and guided her off the dance floor. But instead of heading back toward their table, he turned in the opposite direction. He found a quiet corner, behind an enormous Christmas tree, and faced her. "So when are we leaving?"

She blinked. "What?"

"Do you really think I'm going to let you meet your former fiancé without backup?"

And that was just one of the reasons she loved him. But as much as she appreciated his protectiveness and willingness to rearrange his schedule to be there for her, she wasn't going to let him go all Neanderthal man on her.

"I'm meeting him for coffee at The Cobalt Room—a restaurant in the Courtland Hotel," she explained. "It's a public place, so there's no need to worry about backup."

"You don't want me to come with you?"

"I do want you to come to Springfield with me, but I need to meet with Elliott on my own. I need to stand up for myself. You don't have to like it," she told him. "But I hope you respect me enough to understand that this is something I have to do."

"I don't like it." He touched his lips to hers. "But I understand."

"Do you think you can clear your schedule so that we can stay in Springfield for the weekend?"

"Absolutely."

She took his hands, linked their fingers together. "Good. My parents will be home on Saturday and I'd really like them to meet the man I'm going to marry."

"Does that mean you accept my proposal?"

"It means that I'm hoping you'll ask me again after I've cleaned up the mess I've made of my life."

Julie was more worried about her meeting with her former fiancé than she'd been willing to admit to Lukas. Although she'd never loved Elliott with the same depth and intensity that she loved Lukas, she'd had genuine feelings for him. She didn't regret walking away. She would not be a victim and she would never forgive Elliott for what he'd done, but she still worried that seeing him again might stir up old feelings that she didn't want stirred.

"Mr. Winchester called to say that he would be a few minutes late, but his table is ready, if you'd like to be seated," the hostess told her.

"Yes, please."

She wished she'd accepted Lukas's offer to come with her. She'd wanted to do this on her own, to prove to herself that she could, but now she was regretting her decision. She wanted him there with her. She wanted the man she loved beside her, and she wanted the comforting weight of her baby in her arms. She felt so much braver and stronger when she was with Lukas, and she knew she was capable of doing anything to protect her son.

She ordered decaf coffee and was stirring cream into her cup when she spotted Elliott crossing the room.

She watched his approach, trying to view him through the eyes of an objective stranger. He moved with purpose and authority. He was a good-looking man, charming and charismatic, and he drew attention wherever he went.

She exhaled a grateful sigh at the realization that she honestly didn't feel anything for him anymore. Not even fear. And with that realization, a sense of peace settled over her, calming any residual nerves. He couldn't hurt her. She wouldn't let him. And she wouldn't let him hurt her son.

But could he hurt her father? That was the question that continued to nag at her.

He reached the table and leaned down to kiss her cheek, and though she stiffened, she didn't pull away. She'd wanted this meeting with Elliott to take place in a public venue for a number of reasons but causing a scene wasn't one of them. So she forced a smile and kept it on her face while he seated himself across from her.

"I'm so pleased you called," Elliott said.

"Are you?"

"Of course. I know the situation between us didn't exactly end on a positive note, but I hoped we could find our way back to being friends."

"Do you have a spin doctor on your political team now? Because 'didn't exactly end on a positive note' is an interesting interpretation of the fact that you slapped me around."

He winced at the bluntness of her assessment. "I'd had too much to drink. I lost my temper."

"That doesn't justify what you did."

"I'm not trying to justify it," he assured her. "I know the alcohol isn't an excuse, but it is part of the reason.

"When you left—when I realized what I'd done to make you leave—" he hastily amended "—I hit rock bottom. I finally accepted that I couldn't fix everything on my own. I went to an AA meeting, then I found a counselor who specializes in anger management, and I turned my life around."

"If that's true, I'm glad."

"It is true. But I couldn't have done any of it without Genevieve."

"Genevieve Durand?" She'd met the woman, whose family had been close friends of the Winchester family for years, on several occasions. But she'd never thought that Genevieve and Elliott were particularly friendly.

"Well, she's Genevieve Winchester now."

She just stared at him, still not comprehending.

Elliott's easy smile faded. "You didn't know?"

"Know what?"

"I got married. Four months ago."

"Oh. Well…congratulations."

"I'm sorry—I honestly thought you knew. The engagement announcement was in both the *Globe* and the *Herald*."

She shook her head. "I've been out of town. I didn't know."

If she had known, she might not have stressed for so long

about the possibility that he might want to reconcile for the sake of their child. The child who was, of course, the reason she'd needed to see him today.

"Does Genevieve know what happened between us?"

"I told her everything."

"Not quite everything," she countered.

Elliott's gaze narrowed. "What do you mean?"

She blew out a breath. "I had a child," she finally said. "He was born the first of November."

Chapter Fifteen

It went against every instinct Luke possessed to let Julie meet with her former fiancé by herself. He understood why she wanted to do so, but he didn't like it. And if she left that meeting with even one hair on her head out of place, the aspiring politician was going to be very sorry.

He'd been tempted to follow her, to lurk behind a potted plant in the restaurant or hover at the wine bar. And maybe she suspected that he would do something like that because she'd left Caden in his care. Or maybe she just didn't want the baby anywhere near his biological father.

Julie never referred to Elliott as Caden's father. As far as she was concerned, he might have contributed to her son's DNA but that didn't make him his father. Lukas agreed that biology was only part of the equation, because while there was absolutely no genetic link between him and the little boy, there was an undeniable connection. And there wasn't anything he wouldn't do for the child—or his mother.

Which was undoubtedly why he ended up babysitting while Julie went to meet with the man she'd once planned to marry. The man who had used physical strength and threats to intimidate her.

Thankfully, she'd been strong enough to break away from Elliott. And while he understood that she wanted to prove that she could stand on her own two feet, he suspected that she'd also wanted to keep Luke a safe distance from her ex. Because if he came face-to-face with the man who had dared laid a hand on Julie, Luke knew it was entirely possible that he'd end up in jail on an assault charge.

Which reminded him of one more thing that he wanted to take care of while they were in town.

He'd dropped her off at the restaurant where she was meeting Elliott, and it turned out that the Courtland Hotel was conveniently located across the street from the DA's office. And by the time she called for him to pick her up, he'd made the necessary calls and contacts.

He very nearly forgot the plan when she came down the steps from the hotel lobby, her cheeks flushed, her eyes glowing. Just looking at her took his breath away. And when she planted her lips on his and kissed him, long and hard, right in the middle of the sidewalk, she took his breath away all over again.

"You look…happy."

"I am." She took Caden from his arms and held him close for a minute. "Thank you."

"For what?"

"For coming with me—and for staying away."

"You're welcome," he said dryly.

She grinned. "I've got something to show you."

"Here?" He looked pointedly at the pedestrians moving around them.

"Right here, right now," she said, and pulled a manila envelope out of her purse.

His curiosity undeniably piqued, Luke opened the flap and took out the papers inside. It was a formal legal document prepared, he noted, by Jackson Garrett. As he skimmed through the legalese, certain key phrases caught his attention, most notably "acknowledgment of paternity" and "voluntary relinquishment of parental rights." And it was duly signed and dated by Elliott Davis Winchester III.

"Why are you frowning?" Julie asked him.

He hadn't realized that he was, but he couldn't deny that he was a little perturbed by this unexpected turn of events. "I can't believe that he signed away his legal rights without ever seeing his child."

"I knew he'd be worried about the potential scandal of having an out-of-wedlock child. It turns out, that's only half of it."

"What's the other half?"

"His wife is pregnant."

"He's married?"

She nodded, apparently unfazed by the news. "They had a small, intimate ceremony in Boston four months ago."

"I guess it didn't take him long to get over his broken heart," he mused.

"I never thought I was the great love of his life, but I did think our relationship was about more than politics. But Elliott had a precise plan mapped out for his road to the House of Representatives, and finding a devoted wife was an important part of that plan—almost as important as his carefully documented ancestry and Ivy League education."

"Are you saying that when you left, he simply found an alternate bride?"

"And without much difficulty," she said. "Genevieve Durand's family and his have been close for a lot of years."

"Then I guess she knew what she was getting into."

She nodded.

"How do you feel about all of this?" he asked cautiously.

"Relieved. And ecstatic. My biggest worry was that he would try to make a claim on Caden—now I know that isn't a concern."

"What about his accusation against your father?"

"I didn't even think about that," she admitted. "And really, it doesn't matter anymore, because Elliott has nothing to gain by going public with his claim."

He stopped beside a two-story red brick building. "Don't you want to know if there's any truth to it?"

She looked at the writing on the glass door, then at him. "What are we doing here?"

"I thought, if you really wanted to put the past behind you, we should know exactly what's in that past."

"This is almost scarier than facing Elliott," she admitted.

He held out his hand.

After the briefest hesitation, she took it. And they walked into the DA's office together.

Nerves tangled in Julie's belly as Lukas chatted with the receptionist. After a few minutes, she led them down a long hallway to the conference room where Mr. Chasan was seated at the end of a long, glossy table, reviewing a file folder that was open in front of him.

He closed the cover when they entered and rose to his feet. "Harry Chasan," he said. "Former District Attorney, mostly retired now, but I hang around occasionally and consult on cases. I was hanging around today." He offered his hand to Lukas first, then to Julie, then smiled at Caden.

He gestured for them to sit, which they did. Julie didn't know what to say—she wasn't sure how Lukas had arranged this meeting or what information he'd given, so she let him take the lead.

"I was told that you were the prosecutor in the State of Massachusetts vs. Cosgrove case."

"I can't say the name rang any bells," Harry admitted. "But I pulled the file when your brother called to inquire about it, and sure enough, I was."

Julie looked at Lukas. Apparently he had no qualms about his brother pulling strings to help him get what he wanted. On the other hand, there was nothing unethical about one attorney contacting another for information about an old case.

"Do you remember it?"

"I do now." His gaze shifted from the file to Julie, and he nodded. "You've grown up, Miss Marlowe. I almost didn't recognize you."

She managed a smile. "It's been six years."

"A drop in the bucket when you get to be my age," he told her. "Can you tell me why you're digging into this now?"

"I just had some questions," she hedged.

"What kind of questions?"

"Mainly I wondered why I wasn't prosecuted."

"Insufficient evidence," he said bluntly.

"Who—" She swallowed. "Who made that decision?"

"I did."

"Did you, uh, consult with anyone about it?"

"Yeah, the idiot cop who arrested you."

She blinked at that.

"There wasn't any evidence to justify charges. You should have been released into your parents' custody as soon as you were brought in, but the arresting officer had a real hard-on about the fact that he'd busted a judge's kid." He shrugged apologetically. "Sorry, but there's no other way to describe it."

"So my father didn't pull any strings to get me released?"

Harry laughed at that. "Judge 'Morality' Marlowe? Not a chance."

"You didn't talk to him about the case at all?" she pressed.

"Sure I did. And Reg told me that I wasn't to do him any favors. If there was evidence to charge you, I should charge you.

"Between us now," he confided, "I think he was a little concerned about the path he could see you going down and thought a few hours in lockup might have done you some good. But I reviewed the evidence in this case the same way I would have any other, and the undisputed facts were that you went for a ride in a car that you didn't know was stolen. You made a bad choice, but you didn't commit a crime."

They shook hands with Harry again, thanked him for his time, and left the DA's office.

"I guess I owe you another thank-you," Julie said.

"Does that mean I get another kiss?"

"You're going to get a lot more kisses after we get back to my parents' place and get Caden settled down," she promised.

"When are your parents coming back?"

"Their flight is scheduled to get in to Boston at six-oh-five tomorrow morning, and it's about an hour and a half from the airport to our place." She glanced at her watch. "So we'll have the place to ourselves for about sixteen hours."

"Lead the way."

By the time they got back to the car, Caden was seriously fussing, so Julie fed and changed him before they started the drive to her parents. Sleepy and satisfied, the baby fell asleep within a few minutes. Fifteen minutes later, Luke pulled into the driveway of her parents' home.

He took Caden in his carrier while she gathered the diaper bag and her purse. Inside the door, he set down the carrier beside an antique chest so that he could take his shoes off. But he didn't get a chance before Julie pushed him back against the wall and started kissing him. A deep openmouthed kiss with full body contact. She teased him with her teeth and her tongue as she gyrated against him. And then, just as abruptly as she'd started, she stopped.

"That's just a prelude," she said, and turned away.

He snaked his arm around her waist and hauled her back against him.

"Two can play that game," he warned, and kissed her again, slowly and deeply, using his tongue in a teasing imitation of lovemaking until she moaned and shuddered against him.

"Julie?"

She jolted, dropping her hands from his shoulders and pushing him away. "Mom."

Luke closed his eyes and softly banged his forehead against the wall, cursing silently.

"I, uh, didn't think you were coming back until tomorrow," Julie said, crossing the room to embrace her mother.

The older woman's arms came around her daughter, and she held her close for a long moment. "We caught an earlier flight," she said. "And I'm so glad we did. I'm so glad you're home."

"It's good to see you, Mom. I missed you—so much."

Her mother blinked away the tears that had filled her eyes and turned her attention to Luke, who was hoping like hell she wouldn't notice that he was still partially aroused. Apparently being caught in an erotic lip-lock by a woman's mother wasn't quite humiliating enough to cool his ardor.

"And who is this?" she said, her tone decidedly less warm. "Is this the surprise you mentioned?"

"What? Oh, no. This is Lukas Garrett. Lukas, meet my mom, Lucinda Marlowe."

"I apologize, ma'am, for the, uh, situation you walked in on."

"I'm glad I wasn't ten minutes later." She took a few steps toward the staircase that led to the upper level. "Reginald— Julie's home."

"About that surprise," Julie began, just as her father came into the foyer.

There were more hugs and kisses and tears as Luke tried to blend into the elegant satin-striped wallpaper.

And then Caden woke up.

Several hours later, Julie took her overnight bag up to her childhood bedroom while Lukas was escorted by her father to the guest room on the opposite side and at the far end of the hall. After nursing Caden and settling him to sleep in his portable crib, she tiptoed down the hall in search of Lukas.

"I'm really sorry about this…arrangement," she told him.

"I'm not. In fact, I'm grateful they're not digging a hole in the backyard right now to bury my body."

"Maybe if it was the spring," she teased. "But this time of year, the ground's too hard for digging."

"Well, your brothers are supposed to be here en masse tomorrow. I'm sure between the three of them and your father, they'll figure something out."

She linked her arms behind his neck. "They'll figure out that I'm finally with the right man for me."

"Yeah, that's likely." His words dripped with sarcasm, but he wrapped his arms around her waist and drew her into his embrace.

"Seriously, I don't think either of my parents was as scandalized as you were," she teased.

"It's just that I'd hoped you'd have my ring on your finger instead of my tongue in your mouth when I met your parents for the first time."

"Actually, my dad was still upstairs when your tongue was in my mouth."

"Because that makes a lot of difference."

She laughed softly.

"I wanted to make a good impression."

"There's no doubt you made an impression," she assured him. "Now, about that ring you mentioned."

"You mean the ring you didn't want me to give you a few days ago?"

"If that's the same ring that I couldn't accept until I got my life in order, then yes."

"Are you saying you want it now?"

"I want the ring." She brushed her lips against his. "I want you."

"The ring's in my pocket," he told her.

"Really?" She immediately dropped her arms and began searching the pockets of his jeans, then she looked up at him and rolled her eyes. "It's *not* in your pocket."

"It's not? I was sure I put it there… Oh, right. It's in the pocket of my jacket."

She fisted her hands on her hips. "Are you going to give it to me—or have you changed your mind?"

He crossed to the wing chair in the corner, where he'd tossed his jacket, and retrieved the ring box from the pocket. "I haven't changed my mind," he assured her. "But I thought you might have reconsidered."

"Why would you think that?"

"Because Elliott is out of your life now, completely and forever. You don't have to worry about him making any claims on your baby, so you don't need a stand-in father for Caden."

"I never wanted a stand-in father for my son," she told him. "I want a real father for him. But that has nothing to do with my response to your proposal.

"I love my son, more than anything in this world. More than I ever thought it was possible to love another human being," she continued. "But I'm an old-fashioned girl at heart, Lukas. And I never would have agreed to marry you if I wasn't in love with you."

He felt as if an enormous weight had been lifted off of his

chest. "You told me you wouldn't fall in love with me," he reminded her.

"I didn't want to," she admitted. "But my heart had other plans."

He took the ring—a square cut diamond with smaller channel-set diamonds around the band—out of the box. "You really do love me?"

"I really do love you."

"And you want to marry me?"

She offered her left hand. "Yes, I want to marry you."

He slid the ring onto her finger, then dipped his head to kiss her.

There was no hesitation in her response, but when he eased his lips from hers, her brows drew together.

He rubbed a finger over the furrow. "Is something wrong?"

"Is something wrong?" she echoed. "Is that all you're going to say?"

One side of his mouth turned up, just a little. "What do you want me to say?"

"I'd kind of like to hear that you love me, too."

He skimmed his knuckles down her cheek. "Do you doubt it?"

"No," she admitted. "But it would still be nice to hear the words."

"I love you, Julie Marlowe." He brushed his lips against hers. Once. "With my whole heart—" twice "—for now and forever." And again.

She sighed happily. "Wow—that sounded even better than I expected."

"You'll probably get sick of hearing it," he warned. "Because I'm going to tell you every single day, for the rest of our lives."

"I'm looking forward to it." She snuggled closer to him. "It's hard to believe that only five weeks ago, I was stuck in my car in a ditch and thinking that things couldn't possibly get any worse. And then you tapped on my window, and changed everything."

"*You* changed everything for me," he told her. "You and Caden. Which reminds me—there was one more thing I wanted to ask you."

"What's that?"

"After we're married, will you let me adopt Caden so that I can be his father in every sense?"

Her eyes filled with tears. "You already are," she told him. "But yes, I would be thrilled if you adopted Caden."

"And maybe someday we could give him a little brother or sister?" Luke prompted.

She smiled, nodded. "I'd like that."

"But when we do start thinking about another child, could we try to plan it so that he or she will be due in the spring or summer?" he suggested.

"Why?"

"Because I don't want to chance you going into labor in the middle of another blizzard."

"You mean *you* don't want to have to deliver another baby," she accused.

"I'd rather not," he admitted.

She laughed. "I'll keep that in mind."

Epilogue

Julie stood at the window, her arms folded across her chest, watching the snow fall. Behind her, flames were flickering in the fireplace.

"I'm experiencing the oddest sense of déjà vu," she admitted to Lukas when he entered the family room.

"You said you wanted a white Christmas," he reminded her.

"I was hoping for a light dusting, just enough to make everything sparkly and pretty."

"Obviously Mother Nature had a different idea."

"So much for our plan to attend Christmas Eve church service," Julie noted.

He took her hand and drew her over to the sofa. Of course, Einstein tried to climb up, too, but settled when Julie reached down to scratch between his ears.

"Are you disappointed?" Lukas asked her.

"A little," she admitted. "It's one of my favorite Christmas traditions, and I wanted to share it with you and Caden."

"Next year," he promised. "And the year after that, and every year for the rest of our lives together."

"I like the sound of that."

"Me, too."

She settled into his arms. "I was thinking about a June wedding."

"June? That's six months away."

"A wedding takes time to plan."

"Ava managed to plan Jack and Kelly's wedding in a few weeks," he reminded her.

"And it was a beautiful wedding," Julie agreed. "But it's going to take some time for my mother to forgive me for not telling her that she was going to be a grandmother. I don't think she would ever forgive me if I deprived her of a proper wedding on top of that."

"I don't care about proper as long as it's legal. And my brother has connections at the courthouse—"

"No," she said firmly.

He sighed. "June? Really?"

"Maybe May."

"How about February?"

She shook her head. "Too soon, and the weather's too unpredictable." She tipped her head up to look at him. "Speaking of weather, I'm a little worried about my parents traveling through all this snow tomorrow."

"Your dad has an SUV with snow tires," he reminded her. "And as he assured you, no less than a dozen times, there's no way he and your mom are going to miss their first grandchild's first Christmas."

"I know they wanted us to spend the holiday in Springfield with them, but I wanted Caden's first Christmas to be here."

"No doubt it will be a Christmas to remember, with your parents and my brothers and their families all underfoot."

"It will be chaos tomorrow." And she was already looking forward to it. "But tonight—" she lifted her arms to link them around his neck "—it's just you and me."

"And Caden," he reminded her.

"Who has a full belly, a clean diaper and visions of sugar plums dancing in his head."

He dipped his head to nibble on her lips, and Julie's eyes started to close when she felt a swipe of tongue between her toes.

"And Einstein," she added, giggling when he licked her toes again.

Lukas went over to the Christmas tree and found a package with the dog's name on the tag. "Look, Einstein. Santa brought something for you, too."

He tore the paper off of the conical-shaped rubber toy that he'd prefilled with treats and offered it to him. Einstein raced across the room, his attention immediately and completely focused on the toy.

"That should keep him busy for a long time," Lukas said, returning to the sofa.

"And Caden will sleep for at least a couple of hours," Julie told him.

"If we have a couple of hours—" he brushed his lips over hers "—I have an idea."

His hands were already under her shirt, skimming over her skin, making her tremble.

"Am I going to like this idea?"

"I think so."

A long time later, snuggled in the warmth of his embrace, Julie knew that she had never been more blessed. Because she didn't just have their first Christmas as a real family to look forward to, but the rest of their lives together—and she knew the future was going to be a merry one.

* * * * *

LET'S TALK
Romance

For exclusive extracts, competitions
and special offers, find us online:

f facebook.com/millsandboon

🐦 @MillsandBoon

📷 @MillsandBoonUK

Get in touch on 01413 063232

MILLS & BOON

THE HEART OF ROMANCE

A ROMANCE FOR EVERY KIND OF READER

MODERN
Prepare to be swept off your feet by sophisticated, sexy and seductive heroes, in some of the world's most glamourous and romantic locations, where power and passion collide.
8 stories per month.

HISTORICAL
Escape with historical heroes from time gone by. Whether your passion is for wicked Regency Rakes, muscled Vikings or rugged Highlanders, awaken the romance of the past.
6 stories per month.

MEDICAL
Set your pulse racing with dedicated, delectable doctors in the high-pressure world of medicine, where emotions run high and passion, comfort and love are the best medicine.
6 stories per month.

True Love
Celebrate true love with tender stories of heartfelt romance, from the rush of falling in love to the joy a new baby can bring, and a focus on the emotional heart of a relationship.
8 stories per month.

Desire
Indulge in secrets and scandal, intense drama and plenty of sizzl hot action with powerful and passionate heroes who have it all: wealth, status, good looks…everything but the right woman.
6 stories per month.

HEROES
Experience all the excitement of a gripping thriller, with an inter romance at its heart. Resourceful, true-to-life women and strong fearless men face danger and desire - a killer combination!
8 stories per month.

DARE
Sensual love stories featuring smart, sassy heroines you'd want as best friend, and compelling intense heroes who are worthy of the
4 stories per month.

To see which titles are coming soon, please visit

millsandboon.co.uk/nextmonth